I0720130

STAR-CROSSED CAPTIVE

BLUESHIFT ✦ BOOK ONE

J.E. McDonald

Copyright © 2024 by J.E. McDonald; originally published by City Owl Press on YONDER 2023

STAR-CROSSED CAPTIVE
Blueshift, Book One
2nd Edition 2025

All rights reserved.

This book is human authored. No part of this publication may be reproduced, distributed, or transmitted in any form or by any means, including photocopying, recording, or other electronic or mechanical methods, without the prior written permission of the publisher, except as permitted by U.S. copyright law. Without in any way limiting the author's exclusive rights under copyright, any use of this publication to "train" generative artificial intelligence (AI) technologies to generate text is expressly prohibited. The author reserves all rights to license uses of this work for generative AI training and development of machine learning language models.

For permission requests: contact@jemcdonald.net

The story, all names, characters, and incidents portrayed in this production are fictitious. No identification with actual persons (living or deceased), places, buildings, and products is intended or should be inferred.

Book Cover by Getcovers.com. All stock photos and fonts licensed appropriately.

For information on subsidiary rights: contact@jemcdonald.net

Print Edition ISBN: 978-1-7383952-1-7

Digital Edition ISBN: 978-1-7383952-0-0

Praise for J.E. McDonald

"J.E. McDonald is an exciting new voice
in Sci-Fi Romance."
-Cynthia Sax, USA Today Bestselling Author

"This book was filled with suspense, suspense that kept
me at the edge of my seat and at times breathless."
-Paranormal Romance Guild

"Author J.E. McDonald's debut novel delivers a story
chock full of haunting suspense, humorous dialogue,
scintillating love scenes, and intriguing characters.
The town of Wickwood and its supernatural
happenings are a sure bet to draw in readers, make
them fans, and keep them coming back for more!"
-InD'tale Magazine

"This series starts out strong and just keeps getting
better and better. These books are exactly the kind of
reading I need: magic, romance, adventure, demons,
prophecies, ghosts, and dating apps. Perfection!"
-Lisa Edmonds, bestselling author

"J.E. McDonald weaves the two together so seamlessly that it's difficult to imagine anyone that wouldn't love this steamy and suspenseful story."

-Indies Today

"McDonald's cast of supernatural characters are always impeccably crafted and leave you eager for the next installment of this delightful series."

-Ashley R. King, author

"A fast-paced read with a tension-filled romance and high-stakes plot, Ghost of a Summoning is a paranormal love story you don't want to miss."
-Gabrielle Ash, author of Diamonds & Demons

"A devilishly fun romance."

-Luna Joya, author

"This wickedly compelling story is full of action and romantic tension..."

-J.E. Hunter, author

More Works by J.E. McDonald

https://books2read.com/jemcdonald

WICKWOOD CHRONICLES

Ghost of a Gamble
Ghost of an Enchantment
Ghost of a Summoning
Edge of a Shadow, Part One
Edge of a Shadow, Part Two
Ghost of a Beginning (Prequel)

GOLDENLACH RIDGE SHIFTERS

Captive Wilderness
Caged Fury
Conquered Betrayal

BLUESHIFT

Star-Crossed Captive
Star-Born Anomaly
Star-Cursed Odyssey (Prequel)

CONTENT NOTES

This novel includes sexual content, violence, and other material
that may be triggering or disturbing to some readers.

A complete list of content notes can be found at
www.jemcdonald.net:

To all the fan fic writers out there:
because you're making your
own happily ever afters in
extraordinary ways.

Blueshift: a shift in the lines of an object's spectrum
toward the blue end indicating an object is moving toward
the observer.

The larger the blueshift,
the faster the object is moving.

Chapter One

Elara Five, Deep-Space Medical Station
Outskirts of Sector Five

I won't lose another one.

Blood coated Nia's hands, the by-product of her patient's wound, a defender she'd nearly sent to palliative.

But when she'd put her hand on his arm, felt the vibrancy running through his veins, his *fight*—her heart stuttered. She couldn't speak the words that would have sent him to the last medical bay he would ever see.

The sterilizer at the side of the hover bed whirred. She ran her hands underneath the bright white light, the blood disintegrating beneath the rays. Once clean, she picked up her regenerator tool and held it tight to stare at the unconscious defender with chin-length black hair—his wound went right to the bone.

"You sure about this one?" Ezra asked from beside her, their black medical uniforms matching hundreds of others in the triage bay.

"I'm sure." She turned on the regenerator with a flick of her thumb. It hummed as she brought it close to the exposed femur. *Save this one.* Too many had died already. She took a deep breath. *Focus.* She'd already been on her feet for six non-stop hours.

"Stimulant," she murmured.

Ezra shot the drug into the side of Nia's neck a second later. The triage bay brightened. Her spine straightened, and her heart rate accelerated, thudding heavily in her chest as her hands steadied.

The defender's lifeblood spilled from his thigh to the bed. Ezra hooked him to fluids, lifted the transfusion portal, and paused.

Nia saw why—the dead PALM on the defender's left hand. There was no way to get an identification number, name, or blood type. Without missing a beat, Ezra inserted the portal into his arm, and the synthesized plasma ran into the patient's system.

Shouts from across the triage bay echoed. A new surge of wounded entered on hover beds, shunted into neat rows in the voluminous space. More silver and gray uniforms.

Too many wounded. Too many to save.

Finish with this one. Move on to the next.

Ezra held the leg immobile as she ran the regenerator along the exposed muscle. "He's a big one," the med assistant murmured, hands steady on the man's thigh.

She didn't acknowledge the statement, but had to agree. Even lying down, the defender dwarfed them both. The Tellusians would see this one coming and run in the opposite direction. Her patient twitched but remained unconscious.

Ezra injected another sedative into the defender's bloodstream, and his movements stilled.

The triage doctors shouting orders and the groans of the wounded drowned out the regenerator's hum. Nia's nostrils filled with the familiar but disquieting odor of lacerated flesh. She concentrated on healing each delicate layer of muscle, creating new tissue with her synthesizer. Every stroke of her hand brought the mended muscles closer to his epidermis. As her patient's vitals stabilized, she resisted the urge to take a break and turn on her PALM, her Personal Automated Link to Media that was connected to her ocular implant, and find out what was happening with the nearby battle.

Her forehead beaded with sweat. With plasma and fluids pumping into his system, the defender's vitals strengthened with each beat of his heart. She healed the epidermis of his thigh, the dark hair on the outer edge of the wound singed where the laser weapon had sliced him.

With the last of his skin healed, she turned off the regenerator and braced her hand against the bed. A deep breath fortified her enough to address her patient's second wound: the laser burn that had cauterized a large portion of his oblique abdominals, his uniform partially melted to his body.

Ezra pressed and smoothed regeneration gauze to the newly healed flesh of the defender's thigh. "It's even a pretty scar," he said with a grin, covering the last of the pale pink skin.

She smiled. "You know I take pride in my work."

"That's an understatement."

A shout made them both turn. Nia's heart stuttered, and she froze in place. A defender resisted treatment two hover beds over. The large man swung, knocking a doctor to the deck, then flattened a medical assistant with his next punch.

Without hesitating, Ezra ran and dove, tackling the wounded man to the deck. Defenders on security detail rushed to help while her med assistant held the thrashing man.

"You okay?" she shouted over the noise.

Ezra nodded, his face a grimace until a doctor pressed a dermal syringe into the defender's neck, tranquilizing the soldier.

Swallowing, she returned her focus to the wound on her patient's torso. She lifted the fabric of his uniform where it wasn't melted and—

Blinked, her brain not registering what she saw.

An intricate blue tattoo covered his abdominals. Tellusian blue. Her hands trembled.

Warrior. Terrorist. Slaver. *Enemy.*

She stepped back, a scream lodged in her throat. A hand snaked out to grab her wrist, and she dropped the regenerator. The man's icy blue eyes captured hers.

Her heart froze in her chest.

He swung his legs over the bed and jerked her toward him at the same time. She spun as he whirled them toward the bulkhead. Her scream morphed into a sharp intake of breath as her spine slammed into his chest. A wafting scent of sweat and blood filled her head.

The triage bay muddied into a kaleidoscope of colors. Doctors ran for safety. The defenders on security detail moved, everyone scrambling all at once. They aimed their guns right at her: AL-22s. Set to maximum, it would cleave her in two. Laser sights bounced in her vision.

This can't be happening again. The defenders must have been shouting words, but she could only hear a muffled buzzing in her brain and someone gasping for breath. Her eyes focused on the transfusion portal swinging where it disconnected from the Tellusian's arm, a red stream dripping to the deck beside where her black cap had fallen.

The arm wrapped beneath her breasts was too tight. She couldn't breathe. Nia struggled, kicking her feet. Something cold and narrow pressed against her neck. She tensed, recognizing the shape. *Laser scalpel.* One wrong touch of the controls and her head would roll to the deck.

"Stay still." He spoke with his lips next to her ear, his Common accent throaty.

All the heat left her body. Another Tellusian's voice filled her head from years ago. *Here's a pretty.* Blood, so much blood. And it wasn't from someone's surgery...

"I don't want to hurt you." The voice behind her returned her to the present. "But I will if you keep moving." The laser scalpel pressed deeper into her skin.

She squirmed and grasped his forearm, fingers twitching to grab the scalpel. Could she do it before he could cut her?

"That would not end well for you."

Bile rose in her throat. She swallowed and forced herself to relax. Her feet barely touched the deck. Needing to gain space between them, she dug her fingers into the gap between his forearm and her breasts. His grip tightened, making her gasp, then he loosened his hold a fraction.

She closed her eyes, waiting for the kill order. One doctor wasn't worth risking the entire station. The defenders would kill them both and be done with it. *Please be painless.*

An unnatural quiet fell over the bay. She felt every one of the Tellusian's breaths in her spine.

"Drop her or die, you Tell piece of shit," the lead defender yelled.

Her eyes popped open. They weren't going to shoot her? The defender's visor was translucent, revealing his face: Bradford, one of Calvin's friends.

"Move back or I cut her," the Tellusian barked, his accent guttural in her ear.

The defenders didn't move, didn't fire, their aim unwavering.

She felt the Tellusian's thumb move closer to the laser scalpel's controls. Images of cut throats filled her head, defenders she'd tried to save, blood leaving their bodies at a relentless pace.

"Which way out?" A curl of her hair moved with his words.

A negative sound, a denial, left her lips. She wouldn't help a terrorist escape justice.

His arm twitched around her, then he moved inch by inch toward the nearest exit, her body protecting his. The wall of defenders followed, keeping their formation. Behind the silver uniforms, Ezra stood rigid, his face frozen in horror.

How did this happen? She'd been saving this man's life. He wore a defender's uniform. How had he passed the scans to get on board?

The Tellusian stopped next to a door. "Open it."

Her fingers dug into his forearm. She wouldn't help him. It would only mean her death.

A rough hand grabbed her wrist, twisted, and slapped her PALM against the control panel. A startled cry left her lips as the door slid open.

Three defenders waited on the other side. Laser fire erupted around them. The world blurred and spun with a grunt and a curse. Helmets smashed together with a hollow *thunk*. The scalpel hummed. A leg kicked. Someone gasped. *Pop.* The triage bay door sealed shut when the Tellusian shot out its control panel.

Nia blinked. In only a few seconds, three defenders lay on the deck, dead, and the Tellusian hadn't let go of her. The acrid scent of weapons fire swirled around them. She couldn't look away from the blood coming out a defender's slit throat as it soaked his silver uniform. *It should have been me.*

Her captor tucked the scalpel away and reached for the defender's guns, accessing the controls on their uniforms. She tried to yank free, but the Tellusian pulled her to him again, arm encircling her ribs.

"It'll be okay." He hugged her to his chest. "I just need to get out of here."

His words sank into the calm, rational part of her mind, the place where she could analyze events with detached interest. She reached for that part, wanting to hold it close, needing it to counterbalance the other part of her brain trapped in a continual scream. He would let her go. She needed to believe that. He wanted off the station. He'd leave her here, and she would survive.

A distant blast rumbled, then echoed through the corridor. The shiny, light gray deck beneath them trembled. They paused together, holding their breath.

The bulkheads shuddered with an eerie groan. Dread gripped her chest. That was weapons fire from outside the medical station.

The Tellusian's arm around her tightened. Her feet left the ground as he propelled them down the corridor. She gripped his arm with her fingernails, trying to keep calm.

Boot steps ahead made him hesitate. Her heart leaped when a row of defenders turned the corner ahead of them, blocking their path. Relief shook her body. There was nowhere for the Tellusian to go.

Boom.

The deafening sound split her head in two. An outside blast ripped through the corridor, the force propelling her backward. She and the Tellusian stumbled, a tangle of feet, crashing to the deck. *Oomph.* She landed on top of him.

Ears ringing, she lifted her head. Where the defenders once stood, a void remained. Only the SNAP shielding kept precious oxygen inside the station. Stars blinked at her where a bulkhead was supposed to be. Her mouth went dry, her heart trying to escape her chest.

A flash of light against the darkness of space made her flinch. The Tellusian turned his body, blocking her view as another blast came almost on top of the first. The SNAP shielding sizzled, adjusting to keep as much atmosphere in the station as it could.

He pushed her to her feet, hands on her bottom, propelling her forward as he yelled, "Run! Run! Run!"

She didn't think, just acted. Her feet scrambled beneath her. *Boom.* Another blast shuddered through the deck, the bulkheads seeming to swell around her. She pitched to the side. A strong hand grabbed her upper arm, keeping her upright.

The sound of the next blast felt like it disintegrated every organ inside her. Heat seared her body, her feet lifting. For a second, she had wings.

Then she was turning, spinning, two hands holding her as the deck raced to meet her face.

Chapter Two

Snick snick snick. The sound scratched against her brain, an irritation she swatted away. Her body throbbed.

Nia brushed her cheek, and her fingers came away dotted with blood. Pain pulsed through her wrist. She tried to move, then realized heavy arms held her close.

The bulkheads rattled with another blast. She flinched. *Snick snick snick.* More debris fell onto the deck from somewhere nearby.

Adrenaline spiked through her. The station was under attack, and she needed to find a safe zone. Breaths left her lips in panicked bursts. She pushed against the arms binding her, wriggling free.

His eyes were closed, his body lax. Crawling backward, she turned, scrambling through the debris and broken glass on her hands and knees. Pain shot up her arm.

A hand grasped her ankle. She screamed. The sound cut short as he yanked her toward him. Bits of metal and glass scraped her hands, poking through her uniform into her stomach.

She twisted on her back, kicking, then went cold at the expression of rage on the Tellusian's face. She punched.

He batted her hands away, and her stomach jumped at the skin-to-skin contact.

"Stop," he growled. "We've got to get out of here, *izar*."

His hands spanned her waist. The world spun again when he tossed her over his shoulder. Her breath left her in a whoosh.

"Let me go!" She kicked and slapped, trying to grab anything she could. "You prick-faced, waste-humping bastard!"

The arm wrapped around her thighs didn't loosen no matter how much she wiggled and squirmed. They passed more debris, more sections of bulkhead only held together by SNAP shielding. His footsteps faltered, his body turning...

Laser fire popped through the corridor, the acrid scent wafting a moment later. Then he was moving, quicker this time, his shoulder digging into her stomach. She twisted to see. He stepped over dead defenders like they were space junk.

The corridor quaked again. Red emergency lights flickered. Quieter blasts echoed from farther away. He shifted her weight forward, as if he would set her on her feet, and her heart stuttered. Would he release her? Her hope crashed when he pushed her against a bulkhead, a firm hand on her stomach to keep her still.

His icy eyes flashed. "Make a sound and I'll kill everyone in there."

She shivered, shoved away, but he pulled her against him, chest against her spine and breath in her ear. He lifted her hand and pressed her PALM flat against the control panel. The door slid open a second before he threw an orb inside a maintenance bay.

She heard a shout, then another. People scrambled. A thick fog poured out into the corridor. Another blast rumbled through the station, vibrating through her feet. The Tellusian pushed her into the chaos of the bay.

The smoke from his device shrouded them. Her heart beat in her ears as they wove through ships and people. She yanked her arm, but he held tight, propelling her forward at a swift pace.

A defender stepped in front of them. There was only a second of struggle before he fell to the deck, his throat slit. A whimper escaped her lips. She pressed them together, so tempted to scream, but the Tellusian's threat rang in her head.

She stumbled, tripping on a ship's ramp. Panic stabbed her chest. He tugged her upright by her wrist, and she cried out. His eyes narrowed on her face before he pushed her into a Raven, a scout ship.

She wrenched her arm, gasping at the second stab of pain. "Let me go!"

He pulled her inside, past the hatch, and closed the door with a slap of his hand on the side panel. The ramp rose with a whine.

Clank. The door sealed shut, mocking her last shred of hope. "You said you wanted off the station." All heat left her body, her limbs becoming numb. "You don't need me." Her last words came out in a whisper.

When he shoved her into the co-pilot's seat, she knew she should struggle but couldn't make her limbs work. With quick fingers, he pulled the restraints over her shoulders and between her legs.

She stared at the unfamiliar buckle, her hands shaking as she tried to pry it away from her chest.

The Raven's engines hummed, the Tellusian's fingers flying over the controls. Voices blared from the speakers; someone had left the media feed running when they'd powered down.

"...Calypsons need to be eradicated. They might not be as violent as Tellusians but their influence is insidious, polluting minds, and we—"

He turned it off, then the ship lifted, tilting into a hover. The smoke around them dissipated. With their camouflage drifting away, the defenders on security detail opened fire. Pink shields rippled, enclosing them in a protective cocoon.

Nia stared at the closed blast doors through the Raven's viewer, her heart beating in her head. *No way out.*

An energy pulse left the shuttle. *Boom.*

The bay door crumpled. Bile rose in her throat as debris flung out into space a second before the SNAP shielding initiated. The Tellusian pushed the throttle, and her head jerked against the headrest.

They launched into a war zone.

Laser fire flashed beside them. She screamed, gripping the arms of her seat. Enemy fighters mixed with CORE Marauders. A Tellusian Destroyer loomed in the distance, colossal, its all-black construction an omen of more death to come. The shuttle turned, and she caught sight of the medical station.

Her heart cracked into a million pieces. Most of *Elara Five* was destroyed, including her triage bay. Tellusian pods covered the other sections. *People farming.*

"We're a non-combative medical station." The words whispered through her dry lips as anguish crashed over her in waves. The control panel blurred in front of her as the Raven changed trajectory, the battle through the viewer morphing into indistinct blasts of light against the darkness.

It felt like someone had ripped her chest open.

The Tellusian spoke into his comm in a language she didn't understand. Pods detached from the station to head to the Destroyer. The larger fighters shot away, disappearing into the stars. A high-pitched humming noise filled the Raven a second before they followed.

Tremors began low in her belly and traveled to every limb. She was going to be a Tellusian slave, forced to... She swallowed against the dryness in her mouth. Everyone had heard the stories: people forced into the sex trade, or made to do manual labor until they broke and were tossed out an airlock.

Staring out the viewer, she gripped the straps at her shoulders so tight they cut into her skin. The unmoving stars made it seem as if the ship stood still, but they must be traveling close to the speed of light. A deep breath through her nose did little to calm her.

She didn't know how long she stayed that way, staring at nothing, when a small bit of hope spiked through her. With her uninjured hand, she pressed the cool metal of her locket under her uniform. If she could get alone, she could turn on the inert tracker hiding inside it. Someone *would* save her.

For once, she was grateful she'd listened to her tyrannical mother.

Heart pounding, she glanced at her captor without turning her head, surveying him from top to bottom. She should have realized he wasn't a defender: too-long black hair and a light growth of beard. All the defenders she knew had their hair cut short to the scalp, even the women. Despite his injuries, he'd been strong enough to carry her through the station.

His white knuckles on the controls drew her gaze. She scanned lower, beneath his seat. Blood dripped onto the deck, a small puddle forming.

Her rage and desperation gave way to something else, something she didn't want to feel. She was a healer. The words of her oath upon graduating from Lunar Medical Academy pounded in her head. She would do no harm, help those who needed it. She lived by the mantra every day of her life.

But this man and his people had destroyed her home, killed her friends and colleagues.

Her face flushed with shame, the two sides of her nature warring with each other.

I'll fix him, then *I'll kill him.*

"Release me," she demanded, pulling against her restraints. Her sprained wrist protested. "Now."

He didn't move or twitch, keeping his gaze straight ahead.

"Don't be a twat," she gritted between clenched teeth. "You're bleeding all over the place, and I'm a doctor. Release me."

He turned his head, and she inhaled sharply. *His eyes.* The icy blue looked unnatural, like he could see right through her. Maybe it was a normal shade for Tellusians, but she didn't think so; they seemed to glow.

Skepticism furrowed his brow.

She bared her teeth. "Yes, I'm big and scary. You must fear me."

His brows shot up, a flash of something crinkling the corners of his eyes. Humor? *No.* A Tellusian wouldn't know humor from mercy.

They remained staring at each other, nothing to break the silence but the hum of the ship. Then he undid his buckle and leaned toward her. She held her breath. His hair fell forward, blocking his gaze. Pressing against her seat to avoid his touch, she contracted her stomach and inhaled sharply through her nose as his hand brushed her uniform. She watched closely to see how he undid it: three points pressed at the same time. The buckle clicked.

His unsettling eyes followed her as she stood on shaky legs. Stepping away, she scanned the interior of the ship. Ravens weren't big, but they were built for long-distance travel. The crew should have stocked it with medical supplies.

Compartments ran along the top length of the hull. She opened the first one. Empty. The next one held blankets and emergency rations. The third had a med kit. She snatched it and opened the lid.

It was only half-stocked. Her hand hovered over the laser scalpel. He'd shoved one in her neck. She should return the favor.

Her cheeks warmed with shame—not because she'd had the thought to use the medical tool as a weapon, but because she should feel remorse over the idea, and didn't. Wouldn't anyone in her position feel the same?

Clenching her jaw, she returned to the front of the ship, med kit gripped in her hand. "I'm going to need access to your injury." Her voice cracked, resentment pounding through her.

After a hesitation, the warrior turned, exposing his side. Taking a fortifying breath, she knelt and pulled the ripped and bloody fabric away from his abdomen.

She swallowed her gasp. How could he remain conscious with a wound like this? She met his eyes. Disconcerted by the force of his gaze, she looked away and grabbed the laser scalpel.

He caught her arm before she could aim it. A shocked breath left her lips. They froze, locked in a staring contest, the scalpel between them.

Despite having homicidal thoughts moments ago, she straightened, insulted he would think so little of her. "I need to cut your shirt away," she said between gritted teeth.

A long moment passed before he let her go. She rubbed her arm, trying to remove his heat impression, then grabbed the material of his shirt, splitting the rest with a quick *zip* of the scalpel.

The two pieces hung off his body, baring his chest and exposing the cerulean blue tattoo covering most of the expanse. She pushed the instinctual spike of fear his tattoo invoked.

Ignoring everything else, she passed a scanner over his obliques. Grisly, the charred black outer edges and the red, angry inner flesh surrounded a center of exposed muscle. She'd seen laser wounds like this before, but not on someone alive.

Without looking up, she set aside the scanner and said, "There weren't any paralytics or numbing agents in the kit." It was going to hurt like a son of a bitch.

"Get on with it."

The harshness of his accented voice raised her hackles. With jerky movements, she grabbed the waistband of his pants with her injured wrist and winced as she revealed the bottom of the burn. Her fingers pressed against the uninjured flesh of his hipbone. He twitched.

Freezing, her gaze jumped to his. She looked away to turn on the regenerator with her good hand. Beginning at the outer edges, she removed the charred flesh and healed the skin beneath. It would scar, but without a synthesizer, she couldn't replace the tissue. She kept her hand steady and mind focused, not allowing anything to interfere.

His hands clenched the arms of his seat as she neared the more severe damage. If he passed out, it would be easier for him, but he remained stubbornly conscious.

Turning off the regenerator, she leaned away, but kept her eyes on his hip. "I need better access to your front."

He turned slightly and spread his knees. The bandages on his thigh peeked out between the panels of his torn uniform, glaring at her. She knelt between his legs, her gaze straying to the bulge between his thighs before she blinked and focused on the wound. Heat seared her cheeks.

The regenerator hummed. Nia braced her forearm against the inside of his knee to keep her balance, the heat of his body surrounding her. The scent of new and dried blood, and something distinctly masculine, invaded her senses.

Everything faded into the background as she focused. Time passed as she worked, her energy fading. She nearly asked Ezra to inject another stimulant when she remembered where she was.

How could she forget with the Tellusian's tattoo mocking her?

With a shudder, she turned off the regenerator and sat back on her heels, keeping her eyes on his new scar. "It's done." Not her best work, but he'd live.

"Your turn."

His rough voice made her gaze fly to his. From his grim expression, he wasn't talking about her sprained wrist.

"No," she whispered.

She scrambled backward, but there was nowhere to hide when he closed the space between them.

Chapter Three

Nia's wrist screamed as she tried to get away. Her hands reached blindly, searching for the laser scalpel to defend herself. The Tellusian caught her ankle and flipped her onto her stomach, straddling her hips.

Trying to dislodge his weight on her bottom, she clawed and bucked. "Monster!" she spat.

Rip. Her uniform tore open, cool air pricking her skin. She gasped ragged breaths. Why was he doing this? She'd helped him, and he was going to—

The hum of a medical device made her freeze. Turning her head, she saw the scanner he held. He waved it over her shoulder blade.

"No." She bucked again, trying to break free. "Don't."

The scanner beeped. She thrashed.

He pressed against her harder. "Hold still." The click and buzz of a laser scalpel halted her movements. If aimed wrong, he would slice her right to the bone.

Lava-hot pain slashed her skin. Tears pooled in her eyes, and she shut them tight. Sweat beaded on her upper lip as she tried to stay motionless, even though every instinct in her told her to fight.

The searing pain stopped, but her shoulder throbbed. She felt a moment's pressure as he removed the device the CORE had implanted when she'd become an officer.

"Are there more?"

"No," she gritted through the pain.

Despite her denial, the scanner hummed again, and he waved it over every part of her. When he got close to her feet she kicked harder, trying to get away.

It beeped over her ankle.

"No," she panted, desperate. "It's a lifeline. A family thing. The CORE doesn't know about it." She squeezed her eyes shut. Her mother's shrewd face and father's boisterous laughter filled her mind.

The scalpel buzzed. His body blanketed hers, keeping her still. The pain was too much, the area too bony. Everything that had happened bombarded her brain all at once. She let out a moan of anguish as the blackness claimed her.

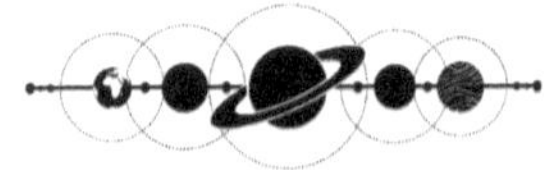

Mace pulled the bloody chip from her ankle. Its pulsing red light slowed, then died altogether from its lack of body heat.

She'd gone limp beneath him, and he let off his weight to collect the fallen regenerator. He regretted forcing her cooperation, but she wouldn't have allowed it otherwise. No one would have.

The tool hummed as the skin on her ankle closed together, barely leaving a mark. He ran the regenerator over her shoulder next, healing it completely. With an absorbent cloth from the med kit, he wiped away the blood from both wounds.

The woman still had cuts on her face and hands from the initial attack on *Elara Five*. He clenched his jaw against a fresh surge of rage. His people's recklessness had decimated her medical station. Whoever Cache had sent for him, it hadn't been Grey. His friend wouldn't have been so messy. Mace had a feeling he knew who'd coordinated the attack.

It was a miracle that he and the woman had survived those initial blasts.

He lifted her hand to examine her wrist, her PALM flickering. They were out of range of the medical station, but the media link was trying to connect with the CORE grid. He pulled the three sensors off her pinkie, thumb, and pointer finger, and the thin film covering her palm came away from her skin. As soon as it disconnected from her body, the device went dead.

Not wanting to take any chances, he tossed it in the reclamation chamber at the stern of the ship. Her trackers went inside next. He hit the "deactivate and disassemble" control.

Returning to the woman, he crouched beside her. With a hand on her shoulder, he rolled her over. Her scent wafted toward him, CORE-issue soap mixed with a floral fragrance. It reminded him of the jasmine blooms his mother used to set on their kitchen table. He settled her head against his thigh to examine her purpling wrist.

The scanner's readout displayed a sprain. He grasped the regenerator and waved it over the injury in a slow and methodical motion. The discoloration slowly faded. Once mended, he tilted her chin and took care of the rest of her scrapes and bruises.

With the last of the cuts healed, he set the regenerator, scanner, and scalpel into the med kit. Carefully, he scooped her into his arms and stood. She weighed next to nothing, had barely reached his chin when standing. Holding her tight, he kicked the side panel on the hull, and a bench lowered with a grating hum.

Mace laid her on her side, then retrieved a blanket from the overhead compartment. When he tucked it around her body, a chain around her neck glinted in the light. He pulled it out of her torn uniform. Etched vines swirled on the surface of the ancient-looking locket. He opened the latch to find it empty, then closed it with a light click and tucked it under her black medical uniform.

Curls fell over her forehead and temples. He brushed one away from her heart-shaped face, examining her wide nose and lush mouth. Dark lashes fanned her cheeks. When she'd glared at him, her russet eyes had flashed with hate. He pressed two fingers to her throat, and her pulse was strong. She was a fighter.

The corner of his mouth turned upward as he remembered the insults she'd thrown at him. What was a "waste humping bastard" anyway? He pulled his hand away, tilting her chin so he could make sure he'd healed all the cuts on her face, ignoring the voice telling him he lingered too long over the task.

Wincing, he stood and stowed the med kit in the hull compartment before returning to the pilot's seat. He sat with a groan. Every part of him ached. It wasn't only the wounds; it was every bone, and his heart too.

He'd lost good people on his last op, young warriors. He wouldn't obsess about the luck and logistics it would have taken to arrive on a CORE medical station as an unconscious patient without being discovered.

Running a hand over his head, he glanced at the woman. He should have left her. Why the hell had he taken her? *Because she would have died with everyone else on the station.* He didn't know that for sure, but it was what his instincts had screamed at him. From the second he woke, he'd planned to leave her in the maintenance bay—until his feet touched the Raven's ramp. Now he was stuck with a captive.

What the hell was he supposed to do with her? He knew, of course. He had put her through processing, what every captive went through as soon as they set foot on a Tellusian ship or station.

Fuck, he was an idiot. If turning around and taking her back wouldn't mean suicide, he'd do it.

Closing his eyes, he leaned his head against the headrest. He needed sleep. Already his energy waned beyond what he could push through on determination alone. He'd lost too much blood, would've passed out, maybe died, if she hadn't healed him.

He glanced at her again. Why had she? Shaking his head, he closed his eyes once more. He'd rest for a moment.

Drifting in and out of sleep, Mace was unsure of how much time passed when he felt the shift in the air as the woman tensed her entire body. He didn't move, kept his eyes closed and breathing level, so he wouldn't startle her.

Disjointed images made her twitch, an achy awareness traveling through her limbs. The hum of a vessel vibrated through her spine. Nia's eyes flew open, her body stiffening beneath a blanket.

A ship. The attack. The Tellusian warrior. It all came back to her in waves.

Trying not to let the panic strangle her, she levered upright. The blanket fell to the deck. He was *right there,* only two meters away. The rise and fall of his naked chest remained slow and rhythmic, and some of her panic abated. He wouldn't attack her again, or force her—not while he slept.

From what she could see, his injury hadn't deteriorated, though she wouldn't know for sure until she gave him a scan. Wanting to stay as far away from him as possible, she remained seated, staring. Even at this distance, she could feel the heat of him, the vitality that had halted her from sending him to palliative when she'd first laid her hand on him.

Relaxed in sleep, he didn't seem nearly as threatening as he did on *Elara Five*. His black hair caught the light of the control panel, and his scruff of beard didn't look as savage.

Keeping her gaze on him to make sure he didn't stir, she rolled her shoulders. The dull ache of a healed wound throbbed through her muscles. She turned her head to get a better look at where her uniform was torn, then ran her fingers over the healed skin. She frowned. *He could have left me to bleed.*

An echoing tingle in her wrist made her take a closer look. She rotated it and felt no pain. A strange feeling infused her stomach. Why had he healed her? He was a killer. Her injuries shouldn't have mattered to him.

She shivered. The cool air of the ship permeated her torn uniform. Nia collected the blanket from the deck and wrapped it around her shoulders. Its warmth calmed the tremors racing through her body.

Another realization slammed through her chest. He hadn't bound her. She was free to roam the small vessel, and could grab the laser scalpel to defend herself.

She glanced around, looking for the med kit, but didn't see it. Her heart jumped when her gaze landed on an escape pod door at the stern of the ship. *I can get away.*

Keeping her movements as stealthy as possible, she slunk to the escape pod's panel, then slid her hand over the screen. Nothing happened. She wiggled her fingers, realizing they didn't feel right. Her PALM was missing.

An exposed feeling squeezed her stomach, worse than when he'd ripped open her uniform. She spun around, scanning the area by the bench, but didn't see it anywhere. Her eyes narrowed at the reclamation chamber next to the escape pod. He must have destroyed it.

Losing her connection to the CORE made her sick to her stomach. How was she supposed to see what was going on in the solar system?

To know her orders? Her ocular implant wouldn't work without her PALM—no data stream for her eyes. She opened and closed her left hand, the flesh moving without the subtle film to cover her skin. *I'm naked.*

Fisting her left hand, she pressed the manual override with her right. A blinking message appeared: Access Denied.

Blast. She glanced at the Tellusian. He'd locked out the controls before taking his nap. *Bastard.*

Maybe she could try to override the lock from the main terminal. Licking her dry lips, she sneaked to the front of the Raven, leaving the blanket on the bench. Two more silent steps and she stopped next to his outstretched legs. She watched his bare chest rise and fall, and counted to a hundred until she was certain he was still asleep.

Swallowing, she braced her hand against the main terminal, then leaned over his legs. Her heart pounded hard in her chest as she searched for the pod's override. She found it on the far side, blocked by the bulk of his half-naked body. Slowly, she reached over, keeping her eyes locked on him for any hint that he was about to wake up. Fully stretched out, she touched the controls. It beeped, making her jump.

Her gaze shot to his face, certain she had woken him. But he remained asleep, his breaths even. Popping onto her tiptoes, she read the message on the panel: Passcode Required.

No! She didn't have any hacking skills, wouldn't know how to generate her own passcode. *Now what?*

The front panel lit up like a festival, beeping frantically. The Tellusian straightened. She hopped to the side, arms flailing to get away from him, and lost her balance.

"I didn't do it!" she shouted out of self-preservation reflex.

Thwack. She landed sideways in the co-pilot's seat. He caught her wrist, pulling her upright. She hissed out a breath and yanked her arm away.

"Does it still hurt?" he asked, glowering.

She shook her head, face heating. He'd touched her skin. Being a doctor, a surgeon, she needed to touch her patients, but that was different. CORE citizens didn't touch, not skin-to-skin unless you knew them intimately, a friend or family member. And even then, the touch was limited.

He faced forward, his fingers skimming over the controls of the ship. "Get strapped in."

His tone had her obeying. With shaky hands, she pulled the straps over her shoulders and between her legs. Then, out of the corner of her eye, something in the deep of space glinted on the viewer.

"What are those?" she asked, the moisture in her mouth evaporating. The ship skimmed over a network of black orbs ranging in size, some moving, some not.

Those can't be what I think they are—

As soon as her restraints clicked into place, he veered them off their trajectory at a furious speed. A scream lodged in her throat. She would have smashed into the roof if it hadn't been for artificial gravity and her buckle. All she could do was stare as he wove through the orbs at a suicidal speed.

We're in a blasted minefield.

Chapter Four

Nia's heart threatened to burst from her chest. The mines went on as far as she could see, packed together tightly.

She glanced at the warrior beside her. He was unhinged, *psychotic*. Even a slight jostle could destroy them. Her stomach rolled. Instinctively, she reached for her PALM, needing a suppressant to tamp her emotions, then flinched when all she touched was her own skin.

With no way to regulate her internal turmoil, she gasped each breath. Her fingernails dug into the arms of her seat as the ship veered sharply. It leveled out, then banked in the opposite direction.

It seemed like they wove in and out of the mines for an hour. Finally, the space between the mines grew wider, allowing the ship more room to maneuver. As her breaths slowed, something large glinted ahead. She squinted.

A space station flashed into existence. Her lips parted. At first, it looked like an elongated version of one of the mines, but as they neared, longer extensions became visible, as well as voids near the center.

In a heartbeat, it was gone again. She blinked. Did she have some sort of brain injury from the attack? But no, it was still there. Faceted shielding fooled her eyes, concealing a station like none she'd seen before. A Tellusian Destroyer docked to the side of the dark, oblong shape, looking like a miniature toy—and those warships rivaled CORE Guardians in size.

The closer they flew, the more the bulk of the station blocked out the minefield. She gripped the arms of her seat tighter, her eyes scanning the ships and shuttles of every size entering and exiting the docking bays. Larger vessels used docking ports like the Destroyer.

"What is this place?" she asked around the lump in her throat, her trepidation growing.

"*Orion*," he said, then switched to that language she couldn't understand. His comm buzzed in his ear, someone's voice on the other end.

How did she not understand it? She was fluent in the main CORE languages and had a grasp of all the others. What dialect was he speaking?

The cockpit darkened. She leaned forward, looking upward as they flew beneath one of the station's long arms. They entered a shaft, the black of the crisscrossed construction and the lights ahead the only things she could see. He stopped the ship, then they descended, surrounded by the metal composite of a chute. She squinted against the bright as they lowered into a docking bay.

Ships moved everywhere, coming and going, settling onto pads or lifting off. She peered through the side viewer, watching people in brown coveralls scurry beneath them. Tiny at first, they grew in size as they descended. The Raven landed with a *thump*. Maintenance workers disappeared under the ship.

When the warrior undid his buckle to rise to his feet, Nia reached for hers. A heavy hand settled on her shoulder, and she gasped, gaze flying to his.

"If you behave, I won't bind you. Do you understand?"

Her nod was automatic.

Heart pounding and limbs made of liquid, she unclasped her buckle. The heat of his hand lingered on her collarbone underneath the fabric of her uniform. He slapped the control by the door, and it slid open to reveal the ramp already half-lowered, whining.

She followed him to the hatch and stiffened when he grasped her upper arm.

"This way." He tugged her down the ramp.

She hated his hand on her, but resisted the urge to yank it away, knowing it would be futile. On the far side of the bay stood a line of people wearing black uniforms, medical officers from her station. Some cried, others had their arms wrapped around their bodies defensively. Armed Tellusians in blue uniforms with hefty guns patrolled the line. Bile rose in her throat along with the panic.

I can't do it. She couldn't just stand by, submissive, while turned into a slave. There had to be a way out.

Someone screamed. A medical officer attacked a warrior. The line fragmented, people panicking, trying to get away. *Pop.* The blast of a laser weapon echoed. Someone else screamed. The warriors moved in a choreographed formation, subduing the captives with barked orders.

But the one who had attacked first was on the ground, unmoving, a laser wound spanning his back. She reached for her PALM again, needing a suppressant, but felt more panic when it wasn't there. Bile rose in her throat. Her legs collapsed. A strong arm caught her around her waist before she could fall, turning her away from the sight.

"Do not look, *izar.*"

Her fingers dug into the skin of his arm, and she shook her head, swallowing the wretched taste in her throat. She'd seen countless laser wounds in her triage bay. The gore didn't bother her. Death was an everyday occurrence in her triage bay.

It was the violence of it. And the loss of an innocent man. One who'd vowed to heal and not hurt others.

"You will not be harmed if you don't resist."

She wanted to resist—to kick and scream and tear this place apart. The strength of her emotions truly startled her. She pressed against his arm, needing him to let go before she puked. He got the message and set her on her feet.

With a slight turn of her head, she saw the dead man being dragged away by his feet. She clenched her hands, her breath leaving her in gasps. The Tellusian stepped into her line of sight, blocking her view. Through her mess of hair, she glared, willing him to justify the death, wanting to hate him more.

His face was a stony mask. Brow furrowed, his eyes swept over her. He opened his mouth to speak when a shout jerked his gaze away.

"Mace!"

Her captor turned, his face relaxing at the appearance of a newcomer. *I would rather not know his name.* She didn't want to humanize him.

A man with dark brown hair cut close to his scalp wove through the foot traffic in the bay. His navy blue sleeveless uniform showed off the tattoos wrapping around his upper arms. A gun was strapped to his thigh, and he wore knives at his waist. A length of metal wrapped around his left forearm, tech embedded in its surface. She'd seen them in images of Tellusian warriors on the media reels.

As soon as they were close enough, both men grabbed hold of each other's wrists before pulling together for hearty slaps on each other's shoulders. She cringed at the crudity of it, the hitting, the skin-to-skin contact. No civil bowing.

"I thought you were dead," the other man said once they'd broken apart. He wore a wide smile, eyes filled with relief.

Cool air swirled where her captor had held her. Free of his touch, she took a step away.

"It was a close thing," Mace replied, his gaze darting to her.

The other man stiffened. "Going to processing?"

Her captor switched over to the other language. When they looked away from her, she took another step back. Heart pounding, she focused on a recently landed transport, its wide hatch humming open. A thick crowd disembarked, moving en masse between ships toward them. Nia flicked her eyes to the two warriors ignoring her and held her breath.

Closer the tide of passengers came, until she retreated inside the crowd, allowing it to swallow her. It pushed and pulled. *I can do this.* She could escape, steal a ship, become a stowaway, *anything* to get away from this place.

A clogged junction ahead had her heart beating an optimistic rhythm in her chest. If she reached it, there wouldn't be a way to know which direction she'd taken. Freedom was so close. *Just a few more meters.*

Mace frowned when Grey stopped talking mid-sentence. "And...?"

Grey's mouth upturned at the corner. "You know your captive ran away, right?"

"What?" Mace spun around and realized Grey was correct. He ran a jerky hand through his hair. "I told her to behave."

"Ah, yes. I've heard all captives are agreeable and do exactly as you instruct."

"Of course." Mace shook his head as they joined the crush of the crowd. He was not cut out to be a warder. He'd lost his captive in the first five minutes on the station.

"You're not going to call it, are you?" Grey asked.

Mace shook his head. He'd find her the old-fashioned way. He didn't want to degrade her escape attempt. Didn't want to scare and humiliate her further.

"We've got a runner!" Grey shouted.

Mace narrowed his eyes at him.

Grey shrugged. "Look, she's right ahead. Easy."

Everyone in the corridor had frozen at Grey's words—everyone except Mace's captive. The circle of bodies around her raised their arms, revealing her position. Mace could hear her hushed and frantic voice as they neared.

"No, no, don't do that. Put your arms down. I just want to leave. Please let me out. Oh, no."

His captive tried to squeeze her way between the people without touching them, angling her body then backing up because they weren't separating for her. Mace knew CORE citizens avoided contact with strangers as much as possible. Not a helpful phobia at the moment.

He broke through the circle of bodies.

She whirled around to confront him, her russet eyes flashing, a snarl on her lips. "You killed everyone."

Mace reached for her upper arm, and she jerked away. Her eyes had gone wild as she searched the crowd.

"You act as if nothing happened." She spoke so quietly he had to strain to hear her broken words.

She fell to her knees before he could catch her, and dry-heaved deep, wracking sounds. His chest ached to hear it. What he'd done to her ate at him. What she still had to go through created a bitter taste in his mouth.

"All clear!" Grey shouted. The crowd resumed its frantic pace.

Still on her hands and knees, his captive looked at his friend with hate-filled eyes.

"Whoa," Grey said, raising his hands in surrender.

"Do you have bindings on you?" Mace hated to do it, but if she tried to run again, she'd get herself shot.

Pressing his lips into a line, Grey reached into his pocket and passed him a thin strip of polymer.

Mace nodded his thanks. "Tell Cache I'll be there as soon as I can."

Sending his captive one last, sympathetic glance, Grey tipped his head and merged with the flow of foot traffic.

Quickly, Mace grasped his captive by the hips and set her on her feet. Taking her two wrists in his hand, he wrapped the binding around her flesh and pulled it tight, leaving only a finger's width of space. If she struggled, it would only get tighter.

Her eyes spat fire at him, her jaw clenched.

"Do you want to be shot by an enforcer?" he said in Common, keeping his voice low.

"Shoot me then. Get it over with."

Letting out a frustrated breath, he tugged on her bound wrists, against the flow of traffic, toward processing.

Nia bent her head, avoiding the stares of the people around her. Misplaced shame wracked her body. She kept her gaze fixed on her bound hands and the fingers pulling her with insistence. The uselessness of trying to escape pressed on her.

Mace. The brutality of his name suited him, a sharp, blunt instrument of death.

They crossed the docking bay, the sound of their footsteps lost among the noise. The line of medical officers had shrunk, but the scent of weapons fire lingered. Two men, faces she didn't know, waited beside two warriors. She took a shuddering breath as they shuffled her into the scanning area.

She watched, her breath caught in her throat, as a red light passed over the men one after the other. Then they were escorted through doors on the other side, disappearing from view.

It was her turn. Mace moved her between two columns of red lights. They pulsed over her body, then turned off. A sexless, disembodied voice announced, "Positive on a necklace."

Her chest tightened, her bound hands flying to her sternum. *My locket.* She needed it if she were to be rescued.

A man in a gray coat, a matching satchel over his shoulder, came toward her, his face a mask of grim determination under his white-blond hair. Panic clawed through her.

"No." She pressed her bound hands against her breastbone, protecting the locket her mother had given her.

"If you don't cede it willingly, we'll take it by force," the man said, features pinched as he jerked his head to the warriors near the entrance.

Mace stepped in front of her. "That won't be necessary." His naked back blocked her view. The air around them crackled. She held her breath, uncertain of what would happen if the warriors challenged him. Then finally, Mace turned toward her.

His brow was furrowed, but his eyes were soft. "It needs to be scanned. They will return it if it checks out."

But would they find something? Or was it scan-proof like her mother had insisted? She kept her hands where they were.

"I promise, *izar*."

Promise. What was the word of a Tellusian? The two warriors behind him shifted their positions until they were on either side of her. Mace tossed them each a scowl. They hesitated, then stepped back.

Swallowing, Nia lowered her hands. He moved behind her, and she closed her eyes. The hair at her nape stirred, his fingers handling the clasp. The chain skimmed against the bare skin of her throat.

When she opened her eyes, the blond man placed her necklace in what looked like a reclamation chamber inset in the bulkhead. Her heart lurched.

"It will be fine," Mace asserted from behind her.

She shook her head, doubting his words. Already she missed its weight and pressed her bound hands to her sternum. The red light of the scanner pulsed over her body once more.

"Negative," came the same monotone voice from overhead. "Please proceed."

Mace's hand settled on her shoulder.

"Commander," the blond man stopped before them. "Would you like to see someone from medical before we carry on?"

"I'm fine," Mace replied.

"He needs a blood transfusion and hydration," Nia contradicted.

His fingers twitched. "I can deal with it later."

The man lifted a brow, looking between the two of them. "Very well. And your vambrace?"

Mace hesitated, then said, "Lost."

"I'll order you a new one." Turning, he cast a glance over his shoulder. "This way." He opened the door, revealing a long corridor.

Her feet wouldn't move.

"This needs to happen," Mace said, his voice rumbling through her. "I don't want to force you, but I will if I have to."

Chapter Five

Mace's tone raised her hackles. Shaking off his hand, Nia lifted her chin and strode forward. The bulkheads of the narrow corridor closed in on her. Her panic renewing, she stepped backward and—smacked into Mace. The door swished shut behind them.

Her heart rate sped up. Terminals and panels ran the length ahead of her. A low hum emanated from behind the bulkheads, accompanied by an occasional click. How many people watched this process? Were weapons pointed at her?

The blond man turned with a long metal rod in his hand. She stiffened, ready to bolt, when Mace's hand settled on her shoulder, holding her still.

"It will render your ocular implant inoperative," the man said, his tone crisp. "You don't need it. You no longer have a PALM or connection to the CORE."

The words turned her stomach, but she held still, given strength by the Tellusian behind her even as his touch unsettled. The blond man pressed the metal rod to her temple. She felt nothing, but the rod squealed shrilly before he pulled it away.

Tucking the rod into his satchel, he swapped it for a knife. Alarmed, she pressed fully against Mace to get away, but the man gripped her bound hands and sliced through the polymer. She flexed her wrists.

A section of the bulkhead lit up where he touched it. "Biometric scans. Place your hands and eyes here."

With Mace's threat fresh in her mind, she obeyed. The scanner hummed, then something pricked her hand. "Ow." She rubbed the skin, seeing a red mark, and scowled at the blond man.

"Blood test for an identity match."

Her stomach sank, her skin growing cold. *They'll find out who I am.* They would ransom her. Only last week, she'd seen two ransom victims returned to the CORE on a media broadcast, swapped for two POWs who had been in CORE prison for years. The two CORE citizens, ruling-class members of the Muller family, had been beaten severely, to the point of near death.

Being ransomed would only mean pain.

Would it be better than what's about to happen?

With fear lodged in her throat, she followed the blond man as he led the way down the corridor. A portion of the panel slid open. He reached inside. "Your new vambrace, Commander."

Mace extended his left arm. The curved piece of tech enveloped his forearm. It hissed itself closed, then beeped, tightening to form a solid piece of metal from his wrist to elbow. The controls on the length brightened in gold.

"This way," said the blond man, walking further along the corridor. "We have a few more things to take care of."

He led the way farther along and placed his hand on another panel, activating it. "What is your name, age, and last rank and position held?" he asked her, his tone impassive.

She licked her lips but didn't speak. Why should she tell them this? Everything could be used against her. They already had her blood.

"If you're uncooperative, we'll assign you a random designation and place you in the manual labor pool." He stated the facts with an unblinking gaze.

"Nia." Her nickname was safe, unknown to the public. "I'm twenty-seven."

The man nodded, entering the information into the panel. "And your last held position?"

She pressed her lips together.

"It'll help us place you in employment," he said, but didn't sound like he really cared one way or another.

"She was in triage on *Elara Five*," Mace answered.

She tipped her face to glare at him. His eyebrows lifted.

The man turned away from her, tapping the panel. "It would be better for you if we knew the specifics of your post, but we'll put your rank as the lowest held in triage for the moment—"

"Surgeon Lieutenant Colonel." She winced. Her pride made her answer. Why should she care if they recorded her as a medical assistant? She pressed her fingers to her throbbing temple.

With raised eyebrows, the blond man entered the information. Another section of the panel popped open. He withdrew two bundles of metal. The malleable ovals looked like jewelry, but she knew they couldn't be.

"Our newest model of bonds," the man said, stepping closer. "Organic metals."

Prisoners' bonds. Her heart thumped hard in her chest. She looked around frantically, needing an escape, knowing there wasn't one, and jumped when they encircled her wrists.

Warm metal slid against her skin. The man pulled a computer palette, slightly larger than his hand, out of his satchel and tapped it. Then the bonds shrank, tightening against her flesh before activating with a beep. She rotated her wrists, watching the metal bend and move. Each had a green light on the side, and a small screen graced her right wrist showing the time: 17:09. Did they use Earth's twenty-four-hour clock like the CORE did?

"Make sure they're synced," the man said.

Mace touched his vambrace.

Her wrists flew together, locking with a click, the metal now solid and immovable instead of flexible, the lights red. She tried to pull them apart, rip the blasted things off, but they wouldn't budge. Another touch of Mace's vambrace and her wrists separated.

Her face burned while the man quickly went over its features: the comm, the embedded tracker, and how she would need to remain within her designated boundary markers.

"Almost done," Mace said from behind her.

And then what? Seconds passed as she stared at the metal encircling her wrists, her new reality sinking in. *I'm a slave.* She lifted her chin to glare at Mace. If she thought she saw regret cross his features, she knew she had imagined it. There was no way he regretted doing this to her.

The blond man's palette beeped. He scanned it, his eyes widening a second later. With a snap of his head, he looked straight at her, lips parted. Then a strange glint entered his gaze—the most emotion she'd seen on him since they'd arrived.

Her heart thumped in her chest. Her blood tests. *He knows.* The remainder of her time with these people would be spent in pain. The Mullers told media reporters that Tellusians tortured them for weeks and healed them only to restart the process. No one returned to the CORE unharmed.

She shook her head, trying to deny her lineage before he spoke a word. The tension between them grew.

"I'll need to inform Commodore Cache at once," he mumbled to himself.

Mace's hand snaked out, gripping the man's wrist to take the palette from his fingers, then froze when he read the information.

Words spewed from his mouth, undecipherable and clipped. The blond man startled, uneasy, then replied in the same language.

A conversation went back and forth, Mace becoming increasingly threatening, the man alarmed, but stubborn in his responses.

Fear and pressure built in her head, and she had the urge to cover her ears and scream. Then something Mace said made the color drain from the other man's face. He glanced at her, then at Mace, locking eyes. The Tellusian who had taken her from her home looked murderous, ready to kill for her.

Why would this warrior step between her and being ransomed?

Finally, Mace's tone softened a fraction. He accessed the controls on his vambrace with a clenched jaw.

The man stared at his palette and nodded once before looking at Nia. "You are now processed," he said in Common. "Your warder has a duty to make sure you're safe at all times. Do you understand?"

With her stomach still climbing her throat at what had just happened, she shook her head. "Warder?"

"Commander Mace will be your warder. You are the ward, protected by Captive Mandate 216 and the old laws." His gaze flicked to Mace.

Her mind raced. Protected? She thought they would turn her into a sex slave or something similar, but they asked about her medical expertise. She scrubbed a hand over her face and encountered her bonds. Her fingers rolled into fists.

She didn't care about a Captive Mandate; she wanted to go home.

Another panel on the left bulkhead popped open. The man reached inside and pulled out her necklace. "It came out clean."

Relief weakened her knees. She reached to snatch it, but he insisted on passing it to Mace. *Not even my belongings are my own.*

But it didn't matter, not anymore. Not when Mace held the chain on either end to clasp it around her throat. All she needed was a moment alone to turn it on.

Averting her gaze from Mace's icy blue one, she turned, presenting her nape and lifting her hair. A moment later, the cool of the chain brushed her neck.

As soon as he'd secured the clasp, Nia stepped away and pressed the locket to her heart. *One step closer to home.*

"We're finished here," the man said. "Good day." He hurried off the way they'd come.

Instead of following, Mace gestured for her to continue along the corridor. They stopped at a rectangular door. He scanned his hand on the panel and the door slid open, revealing a small room, brightly lit.

Her breaths shortened. What would come next? The white bulkheads gave her no comfort.

"I have to follow the rules." Mace's voice rumbled loudly in the tiny space. "You'll need to remain bound in the general population."

Stomach fluttering with nervous tension, she swallowed against the sudden dryness in her throat. *Click.* Her wrists snapped together. She glared at him, her chest burning.

Another scanner was positioned on the opposite bulkhead beside a white door. This one opened into a corridor with metal grating on the deck and gray bulkheads. The murmur of people pulsed from nearby.

Fingers gripping her elbow, Mace guided her out. The vacant corridor led to a densely packed one. She tensed, and Mace pulled her closer, heading toward the noise.

So many people. They merged into the crowd. Garish fashions intermixed with uniforms of navy blue, brown, and white. Banners hung from the bulkheads at intervals, each with a swirling symbol at its center, reminiscent of water. She'd glimpsed something similar graffitied on *Jupiter One* once—before the bots had scrubbed the mess.

She tried not to touch anyone, but it drove her closer to her warder. *Blue tattoos everywhere.* The face tattoos made her stomach roll. *Here's a pretty.*

She buried the memory and looked up. Light shifted through the latticework metal as people walked in the corridor above them. A rush of water gurgled from somewhere, like a stream, but she couldn't see one. Vines climbed the bulkheads, mixing with bushy shrubs in round pots. People sat on benches tucked into alcoves.

Corridors are for walking, not mingling.

A man stumbled toward her, and Nia shrank away—right against her captor's naked chest. She yelped, jerking sideways. Mace tugged her bonds in the opposite direction, then steered her behind him, his body partially shielding hers. The people in the corridor parted as if he were a scavenging plow.

The scent of hot food wafted toward them. Her stomach clenched painfully. How long had it been since she'd eaten? Twenty hours? More?

They turned another corner, and the crowd thinned. She caught her breath. Welcoming beams of light flooded the open space ahead. She veered right, walking straight toward it. Mace didn't stop her.

Placing her bound wrists on a railing, she leaned forward. They stood on the second level of a tall atrium, fixtures dispersing dazzling rays from the overhead five decks above. At ground level, tables of varying sizes spread throughout the center. Vendors skirted the outer edge.

Her side warmed as Mace stood beside her. She wanted to shift away from his heat but kept herself still, then jumped when a red parrot flew in front of her face.

"Birds?" When was the last time she'd seen an actual bird? Maybe her last visit to *Jupiter One*. Her heart thumped with wonder as she watched it soar.

"They escape the arboretum from time to time." He shifted his weight, the movement bringing him closer.

The parrot swooped, landing on the uppermost railing with others. Her feet twitched, wanting to head there for a closer look.

"We need to go," Mace said, his tone kind.

She hated him for it.

Swallowing, she turned away from the sight. He gripped the section of bonds between her wrists and tugged her toward a lift.

Once inside, the doors shut, and the lift descended deck after deck, giving her another sense of *Orion's* size. It stopped, the door opening, and she tugged her hands free to step out on her own. This corridor was smaller than the previous one, with the bulkheads a lighter shade of gray. She raised her gaze to his in question. He gestured to the left, keeping his distance.

Holding her body stiff, she walked ahead of him. A man strode away from them at the far end of the otherwise empty corridor. A guffaw of laughter came through one of the closed doors, a woman yelling from another. Nia cocked her head when she heard a baby cry farther along.

Mace stopped at a door marked CSL92-264 and scanned his hand. The door slid open, and he waited for her to enter. Once through, he touched his vambrace. Her bonds separated, hands falling to her sides.

She scanned her surroundings. They were large quarters, bigger than hers on *Elara Five*. The countertop in the kitchenette gleamed. A table sat next to it, two chairs tucked in efficiently, and a skinny sapling in a brown pot at its center. Mace walked to the refrigeration unit and opened it.

Her heart thumped with uncertainty. Why didn't he throw her into a cell?

A wall terminal occupied the bulkhead on the other side. Inactive, the black surface reflected their distorted forms. A large bed was built into the construction of the rear bulkhead, only accessible from one side. Fluffy ivory blankets billowed upon it like clouds.

A pile of dark blue cloth at the end of the bed contrasted with the pale color. She walked closer. It was clothing, a warrior's uniform.

She whirled around, heart pounding in her throat. "These are your quarters," she choked.

He paused at the exit. "Yes. Make sure you eat something." He nodded to the open refrigeration unit.

"Where am I to sleep?" She gritted the words between clenched teeth, looking for another room. There was one other slender door. It had to be the washroom, not separate sleeping quarters.

"The bed," he said, nodding to the monstrosity behind her. "Or the deck, if you prefer."

Her heart beat hard in her chest, threatening to break free. "I will never sleep with you."

Her words came out in a strangled whisper, but she knew he heard her when he said, "The deck it is, then."

She screamed and charged. When the door closed between them, she grabbed the closest thing.

Chapter Six

*C*rash. Something smashed inside his quarters, the sound reverberating off the bulkheads. Dull thumps followed. Was she kicking the door? Mace cringed.

An off-duty subordinate passed him by with raised eyebrows. He gave the young man a nod, then ran a hand through his hair. This was utter madness. He'd locked a raging captive in his quarters, and he was going to leave her there. On her own.

And he'd spent a sizeable chunk of his saved creds to keep her safe—enough for the processor to never want for anything in his life ever again if he kept her lineage buried.

Mace closed his eyes. Out of everyone he could have taken on *Elara Five*, he had to steal away a member of the CORE's ruling class. He might have been able to convince himself he'd kept her because she would have died, but now he'd put her in more danger. The processor wouldn't speak for fear of his personal wellbeing, but the only way to keep her safe, to keep her away from everyone else, had been to invoke the old laws. Everyone would think... stars above, what had he done?

He rubbed a hand over his face. She had to be scared shitless. *I should have left her to die.* It would have been the merciful thing to do.

He'd seen the dread in Nia's eyes when they'd taken her blood. Mace didn't need to worry she'd betray herself. She understood the consequences of revealing her identity.

Nia. The name suited her, short and feisty.

When silence reigned on the other side of his door, he headed toward the lift. Once on, he hit the control to take him to the fifth level of the atrium and training, his favorite place on *Orion*. When not on missions for Cache or taking shifts in the command center, it was where he spent most of his time. The door slid open, and he walked close to the railing, eyes alighting on the birds Nia had seemed so enthralled with, the same birds he had paid little attention to until now.

The entrance to training opened into a wide corridor, doors on either side leading to lockers, showers, and barracks. Beyond was the matted sparring arena, rivaling the atrium in size. Mace stopped for a quick steam shower. It almost made him feel normal.

Alone in the changing room, he ran his fingers over his ribs. She had done a good job of healing him. The scar was minimal, his ink missing in one large section, faded in others. He would need to get it reworked someday.

With a towel slung low on his hips, he crossed to the lockers and found a new uniform in his assigned cabinet. The familiar weight of the material settled on his shoulders. Boots tied and a fresh gun strapped to his leg, Mace left training, nodding to the warriors and tyros milling around in the common area. He headed to the command center in Section A and didn't dread his upcoming confrontation with Cache as much as his next one with Nia when he returned to his quarters.

Stepping off the lift on deck one, he went through the security checkpoint, a tunnel-scanner recording his biometrics, then strode into the brain stem of *Orion*. Three stories tall, the spherical space buzzed with activity. Each level held science stations, tech posts, and warriors on security duty.

Commodore Cache was at the center of it all, her black hair bound tight in a tail. Her posture tense, she stood next to the main holotable, a frown wrinkling her brow. The uniform style she'd chosen covered her like a second skin, one gun strapped to her thigh like his. The techie in front of her spoke quickly, his gaze averted. Whatever he said wasn't pleasing her. Grey stood nearby, his eyebrows raised at the exchange.

When the techie noticed Mace walking over to them, he let out a long breath, probably assuming Cache would direct her attention elsewhere.

And that she did. Her eyes flicked to Mace, narrowing, before returning to the techie. "See it never happens again." She jerked her chin toward the tech terminals. "Report to Mouse for your new assignment. Dismissed."

"Yes, sir," the techie muttered, then scurried away.

She turned away from the holotable. "Commander." Her emerald eyes might be hard, but there was relief there too.

"Commodore." Hands clasped behind his back, he faced the woman he'd known since they were tyros. Grey stepped to the side, the third point of the triangle.

"Report."

His chest squeezed. This was one report he didn't want to give. "Your plan to attack the weapons armada was solid, but I believe the CORE obtained inside information."

She twitched. "Explain."

"We boarded the disabled ship, one venting air. Two squads of defenders met us instead of the freighter crew. Our CORE uniforms provided some confusion, but not enough."

Those last moments played through his head. It hadn't been his regular team. Cache had wanted the younger warriors to gain experience on what was supposed to be a straightforward mission. Instead, they all died.

"They fought bravely," Mace said, his throat tight. "To the bitter end." And he would tell each of their families the same thing as soon as this meeting was over.

If he hadn't known her so well, he would have missed the regret shuttering her features. "I'd thought you were dead until the signal flare."

Mace blinked. A signal flare. The moments after the ambush were disjointed in his mind. He must have sent it out of self-preservation instinct on the way to *Elara Five*.

"How did you survive?" she murmured.

"Honestly, sir. I'm not really sure."

"Elaborate."

He shook his head. "The defenders must have thought me dead with the others, but when cleanup personnel dealt with the bodies and my heart was still beating, they sent me to medical instead of reclamation because of the CORE uniform."

It still seemed too unbelievable to accept. The look on Cache's face said as much.

"I woke up in the middle of surgery," he added. And there was Nia, frozen in shock, with him seeing only one chance for survival.

"So you took her captive."

Tension raced down Mace's spine. "Yes, sir." But if he'd known about her lineage, he would have left her to die. If her bloodline were discovered, it would have been the kinder choice.

Cache's mouth upturned for a brief second, like she resisted the urge to poke fun at him. He'd always been outspoken about captive rights, the barbarism of an indentured class propelling their economy, and wanted to abolish the system altogether.

"What would you have done if I hadn't sent Foley and the *Bellicose* after you?"

Mace met Grey's eyes before he returned his attention to her. "That was Foley's strike?" He had suspected as much. Foley, the commander who headed security, never had much finesse.

"He was following orders."

"You ordered him to destroy a medical station?" Mace understood she'd given no such order, knew Foley had embraced his sadistic side.

Cache's eyes flashed. "Watch it."

He heard the challenge and ignored it, having no desire to overthrow her position and take on all the bullshit that went with it.

"You would have been better off sending Grey." His attempt to appease made her eyes flash again.

But Grey cut in, diffusing the tension. "That's what I said."

Cache took a breath, glancing between them. "I couldn't risk losing both of you on a retrieval mission, so I sent Foley."

He shared a glance with his friend. *Good to know Cache thinks Foley expendable.* Especially when they knew the commander earned his position here through his connections with Admiral Ricker, a man who shared his sadistic side.

Mace changed the subject. "What's on the docket, Commodore?"

Cache turned to the holotable, accessing three-dimensional images of ships, data running along the glossy surface. "They've stopped everything in Sector Five since your mission. We can't find any trace of them, but," she paused, swiping her hand across the table, "we've received some good information about possible gun running in Sector Four, here."

She magnified a small section of space on the edge of CORE territory. "We're concentrating our efforts at this location since the new manufacturing plants won't be operational for another month. We're waiting to hear from our contact."

"What's this?" he asked, gesturing to a red beacon on the other side of the map.

Cache enlarged the area, her expression turning stony. "We were tracking a CORE civilian vessel heading to Sector Ten. They didn't heed our warnings, and have passed the point of no return now. Short of locking weapons, there wasn't anything we could do."

Mace shook his head. He didn't understand why anyone would choose to go to Sector Ten voluntarily. Once a vessel went into the man-made nebula controlled by Calypsons, it never returned, basically amounting to suicide—or some sort of twisted religious pilgrimage where no one on the outside understood the end result.

Cache met his eyes. "Return to your regular duty roster tomorrow." When he opened his mouth to say he was fine now, she added, "That's an order."

"Yes, sir."

Dismissed by her nod, both he and Grey strode to the exit, then through the security checkpoint.

"I have some families to speak to," Mace said when they stopped in front of the lift.

Grey nodded, slapping the control to call it to them. "Right beside you."

Nia's locket lay cool in her palm. Her heart beat fast in her throat. It was time to turn the tracker on.

Sitting on the edge of the bed, she glanced around Mace's quarters, pleased with the carnage she'd wrought. Destroying the potted plant hadn't been enough. She'd grabbed anything she could get her hands on. After she'd eaten as much as she could from the refrigeration unit—too much because she'd gotten sick immediately after—she'd demolished the rest, hoping he wouldn't have any food rations for the next month and would starve to death. As a precaution, she'd taken a shard of the pot to use as a weapon, and it lay beside her hip.

A tiny voice in her head poked at her. *He won't hurt you. He kept you from being ransomed.*

Ignoring that voice, she ran her thumb over the etched vines decorating the locket. She needed to turn it on but hesitated. As far as she could tell, there weren't any recording devices in Mace's quarters. But what if there were? What would happen to her if they found out what she held? Once activated, would those enforcers pound on her door? Would they think twice about shooting her, or kill her with the same swiftness as the medical officer who'd resisted?

But if she didn't turn it on, then she'd have no chance of escape. Orion's tight security measures and heavy fortifications prevented her from escaping on her own.

Would Calvin be looking for her? She and the administrator of *Elara Five* had a brief, uninspired relationship. The only way she'd enjoyed being with him was when she'd taken enhancers. When she'd realized he'd only been using her for her connections, she'd ended it. But he'd never let go of his entitlement to her time. She'd hated him for continually stepping into her business, but if he sent people after her now, she wouldn't complain.

Maybe Calvin couldn't. Maybe he had his hands full putting *Elara Five* back together. *If he's still alive.* Nausea rose in her throat when she thought of how many must have died in the attack.

After someone informed her parents that she had been taken, they would do everything to find her. They had the resources and influence to move fleets of ships. Did they already know? *Probably.* News traveled fast when connected to the grid.

Nia wiggled the naked fingers of her left hand, looking at the tiny ports where her PALM was supposed to connect. Would the Tellusians remove those too? *Most likely.* They'd already rendered her ocular implant useless.

She clenched her hand into a fist, then forced herself to relax and clicked the locket open. The overhead lights glinted against the gold of the empty ovals. With a deep breath, she pressed her right thumb to the left side. The metal warmed beneath her skin, and adrenaline pumped through her blood.

In the other oval, a white line hovered across the middle. It fluctuated in the rhythm of her heart, like the stats of a med bed. *There.* If she survived, someone would rescue her. She allowed the locket to fall to her chest, then flopped onto the bed. Crisscrossed overhead beams filled her view.

Turning on the tracker lifted a suffocating load from her mind, but the resulting weariness settled into every limb. *So blasted tired.*

Under no circumstances would she allow herself to fall asleep, to be vulnerable. She needed to protect herself. If she fell asleep... her mind had conjured a thousand horrific scenarios.

Blink. She kicked off her CORE-issue boots and rolled on her side to stare at the door. *These blankets are too soft.* If she closed her eyes, she would still be able to hear when he returned. *Just for a moment.*

Chapter Seven

M ace had thought it was a good idea to allow Nia some time alone, some space, but when he walked through the doors of his quarters, the sight before him made him take an involuntary step back.

She'd demolished everything. Fruit peels and juices smeared the bulkheads and deck. All the shelves from the refrigeration unit were pulled out and tossed. She'd emptied the ration tubes and thrown them.

I should have kept her bound.

The only thing remaining in its original location was the table—probably because it was bolted to the deck. One chair lay in the center of the room, the other was beside the far bulkhead. It looked like she'd chucked the thing at the terminal. He squinted at it. *Yep.* Definitely a dent in the middle.

The destroyer herself lay on her side, her hands tucked under her chin, knees bent to reveal her socked feet. A wrapper hung from the overhead beams, threatening to fall on her head.

His next step inside crunched on the broken pot of his orange tree.

What the hell was he supposed to do with her? He ran a hand over his face. Waking her was probably a good start, but he wasn't looking forward to defending himself against her. He rather enjoyed owning eyes and testicles.

Mace collected the chair in the center of the room and placed it on its feet before sitting. He cleared his throat.

She shot to her feet like a fighter out of a launch tube. Standing on the bed, she clutched a piece of plant pot in her hand, holding it in front of her like a weapon.

"Stay back," she yelped, her voice cracking.

His chest tightened. Placing his hands on his thighs, he leaned back in the chair. Her eyes were fixed on his and didn't waver. He kept still, waiting for her to calm and adjust to his presence.

"I will not hurt you, *izar.*"

Her hand shook on the makeshift weapon, almost imperceptibly at first, then her whole arm trembled.

"What do you want?" she finally asked, lowering the weapon a centimeter.

"I came to check on you and to see if you wanted new clothing."

"Clothing?" Her weapon lowered farther. She glanced at the torn material on her shoulder, and his gaze followed. Alabaster skin contrasted with the black of her uniform. With one hand, she tried to lift the flap, but it flopped forward. She gave up, grasping the weapon with both hands and pointing it at him with a jab. "What do you mean by clothing?"

"Clothes. The normal kind. Pants go on one leg at a time. Shirts over your head."

She didn't break a smile at his attempt at humor, didn't even blink.

Mace exhaled. "I'll take you to a shop. You can pick out what you like."

Her face tightened.

"There's a nice place in the atrium where we were earlier."

Her features relaxed, and she lowered the pot shard. Maybe she thought she could gain her freedom in such an open space. Emotions played across her face, like she were having a conversation with herself in her head.

Finally, she hopped to the deck and primly set the shard on the edge of the bed. She stooped to pull on her boots before smoothing the front of her bloodstained uniform.

"Clothing would be appreciated, thank you."

He almost shook his head at her forced manners. CORE citizens were nothing if not polite. Standing, he walked to the door and waited for her to join him. She strode through the carnage with her head held high, stepping over each smear of mess with a dainty hop. He might have found it comical if it hadn't been his quarters.

When she stopped beside him, he touched his vambrace, and her wrists clasped together with a click.

A strangled sound came from her throat as she turned her gaze to his, her jaw clenched. He had the urge to undo the bonds but knew he couldn't. Not without repercussions to both of them. He turned away from her infuriated eyes and stepped into the corridor.

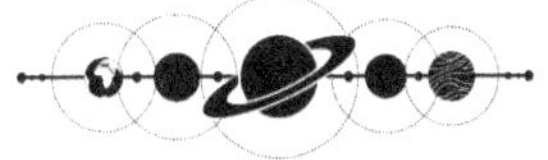

Jaw clenched, Nia kept her gaze glued to Mace's back, watching the play of muscle beneath the skin-hugging material as they walked the corridor. He'd changed into a warrior's uniform, like the one his friend had been wearing the day before, but Mace's had long sleeves. The dark blue suited his olive complexion. He'd shaved too. It almost made him look...respectable? Less threatening?

She shook her head, eyes lowering. Stars above, why did Tellusians wear such tight pants? He might as well be naked given how little they left to the imagination. *Gluteus maximus, gluteus medius, tensor fasciae latae.* Medical terminology helped her keep it professional instead of appreciating the way his muscles bunched and shifted.

Her eyes rested on his gun. All the warriors she'd seen yesterday in the corridors had at least one gun strapped to their thigh, some with two, and numerous blades as well. Mace only had the one, no knives.

They arrived at the lift, and he turned to her, catching her stare. She stepped back, heat flooding her neck and face.

He held her gaze, his brow puckering. "That would not end well for you, *izar.*"

She shivered at the threat given in such a soft tone, was about to deny she'd been thinking about grabbing the gun, when he touched the panel beside the lift.

The door slid open. He gestured for her to enter ahead of him. They both turned, and the lift doors closed, sealing them inside. As it rose, she cast him a glance out of the corner of her eye. She'd thought him intimidating before, but in his Tellusian uniform, with a weapon on his thigh, it was ten times worse.

The lift stopped, the door opening. Mace sent her a brief glance before leading the way out. She followed him onto the third level of the atrium, to a door marked CAL3-027. It slid open when he touched the side panel.

Mace stepped through first, and she followed, hesitant. The space was as large as his quarters, but bolts of fabric covered the bulkheads with bright colors and bold patterns. Nia squinted against the offensive glare. Some fabrics were even changing color and pattern.

A woman sat on a stool beside the counter at the rear of the space and lifted her head. Her eyes widened. "Mace."

Her black hair was styled elaborately on her head, and she'd outlined her eyes with dark makeup. The red dress she wore had cutouts everywhere, revealing more flesh than it covered, despite the skirt being floor-length. *So much skin.*

The woman said nothing for long seconds, only stared, then she shot to her feet before moving toward them, her eyes jumping from Mace to Nia, then to her bonds. Nia flexed her fingers.

"Welcome. Come on in." The woman's accent wasn't as thick as Mace's, lilting in a different cadence, almost musical.

"You look well," Mace responded with a smile.

His genuine pleasure made Nia's stomach flutter. She glowered, turning her head to stare at the woman's tattoo. A thin line of words, in a language she couldn't read, spiraled its way from her pinkie finger to her ear.

She met Nia's eyes, brow crinkling, then blinked at Mace. "You need some clothes?"

Mace nodded as he touched his vambrace, and Nia's wrists fell apart. "Whatever she needs."

"Budget?" she asked, eyebrows raised.

Mace shook his head.

Her eyes brightened. "Great!" The woman grabbed Nia's elbow, and she instinctively pulled away.

Beside her, Mace took a step forward to separate them.

The woman frowned. "It's okay," she said to Nia. "I won't hurt you."

Her cheeks burned. She hadn't thought the woman would hurt her; she just didn't want to be touched. Nia pressed her lips together. She shouldn't have to say it.

"Let's go into the back," the woman said after an awkward beat, pointing with excessive gestures like she had a hearing problem instead of a touching problem. "I can get you started."

Nia glanced at Mace. He was leaving her here? Tightness squeezed her chest.

"How long will you need?" he asked, a strained expression on his face as he glanced between them.

Without looking at him, the woman waved over her shoulder. "Give us an hour."

"Thanks, Dee." Shooting Nia one last glance, he left.

Unreasonable panic shot through her a second later.

The fragile expression on Nia's face was almost too much. But Mace knew not to worry. Dee was safe, reliable. She wouldn't do anything to upset or hurt his ward.

Running a distracted hand through his hair, he strode to the lift, then hit the control panel for the fifth deck. He had an hour. One hour to relieve the strain in his shoulders and try to rid himself of the protective, *possessive*, feelings that arose whenever his ward was near. Emotions he had no business having.

Striding past the barracks, Mace walked through the double-wide doorway of the sparring arena and jogged down the set of stairs immediately right. Grey, along with two other of his top instructors, worked with the new batch of tyros. The novice warriors were unarmed—standing orders until some of the more eager ones understood what control meant.

Mace gave Grey a two-finger salute and kept walking until he passed through the wide doorway leading to the target range. Returning the nods of the warriors who acknowledged him, he kept going until he reached the end of the corridor.

Four private rooms occupied the rear corner, and two of them were empty. He scanned his hand and stepped into a small sparring space, everything matted from deck to overhead. One bulkhead held numerous weapons, but he didn't reach for one, instead, pressing the control beside the door.

A cylindrical matted column rose from the deck until it connected with the overhead. Mace didn't bother to wrap his knuckles before he beat the shit out of the thing.

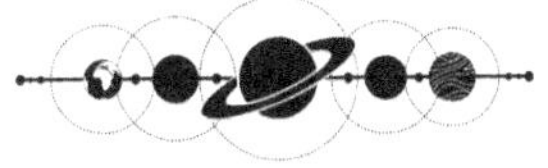

The woman disappeared through a doorway behind the counter while Nia remained frozen in her spot. *Abandoned.* He'd left her there.

Black hair and outlined-eyes poked around the other side of the bulkhead, then she stepped fully into view. "I'm Deesha, by the way. Everyone calls me Dee." Cocking a hip, she raised her eyebrows expectantly.

Nia cleared her throat. "Nia." She pushed at the torn edge of her uniform, trying to cover exposed skin, but it flopped forward again.

"Nice to meet you." Dee waved her closer, gesturing to the counter. "Why don't we look at a few things first, get used to each other."

Forcing one foot in front of the other, Nia joined her, the counter separating them.

After a few taps on its glossy surface, Dee said, "Let me know if you see anything you like."

Images of different fashions materialized in front of them, and Nia's jaw went slack. It was beautiful work, but Dee couldn't expect her to wear this stuff. She might as well walk around naked.

A few more pages of three-dimensional outlandish fashion and finally Dee arrived at more conservative styles. They still weren't anything Nia was used to.

"Stop, please. That's nice," she said, pointing to a woman wearing a long-sleeved tunic top with leggings underneath. Despite it being rather formfitting and having a wide neckline, it would cover most of her skin, more than most of the styles she'd seen.

"Good choice." Dee scrolled through more images. "Anything else catch your eye?"

"No. Thank you." She stepped away from the counter so she wouldn't have to look at the revealing fashions anymore.

Dark-lined eyes blinked at her. "What? No. You've got to take advantage of Mace's creds while you can."

Nia's cheeks burned.

"Look," Dee said when Nia didn't respond. "I'll fabricate the first one, and we'll go from there." Her hand stretched out, like she were going to grab Nia's elbow, then she stilled and dropped it to her side. "The change rooms are in the back. We need to get you out of this icky stuff."

Following Dee, Nia smoothed the wrinkles in her uniform. Three frosted glass doors lined one side of the narrow space.

"Get out of your clothes," Dee said, sliding one door open with a touch of her finger. "Boots too. All of it. I'll make you some underwear. The room will scan your measurements, and I'll return momentarily."

The door to the changing room slid shut behind her. Hesitating a moment, Nia kicked off her beaten-up boots and undressed. As soon as she stood naked except for her bonds and locket, the room scanned her with white light. Her mind returned to her first few minutes on this station, and she breathed faster. Exposed, she crossed her arms over her chest and stared at the frosted glass door instead of the floor-length mirror. She didn't want to see the defeated circles under her eyes.

Fabric flew over the top of the door, making her jump.

"Start with these," Dee called.

Black leggings, a purple tunic top, and nude undergarments hung over the glass. Nia yanked them over and quickly slipped them on, this time facing the mirror. They were tighter than she would have liked, but they would do.

"Can I see?" Dee's voice came through the door. "I want to make sure the seamer got your measurements right."

Nia touched the control, and the door slid open.

Dee smiled. "You look great. Prefect fit." Her eyes went right to the locket hanging against Nia's sternum. "Oh, wow. That's beautiful. Antique?"

When Dee leaned closer to peer at it, Nia covered it with her hand.

Chapter Eight

Nia's heart pounded, the threat of discovery fogging her vision. It was a foolish reaction. If enforcers hadn't come running already, then no one knew she'd signaled her position to the CORE.

Dee stepped away. "Oh. I didn't mean to pry." When it looked like she was about to say something else, she shook her head and forced a smile. "I have some other stuff for you to try, but I'll get this one in green too. Be back in a moment."

When the door closed, Nia's heart rate lowered. She opened her palm and realized she'd squeezed the locket so tight, an impression remained where her PALM should have been.

Dee threw more garments at her, most too bold or bright, too revealing. Nia approved the ones in darker colors that covered most of her skin.

After forty minutes, Nia called a halt to the fashion show, exhaustion setting in.

"You've picked some great stuff." Dee smiled, tilting her head. "Get yourself changed, and I'll package everything to be delivered."

Left alone, Nia chose the first purple outfit to wear. Dee had new black flats waiting for her beside the counter. Nia slid into them easily, her feet cushioned on what felt like pillows. She cleared her throat. "May I ask you something?"

"Just ask." Dee's eyes crinkled in mirth. "You don't have to ask if you can ask."

Nia's face heated. "Why were you so shocked when I came in here?"

Dee seemed to consider her answer for a moment before saying, "Well, Mace is quite outspoken against people farming. Taking you pretty much contradicts anything he's said since he took his command post here."

Nia frowned. Tellusians against people farming? Wasn't it what they lived for?

The door to the shop slid open, and Mace stepped in, pausing mid-step. He looked like he'd gone for a run, his skin tone brightened by exertion, a fiery light in his eyes.

"You ladies finished?" he asked, entering the shop fully.

"Yep!" Dee replied. "Everything will be delivered to the common holding within the hour."

"No," he contradicted her. "To my quarters."

Dee opened her mouth, eyes wide. She slowly nodded, her jaw still hanging wide.

"Thanks Dee, I owe you one."

She snapped her mouth shut. "Nah. You paid plenty. How's the orange tree doing?"

"Could be better."

"Mace! I told you it needed care and attention. You can't ignore the thing, or it'll die." Dee shook her head at him.

Cheeks heating, Nia focused on the versatile fabrics changing color next to her. There'd only been one plant in his quarters, and she'd mangled it. She held her breath, waiting for him to say what she'd done, but he gestured toward the exit.

Nia moved closer, aware of how her clothes clung to her body. The urge to pull the fabric away from her skin, to make it bulkier, gave her a full-body flush. She should have gotten Dee to design something similar to her unisex CORE uniform, a garment she practically lived in.

When she glanced up at Mace, he touched his vambrace without looking at her. Her wrists snapped together.

Blast, she hated that.

With one last glance at Dee and the disbelief underlying her expression, Mace followed Nia out, but kept his distance. His ward kept walking until she overlooked the common space of the atrium. A strange sensation rolled through his gut at seeing her out of her uniform.

She leaned over the railing, the fabric of her new shirt stretching across her shoulders. Mace nodded to a warrior under his command who walked past, before taking a breath and closing the gap between them.

He leaned forward to see what Nia was seeing. If he concentrated on the people below, then maybe he wouldn't stare at her. Her uniform had been formless and unflattering. This new top and leggings were anything but.

Straightening, he strangled the railing like it was his own neck, then cleared his throat. "You've been placed in a medical bay."

She stiffened and shot him a side-glance. "To work at." Her tone flat, she refocused on the people sitting around the tables below.

"To work at," he agreed.

A breath shuddered through her. "And if I refuse?"

"Then you can't earn any creds." He couldn't force her to work.

"And I could earn enough creds to buy my way off this place?" Bitterness coated her words.

If only. "It doesn't work that way," he replied.

Nia narrowed her eyes at him. "Then tell me how it works."

How could he even begin to explain the intricacies of the processing system centuries in the making? So convoluted, laws within laws, especially for new captives. The old laws he'd invoked to keep her with him were barbaric—and that was a kind word for them.

At his silence, she returned to watching the crowd below. "When would I start?"

"Now, if you like. They placed you in a bay manned only with medics, not doctors. We currently have a shortage."

"And that explains why you people farmed at *Elara Five.*" She spoke between gritted teeth.

"Yes." There was no disputing it. Every warrior who took captives would earn a percentage of their income—an incentive that needed to be abolished and one he'd waived.

"But it doesn't explain its destruction." Her voice had gone soft.

His chest squeezed. Cache had sent the raid to rescue him. It was Mace's fault her people died.

A sharp beep emitted from his vambrace, distracting him from the weakness of his guilt. Cache's command insignia flashed at the top of the communique. He swiped the message away, not wanting to rush Nia through her decision.

She took a deep breath and stood straighter to meet his eyes. "I will work."

Unwarranted pride swelled in his chest at her determined expression. She might be tiny, but she was filled with fire. It would have been easy for her to stay in his quarters and give up. But her spirit wouldn't be quelled—perhaps one of the reasons he hadn't been able to leave her on *Elara Five* to die.

Mace pushed away from the railing, muscles rigid. "This way," he said, cocking his head toward the lift.

The medical bay was located towards the docking bay where they'd arrived. Nia buried her disappointment. It would have been nice to be close to the welcoming light of the atrium.

Stopping in front of the door, she read the words printed in Common below a script she couldn't read. She stiffened. "Family medicine?" She met Mace's gaze.

A frown pinched his brow. "Is there a problem?"

Nia closed her eyes briefly. Her family medicine rotation at the Lunar Medical Academy had been the longest of her entire medical training, rivaled only by her stint in pediatrics. She didn't understand young people, was always awkward around them, and had been relieved when she'd completed that chapter of her life. Children smelled funny and had sticky fingers.

"I'm a surgeon," she said, voice hoarse. "Post me where my skills are useful." She tugged against her bonds, stepping aside when someone needed to pass them in the corridor. "How do you know I won't hurt someone in there?" This was beyond ridiculous.

"Will you?"

"Of course not!" She winced at her honesty. "Just—" She stepped to the side again, allowing another person by, then glanced down the corridor. "Put me somewhere else." *Anywhere else.*

"This is where you're needed." He ran an agitated hand through his hair. "You'll have a four-hour shift to start." Pressing the side panel, the door slid open. He all but pushed her inside, hand on the small of her back.

All activity stilled at their entrance. Every head turned in her direction. Three medics stared at her, their white jackets standing out against the gray of the bulkheads. She heard the beeping of Mace's vambrace, and her hands parted.

The medics resumed their tasks, but the patients, both child-sized and not, remained focused on her.

Nia forced a smile. "Get me another post," she said, trying not to move her lips.

"You're good. I've seen your work. You'll be fine here." His words made her break the staring contest she was having with a toddler sitting on their mother's lap.

She ignored the rush the compliment gave her and turned her back to the room. "No. I won't," she said under her breath.

Head tilted slightly, he stared at her. For a second, she believed he would give in, then he shook his head. "I'll return for you at the end of your shift."

She wanted to throw something at his retreating back. When he paused at the door, she breathed a sigh of relief. Then he said, "Don't try to leave."

"Why not?"

He kept his voice low. "Your bonds will shock you once you cross the threshold."

She stared at her wrists, unsurprised.

But he continued, "They increase in intensity with each attempt. Could eventually kill you if you kept at it."

Nia inhaled sharply as the door closed behind him. She looked at her bonds, then at the door, then at her bonds—a sick feeling settled in the pit of her stomach. The voice of her basic training instructor pounded in her brain. *Better to kill yourself than to be used and abused by Tells. If you have an out, take it.*

Her stomach rolled. The suicide option had never sat well with her. She turned around, and a medic stopped in front of her, looking her up and down.

"You're a doctor?" His tone held derision.

Nia tensed. "Yes, a surgeon."

He threw a short white jacket and a scanner at her. "Get to work or get out of the way."

Her spine snapped straight, jaw going slack. *What an asshole.* That sort of insubordination would have earned him a reprimand where she'd come from. Her eyes followed him as he returned to the woman he'd been tending.

Trying to put her wounded sense of hierarchy aside, she donned the jacket, zipped it closed, and noticed the sleeves stopped short of her bonds, ensuring they would always be exposed.

Hand clenched around the scanner, she approached the first unattended person—a child. He sat on a med bed, face flushed, his mother beside her. Nia stopped in front of them, and he sneezed.

She stepped back.

When Mace entered the command center, he knew something was wrong. All the commanders and sub-commanders were already there, one for each section of the station, eight in total. At the head of the holotable, the commodore threw him a displeased expression. The rest stared at him with raised eyebrows.

Ignoring them, he took his place beside Grey and homed in on Foley across the table. Narrow face, long nose, and his muddy-colored hair swooping over his pale forehead, Foley appeared as self-satisfied as he always did.

Mace clenched his fists, ready to call him out, but Cache touched the holotable, retrieving three-dimensional images of a decimated ship. A tense hush settled over them.

"We've lost another Destroyer," she began without preamble. A rumble of unease passed between the commanders. "Three Guardians attacked the *Bellicose* while it escorted five transports to Saturn."

Air escaped from his lungs like he'd been punched. He'd had many friends on the *Bellicose*. Snippets of recordings streamed across the table's surface, one where the Destroyer exploded. Fury seared through him, hot, escalating his need to lash out.

Retaliation. The CORE had done this because of the attack on *Elara Five*. Mace's eyes went to Foley again. The other commander kept his eyes on the recordings, arms crossed, and had more to answer for than the destruction of a medical station.

"Survivors, sir?" Commander Poole asked from beside Foley, his features wide where Foley's were narrow.

Cache took a breath. "They kept a few to make an example of and executed the rest." Grumbles of anger and unease rippled across the surface of the table. "The ones who survived are scheduled for the airlock in two days' time. The CORE didn't seize the transports caught in the crossfire. Some are being diverted here for medical attention and should arrive by tomorrow."

Tension cascaded off the commanders around the table, the mood shifting from alert to volatile. Everyone wanted to fight, to get even. *Blood for blood.* Mace kept his eyes on Foley, waiting for Cache to call him out for his misstep. The reprimand never came.

"Do we have a target in mind, sir?" Grey asked from beside him.

"No."

Everyone's gazes snapped to hers.

She raised her hand. "I know. We all want to take action, but my orders came from the top. Admiral Krispin and the others want us to focus on

Sector Four. If we retaliate now, we lose our chance of finding out what's going on there. We need to stay focused, even if it kills us."

Distracted from his need to put a knife through Foley's eyeball, Mace raised his eyebrows at her.

"I'm serious." Everything in her posture said she was speaking the truth.

He nodded, knowing if the admirals were breathing down her neck to stay out of the way, they meant it.

"What about those who are going to be executed?" Grey asked. "Are retrievals scheduled?"

Cache didn't answer right away, and a hard knot settled in Mace's stomach.

"We've been told to stay out of that as well." A stunned silence fell over the table. Cache kept her eyes fixed on the images hovering above the table. "We'll reconvene when I have something new to report. Dismissed."

Mace wanted to argue, to demand a way to make the CORE pay for what they'd done. His focus shifted when Foley pushed away from the table and headed toward the exit.

Before he could follow, Cache stepped into his path. "You were late."

She might be itching for a fight, but she wasn't the one he needed to confront. He stepped around her and kept walking, then felt her eyes boring into his spine. It didn't stop him.

There was blood he needed to spill.

Chapter Nine

The lift door slid open, and Mace stepped out. At the end of the corridor, Foley walked away from him, Commander Poole at his side. Fury burning in his gut, Mace jogged to catch up.

"Hey, Foley," he said, tapping him on the shoulder.

Mid-sentence, Foley turned. In the next instant, he was on the deck, holding his nose, blood coating his mouth. "What the fuck?" His nasal voice went high-pitched.

At his side, Poole tipped his head, looking from one of them to the other without intervening.

Mace shook the sting out of his hand. "That was for *Elara Five*."

"*Elara Five*?" Foley whined. "I saved your ass on *Elara Five*."

Mace clenched his fists, needing to hit him again. "You destroyed a non-combative medical station and nearly killed me."

With his hand holding his nose and blood dripping down his chin, Foley's face puckered in confusion. "I was following orders."

"Cache did *not* order you to destroy the place."

"Cache *ordered* me to take as many medical officers as possible because we're so short. Do you think if we'd sidled up and parked nicely, they would've hopped on?"

Mace ran his hand over his face. More guilt pressed down on him. Poole pulled Foley to his feet.

"What is this really about?" Foley wiped the blood off his upper lip and flung it to the side. "You want my position?"

"I don't want your fucking position." Being *Orion's* head of security was the last thing he wanted. He'd found his place training tyros and loved it. It was the only thing he cared about, really. He didn't want to become Cache's glorified enforcer.

Wiping more blood onto the sleeve of his uniform, Foley said, "You should be thanking me. Everyone's heard about the captive you kept to play with and—"

Mace's fist connected with Foley's face for a second time, in the exact same spot as it had before.

Foley's head snapped back, but he stayed on his feet. "What the fuck?" he roared, charging forward. Mace braced, ready to do more damage, when Poole stepped between them. Grey was there a second later.

Mace's body slammed into his friend's. "Get out of the way," he gritted.

"Think about what you're doing." Grey murmured the words, but there was steel in his tone.

But the urge to kill Foley was so strong, he could hardly see straight. He wanted him to pay. For everything.

For attacking *Elara Five*.

For almost killing them.

For Mace taking Nia instead of leaving her behind.

The thought was a cold spray of water in his face. As angry as he was at Foley, he was more enraged with himself. He'd used her as a shield like a coward. If there'd been another way to survive the situation, he hadn't seen it.

But I should have left her to die.

Mace straightened, digging his hand into his hair, and watched as Poole restrained a thrashing Foley.

"You need to blow off some steam," Grey said under his breath.

Mace stepped back. "Yeah."

With Foley still vowing in three different languages to bring hell on his family, Mace turned around and headed toward the lift, Grey beside him.

Before the lift door closed, he met Foley's gaze. The commander had stopped fighting Poole. Blood dripped down his face as he stared at Mace with an expression that promised retribution.

As the lift ascended, Mace stared at his reflection in the shiny surface of the control panel. Then he punched it, a dull crack reverberating in the small space. "Fuck!"

Breaths labored from exertion, Mace wiped his neck and chest with the towel and threw it to the deck. He flexed his fingers, wincing. The cuts and bruises shifted over the bones of his knuckles.

The confrontation with Foley kept bouncing around in his head. He'd owed the man the first punch, but with the second, he may have started a blood feud. He should have regretted it, but didn't. Mace wanted more of Foley's blood spilled. Then maybe his mind would finally settle.

Because no matter how much he pounded the shit out of the padded column, he couldn't erase the sound of Nia's voice when she'd begged him to leave her on *Elara Five*.

He *shouldn't* care. Compassion for his pint-sized ward would only lead to weakness.

I am not weak. If other commanders and those below him thought he couldn't handle his job, then there would be no end to the challenges for his position. Hell, Cache would call him out herself if she thought him unfit for duty.

And all because he was stupid enough to care about what happened to one CORE doctor.

His vambrace beeped. It was the end of Nia's shift. Bending, he scooped his shirt from the deck and pulled it over his damp body. He'd shower later.

Grey gave him a wave, eyes concerned, as Mace walked the outer edges of the sparring area and took the stairs two at a time to the barracks level, then out into the atrium. He kept his pace quick as he strode to the lift and rode it down.

A few more corridors later, Mace stepped into the medical bay. Three medics glared at Nia's back while she attended the only patient in the room. They abruptly scattered when they saw him, trying to look busy with their duties.

Nia sat on a stool, a boy's foot in her lap. The kid's father stood beside her, arms crossed over his chest, looking as grumpy as the medics.

Completely focused, she moved a regenerator over the boy's ankle. A strange sensation unfurled in his chest as Mace leaned against the door frame to watch.

The boy twitched, and Nia's head snapped up.

"Are you okay? Has the numbing agent stopped working because—"

She stopped talking when the boy shook his head. "It tickled."

"Oh." She let out a heavy breath, then a strained chuckle. "That's okay then. I'm almost finished."

She returned to her task. Curls fell forward to curtain her face, and Mace had the urge to go over there and tuck her hair behind her ears so he could watch her expressions. He clenched his fists, the freshly bruised skin of his knuckles protesting the action.

Straightening, Nia said, "There. You're all done." She slid on his sock and shoe before helping him hop off the bed. "Don't do any backflips for a while."

Mace saw her glare at the father as she said it. His answering glower made Mace want to punch him. He kept his eyes on the pair as they left the medical bay. Nia's cheeks turned pink when she saw him standing near the door.

"You ready to go?" he asked, noticing the dark circles under her eyes. His chest constricted knowing he'd been the one to put them there.

"Gladly," she said, tossing a glance at the three medics who fumbled around the supply shelves. She shrugged out of the white jacket and hung it on a hook with others near the door. When he reached to touch his vambrace to engage her bonds, she stopped him by grabbing his hand. His whole body twitched.

"You're injured," she said, examining his knuckles. "How did this happen?"

Nia pulled him over to the med bed, and he followed, unable to resist the tug of her warm fingers. Tingles radiated up his arm from where her skin connected with his. Grasping a regenerator, she adjusted the settings, then raised her eyebrows, waiting for his answer.

Mace cleared his throat. "I hit something."

Her brows pinched together before she focused on the injury. The regenerator hummed in the otherwise silent room. With his hand resting in her much smaller one, she healed each of his knuckles in turn.

The damage wasn't bad. He could have healed it himself without a problem, but hadn't been thinking. He should tell her he'd do it himself later—he didn't.

Mace couldn't pull his eyes away from the sight of his hand in hers. He focused on the differences between them. Her skin was pale, flawless, but still had the slightly red contact points of her PALM on her thumb, forefinger, and pinkie. His hand seemed so bulky compared to hers, his skin darker. He became overly conscious of where they connected, how her thumb pressed on the side of his hand to keep him from moving.

It was all over too soon, each of his knuckles unblemished. He didn't move his hand when the regenerator stopped humming.

"I'm assuming the other one is damaged?" she asked, keeping her head bent.

Mace removed his hand and placed the other in her upturned palm. Heat traveled through his arm from the fresh contact, and it had nothing to do with the regenerator humming over his knuckles. His fingers twitched. Nia stilled her movements for a second before continuing.

With all his knuckles mended, Nia let go of his hand and turned off the regenerator. She set it with the other tools next to the med bed before heading to the exit, casting a glance at the medics over her shoulder. The pink on her face darkened to red. Mace touched his vambrace, her bonds clicking together, and they headed out into the corridor.

"What was that all about?" he asked as they stopped in front of the lift.

Her wide eyes flew to his, confused, until he jerked his head toward the medical bay. "The medics?"

The question set her off.

"They didn't even know how to treat a compound fracture. Can you believe it? What are they doing in there if they can't treat something simple? That boy came in, and the one medic, he was going to make a mess of it, so I told him to get out of my way. I wasn't going to put the child at risk of chronic pain for the rest of his life. Not on my watch." Her breath left her in a whoosh.

Mace had always thought the CORE's Common accent was snobbish at best, their pronunciation of words exact, consonants hit precisely. But in her irate state, his ward wore it well. It made her even more appealing.

He cleared his throat. "I told you we had a shortage of doctors." He touched the lift's control to call it to their location.

"I know, but I didn't think it would be that bad..." Her voice trailed off.

The lift arrived, and they stepped inside. "And the father? He didn't look happy."

Mace didn't know it was possible for her to redden further.

"I *may* have asked him how the boy sustained the injury, and I *may* have insinuated I didn't believe his answer."

His eyebrows jumped. She really knew how to make friends. Her heightened color didn't recede as the lift doors opened and they exited onto the deck with his quarters. Her fingers tugged at the hem of her shirt as they walked, drawing attention to areas of her body he'd been trying to avoid.

Mace focused on the corridor ahead instead of his ward's body. After scanning his hand on the panel next to his quarters, he ushered her through and disengaged her bonds. She turned to him, face flushed and vibrant.

He retreated into the corridor. "Feed yourself, get some rest."

"Wait!"

He raised his eyebrows at her shout.

Nia bit her lip. "Is there a way for me to contact the captives from *Elara Five*?"

The hope in her eyes was enough to cool his emotions. "No. It's not allowed."

Her gaze fell, and he tried to ignore the resulting pang in his chest. He needed to get out of there before he considered breaking Captive Laws to give her what she wanted.

The door closed between them, and Mace exhaled. He couldn't be in the same room as her, not when his emotions were so volatile and he didn't know which way was up.

He flexed his healed knuckles and knew he needed to bruise them again.

Chapter Ten

N ia drifted in a safe space, warm and cozy.

Waking increments at a time, she realized she hadn't had one of the bizarre dreams, memories, that usually woke her. No images of birds eating eyeballs. No double-edged knives waved in her face. No voice saying, "Here's a pretty."

She sighed, contentment seeping into her limbs, then snuggled deeper into the plush bedding. Her face pressed against something smooth but hard, her knee cocked upward, and her one hand was wedged between two warm thighs.

She froze. *Thighs. Oh god.*

Her eyes flew open. *Mace.* Her whole body was squeezed against him.

She pushed away. "Don't touch me!" she screamed, shooting to her feet to hunch against the bulkhead. Her whole side was warm from his body heat. She rubbed her hands against it, trying to erase the sensation. A flush traveled up her throat.

"I wasn't," Mace replied, his hands stacked behind his head, fully clothed. He hadn't moved.

Her cheeks burned. She'd been using him like a pillow.

"Sorry," she muttered, then shook her head. Why was she apologizing? Amusement flashed across his face.

Nia narrowed her eyes. His uniform clung to his body, outlining his pectorals and abdominals. She knew each of those defined muscles from when she'd healed his wound.

Tearing her gaze away, she stared above him, at the crisscrossed overhead beams, and fisted her hands. "I need to use the washroom," she said between clenched teeth.

"Go ahead," he replied, remaining where he was.

A huff of disbelief burst from her lips. He wasn't going to move? *Fine.* She shuffled to the side, keeping her spine against the bulkhead, then nudged his socked feet with her toes. They jiggled, but he didn't move out of the way.

So she kicked him.

Averting his face, he rolled to his feet, and she could have sworn he swallowed a chuckle. *A chuckle!* Cheeks burning, she hopped off the bed and scurried to the washroom. The door slid closed behind her, lights illuminating the small space a second later.

She turned to the digital mirror, but it was off.

"Viewer on," she murmured. Nothing happened. "Mirror on." It remained inert. Then she noticed the button on the bulkhead and pressed it. Her image flickered to life.

Why is nothing voice activated here?

Her shoulders tense, Nia stared at herself, her heightened color blazing at her. She really wished she didn't light up like a fixture every time she felt embarrassed. It plagued her existence. She was a doctor, not a ten-year-old.

Still agitated, she used the toilet, then the steam shower. The clothes Dee had made for her had been waiting in neat piles on the bed when she'd arrived yesterday, but she hadn't thought to grab a new set in her haste. There'd been some other changes in Mace's quarters too. Someone had cleaned the room, and none of what she'd destroyed remained. The refrigeration unit had been coded to her biometrics, as well as one of the clothing compartments under the bed.

The only evidence of yesterday's tantrum was the sapling missing from the table.

After redressing in the purple top and black leggings, she returned to the main room. Mace sat at the table eating rations. He wasn't facing her directly, but she could still feel his amusement.

Blood rushed to her face. He thought she was something to laugh at? Was she here to entertain him? He'd abducted her, and he was *amused*?

Striding to the table, every nerve ready to do battle, she faced off with him. "What do you want from me?"

He looked up from his meal, pale blue eyes sparking.

She waved her hands at the room. "What's my job? A media performer? Is it funny that I'm here? A joke? Have you laughed with all your warrior fucking buddies about killing my colleagues?" The last sentence almost came out as a sob. Her hands fell to her sides. "What do you want from me?"

Mace's face changed from startled to a steely mask by the end of her tirade. He swallowed his mouthful, stood, and walked to the door.

"Your shift starts in ten minutes," he said, looking above her head. "Six hours this time."

Nia exhaled, shoulders slumping, and went to stand beside him. What else was she supposed to do? Sit in his quarters and stare at the bulkhead all day until the end of time? She'd go mad. The suicide option would become more appealing with each passing hour.

Until the end of time. Her fingers twitched, wanting to touch the locket beneath her shirt. Someone would rescue her. Her family would come for her.

Mace touched his vambrace, and her wrists clicked together. She glared at him and caught his gaze—regret?—before he looked away.

Nia set her shoulders and held her head high throughout the journey to the medical bay. They rounded the last corner behind the two medics who'd been hostile to her the day before, Faas and Mayra. Both seemed unaware that she and Mace were only a couple of meters behind them.

"I'm a surgeon and soooo much better than you. Thank you," Mayra said, affecting an exaggerated CORE Common accent.

"Pleeeaase. Keep your dirty Tell hands off me," Faas said, pitching his voice high.

Nia's face flamed as she glanced at Mace, wondering what he felt about the barbs directed at her. A frown pinched his brow.

Faas laughed. "From the way he looks at her, I bet the commander has her bent over a table day and night. Did you hear he—"

Mace clapped a hand on each of their shoulders. Nia's heart jumped in her chest. Both medics sputtered.

"Commander. I meant no disrespect. I mean—I didn't think—"

Mace cut off Faas's blubbering. "If I hear either of you speaking disrespectfully again, I will see you removed from your posts at this station. Is that understood?" He spoke each word with deadly quiet.

"Yes, sir. Sorry, sir." They both scurried into the medical bay ahead of them.

Mace disengaged her bonds but touched her hand before she could reach for her medical jacket. Her pulse jumped beneath the light pressure.

"If you have any trouble, you contact me." His eyes flicked to her bonds.

Nia nodded, aware of how warm her skin felt beneath his fingers, how wrong his touch should feel. But instead, it was... pleasant.

Mace ran a shaky hand through his hair. What the hell was wrong with him? He'd touched Nia when he knew how much she hated it.

And last night, when he'd returned to his quarters after training the tyros longer and harder than he should have, he'd seen she was asleep and had lain beside her on the bed instead of leaving and staying in the barracks. Curled against the bulkhead, she'd seemed so small and vulnerable. He'd kept to the edge of the bed, a barrier against the rest of the system.

But, one centimeter at a time, she'd moved closer, until her body pressed into his—and she'd sighed in contentment.

It was her sigh that cracked something inside him.

He hadn't done the noble thing and broken the contract—or woken her to let her know what she was doing. No, he'd stayed still and allowed her to melt into him, taking the warmth her soft body offered.

Then she'd bared her soul while shouting questions, and he hadn't a response, couldn't speak for the tightness in his chest.

He needed to get her face out of his head, the feel of her skin off his flesh.

His movements jerky with agitation, Mace strode into training. In the sparring arena, Grey had the tyros in two lines facing him. Mace jogged down the steps and stood beside Grey. A frown creased his friend's usually relaxed face.

"Something wrong?" Mace asked, cocking his head.

"We have a traitor in our midst."

"Ah," Mace said, standing with legs braced apart, hands clasped behind his back. "What do you propose we do?"

Grey would need to take the lead on this one. Mace hadn't been present of mind the last couple of days and didn't know what had made his friend choose this particular exercise.

"The usual." Grey continued to survey the tyros. A few of them looked worried, but most appeared confused. It was the cocky ones who had it coming, the ones who thought they knew what would happen next.

"Interrogation techniques," Grey said, letting his voice ring through the space. "Who thinks they know anything about interrogation techniques?" No one spoke. "Those who think they know one interrogation technique, step forward."

The entire group stepped forward, a few hesitantly, but there wasn't one who didn't take a step.

Grey pointed to the first person in line. "Name one."

"Torture, sir," she answered.

Grey cocked his head to the side. "Pretty broad topic. Can you be more specific?"

The girl looked to her left, then her eyes snapped forward once again. "Medical torture, sir."

Mace raised his eyebrows. Grey gave him a look, then his focus returned to the tyros. He pointed to the next person in line. "Another technique."

"Deprivation, sir."

"Be specific."

"Food, water, time, rights. Take it all away, sir," the boy replied.

Grey was silent for a moment. "Another," he ordered the next girl in line.

"Weaknesses, sir," she mumbled, and Mace shifted his weight, crossing his arms over his chest.

"Be specific," Grey ordered.

She cleared her throat. "Exploit what's most important to them."

Silence followed her words. She looked at both Mace and Grey before refocusing on whatever spot she'd been staring at.

"These are all interrogation methods, but do they work? Will they find out the truth when you're running out of time?"

Grey paced in front of them, his brow furrowed. "Today we'll find out. You will all be locked in a room together to identify the traitor. Many methods will be at your disposal. You will discover the truth together, and you won't be released until you do. Is that understood?"

There were no cocky faces left, only the confused and the terrified.

"Sir! May I ask a question?" asked one boy near the end of the front row.

"Of course," Grey answered.

"What was the act of treason, sir?"

"Ah," Grey replied. "An important question." He stopped walking and stood front and center. "Upon your arrival as a unit, you received instructions to stay in the barracks during the first six weeks of training. This was disobeyed. One person left yesterday and was absent for fifty minutes and six seconds. I can only assume this person is working for the enemy. Therefore, they are a traitor to their unit."

"Um, sir." A boy in the back row lifted his hand. "There could be a lot of reasons a person left the barracks. They might not be a traitor."

"Front and center!" Grey yelled at the boy, who jumped and scurried to obey, stopping a few feet in front of him. "Why would you say this? Were you the one who left the barracks?"

"No, sir. I didn't—"

"Then you're protecting the one who has."

"No, sir, I was—"

"Enough." Grey didn't yell the word, but it had the same effect.

He scanned the rest of the tyros. "Who here believes Parry is guilty and should be punished for his betrayal?"

No one lifted their hand.

"We can't know for sure until we interrogate him. Who will volunteer to wrest the truth from him?"

No one moved for a second, then a blonde girl at the end stepped forward.

"Freya." Grey looked at Mace, then the blonde girl. "You volunteer to interrogate Parry?"

"No, sir," she responded, keeping her head high.

"Why did you step forward?"

"I was the person who left yesterday."

Grey didn't respond. A boy stepped forward. Grey looked at him. "Ketchen, explain yourself."

"I was the person who left yesterday."

After he said the words, more stepped forward, echoing his sentiment without being asked until the whole group had declared they were the ones who'd left.

Once they'd quieted, Grey said, "Return to your positions." They all scurried into two neat rows. Grey looked at Mace. "I'm going to let Commander Mace take over from here." He stepped back, and Mace took his place.

"What was the first thing I made you say together upon arrival?"

"We are a unit," they spoke in unison.

"One of you forgot that yesterday. Don't forget it again." He glanced at the end of the group. "Freya, what interrogation method did Grey use to discover the truth?"

The girl startled, then stared straight ahead, flushing, reminding him of a brunette with curly hair. Mace clenched his fists. Even in a fucking exercise, he couldn't keep his mind clear.

"He exploited a weakness," Freya said quietly.

Mace's eyes flicked to Parry in the back row, also red in the face, eyes straight ahead. "The relationships in a unit are sacred. No one person is more important than another. Relationships can also be a weakness. They can be used against you."

Words he'd said a hundred times to different tyros, but this time his stomach swirled with nausea. *What the fuck?*

"The whole of the unit is more important than the individual." He waited for the silence of the room to become annoying before he said, "Pair up. It's time to get serious."

The tyros broke their lines to match partners. Parry and Freya stayed far away from each other.

Grey rejoined him. "You didn't go into the long-winded version," he said. "That's different."

"Didn't have it in me today."

"You okay?" Grey asked as he turned to face him fully, like he was seeing Mace for the first time.

Mace ran a hand through his hair. "Fine, just preoccupied."

"I can see that."

A boy hit the mat with a groan nearby.

"On your feet, tyro," Mace ordered, and the boy scrambled to stand, facing off with the girl once more. "A couple of hours of training will focus me."

He'd said it with conviction but wondered who he was trying to convince, himself or Grey.

Chapter Eleven

Nia concentrated on the wrist of her patient, a boy with a strained ligament. The extra two hours made the shift seem incredibly long. Funny, since she was used to twelve-plus hours on *Elara Five*. There she'd had the benefit of stimulant injections. Now, weariness infused her bone deep.

Faas and Mayra were determined to be as difficult as possible. Access to supplies and prescriptions, receiving patients according to skill level—everything became a battle. The third medic, Kessy, hadn't been there the day before, but remained distant. The other two had been talking to her at the beginning of the shift.

Nia finished with the boy, saw him out the door with his mother, then rolled her neck, trying to work out the kinks. Stars above, she needed a three-hour soak in a regeneration bath. Did they have them here?

The door to the bay slid open. A man strode through, his dark blue uniform like Mace's in style, except he wore two guns, and the most blades strapped to his waist as she'd seen on any warrior. His brown hair swept forward, covering much of his forehead, and his nose was long and curved.

A strange silence descended in the med bay. Nia glanced over her shoulder. All three medics had frozen in their work, staring at the man who entered, a touch of fear in their eyes.

Nia swung her gaze back to him. *Must be important.* And she was the only one without a patient.

"This is family medicine," she said, and someone gasped from behind her. "Are you in the right place?" There had to be another med bay warriors used.

The man's gaze landed on her and didn't leave. A smile curved his lips. "I'm in the exact right place."

Her stomach clenched at his tone. The look in his eyes reminded her of how Calvin would get sometimes, like he was owed something.

Squaring her shoulders, Nia tipped her head toward the nearest med bed and asked, "What is your medical issue?" If he didn't have one, then she'd ask him to leave. The medics behind her had resumed their tasks, but there was still an air of caution in the bay—one exuding from the patients as well.

He hopped onto the med bed, then lifted his hand. Blood coated his fingers. "I seem to have cut myself."

She swallowed at his nonchalant tone. Shaking herself, she grabbed the scanner. He was tall, and the way he sat, she could only access the injury by standing between his legs. Unease crept up her spine, and she couldn't help but compare this to when she'd healed Mace on the way to *Orion*. Even surrounded by people, this somehow felt more threatening.

Pushing the eerie sensation aside, she ran the scanner over the palm of his hand, eyes narrowing as she read the screen. As a trauma surgeon, she had a mental catalog of injuries, and this one wasn't some accident. It appeared self-inflicted.

A sense of self-preservation made her forgo the regular round of questions in favor of getting him out of the med bay as quickly as possible. She could feel him staring at her as she ran the sterilizer over his skin, cleaning the blood away. The regenerator hummed next. The cut was fresh and deep.

Three quarters through the heal, a teenager strolled in clutching her wrist, face pale with pain. Her eyes widened when they landed on the warrior.

Why did everyone fear this man differently than what she'd seen with Mace?

"Sit right there," Nia said, jerking her head to the closest med bed. "I'll be with you next."

Finishing up with his hand, it no longer looked like he'd been injured, the skin smooth. He flexed his fingers, curling them into a fist.

Nia stepped away from the bed, but he stopped her with a hand on her arm. Her stomach squeezed with nausea.

"I'd heard you were good." He said it like he meant something other than medical expertise.

Trying not to react to his innuendo, she said, "I have patients to attend to."

When she jerked her arm out of his grasp, he let her go. Swallowing, she turned to tend the teenager, giving him her back, and tried to concentrate through the erratic pounding of her heart.

He didn't leave for a long while, and her spine burned from his stare. A collective breath was released from everyone in the bay when he finally left.

Nia lifted her head, meeting Kessy's gaze. The medical assistant's eyes were wide, but there was relief there too. What had Nia escaped?

She tried to push the whole incident aside, the rest of the day passing in a blur. Only a few minutes remained of her shift when the bay emptied of patients.

But Nia didn't have time to take a breath.

The lights in the room changed abruptly, flashing red. Cursing, Faas ran to the wall terminal, reading the information scrolling across its surface. He whipped around to Nia. "What kind of surgeon did you say you were?"

"Trauma," she replied with a hint of pride.

"Shit. We're getting incoming trauma patients. They would usually redirect them to the main trauma center, but since you're here—"

A chute opened in the bulkhead. Three hover beds rolled inside via an automated system with two teenagers and one child in stasis.

Nia's body tensed. The youngest boy had blood all over him. The medics turned wide eyes on her. From what she'd seen so far, they didn't have enough training to work with these patients. Maybe someone sent them here because the primary trauma center was already overwhelmed.

Silence echoed in the room, disconcerting while paired with the crimson lights, like the four of them were bathed in blood like the patients.

Time. Every triage doctor knew time was the biggest factor when treating trauma patients. And these three might not have any left.

Nia's training took over. "Kill the alarm." She strode to the hover beds. Burns covered the girls' bodies, and their stasis only had minutes left on the clock.

"You," Nia said, pointing to Faas. "Take this one. Give her a sedative immediately upon exiting stasis. Start with the worst of the burns using a broad-spectrum regenerator set to level—" Nia checked the girl's stats again, "five point two six. Plug her into fluid and blood transfusions. By the time you get to the first-degree burns, your regenerator should be at about three point three one. Once all the burns are healed, cover all affected areas with two layers of regeneration gauze."

Nia went over to the other hover bed. "And you," she said, pointing to Mayra. "You do the same with the other girl but start the regenerator at six point one."

They both stood staring at her, jaws dropped.

"Move," Nia ordered between clenched teeth. They jerked out of their daze, scampering to the beds. When they took the girls out of stasis, momentary cries of pain and alarm echoed before they were put under.

Nia gestured to Kessy. "You're going to help me with the boy."

The panel on the side of the bed read his name was Kilian, and he was ten years old. The leg had been newly amputated, but from his stats, the work had been done quickly and without skill.

"It's a dirty wound," Kessy said, reading the panel on the other side of the bed.

Nia dropped the stasis field, glad the boy was sedated. Kessy plugged him into the hydration and blood transfusion portals without her having to ask.

"Retrieve a dose of nanos to remove the infection while I re-cut the limb." Kessy hurried to the dispensary on the bulkhead. "We're going to need to remove all the shattered bone in the wound," Nia said when the assistant returned. "Do you have access to prosthetic limbs on this station?"

Kessy injected the nanos. "Yes, but—"

"Good. We'll need to keep it open-flap for the bonding process. A PK576 model or whatever equivalent you have here would be best for his age."

"Yes, sir," Kessy replied with wide eyes.

"You can call me Nia."

"Yes, sir."

Kessy placed a tray of laser scalpels beside Nia, then used the sterilizer at the end of the hover bed. Nia did the same before examining the tray, selecting the appropriate scalpel, and testing its charge.

After taking a quick look at the other two medics to make sure they were doing as told, Nia returned her attention to the boy. Kessy removed the rest of his pants, then held his thigh immobile.

Nia focused, everything else fading into the background as she began her first incision.

A strangled sound made her lift the scalpel.

"She's CORE!" an unfamiliar voice shouted, then she went flying.

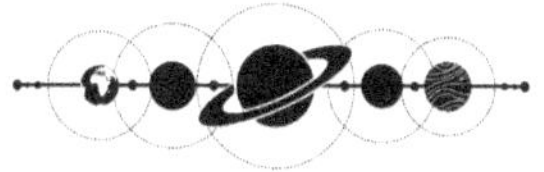

Mace strode toward Nia's medical bay, recently notified she'd received trauma patients from the inbound transports. He didn't doubt her skills as a surgeon, but something made him quicken his pace.

In the last corridor, a man entered the med bay ahead of him. A moment later, someone shouted.

Battle readiness licked up his spine. Mace ran the rest of the way, touching his vambrace to summon a security team. He bounded into the med bay, his first thought to make sure Nia was okay.

She lay on the deck beside a hover bed. His heart lurched in his chest, rage darkening his vision. She wasn't moving, and blood smeared across her temple. A medic crouched beside her as two others restrained a man who looked ready to assault Nia again.

A primal shout ripped from Mace's throat.

The attacker, a man with light brown hair and a weak chin, went limp in the two medics' arms. If it weren't for his frailty, Mace would have killed him right then.

Clenching his fists, he strode to where Nia lay. "Is she okay?" He squatted beside the medic.

"Yeah," she replied, running a scanner over Nia's head. "Knocked unconscious. Concussed. Quick heal."

"How did this happen?" Mace asked, moving Nia's hair away from her face.

"He pushed her away from the kid, and she hit the next bed over."

Mace swallowed his growl and swept Nia in his arms to place her on the vacant med bed, taking extra care with her head injury.

Then he turned, every part of him coiled to strike, and faced off with her attacker. He wanted blood, but the man was unarmed, his eyes wild. Bruises covered his face, burns on his hands.

A frantic beeping trilled from the boy's med bed. The medic rushed to his side, raising the foot of the bed and plugging another portal into his arm.

"Save him. Save my boy," the man moaned, straining against the medics.

"You incapacitated the only surgeon in the room," the medic spat. The beeping subsided, and she ran a scanner over the boy's body. "He's stable for a moment, but the doctor needs to see to this artery."

"Can you wake her?" Mace asked, brushing the hair away from Nia's face, then gripped the edge of the hover bed, his knuckles turning white at the effort it took him not to drag her attacker into the bowels of the station where he'd never be found.

"Yes." The medic came over and touched a dermal syringe to Nia's throat.

Her fingers moved first, then she opened her eyes. Seeing Mace hovering above her, she bolted upright, pushing him away. Her hand flew to her head with a groan.

Mace nudged her down. "Take it easy. You've had a fall."

"A fall?" Her voice came out in a croak. "No." She sat up again, and this time he helped her. "Someone pushed me."

Her outrage calmed his nerves.

Nia's gaze flew around the room to rest on the man being restrained by the two medics. Her brows pinched together as her hand moved to the side of her head, coming away with residual blood. Mace's heart beat hard in his chest. She looked at the boy.

"How's Kilian, Kessy?"

"Went into hypovolemic shock. Tibial artery."

Nia jumped to her feet and swayed.

"Whoa," Mace said, putting a hand on her shoulder. "You need to rest for a minute."

"No time," she said once she'd regained her balance, then pushed away from him.

"He's stable now, but we need to re-amputate and seal off the artery," Kessy explained.

"Don't touch him, you CORE filth!" the man screamed. "Your kind put him there. You've no right to touch him."

Mace allowed his rage to take over and took a step toward him. The door to the med bay opened. A team of four enforcers entered, guns aimed at all present.

"Commander?" the lead warrior asked.

Mace grimaced and exhaled a slow breath. He'd forgotten he'd called the team. With regret, he cocked his head to the man being restrained. "Take him to the brig and make sure I'm the first in line. No questions."

"Yes, sir."

The man yelled, trying to break free from the warriors. The door slid shut, cutting off his insults.

With one last glance at Nia, Mace strode toward the door, intent on following the team to the brig.

A hand on his wrist stopped him. Nia stood there, eyes round. The heat of her fingers below his vambrace sent tingles flowing across his skin.

"What are you going to do?" she asked.

"Don't worry. He won't be bothering you again."

"No, no. That's not good."

Mace frowned. "You want him to bother you?"

"No, of course not."

Mace shook his head. She didn't make sense. Maybe it was the effect of the head injury. When she removed her hand, he had the urge to return it to its place.

"Don't hurt him. He's been through a trauma," she continued. "Some people don't know how to deal with extreme situations."

"The man assaulted you," Mace ground between clenched teeth.

"I know, but he was injured too. Once he's calmed, we can talk—"

"Once he's—?" Mace needed to stop speaking and shook his head. "He'll get nowhere near you again. I'll see to it."

Without looking back, he strode through the door.

Chapter Twelve

As soon as Mace stepped onto the lift, his vambrace beeped with a communique with Cache's insignia, priority one from the command center.

His hand hovered over the controls. He wanted to ignore the summons, to follow through with his need to gain vengeance for Nia, when her words rattled in his mind. *Some people don't know how to deal with extreme situations.*

She might as well have been talking about Mace, because he wasn't dealing with her attack and injury well at all.

He tried not to notice how his hands shook when he touched the control for the command center. With a deep breath, he realized this was probably a good thing. Walking into an interrogation room enraged was a mistake.

By the time he strode through the command center's security scanner, he'd regained control of himself. Mostly.

All the commanders and sub-commanders had already arrived ahead of him again. Foley's eyes tracked him as he walked toward the group, his arms crossed. If the commander wanted to have a go at him, Mace was happy to oblige. It would relieve some of what boiled inside him. But when they locked eyes, Foley's expression turned into a grin. Unsettled, Mace took his place beside Grey.

Cache clunked a gun onto the holotable. Everyone leaned in for a closer look.

Pushing his volatile emotions aside and ignoring Foley's disquieting stare, Mace focused on the weapon. He had seen nothing quite like it. About the same length as a pulse cannon, it was made of black metal composite, sleek, the barrel about fifteen centimeters in diameter. A void occupied most of the shoulder rest, like it was incomplete.

Cache waited for the murmurs to settle around her. Meeting each of her commanders' gazes, she narrowed her eyes at the weapon. "One of our scouting missions came across a rogue cruiser in Sector Four. They found this," she said with a jerk of her chin, "on board."

"It looks like it's missing something, sir," Mace commented, crossing his arms over his chest.

"Yes, it's the charge and the payload," Cache replied. A collective wince shuddered through the commanders, and she didn't have to say her next words. "We're talking bio-weapons here, people."

"Proof?" Commander Sheefra asked.

If they had proof, they could pull out their existing treaty with the CORE and wave it in their sanctimonious faces.

Cache shook her head. "Not in this catch. We have the hardware, but none of the ammo."

"How do we know it's a bio-weapon then?" Grey asked.

"Commander Foley has been interrogating the occupant of the cruiser. We've received solid information from his efforts. The man was on his way to meet a contact."

Mace's gaze flicked back to Foley. Satisfaction hung around the other man like a cloak.

"This weapon wasn't the only one on the ship," Cache continued. "There were fifty disassembled and integrated into the cruiser's construction."

A low murmur rumbled around the table. That amount of prototype guns hiding in such a small ship meant the CORE had been planning this for a while.

"I shouldn't need to emphasize how important it is to find out what the CORE's agenda is and put a stop to it." Cache stared at each of her commanders in turn. "The day they use bio-weapons on Tellusians again is the day we really go to war. I have orders from Admiral Krispin to use everything at our disposal and to contact our assets." Her eyes rested on Mace a moment longer than necessary. "And I mean everyone."

Mace raised his eyebrows at her. He wouldn't endanger Lexi unnecessarily, not with her position so vulnerable.

"Dismissed," Cache said, and the commanders scattered.

Mace remained where he was, but his eyes followed Foley as he strode to the nearest lift. Beside him, Grey grasped the gun to examine it closer.

"It's pretty," Grey said, stroking the barrel and lifting the weapon to his shoulder. "Light too. Point and shoot. Couldn't be easier." Grey set the gun back on the holotable and leaned forward, bracing his hands. "Fuck, what are they planning?"

"Nothing good," Cache replied, crossing her arms over her chest before jerking her chin at Mace. "You need to contact Lexi. Find out what she knows."

"You know I can't do that, sir," Mace replied.

"Dammit, Mace." Cache seized the gun, and with her eyes flashing, shoved it at his chest. "This is a game changer, and it's on my watch. My territory."

His hands wrapped around the barrel. Grey was right. It was lightweight, the sleek composite material comfortable in his hands. Mace stared down the sight and the opposite side of the command center came into focus. *Point and shoot.*

A chill ran down his spine at the idea of the CORE making bio-weapons this easy to use. "What about the prisoner's contact?" Mace placed the gun on the holotable.

"No show. They were probably going to send another set of coordinates before the real drop point." She narrowed her eyes at him. "If you don't contact her, I will."

"And you'd be giving her a death sentence. Do you want that?"

Cache's nostrils flared. "No, of course not." She took a breath. "But with bio-weapons, no one's safe. Use proper channels if you must, but we need what information she has ahead of the regular schedule."

Mace's stomach twisted. The only way his sister remained safe was if they didn't contact her. Too many variables were involved, and the CORE could intercept long-distance communications.

But at least Cache was being reasonable enough to wait for proper channels. "I'll see what I can do, sir."

"That's all I ask." She turned on her heel, black hair swooshing over her shoulder, and headed to the far side of the command center, a group of techies scurrying as she yelled orders.

Mace stared after her for a minute before heading to the lift outside the security checkpoint. Grey fell into step beside him.

"Are we off to training, then?"

The lift door opened, and they stepped inside. "I need to make a stop first." He hit the controls. Grey got off on the training level, but Mace remained, descending into the belly of *Orion.*

The corridors of the brig were brightly lit, a grid-like deck full of both cells and interrogation rooms. Mace strode to the intake desk and spoke to the warrior on duty.

"There was a man arrested in Section C, family medicine. Where is he now?"

Her fingers skimmed the terminal in front of her. "Cell twelve," she said, looking up at him.

"Has anyone been in there?"

"No, sir," she said. "My orders were to wait until you arrived before following procedures."

Mace nodded his thanks. "Send for a doctor. He'll need one when I'm finished."

Her eyes widened a fraction at his words. Realizing how he sounded, Mace shook his head before continuing on. Marked doors lined the sterile gray bulkheads.

He stopped in front of the cell and ran a hand through his hair. Remembering Nia's last words to him, he took a breath. She was a healer. She'd asked him not to hurt the man, and knew trauma induced recklessness.

None of that should matter to him, but it did.

After taking another calming breath, he pressed his hand to the panel. The door slid open to reveal the man hunched on the deck in the corner of the empty metal room, head pressed against his knees.

When Mace stepped inside, the man scrambled to his feet using the bulkhead as support. Mace's fingers twitched as they stood staring at each other.

Finally, the man asked, "Is my son alive?"

"He was when I left him in the doctor's capable hands."

The man sneered. "She's CORE. They should all be sent out an airlock."

"She'll probably save your son's life. She saved mine."

For a second, it looked like the man would argue the issue but stayed quiet when Mace took a step forward.

"What happens to me now?" he asked.

If I don't change my mind and decide to kill you? Fists clenched, Mace crossed his arms over his chest. "You'll be charged with assault." Maybe more. It depended on what other charges he felt like adding on. "If you're eventually released, you are not to enter my ward's med bay. You are not to come within a deck of her. Do you understand me?"

"But if my boy—"

Dropping his hands to his sides, Mace took a step forward. "Do you understand me!"

The man swallowed and nodded, back pressed into the corner.

Mace forced his fingers to unclench one by one. He stepped back, breaking the man's wary gaze. There was nothing honorable about beating someone weak and unarmed, but let him be afraid if it meant he'd stay away from Nia.

A medic waited in the corridor, a med kit clutched to his chest.

"He hasn't seen a doctor since arriving from the transport attack," Mace explained, cocking his head toward the door.

"Yes, sir." The medic hurried inside.

Mace finished charging the man, Sorley was his name, then returned to the med bay to retrieve Nia. It was well past the end of her shift.

He found her talking with one medic beside the boy's bed. The other two medics were gone, but each of the girls who'd been in earlier had an adult nearby, regeneration gauze on their skin. *More victims from the transport attacks.*

Mace came alongside the boy's bed. "How's he doing?"

Nia turned to him, her head clean of blood. He noted her tense shoulders, how she held herself away from him.

"Good," she said, voice tight. "Better. We almost lost him there, but he pulled through. He's tough." She rubbed the middle of her forehead. "Why does everyone keep telling me I have to ask you about prosthetic limbs?"

"We can talk about it later."

"He needs the bonding process to begin right away. Any delay could mean complications—"

"We can talk about it later."

Nia's breath left her in a rush as she dropped her hand and narrowed her eyes at him. "Fine." She turned to the medic. "Is there a way to contact me if his status changes?"

Kessy nodded. "I can contact the commander if there's any change."

After scanning the boy's vitals one more time, Nia headed to the door to hang her white jacket on a hook. Mace coded his vambrace, and they returned to his quarters in silence. Once her wrists were disengaged, her posture caused him to stop instead of immediately backing out of the room to give her space.

"Are you okay?"

She looked over her shoulder at him, her complexion paler than normal.

"Yeah, need to sit…" She'd barely finished the sentence when she collapsed to the deck.

"Fuck," Mace breathed. He tried to catch her before she hit, but didn't reach her in time. At least she didn't smash her head against the corner of the table and make things worse. Mace swept her up, cradling her against his chest before striding to the bed to lay her down. He felt for the pulse in her throat. A strong rhythm. She'd only passed out.

Mace moved her knees to sit beside her and ran a hand through his hair. He'd done this to her, worked her to exhaustion. He felt like an ass. First the attack, then this. She needed sleep. A huge chunk of it.

He sent a quick message to Grey, telling him he wouldn't be in until the next day. Lifting her back into his arms, he scooted to the back bulkhead, then let the length of her body rest between his legs.

Mace didn't examine the feelings rioting inside him at the familiar contact, how good it felt. Instead, he covered Nia with his blanket as best he could in their position, closed his eyes, and rested his head against the bulkhead. The only thing he cared about right now was making sure she stayed safe.

Chapter Thirteen

N ia's stomach growled, then clenched. *So hungry.* She didn't know how long it had been since she'd eaten anything. But she was comfortable and didn't want to move, even to relieve the insistent pressure of her bladder.

Something beeped.

"Five more minutes," she whispered, snuggling deeper.

"Okay, five more. But that's it."

The accented voice rumbled beneath her cheek. Her fingernails dug into fabric and felt pectoral muscles with no give. Her cheek was pressed against abdominals, her shoulder against—

She pushed away, scrambling. Mace's arms and a blanket dropped from her shoulders, and the cold of the room rushed in, chilling the exposed skin of her throat and hands. Against the opposite bulkhead, she shivered and wrapped her arms around her body, willing away the involuntary reaction she'd had to his nearness.

Amusement twinkled in his eyes. Nia clenched her hands. The embarrassment heating her cheeks was quickly replaced with anger. Exhaling an irritated breath, she jumped off the bed and dashed to the washroom. Her limbs shook as she braced her hands against the edge of the counter. She blamed it on fatigue and hunger. It took her a minute to collect herself and use the facilities, finishing with a splash of water on her face. Her stomach cramped again.

Leaving the washroom, her gaze went to Mace sitting on the edge of the bed, legs over the side. Eyes narrowing, she aimed past him for the refrigeration unit. She needed carbs and protein first. Halfway there, Mace stopped her with a hand on her wrist.

She glared at his fingers, hating how his touch no longer repulsed her—if it ever had.

"Are you okay?" he asked.

Her gaze flew to his, and her heart squeezed at the concern in his tone, the way his eyes searched her face. Nia swallowed around the sudden dryness in her mouth and touched her overheated cheek. "What do you mean?"

"You passed out when we returned yesterday."

"I did?" She scanned her memories of the previous day, knowing she'd been exhausted when they'd returned to his quarters. She'd just needed to rest and thought she'd fallen into bed. *Apparently not.*

He hadn't let go of her wrist, the warmth turning into pleasant tingles. She licked her dry lips. "It was probably from fatigue, dehydration, and lack of food."

When he pulled her closer, she didn't resist, and stood between his legs, the heat of his thighs warming her hips.

"Fatigue and dehydration?" His deep voice rumbled through her, doing unwanted things to her blood pressure. "Doesn't sound healthy, Doctor." He was close enough that she could feel his words in her chest, and see the lights above reflected in the blue of his irises.

The hand on her wrist increased in temperature with each passing second. Nia cleared her throat. "I'm used to pumping myself full of stimulants during a shift. The medics here don't seem to indulge, so I didn't either." And for the first time, reaching for a mood modifier seemed odd when no one else was doing it.

"And again, Doctor, that doesn't sound very healthy."

"It's not," she said, staring at his mouth. How could his lips look soft? They'd been so angry yesterday. He'd threatened that man. He'd abducted her from her home, destroyed her station. *Killed people.* It was what he did for a living. A killer.

Struggling between her emotions and common sense, Nia pulled away. He let go of her wrist. She retreated to the kitchen, keeping her face averted as she searched for each of the four food groups in his refrigeration unit. She continued to ignore him as she sat at the table and ate her meal, but felt his eyes on her. Finally, he rose from the bed and went to the washroom.

As soon as the door closed, her shoulders sagged forward, hands shaking.

He scared her—and not in the way he was supposed to, not as a Tellusian, her enemy. It was something different altogether, something that made her more aware of him than any other man in her life.

The thought took her back to *Elara Five*, where she'd dated because *why not?* No person had caused her heart to race the way it was now. When she'd been with Calvin, she'd needed enhancers to make their intimacy tolerable. Now every touch, every look of Mace's, caused her stomach to flutter and her chest to squeeze.

It has to be because I'm stuck here. It had to be because he was the only man she spent any length of time with, and her psyche was latching onto him—any other reason created a tide of panic.

She embraced her anger instead, the injustice of it all, even as her hand itched to touch her PALM and order a suppressant to calm her. Mace had taken away her choices, taken away everything. It felt good to get herself worked up, to block all the other uninvited emotions.

When he stepped out of the washroom, she jumped to her feet to confront him.

"Why do I need to ask you about the prosthetic?" It made little sense. She should have been able to order it through the med bay, but no one allowed it, not even Kessy, who'd turned out to be sensible.

After a hesitation, he stepped around her. "What do you need?" he asked over his shoulder, heading toward the refrigeration unit.

Her ire deflated at his question. After encountering so many obstacles yesterday about it, all he asked was, *What do you need?*

Licking her lips, she rattled off the specs for the prosthetic she wanted for Kilian and watched as he ran his fingers over his vambrace like he was ordering it right then and there.

When she fell silent, he raised his eyebrows. "That's it?"

She nodded once.

"I'll find it." He sat down to eat his meal.

Nia remained in the middle of the room, staring. Her conflicted emotions continued to tumble inside her, making it hard to concentrate.

He pointed at her uneaten rations. "Are you going to finish?"

She shook her head, face heating. "I don't want to make myself sick." But really, she didn't want to sit across from him, didn't want to act civil when all she wanted to do was scream at the absurd nightmare she'd found herself trapped in.

His eyes narrowed on her, then after a hesitation, he scooped all the remains off the table and took them to reclamation.

They left his quarters in the same way they had on previous days, her hands bound, and walked in silence to the med bay. Nia stopped short when she noticed a new addition to the room, a blond warrior who introduced himself as Elec and spoke to Mace with deference before her warder left.

She stared at the young man, realizing he was only there for her. *I've turned the med bay into a prison for everyone.* She couldn't decide if she was mad at Mace for the added security, or if it was thoughtful of him to care about her safety.

Her brain struggling with contrary emotions, Nia moved to Kilian's bedside. Kessy ran a scanner over the unconscious boy's head, torso, and leg. "He's doing remarkably well," she said with a smile, tucking a lock of brown hair behind her ear. "No complications overnight."

Nia returned the smile, liking the other woman's enthusiasm. "That's great news."

"Should we wake him?" Kessy asked. "I was waiting for you."

Glancing around the bay, Nia noted all the patients were being attended to, and the teenagers who'd arrived yesterday with Kilian looked to be recovering nicely with an adult each at their bedsides. She ignored the hostile looks Mayra and Faas sent her way.

Nia nodded at Kessy. "Let's do it."

The medic pressed a dermal syringe to Kilian's neck while Nia raised the head of the bed.

Kilian's forehead crinkled first, then his eyelids opened. The boy saw them both, jerked upright, and tried to scramble off the bed. There was a jumble of words in a language Nia didn't understand before he asked in Common, "Where's my dad?"

Nia laid a gentle hand on his shoulder, nudging him against the built-in pillow of the med bed. "It's okay. You're okay. Lie down a moment."

He stared at Nia's bonds and thrust her hands away from him. "No! Don't touch me. You're CORE. I'm not supposed to be around anyone CORE. They should all get thrown out an airlock." His accented words turned into deep sobs.

Heart pounding, Nia stepped back. Elec moved toward them, but she gave him one shake of her head, and he returned to his post next to the door. Kessy tried to calm the boy with hushes and gentle hands.

Nia didn't know what to do. Kilian hated her on sight. How was she supposed to be his physician?

"Where's my dad?" he asked again when his sobs subsided.

Nia remained where she stood, arms at her sides. "Kessy, could you see if you can find Kilian's father, please?"

Kessy hesitated, then nodded before heading to the wall terminal.

The boy stared at his amputated leg, eyes refilling with tears. "I'm a freak."

Nia's chest tightened. "No, you're not. Not at all."

Ignoring her, he cried with silent sobs.

Nia's heart pounded an erratic rhythm as she tried to think what to do. Kessy returned to the bedside, glanced beyond Nia's shoulder, and grimaced.

Nia's spine straightened. One of the other medics was going to suggest they take over Kilian's care. *Unacceptable.* She wouldn't allow anyone to insinuate she gave substandard care, no matter the situation. She acknowledged it was her pride talking and didn't care. The other two medics were complete assholes, and she would not stand their interference.

Taking a breath, she stepped forward and resumed her place beside the med bed. "Can I tell you a secret?" she asked, keeping her voice gentle.

Kilian turned his head so fast that she realized he hadn't been aware of how close she stood. But instead of retreating, she held her ground. "It's an important secret," she added.

Interest lit the boy's eyes before he scowled. "I'm not supposed to talk to CORE people. No matter what."

Trying to keep her face neutral, Nia ignored the comment and leaned forward. "Do you want to know the secret or not?"

Kilian stared at her, then nodded. Nia bent close to his ear. "I know what to do to make your leg better than new."

His eyes widened. "Really?"

Nia straightened, smiling. "Yes. The proper prosthetic will make you the envy of all the other kids."

Kessy made a strangled noise. "Doctor, can I speak to you for a moment?" She jerked her head away from the table. "In private?"

"Yes, of course." Nia glanced at the other two medics, who'd returned to their patients.

Kessy pulled her out of earshot of the boy. "You shouldn't have spoken about the prost—"

"Did you find Kilian's father?" Nia interrupted. The prosthetic didn't worry her. Mace had said he would find the right one. She believed him.

"Sort of," Kessy answered. "He was in the brig until a short time ago. They're not from *Orion*, so I'm not sure where to check next. We'll have to wait until they're assigned quarters or—" Kessy stopped mid-sentence when the door to the medical bay opened, her mouth freezing in an O.

Nia turned, every part of her body going on alert at the sight of Kilian's father. Mace hadn't killed him. Her relief was replaced by the sharp sting of anger at what the man had done to her until he rushed to his son, his shoulders shuddering as they hugged each other. Heads bent, their light brown hair matched.

Hand on his gun, Elec spoke low into his comm.

"Are you okay, boy?" Kilian's father asked. "Did they hurt you?"

"I'm okay, Dad. My leg feels better than it has—" Kilian wiped his tears with the sleeve of his shirt. "The doctor said she could fix me better than new."

The father's narrowed eyes swung to her, lips twisting in a snarl. "What's this about?"

When Nia stepped forward, Kessy tried to stop her with a hand on her shoulder. Nia lifted her hands, fingers spread wide in a placating gesture. "I started to explain about prosthetics to Kilian." She shrugged off Kessy's hand and kept moving forward. "With the proper one, it'll be like he has his old leg back. I promise."

"I don't want you to give him false hope," he ground out, still clasping his son.

"It's not a false hope." She kept her hands up to make sure he knew she meant no harm. "I'm a trauma surgeon by trade, and I've dealt with amputations in the field. With the surgery I performed yesterday, Kilian's leg is primed to take a prosthetic."

A glimmer of hope entered the man's features, and Nia gave him a nod of encouragement. She wanted the best for his son, no matter where she came from or what he'd done yesterday.

The man's face relaxed. He bent his head, nodding, and Kilian wrapped his arms around his father's neck.

She lowered her hands. It would work out. Kessy came alongside her to give her shoulder a light squeeze. Nia didn't shy away from the touch, needing the support the medic gave.

Then Mace stormed in and ruined everything.

Chapter Fourteen

"I told you to stay away," Mace growled, prepared to rip off Sorley's arms.

He took two steps inside the med bay when Nia suddenly blocked his way, her face flushed. "Stop! He hasn't done anything. He—"

Ignoring her squeal of alarm, Mace grasped her elbows, lifted her, and plopped her out of his path. One more step and she was in front of him, hand on his chest, pushing him back. He ignored the awareness spreading through every part of his body from her touch and encircled her wrist above her bonds to tug her behind him, but kept hold. She wouldn't be able to block him again.

Arms at his sides and face pale, Sorley straightened to his full height, but Mace didn't stop advancing until their faces were only inches apart. "I told you not to return."

Sorley visibly swallowed. "I know, but I had to see my boy."

"Kilian needs his father," Nia said, twisting to the side and yanking on the wrist he held. Mace tugged her behind him. Her frustrated breath heated the side of his arm.

Trying to ignore her squirming, Mace stared at Sorley his ire continuing to rise. This man attacked Nia, hurt her, and Mace had every right to retaliate. Fuck, it was the law. And he would have educated the man on how precariously the rest of his life hung when something small bashed against his calf.

Mace twitched and whirled around. "Did you kick me?" he asked, incredulous.

"Yes." Nia yanked on her arm again. "Stop jerking me around." Her russet eyes flashed at him.

Mace guided her beside him, loosening his grip to hold her hand instead. "Then stay put." He returned his attention to Sorley but couldn't help but note the way his side warmed as they stood together, how small her fingers felt in his, and how she didn't move away.

"If you touch her again," he said to the man in front of him, "I'll kill you." The boy behind him was shaking. The fear in his eyes as he stared at Mace twisted something in his chest. A child shouldn't fear him; he would never hurt an innocent. But this man had *attacked* Nia.

"I'd deserve it if I did," Sorley replied immediately, meeting his gaze straight on.

The quick response gave Mace pause. Hesitating, he glanced at Nia, who stared at their joined hands as if frozen. It had only taken minutes for her to sway Sorley with her charm.

"Are we good here?" he asked, and her eyes snapped to his.

Her gaze jumped between him and Sorley, then she nodded. "Yes. We're good."

Mace loosened his hold with reluctance, allowing her fingers to slip through his. Her face flushed as she looked anywhere but at him.

A charged silence had settled over the medical bay. He scanned the rest of the occupants, meeting everyone's gaze in case they thought they could get away with hurting Nia.

When everyone seemed suitably respectful, he strode to the door to speak to Elec. "Anytime he's in here, I want to be notified. Don't leave for any reason while he's here. Understood?"

"Yes, sir."

"Any threat he makes toward her, you shoot first and ask questions later. Understood?"

"Yes, sir."

One last glance over his shoulder revealed everyone's gazes still fixed on him, including Nia's. Brow furrowed, confusion swam in her eyes.

No one would have the opportunity to hurt her again. He would make sure of it.

And that included himself.

Running an agitated hand over his face, he strode out of the med bay, down the corridor, and slapped the panel to call the lift. When the door opened and he stepped inside, he released a slow breath.

As the lift ascended, his emotions tumbled over themselves, trying to gain a foothold. The need to beat the shit out of someone or something raged against the desire to take over Elec's post and glare at anyone in the med bay who so much as looked at Nia wrong.

The way she tied him up inside didn't make sense. If he took an objective step back and reviewed his choices over the past few days, he knew it looked bad. None of what he'd done since returning to *Orion* fell into familiar patterns. Attacking a fellow commander, bribing a processing official, keeping a captive in his quarters instead of sending her to common holding—Cache had the right to give him displeased glances and question his commitment level.

That being said, he still had a ward to look out for. He would protect Nia, but he wouldn't allow her to become a weakness. His work with the tyros, his command here, stopping the CORE from whatever plan they concocted in Sector Four, *those* should be his priorities.

Feeling empowered, like he'd come to some sort of profound conclusion, Mace stepped off the lift on the fifth level of the atrium and headed for training. He'd only left because Elec had signaled Sorley's return.

Once through the main corridor, he jogged down the steps to Grey's side at the edge of the matted arena. His friend raised his eyebrows in question.

"It seems I need to—" Mace stopped when he saw what the tyros were holding. "What in the...?" They all had knives. It was his turn to raise his eyebrows at Grey. "I was only gone a few minutes."

Grey shrugged. "They pushed me. I thought they could learn a lesson."

Mace winced as one tyro got cut. Then again. And again. *Stars above.* "You're so easy to manipulate when I'm not around. Grey, they're not ready."

"I know that. But they didn't."

"They're going to kill each other slowly with flesh wounds. They'll bleed from scratches overnight and be dead by morning."

"I called in a couple of medics," Grey jerked his chin to the side, "but told them to stay put until something serious happened."

The pair of medics seemed to exist in a constant state of wince, one covering his face with his hands and peeking through his fingers, the other with her shoulders hunched by her ears.

One more slice, and another gasp, and Mace had had enough. "Hold!" he shouted over the din of hisses and groans. Panting, everyone stopped their sparring.

Mace strode to the pair he'd been watching, Shand and Freya, and the rest of the tyros formed a loose circle around them.

"What the hell?" Mace asked, grabbing Shand's arm to examine the cut along his knuckles. "Why did you take the slash?"

"When using knives, expect to get cut, sir," Shand replied, keeping his eyes straight ahead.

"Did Sub-Commander Grey spout that bullshit to you?" Mace asked, not needing to look at Grey to know the answer.

"No, sir."

"Do you know why he would never spout that bullshit to you?"

"No, sir."

"Because it's bullshit." Mace directed his next to the entire crowd. "Expect to get cut doesn't mean to *allow* yourself to get cut. Who here is unharmed at this point? Who doesn't have a cut on them?"

No one raised their hands.

Mace shook his head, then glanced at Grey briefly. "We're going to need more medics."

His friend shrugged.

Mace returned his focus to his students. "Who here wants to learn how to use a knife?"

They all raised their hands.

"First lesson: a knife isn't in your hand to *use*. It's there to kill. Don't fool yourself. You're never going to waltz up to your enemy and have a knife fight like you're having right now, with dainty-ass jabs and pretty slices of flesh. In battle, we use a knife to kill, not to injure. Now, if that's *always* your *only* objective, answer me this: who here is ready to learn how to wield a knife?"

No one raised their hands.

Mild surprise whipped through Mace. "Smart unit. Put the knives away. Get your wounds seen to, then clean up your sorry asses. I don't want to see your faces again until this evening after your schooling. Dismissed."

The tyros scattered, tossing their knives into the cleaning stations in the bulkhead and forming two neat lines to await their turn with the medics.

Mace ran his hand through his hair and stared at Grey. His friend's mouth quirked at the corner before he said, "And they learned their lesson."

Nia knew, without turning around, that Mace had returned to collect her. She didn't need Sorley's back straightening, the slow nod he gave toward the door as he sat beside Kilian's bed, or the soft, "Yes, sir," from Elec. She would have known from the way the air in the medical bay shifted and changed with Mace's presence.

Holding a regenerator firmly in her hand, Nia ran it over the girl's knee once more, ignoring the intrusion. "And straighten it," she encouraged, and the girl responded by resting her knee flat against the bed. "Good job. Almost done."

She began at the top of the kneecap again, ensuring she repaired all the ligaments and that the dislocated knee joint was healed to her satisfaction.

Assisting the girl off the med bed and discharging her into her mother's care, she then went to Kilian's side to make sure he was comfortable. She didn't have to, but derived a perverse pleasure in making her warder wait—and felt his eyes on her the entire time.

After stalling as long as she could, Nia turned to the door and met Mace's gaze. His brow was furrowed, his eyes sharp. She broke his stare to take off her white jacket and hang it on the hook by the door.

Ever since he'd left after confronting Sorley, he hadn't been far from her thoughts, making it hard to concentrate. She resented that. He shouldn't be able to consume her brain space. But instead of being able to push thoughts of him aside, the memory of him defending her, of cradling her hand, kept intruding over and over again.

"Ready?" he asked, his voice rumbling through her abdomen.

Breaking his gaze, Nia nodded. He touched his vambrace, causing her wrists to lock together. Head held high, she followed him out the door.

Watching the play of the muscles of his back beneath the fabric of his uniform as he walked ahead of her, she knew she should probably see the station's psychologist. Did captives have mental health support on *Orion*? But maybe if she confessed her confusing thoughts and emotions, they wouldn't stay private. Her cheeks burned. When she started, no one had given her any procedural directives. No one had said Tellusians kept the same sort of doctor-patient confidentiality as CORE physicians. The reckless nature of their medical system made her shake her head.

They stepped onto the lift in silence, and as it descended, Mace cleared his throat. "I've found the prosthetic you requested."

Distracted from her tangent thoughts, her heart fluttered. "Really? That's great." She bounced off the lift when the door opened and met his gaze. "For a while there, I thought maybe you couldn't get it because of how everyone was acting." Her chest felt lighter than it had been a moment ago.

He followed her out. "It'll be delivered to your med bay in the morning."

"Fantastic news." She couldn't stop smiling as they walked side by side. "Thank you. Kilian will be so excited." With a bounce in her step she hadn't felt in a long time, she envisioned the boy's face lighting up, and the image propelled her the rest of the way to Mace's quarters.

He scanned his hand, and she hopped into the room. When she turned to face him, he was moving backward into the corridor.

"You're leaving?"

His eyebrows lifted.

"I mean—sorry." She shook her head to clear it. "I was wondering if I could have access to the terminal?"

His eyebrows lifted more.

"Books," she blurted, feeling like a complete idiot now. "I wanted some books to read. Please. There's not much to do in here, and I've been going a bit stir-crazy." She lifted her arms and dropped them again, knowing her face reddened as usual.

Mace hesitated, then crossed to her in two steps. Taking hold of her hand, he tugged her toward the terminal.

Nia inhaled sharply, her eyes fixed on where his hand held hers—how she didn't pull away, and her fingers curled naturally inside his like they'd done earlier in the day.

Before she could fully examine her treasonous reaction, they arrived at the terminal. He dropped her hand to press his against the scanner. The shiny black surface activated, and Nia kept her eyes averted from the huge dent she'd made her first day.

When he took her fingers again, she twitched. His palm warmed her knuckles as he pressed her hand flat against its surface. After the scan, he took his hand away before punching in more codes, both on the terminal and his vambrace.

Nia curled her fingers into her palm, trying to squeeze the tingles away.

"I've given you access to some of the station's libraries," he said, his fingers slowing. "You're not supposed to, but I've overridden the system."

"Thank you." The names of libraries scrolled across the screen in three languages, one she couldn't read: Library of Law, Library of Architecture, Library of Fiction. Nia read each heading to distract herself from the fact Mace hadn't left yet, hadn't moved away, and his body continued to warm her side.

After a long, quiet minute, she looked up at him. His furrowed brow smoothed when she met his eyes.

"I've got to go," he said, but still didn't move away.

Nia nodded, heart beating strangely in her chest. Why did it feel like the entire station had tilted on its side when her feet remained firmly on the deck? Her breaths shortened, almost to the point of panic. Why was he making her feel this way? Her fingers twitched, this time stopping before she could reach for her PALM and a dose of suppressant.

Mace straightened suddenly, like he'd been struck with a power surge, and headed to the door without saying another word.

Chapter Fifteen

Nia knew with certainty she was once again near Mace when she woke the next morning. Not only because of the unrelenting warmth coming off his body, but because she'd had a dreamless sleep.

That wasn't quite true. She'd dreamed of her parents. But the nightmares of cerulean birds eating eyeballs had stayed away.

Curled on her side, she felt waves of heat moving into her spine. They weren't touching, but she was certain that if she rolled onto her back, she would meet his body.

Nia lay there, eyes closed, debating whether to test out her theory when the blanket covering her shifted. Cool air seeped against her skin as he left the bed. The door to the washroom whooshed shut a moment later.

The steam shower hummed. She kept still, listening, and an image of Mace's chest filled her mind, beads of moisture running through the grooves of his muscles, traveling downward...

Nia swallowed, heart rate speeding up. Something had shifted between them yesterday. She didn't like it but couldn't seem to stop it. She'd been *aware* of him from the second he'd landed on her table on *Elara Five*, but that awareness had turned into appreciation or something like it.

Self-loathing consumed her, and she gripped her locket through the material of her shirt. This softening toward him couldn't continue. There should be nothing but hate in her heart.

But thinking the thought didn't make it true.

With defeat rolling through her, she squeezed the locket, then let go. Escape was the only thing she should worry about. Brushing the hair out of her face, she rose from the bed. While she had privacy, she opened the compartment under the bed and changed her outfit, stuffing the other one in the sluice beside the washroom to be laundered.

The narrow door slid open. His black hair damp, Mace wore his uniform, his vambrace contrasting with the navy color.

Quickly, she retreated, ignoring the way her heart pounded at his nearness and the fresh, minty scent coming off him in waves. Stopping on the other side of the kitchen counter, she stared at the refrigeration unit.

Mace followed and reached around her to open the door. "Are you going to have something to eat?"

She grabbed the first thing without looking at it, then sat at the table before opening the packet of concentrated greens. Not her favorite, but whatever. Convincing herself she meant to grab these greens, she bit into the corner and chewed, and followed Mace's movements out of the corner of her eye.

Instead of sitting at the table, he remained where he was, leaned against the counter, and crossed his ankles to drink his compound beverage. Her mind kept returning to the events of yesterday, but she felt his gaze bore into her while she ate.

They both kept silent, the tension between them growing.

Swallowing the last lump of greens along with her unwanted emotions, Nia stood, shoved the packaging in reclamation, and walked to the door to wait. She told herself it was to get to the med bay as quickly as possible, to see Kilian's new leg, and not her need to escape the man who'd become a vulnerability to her sanity.

Neither of them spoke on the walk to the medical bay. Nia kept her mind on the prosthetic and the rehabilitation process Kilian would need to undergo after the surgery, instead of all her other rampaging thoughts.

The door to the med bay opened, revealing the place crammed with people. As soon as Mace disengaged her bonds, Nia's triage skills kicked in and she began with the more urgent cases.

She didn't hear Mace leave and barely had the chance to say a quick hello to Kilian and Sorley. A broken arm, a jammed finger, a bruised collarbone, and a multitude of runny noses and fevers, Nia didn't have a moment to spare until well into her day.

When the bulk of the crowd had thinned, with the patients either discharged or remaining on med beds for observation, Nia finally had a minute to look at the prosthetic for Kilian. She pulled it out of its foam-inlaid box, the length of the limb covered in transparent sterilization film. It was the exact model she'd requested, a PK576.

But the packaging made her heart lurch. This... was exactly how it would look if she'd ordered it directly from the CORE herself. Where had Mace gotten it from? Why hadn't she asked how it would be obtained? It had to have been stolen from somewhere.

She had seen daily newsreels reporting on Tellusians raids of medical freighters and medical stations like *Elara Five* for supplies and people. It was what Tellusians did.

Why would she have expected anything else?

When Sorley joined her, Nia forced a smile, pushing all her muddled thoughts aside. She couldn't change how the prosthetic had arrived and needed to focus on her current patient. But Sorley's dour expression made the dread inside her intensify.

"I don't think I can afford this," he said, his voice almost a moan, his head bowed.

Nia's fingers twitched on the artificial limb. "What?"

Sorley lifted his hand as if he wanted to touch it, then let his arm fall. "We were on the transport to Oberon because I was moving where the work was. Things have been tight lately. And after a night in the brig, no one wants to hire me here." He looked away from her, shoulders slumped.

Nia blinked, a hard knot solidifying in her stomach. The CORE government would cover the cost of a medical procedure like this—necessary for the person to function as a productive member of society. She hadn't realized it could be any other way. Nia glanced over her shoulder. Kilian strained to hear what they said, his face so eager, her heart shattered.

Her hands tightened around the limb. "Someone had to pay for this?"

"If your commander was the one who acquired it for you, he was the one who paid for it."

"He's not my commander," Nia muttered, angry at everything in the solar system. With one more look at Kilian and she squared her shoulders. "I promised your son, and I'm not about to break my promise."

"But I can't afford this."

"I'll pay for it. Or Commander Mace can take my creds until it's paid for."

Sorley straightened in surprise. "You don't have to do that."

"I do. And I will. End of discussion." Nia carried the limb to Kilian's bed, shoulders squared as she offered him a smile. "It's perfect, Kilian," she said, easing the worry etching his face. "Kessy, I'll need your help with this."

"Yes, sir," she said, leaving the new shipment of tools she'd been unpacking to join her.

Nia's eyes lingered on the CORE packaging there too. Then, she shook herself. They sterilized their hands, and Nia unwrapped the prosthetic. Accessing the control panel on the back of the knee, she waited for the limb to beep before settling it in line with his thigh.

After Kessy injected a mild painkiller and numbing agent into Kilian's leg, Nia removed the regeneration gauze from his wounds. Using her fine detail regenerator, she stimulated each of the nerve endings and ligaments that would grow into the limb itself.

Kilian hissed.

"Are you uncomfortable?" Nia asked him, pausing in the work.

He nodded. "A little."

"Kessy, another, please."

"Yes, sir."

Once administered, Nia continued, and this time Kilian remained comfortable. The ligaments primed, they fitted the prosthetic over the stump. With one touch of a button on the back of the knee, the four plates and the top hissed and shrank to fit the diameter of Kilian's thigh.

"This is the hardest part," Nia said, wanting to squeeze his hand, but stopped herself, frowning. She'd never wanted to squeeze the hand of her patient before. It wouldn't be proper. Touching was acceptable only in a medical context.

Kilian's brow wrinkled, sweat beading on his upper lip.

"Kessy, one more dose, please," Nia said.

"Yes, sir."

Nia shook her head at the medic's insistent formality, then returned her focus to the prosthetic when the limb beeped once more.

"There," she said to Kilian. "Now all you have to do is stay put for a day while your body does the work. By tomorrow, you'll be standing on your own."

"Really?" Kilian's eyes rounded, drops of moisture gathering in the corners.

She blinked away a sudden stinging in her eyes, her fingers twitching to call a suppressant. She shouldn't be having these feelings while tending a patient. "Yes, ah." She swallowed around the lump in her throat. "The tissues in your body need to integrate with the limb. It takes time." She motioned to the top part of the limb above his own knee joint. "This will always stay on. You can remove the bottom part, but you won't need to replace the limb as long as it's working properly. It will adjust as you grow to accommodate height and weight."

Focusing on the specifications of the limb helped her ignore the adoration coming from the boy and the uncomfortable sensations in her chest. She needed to step away before she became truly emotional.

Turning, she froze with a gasp when Sorley touched her hand.

A sharp word in another language cut through the room from the doorway. Everyone's head whipped around to see Mace standing there, blocking the whole door with his bulk. Sorley dropped his hand and met Nia's eyes.

"I was going to say thank you for doing this," he paused, "all of it. You didn't have to after the way I acted. I'm sorry for how I treated you in the beginning. There was no excuse for it."

"That's..." Her throat tight, her eyes strayed to Mace. "You're welcome."

He looked like he had yesterday, positively murderous. With all the other potent emotions swirling around inside her and no way to block them, his added presence only made her panic. She didn't want a repeat of what had happened yesterday, but not knowing how to stop another disastrous encounter, she remained stuck in her spot.

The tension in the bay grew, everyone else as frozen as she was. But when Kilian squirmed uncomfortably in his bed, his face a mix of fear and worry, protectiveness washed over her. She shot Mace an accusing look. *I will not allow him to agitate this child.*

Nia moved to the end of the med bed, blocking Kilian's view of the door, then crossed her arms over her chest. "Why are you here?" She'd only completed half her shift.

His eyebrows jumped into his hairline, and he glanced around the room. He looked... embarrassed? That couldn't be it.

Shaking her head, Nia walked closer but kept her arms crossed. "What is it?" she asked, stopping close in front of him. Did he have a medical issue? She glanced at his knuckles. No bruises or cuts today.

"Um," he started, then stopped, running a hand through his hair.

She cocked her head to the side, totally baffled by this new hesitancy.

"I wanted to make sure you ate something," he finally said.

Nia's arms dropped to her sides, her stomach fluttering.

His eyes narrowed. "Did you?"

She shook her head slowly.

He scowled. "Then eat."

"Okay." She pursed her lips. "That's it?"

"Yeah. Eat." He spun around and left.

Nia blinked and stared at the closed door. Mace's appearance, his demand, muddled her already turbulent emotions. She pressed a hand to her stomach. What the hell was happening to her?

Turning around, she realized everyone was staring. Nia grimaced, then returned to Kilian's side.

"Rather intense fellow," Sorley said, a pucker of concern marring his brow.

Ignoring the comment, she explained Kilian's rehabilitation process and tried to invalidate the way her heart beat uncomfortably in her chest.

Chapter Sixteen

M ace watched the tyros grapple, giving pointers when someone did something truly asinine, but couldn't stop glancing at his vambrace every other minute to check the time. As soon as he realized what he was doing, he made himself stop.

"Distracted?" Grey asked, jogging past him with one tyro at his side.

Mace didn't bother answering. Grey was already halfway across the arena by the time he'd thought of a suitable response. That last pass had marked the second time he and the student had been around.

"Parry, stop dancing and hit your opponent," Mace ordered.

The tyro straightened and received a shot to the head for it. Mace shrugged. He'd sort of deserved it.

"Keep low," Mace added. Though flat on his back, Parry couldn't get any lower.

His eyes might be on his students, but his mind remained in Nia's medical bay. He couldn't get her face out of his head. She'd challenged him like a fierce mouse. To see her embrace her own authority, to act like a Tellusian... it did something to him he couldn't explain.

"I feel as if your mind is elsewhere," Grey said as he jogged by again, the tyro trying to keep up. Earlier, Grey had barked something about stamina to the kid.

Mace glanced at his vambrace again. Nia's green light remained in the med bay. Elec gave him regular updates. He needn't have had the desire to return and make sure she'd eaten.

He shouldn't be thinking of her at all.

"Is there a worry in your thoughts?" Grey asked, jogging by once more, the tyro lagging a few meters behind.

Mace shook his head, tracking his friend's movements as he circled the perimeter of the sparring area, timing Grey's pace.

"Good hit, Parry," Mace barked. "Now don't get cocky."

The boy got cocky, and his opponent laid him out on the mat with a punch to the gut. She stood above him, smile wide. "Don't get cocky either," he said to her as she helped Parry off the mats.

Mace stuck out his foot.

Whatever Grey had been about to say, garbled into a whoosh of air and a half-laugh as he tumbled, tucked, and somersaulted to his feet.

"Took you long enough," Grey said, rolling his shoulders like he was working out a kink.

Mace shook his head at his friend. "Back at it!" he yelled to the sparring tyros who'd gotten distracted by their instructor's almost-inelegant fall. The tyro who'd been running with Grey kept going. *Smart.* He hadn't dismissed the boy yet.

"Want to talk about it?" Grey asked, standing beside him, duplicating Mace's crossed-arm posture.

Mace lifted his eyebrows at him. Was he a therapist now? Shaking his head, Mace remained silent.

After a few minutes of watching the tyros, he glanced at his vambrace. "Nia's shift is almost over."

"Ah."

"Ah?" Mace looked at him. "What does 'Ah' mean?"

"Just 'Ah.' Nothing else."

Eyes narrowed at his friend, Mace refused to fall into whatever verbal trap his friend wanted to lay, and instead backed away with a tilt of his head, leaving the tyros in Grey's capable hands. If he hurried to Nia's medical bay faster than was warranted, he wouldn't dwell on it.

Dismissing Elec, he leaned against the bulkhead, nodding to Sorley when the man acknowledged him. Nia stood beside the med bed furthest away from the door, tending a small child, probably no older than two. The child was watching the scanner with a leery eye, but Nia had turned it into a game, hiding it, then making it talk.

The little girl giggled. For someone who'd resisted family medicine like it was plague-ridden, Nia appeared to be a natural with kids.

"I'm Mrs. Scanner." She pitched her voice high as she opened and closed the device. "I'm going to make a funny beeping noise. Beep boo beep." Somewhere in there, the scanner actually beeped, taking the girl's stats. "Bye, bye," the scanner said before Nia placed it on the worktable.

"Bye bye," the girl said, waving at it.

Mace pressed his fingers to his sternum, a sudden tightness there. Was he developing a gastrointestinal reflux condition?

After Nia gave instructions to the girl's father, the pair left with the girl saying "beep boo beep" repeatedly.

Then Nia noticed him standing there. She straightened, face flushing pink. "Is it that time already?"

"Yeah."

With a slight nod, she smoothed the front of her white jacket, took a glance around at the last two medics on duty, then walked towards him. Once she'd hung her medical jacket on an available hook, he pressed the control on his vambrace to bind her hands.

An awkward silence descended between them on the return trip to his quarters. Nia kept casting him glances, like she wanted to say something, then thought better of it. He waited while she sorted through her thoughts.

On the lift, halfway between the atrium level and his quarters, the lights changed, pulsing yellow. Battle readiness whipped through him. As soon as the lift door opened, he took Nia's upper arm in a firm grip and ushered her toward his quarters at a near jog.

"What's going on?" she asked over the noise of the alarm.

"Proximity alert." The door to his quarters opened. He disengaged her bonds and was already jogging back towards the lift before the door closed.

The ride to the command center was too slow. Mace checked his vambrace for updates on the way. When he finally stepped into the command center, every cell of his body was ready for the fight to come. Commodore Cache stood at the holotable, half of the commanders also present, everyone with their eyes glued to the three-dimensional image hovering above the table.

"A Guardian," Cache said as he joined her. "They're scanning."

A collective hush descended as they waited to see what the Guardian would do. It had been a long while since a warship had entered the area. Too large to traverse the minefield without blowing itself up, it could only rely on scans to gain information within the field.

The CORE itself set up numerous fields just like this one to corral Tellusians in certain sectors. Centuries ago, while the CORE remained unaware, the Tellusians gradually claimed this field for themselves, one mine at a time—the perfect place to shroud the existence of their deep-space station on the edge of CORE space.

The Guardian's scans would only show the minefield, nothing more. *Orion's* faceted shielding had kept this location secure for a hundred years.

But a wary feeling infused Mace's body, his instincts flaring. Something was off. "My recommendation would be to prep the station for relocation, sir," he said, voice low under the hush of the quiet.

"It would flag our position. We wait," Cache said, eyes never leaving the image.

More commanders joined the group, the tension climbing with each passing second. Mace wanted to suggest again they power up—it took a long time to get a beast like this moving—but Cache didn't need the reminder. She knew her options.

The Guardian remained outside the field for thirty minutes, scanning, adjusting trajectory, then scanning again. Eventually, it moved off at a slow pace.

Everyone released a collective breath.

"No need for drastic measures," Cache said, straightening, her tone confident.

"You were right," he agreed. If they'd initiated propulsion, they would have exposed themselves.

She tipped her head, acknowledging the statement, but her eyes spoke other words, how easily she could have been in the wrong. Neither of them admitted their weaknesses aloud, content to leave them unspoken because of their long friendship.

With a tap of her fingers on the holotable, the proximity alert lifted, the lights returning to normal. Most of the commanders scattered.

"I want to follow, sir." He wouldn't rest easy until the ship was well out of the sector.

She pursed her lips. "You know what I'm going to say."

"That I'm being paranoid."

Cache stared at him, waiting for him to justify the request that could signal their position as much as powering their engines would have.

"Paranoia has kept us both alive," he said.

Cache turned to the image of the Guardian, bracing her hands against the table. "Assemble your team, follow, and appease your paranoia." She touched the tabletop, replacing the image with another sector further out. "And while you're out and about, I'll get you to do some reconnaissance here." She pointed. "We've had some recent activity and need to find out more." Cache glanced at her vambrace. "It's not a long journey. I'll expect your return in nine hours."

"Yes, sir."

"And Mace, this is a reconnaissance mission, not a raid. Even if you find something juicy, you leave it be. Understood?"

"Of course, sir."

The lift of her eyebrows told him she didn't believe his quick agreement. He just smiled.

The blackness of space stretched before them, endless, interrupted only by the smudge of gray the freighter created with its presence.

"You know, it would be fairly easy to force an airlock and take their cargo," Grey said from beside him. "Whatever the cargo might be."

Mace analyzed the data streaming across the main terminal of the Cetan, their stealth vessel, as they traveled concealed in the freighter's energy wake. They'd trailed the Guardian until it had finished its scans and left the sector and now followed this anomaly in the middle of nowhere.

"I agree," Spiro said from behind him. Mace always included him on missions because of his aptitude for jamming signals and scans. "This juicy peach is waiting to be plucked."

Mace turned at Spiro's words and regarded the man whose dark glasses concealed his expression and contrasted with his copper skin. Spiro went on, "Send Betel in the Griffin for the forced airlock, and we'll swoop in behind. Easy." Eager for any chance to kill defenders after what had happened to him as a POW, his suggestion didn't come as a surprise to Mace.

Beside Spiro, Betel grunted his agreement. A man of few words, he sat with his arms crossed over his chest. The scar over Betel's left eyebrow contrasted with the umber tone of his skin. Out of all of them, Betel flew the Griffin housed within Cetan the best. He was also unstoppable at tactical and couldn't seem to miss a target.

Mace cocked his head at his team before turning back to the controls. "I have two thoughts."

"Please do tell," Grey said, using his most pompous tone.

Mace lifted an eyebrow. "One, if we take this ship, we lose any hope of finding out where it's going and what it's doing here." He turned to Spiro. "Speaking of which, have you figured out what it's carrying?" Mace asked.

"This peach is brimming with fighters. Not sure if they're Marauders or Condors, but there are at least thirty of them."

Grey let out a low whistle.

A truly tempting raid. Not only in terms of the hardware the fighters would provide but for the dent it would put in the CORE's inventory.

"What was your second thought on the subject?" Grey asked, swiveling in his seat.

"This juicy peach stinks of ambush," Mace said, scowling at the freighter through the viewer.

"Stars above, I could really use a peach," Spiro murmured. "Haven't had one in weeks."

Mace knew he wasn't talking about fruit, and ignored him to say, "When was the last time we found an unescorted freighter traveling this slow?" He looked at each of them.

"Sometimes fruit is just fruit," Spiro grumbled.

"And sometimes it has a grenade in it," Grey replied.

Spiro's eyebrows rose over his glasses. "What sort of peaches have you been partaking in?"

Mace continued as if he hadn't spoken. "If we knew for sure this was the only freighter traveling this route, I wouldn't hesitate to raid it. But blowing our cover now means risking a bigger future score." He'd follow Cache's lead when it came to acting hastily.

The other three remained silent. With no further disagreement, Mace turned to the controls. "Spiro, tag it."

The digital marker would allow Cache to send a fleet of Cetans to see what was going on.

Mace reduced their speed until the freighter disappeared from sight, the Cetan's heat signature concealed in the other ship's energy wake. When it was safe, he turned the ship around and headed for home.

A two-hour flight and they'd be back at *Orion*.

For the first time in a long time, the thought of returning home not only contented him, but he was becoming downright buoyant—all because of a certain curly-haired doctor.

What the hell is wrong with me?

Chapter Seventeen

N ia glared at the door, her palms flat against the cool metal of the table, her spine pressed against the chair. Grit lived in her eyeballs, making the room around her blur. She swayed with exhaustion. It had been hours since she'd been waiting, ready for Mace's return.

At first, she'd been annoyed. He'd left so suddenly, not telling her anything, and she'd expected him to return with information, to explain what was going on and who, or what, had started a proximity alert.

The yellow alarm had stopped, and he hadn't returned. Her annoyance turned into frustration. Hours passed, and she'd gotten angry. Now she seethed with rage, fingers flexing against the tabletop.

She'd only got a couple of hours' sleep between frustration and anger, and she wasn't moving until Mace returned. He had to collect her for her shift at some point, right?

The door slid open. Nia jumped to her feet, grabbed the orange sitting beside her hand, and whipped it at his head.

At the last second, Mace ducked out of the way, lips parting in shock, eyes wide.

She had another orange ready and threw it. This one he deflected. She grabbed the peach and whipped it. He caught it with one hand. Ripe, it made a sloppy, squishing noise when he squeezed it.

Swallowing at his expression, Nia reached for the next peach. Nostrils flaring, Mace advanced. He deflected the second one, skirted the table, and grabbed her wrists before she could reach for another.

Tugging, he pulled her close, until they almost touched. "What the hell are you doing?" he asked, his voice deadly quiet.

"I'm pissed off." Nia tried to yank her arms away, but he held firm. Her chest heaved with each angry breath. She tilted her head to meet his eyes.

Icy blue flecks flashed at her. "Pissed off?"

"You left me here with the lights flashing and didn't come back!" Her voice rose in volume with each word, her rage igniting like a spark in a room full of combustible gas. She yanked on her arms but couldn't break free. "Let me go so I can finish," she demanded, jerking her chin at the table full of all the food she'd emptied from the refrigeration unit.

His grip on her wrists loosened, but he didn't let go. Instead, he pulled her hands around until her arms wrapped around his hips in a hug. Her breasts squished tight against his chest, her locket a hard mass between them.

Her nerves tingled at the contact. She swallowed at the look in his eyes while her heart beat at an uncomfortable pace in her chest. His eyes had darkened to an electrifying shade of cobalt.

"There was a Guardian in the area." His warm breath brushed her cheeks. "It's gone now."

"A Guardian?" She couldn't keep the hopeful tone out of her voice.

Mace's eyes narrowed, hands tightening on her wrists behind him. "Don't get any ideas."

All the cumulative frustration from a long night of uncertainty bubbled inside her. "What the hell would I do?" She struggled against him. "Stick my arm out an airlock and wave?" Her knee jerked toward his groin.

He spun her around so fast his quarters were a blur until she faced the bed, his arm a band around her middle. With her hands pinned to her sides, he pressed his lips to her ear. "That would not end well for you, *izar.*"

The position and the words brought back memories of her last day on *Elara Five*, how he'd ripped her from her home and killed her people. With a scream, she threw her body backward, snapping her head, kicking where she could reach. She thought she'd gained an inch of space when he pushed her forward until her knees hit the bed. Bent over, his groin pressed against her ass, her hands trapped against the bed frame.

"Let me go," she spat over her shoulder and pushed against him. The part of him pressed between her thighs hardened. Every part of her went tense.

"I'd stop doing that if I were you," he said, voice low.

The air around them crackled and shifted. She froze. A shiver tickled along her spine. Her cheeks burned at having his body pressed so intimately against hers.

The fight left her, and her body sagged. Heat settled in the pit of her stomach. She leaned forward until her forehead pressed against the bedcovers. With sheer willpower, she held herself still.

"Mace." She groaned, barely resisting the urge to move suggestively against him. His hand hovered over the middle of her spine, like he was about to press her further into the mattress.

"Mace—" Nia stopped speaking. Heat settled between her legs. *Oh, hell.* What was going on with her body? Why wasn't she screaming at him to stop touching her?

He shifted, releasing his hold, and freed her arms.

Nia exhaled and braced against the bed to stand on rubbery legs. By the time she'd turned around, she stared at an empty room, the smashed fruit on the deck and the thrumming of her body the only indications he'd been there.

Mace ran a shaky hand over his face, leaning against the bulkhead beside the door to his quarters. What the fuck? He had nothing in his brain except that. *What. The. Fuck.*

He needed to stay away from her. Nia was his responsibility in every way. He needed to protect her, even if it was from himself. The way she'd said his name... an accented purr making every part of his body harden.

Pushing away from the bulkhead, he stalked the corridors until his brain slowed to an acceptable speed. Unfortunately, his cock remained as hard as it had been when he'd held her in his arms.

Walking and taking deep breaths for long minutes, Mace circled back to his quarters. The door opened, and he found Nia sitting on the edge of the bed, her arms wrapped around her knees. He lifted his gaze above her head so he wouldn't see her wounded expression.

"Your shift starts soon," he said, speaking to the bulkhead.

Nia rose and walked toward him. He refused to look at her as he engaged her bonds and continued to the lift. When he finally turned, he realized she hadn't followed. She stood by the door to his quarters, wrists clasped, and stared at him.

The sight of her bound had never hit him so wrong as it did right at that moment. An emotion akin to panic wrapped around his chest and squeezed. There was no way to fix this situation, and he'd made it worse. He stood frozen to the spot.

Finally, she walked toward him with slow steps, counted only by the stuttered breaths in his tight throat. She stopped in front of him, her gaze searching his, the color high on her cheeks.

The lift door opened, but neither of them stepped inside.

"Am I safe with you?" Nia asked, chin jutting. Confusion and challenge swirled in her eyes. "On my first day here, you said you wouldn't hurt me."

It felt like someone's hand punched into his chest and squeezed his heart slowly. "I won't hurt you."

He had to make this true. He couldn't overpower her again. She was his ward, and he needed to protect her. If staying away from her was his only option, then that was what he would do.

She stared at him, eyes searching, then gave him one nod, like she believed him, before stepping onto the lift.

Nia focused on her patient, a boy with a sprained wrist, and tried to clear her head of everything else.

It wasn't working.

She'd been angry—beyond angry—for being kept in the dark about the proximity alert. Attacking him with fruit had been juvenile and stupid, but she'd needed some sort of release.

But it had turned into something completely different.

It made her mad all over again. She shouldn't feel attraction towards her warder, a Tellusian. She shouldn't want to get to know him better. But no matter what she should or should not be doing, she found herself craving both.

Instead of dwelling on all the confusing emotions in her head, Nia focused on work.

The day merged into the next, and the one after that into another. Nia became used to the routine of family medicine, the rhythm. Ignoring the occasional snide comment wasn't hard. Kilian was booked to see a physical therapist and was discharged. The debt of the prosthetic hung over her head.

And it didn't take long for Nia to realize Mace was avoiding her.

He didn't sleep in his quarters anymore, didn't even speak to her except for the bare minimum. He collected her at the start and end of her shift. And with the lack of him in the bed, her nightmares of a face covered in a blue tattoo and birds eating eyeballs returned.

What she wouldn't give to order a sleeping aid in the middle of the night with her PALM, but things didn't work like that here. There wasn't a dispensary in Mace's quarters or every few meters in the corridor.

Mace had been so dedicated to his silence that when they walked side by side toward the med bay and he actually spoke to her, she jumped.

"We need to go to processing after your shift."

"Why?" She barely resisted the urge to grasp her locket protectively. Had someone figured out she was wearing a tracker? She swallowed against the lump growing in her throat.

"Captives need to be interviewed within two weeks of their arrival. It's mandatory." He spoke in a flat tone.

"And you don't want me to be interviewed?"

He didn't answer, instead leading the rest of the way to the med bay in silence.

Tension rolled through her stomach for her entire shift. Scenarios raced through her head, ones where she was thrown into the brig for her tracker. Ones where her lineage was exposed, and they tortured her for being ruling class. Ones where she was locked in a cell instead of being allowed to work.

By the time Mace retrieved her, she'd put herself in a right state. The calm she'd attained over the past few days evaporated.

With her hands bound in front of her, the walk to processing felt like a death sentence. They arrived through the docking bay, the same one as on that first day. Her body trembled remembering the line of medical officers, and the one who'd resisted and was murdered.

Mace led her past the area where she'd been scanned, to a door beyond. After tapping his vambrace, it opened into a long corridor, blank doors alternating on both sides. He glanced at his vambrace and strode forward.

For a moment, her feet wouldn't move, then Mace threw a scowl over his shoulder. Glowering back, she stepped over the threshold, and the door slid closed behind her.

He stopped at a door on the right and tapped on his vambrace. It slid open with a soft whoosh. A sterile scent assaulted her nose, not unlike the smell of a medical lab. Two chairs and a slender metal table sat in the middle of a small room, one entire bulkhead filled with a viewer set to opaque. She couldn't tell if there was anyone on the other side.

When she felt the warmth of Mace's hand on her lower back, she stepped forward. Her bonds separated.

Not five seconds later, a man wearing a long gray coat stepped through the door on the side. She tensed. It was the same person who'd processed her on her arrival. He bustled to the table, an aura of hurry surrounding him.

He sat, then sent her an expectant expression. The door closed with a hush, and she spun around. An immediate sense of abandonment tightened her stomach.

Mace had left her there.

CHAPTER EIGHTEEN

Panicked, Nia whipped around again and stared at the blond man in confusion.

"We keep these interviews confidential," he said, answering her unspoken question. His palette lay on the table in front of him, and he gestured to the free seat.

Stomach twisting in knots, she stepped forward and settled in the cold chair.

His face blank, he glanced at his palette. "Have you been given appropriate food and clothing?"

"Yes."

"Has your warder mistreated you in any way?"

Nia's face flamed thinking of what had happened between them only days before, but Macc had walked away and stayed away ever since. "No," she said.

The man squinted at her before continuing. "Are you satisfied with your living arrangements?"

She straightened, confusion replacing her wariness. "I can choose to live somewhere else?"

"There's the common holding where captives live. They might or might not assign you to manual labor." His expression changed, brow wrinkling. "Probably not, since you've already established yourself as a doctor."

"If that's where captives live, why am I in Mace's quarters?"

The man shifted in his chair, eyes darting to the side. "Commander Mace invoked the old laws."

"Old laws?" she asked with a shake of her head, not understanding.

The man cleared his throat, his eyes fixed on his palette. "Tellusians have come a long way regarding captive rights over the last century. There's the Take and Keep law, where the warrior keeps his spoils of war. He kept you."

"He kept me," she repeated.

The man nodded, mouth tight as he met her eyes.

"And this doesn't happen often?"

He shook his head slowly.

Nia's face warmed all the way past her forehead. There was more here than the man was telling her, but from the set of his jaw, he wasn't inviting more questions.

He glanced at his palette. "Are you satisfied with your living arrangements?"

She stared at him. What would happen if she lied? What would happen if she claimed abuse?

But Mace had said she was safe with him.

For some reason, she believed him.

When she'd arrived, something had transpired between this man and her warder. Mace had secured protection for her, hidden her lineage. If she moved to common holding, what sounded like communal living, would the person in charge find out about her identity and sell her off for ransom?

The devil you know.

She had access to the terminal for reading. She had privacy, and Mace left her alone.

"I'll stay," she said after a long, tense minute.

"Very well." He tapped on his palette. "Have you been given a chance to earn a wage?"

"Yes. I mean, I think so. But no one has given me money."

"I'll be in charge of that today. Yes, here it is," he said, reading from his palette. "You've earned yourself a fair amount of creds. A lot of captives refuse to work." He tapped the palette, and her bonds beeped. On the inside of her wrist, an amount appeared. "The bonds work as a cred exchange too."

Her eyes widened. She wasn't sure how CORE and Tellusian currency compared, but if they were remotely similar, it surpassed what she'd earned on *Elara Five* in a week. Not enough to buy a ship, but definitely enough to live on and have some tucked away for an emergency.

Enough to pay off the debt of a state-of-the-art prosthetic? *Hopefully.*

"That wraps it up. Do you have any questions?"

Nia's brain ran amok with them, but most she didn't think safe to ask this man. His apathetic and formal demeanor, so much like the CORE, should have put her at ease, but it only made her anxious.

She cleared her throat. "What language is everyone speaking here?"

"Tellusian."

She shook her head. Like everyone else educated through the CORE's education program, she's learned all the languages of the system, including Common. There was nothing called Tellusian. "I don't understand it." Her cheeks burned at the obvious statement.

His smile wasn't kind. "That's the point." He glanced at his palette, his expression dismissive. "Any other questions?"

With her hands clenched in her lap, she shook her head.

"Very well." He stood. "Good day to you." Palette tucked under his arm, he exited the way he'd come, leaving her alone.

She stood, feeling trapped, when the other door slid open, revealing Mace. An uncharacteristically hesitant expression pinched his face. "You chose to stay with me."

She lifted her chin. "Unless you want me to go."

His eyes narrowed a fraction, penetrating, until she couldn't stand it anymore. She dropped her head and saw the cred amount on the inside of her wrist.

"Take them," she said, lifting her arm toward him.

His head jerked. "What?"

"My creds."

He shook his head, frown increasing in strength. "I'm not taking your money."

"Yes. You will. For Kilian's prosthetic."

He shook his head again.

"I will *not* be indebted to you," she ground out between clenched teeth. She already was, for whatever he'd arranged with the processor, despite the circumstances that brought her here.

Mace stared at her for a long while, then said, "We can talk later." Touching the control to bind her wrists, he gestured for her to precede him out.

The return journey to his quarters took them on a similar path as the first day: too many people, too much noise. Mace led the way, and the crowd parted for him. Nia followed, staring at his spine. He didn't look back once to see if she kept up.

What would happen if she turned around and walked in the other direction?

Before she could muster the courage and energy to test out the thought, they arrived at his quarters.

As soon as she stepped inside, her wrists separated.

"Did the processor inform you of your day off tomorrow?"

She spun around. "What?" First, she was paid, and now she got the day off?

"Mandatory," he said with a nod.

She squinted at the room. "I have to stay here all day?" She'd rather be in the med bay than go stir crazy, no matter how well-stocked their libraries.

But he shook his head. "You'll need to stay in Section C, but you have six hours of free time. Your bonds would let you know if you crossed the boundary line."

She understood Section C to be quite large, so the prospect of being confined within its limits didn't bother her. "What about my patients?" Kilian was supposed to return for a follow-up.

"They would notify anyone looking for you at family medicine that you have the day off."

Her next thought splashed cold water on her newly gained good mood. "Do you need to stay with me the entire time?" The words came out garbled.

He hesitated. "Someone has to at this point. I could assign an enforcer if you'd rather have someone different."

"No." The word came out fast. "I mean, as long as it's not too much trouble." She winced. Stars above, she didn't want him to babysit her. He probably had duties as a commander.

"It's fine."

She shook her head. It was anything but fine, but a day off... she couldn't refuse.

The liberating thought of a bit of freedom kept her up half the night. By the time the morning hour rolled around, Nia was both exhausted and wired with anticipation. With automatic movements, she smoothed the covers of the bed, trying not to notice the coldness of the unused half.

She turned around at the sound of the door opening. Mace stood there wearing his dark blue uniform, his arms hanging loosely at his sides. Her stomach flipped pleasantly. She hated herself for it.

"Have you eaten?" he asked, stepping inside.

She nodded.

"Then you're ready to go?"

Nodding again, she moved toward him. He reached for the controls on his vambrace. Instead of her bonds snapping together, the light on them turned blue. Meeting his inscrutable gaze, she raised her eyebrows.

"You have six hours. You'll remember?"

Her heart raced in anticipation. "Yes."

She stepped out into the corridor, shoulders tensing at the thought of being shocked, but nothing happened. Exhaling a slow breath, she cast one last glance at Mace over her shoulder and hurried toward the lift. A couple passed her by with a baby in their arms. Someone coughed behind a closed door.

She stopped in front of the lift. Instead of waiting for Mace to call it to them, she pressed the control panel like she'd seen him do.

It worked! The door slid open as Mace stopped beside her. She schooled her pleased expression and looked up at him.

"Don't fret," he said, stepping onto the lift beside her. "You'll have space." He touched the control panel inside.

It hadn't been what she was thinking at all, but now he said it, she worried he'd be hovering for her whole day off.

They rode the lift upward, then the door slid open on the ground floor of the atrium. She stepped off and felt the heat of Mace following against her spine. For a moment, the amount of people pressed in on her, her chest squeezing tight. *Too many.* It always seemed the case with Tellusians. Too much. Too many.

The crowd thinned, people leaving, sitting, carrying things in their arms. Her eyes darted around, taking it all in. She took another step forward, throwing Mace a glance over her shoulder, but he was gone. Frowning, she turned around fully. He hadn't been lying when he'd said she would have space.

With tentative steps, Nia walked forward between the tables. Being on the ground level was so much different from watching from above. Music played from somewhere, the rhythm hitting her deep in her abdomen, but she couldn't tell where it came from. Every table had at least one person at it, groups of gray and brown clad workers at several.

A group of warriors sat on one side, their voices loud. She wasn't sure if they were happy or angry at each other from all the shoulder-slapping and guffaws.

Standing on the other side of the wide space, a woman and a man spoke animatedly in Tellusian, waving their hands furiously between them. No one else seemed concerned by the display of... affection?

Skin. Everywhere. Nia pulled at the hem of her shirt. Why did some of these people bother getting dressed at all?

It was then she realized there were captives mingling among the Tellusians, bonds on their wrists. She scanned faces, looking for someone familiar, someone from *Elara Five*, but no one stood out. One laughed at something a Tellusian said.

How could they sit there so calmly? How could they act happy? Anger swept through her body, heating her skin. The urge to storm over there and demand answers almost overwhelmed her, but she held herself back. Shame followed her anger. Wasn't she as guilty of integrating herself over the past days? Hadn't she had inappropriate thoughts about her warder? Nia averted her gaze, indecision freezing her to the spot.

Viewers peppered the perimeter. Advertisements and public announcements flashed. A section of screens showed some sort of brutal and bloody game, making her wince. One viewer caught her eye: a CORE newsreel. Three translations scrolled along the bottom.

Chancellor Feering was making a speech. Members of the ruling class stood behind with stoic expressions, including the Xus and Mullers.

Nia swallowed the tight lump in her throat. She couldn't tear her eyes away from the familiar faces until the news story changed to another.

A hard knot of nausea settled in the bottom of her belly. Pressing a hand against her stomach, Nia distracted herself by walking the outer edge of the area, where shops lined the perimeter: children's toys, items made from what looked like natural materials—wood? really?—a salon, a tech exchange, and food vendors with sizzling confections. She strolled by a wide, curving staircase winding its way to the second level before her feet stopped in front of a weapons manufacturer.

Chest squeezing, Nia watched a warrior test the sight of a gun about the length of her arm. Seemingly pleased with its construction, he purchased the item through his vambrace cred exchange. She'd healed injuries created from those sorts of weapons, ones that would slice a limb off like a laser scalpel on steroids.

The neat row of knives in front of the guns drew her eyes. *So many blades.* Nia couldn't pull her gaze away. In the infancy of her profession, surgeons used knives to cut into their patients, a crude way of healing to be sure, but these knives weren't meant for anything so noble. These blades were meant to kill, some serrated, others double-edged. *Here's a pretty.*

Quick movements out of the corner of her eye had Nia turning. An enforcer moved toward her, the woman's hand on her gun, eyes on Nia's face. Another came at her from the side, his expression fierce, an intricate blue tattoo climbing his throat.

Panic set in. Nia turned back to the weapons vendor, who was also staring at her, a frown puckering his brow. She'd done something wrong. *I shouldn't have stopped here.* But her feet wouldn't move. Her limbs began to shake.

And the enforcers kept getting closer.

Chapter Nineteen

I f Nia acted any more suspicious, she'd gain more attention than that of two enforcers.

Mace caught Glade's eye and waved her off. He'd only left Nia to her own devices for ten minutes, and already she'd have a report written up about her. Sliding behind her, he gave the weapons vendor a nod.

His ward wasn't a danger to the people here no matter how she looked right now. He'd bet his life on it. If she grabbed a knife to hurt those around her, he'd slit his own throat.

When he settled a hand on her shoulder, she jumped as if he'd screamed in her ear.

She spun around, relief flooding her eyes when she saw him. "I wasn't doing anything!" Her words were heated, but her tone was quiet.

"I know, *izar*." He slid his hand to the small of her back, coaxing her from the hazard. "Come."

Ignoring the stares sent their way, he wove her through the crowd to a narrow gap in the bulkhead, on the other side of the atrium. The dark corridor snaked with a twist and turn, then opened into a vast space, the air thick with moisture and the scent of earth.

Nia's gasp of wonder made him look around the arboretum with new eyes.

Trees towered, reaching toward the special lights crisscrossing the overhead five levels above. Evergreens, redwoods, birches, palms, ferns, and flowering bushes grew close together. Pathways and landscaped sections separated them at intervals. A green flavor filled his nostrils. Air pumped in through the ventilation system, rustling leaves. Water gurgled from farther along.

Beneath his hand, tension leaked from her body in a whoosh of breath. "It's beautiful."

She stepped away from him, and his hand dropped to his side. Tilting her head, she walked along the winding composite path to the bright red bridge ahead.

"A stream." She stopped halfway across and stared at the flowing water.

"It's a self-contained ecosystem," he offered.

She startled as if she hadn't remembered he was there, then straightened. His chest stung when the joy on her face melted away.

"It even has fish in it," he said, hoping to bring back that look of delight.

Her expression softened. "I've seen nothing like this except in the Lunar colonies and Mars." She shook her head. "Is this why I hear water running in some of the main corridors?"

He nodded, stepping closer. "It's all connected."

Her eyes followed the line of the closest conifer as it reached to the overhead. "How are the trees so big? Genetic manipulation?"

"They're just old."

She glanced at him, questions swirling in her eyes. No doubt wondering how long *Orion* had been here. But he couldn't get more into the history of the station than what she would have been able to read through his terminal.

The grounds beyond the path swelled and dipped in man-made slopes. At the top of one, a young couple sat side by side with their heads bent together, whispering. Others strolled along the path, some taking shortcuts to other parts of the station. From somewhere farther along, a child squealed with delight.

Turning on her heel, Nia continued along the path. Mace followed at a distance. When the trail crested a hill, she stepped off and strode up the grassy incline, pausing where aspens circled a clearing. She spun around, arms spread wide, face upturned toward the lights, before dropping to lie spread-eagled on the grass.

His chest panged at the sight of her enjoyment. He turned slightly, intent on giving her privacy, when her sultry voice rang across the space between them.

"Why did you become a warrior?"

A couple passed him on the path. He gave them a nod, then headed up the incline toward Nia.

Her eyes were closed, the rise and fall of her chest even. He could be doing a hundred other things right now, but none seemed important at the moment. He'd stayed away from her this past week as much as he could, but right now, none of his reasons seemed to matter.

When he didn't answer, she tipped her chin and opened one eye to capture his gaze.

Exhaling, he broke eye contact and strolled to the closest tree. When he turned around, she still stared at him with that one russet eye.

He leaned against the trunk. "I always knew I was going to be one," he said loud enough for his voice to carry. "From the time I could walk, I'd always wanted to be like my parents."

Her eyes widening, she sat up. "They're warriors?"

"Were." An ache throbbed in his chest like it always did when he thought of them. "Both died in battle."

His father and mother had given each other strength. But Mace also knew their emotional attachment had killed them. During their last mission, his father wouldn't leave his mother behind to save himself. After all the lectures he'd gotten from his father about never being weak, never showing vulnerability, it was his own that had killed him.

Mace couldn't find any shame in the way they'd died.

"I'm sorry. I shouldn't have asked."

He waved her comment away, sliding down the trunk until he sat with knees bent. "You can ask me anything you like."

Hesitating, she wrapped her arms around her knees and asked, "What were they like?"

"I guess my father was a lot like me." He tilted his head. "Or I'm a lot like him. His father had been a warrior, and his father before him. It was expected of me, but if it hadn't been, it would have been my choice. It's what I'm good at."

Throughout his description, her eyes lit with interest.

He continued. "My mother was a lot gentler."

Nia's eyebrows jumped. "Gentle? A warrior?"

Her surprise amused him, though he tried not to show it. "She became a warrior as an adult, unlike most of us who were raised as warriors. She'd had a life of science before that."

"Why did she become one then?"

Memories of his mother assaulted him, of the sometimes-sadness in her eyes. He'd asked her once why she would get tattoos on her wrists like her old captive's bonds. *It reminds me of where I came from.*

But he didn't want to tell Nia this, to draw the similarities of how she'd come to *Orion* compared to his mother. "Circumstances changed for her, and it seemed her best option."

A frown gathered on Nia's brow, her eyes distant.

"What about your parents? What are they like?"

He regretted his question when her spine snapped straight. She glanced around, her expression wary, before resettling on him.

"Um." She licked her lips. "My mother is stern, very driven. She wanted different things for me, but I rebelled." Turning her head, she focused on something in the distance.

"You were far from home." He'd never heard of anyone from the ruling class working so close to the front lines.

"Yes," she agreed, meeting his gaze once more. "Our different viewpoints created obstacles in our relationship."

"And your father?"

"He just wanted me to be happy." Her expression softened. "Growing up, I received the most affection from him. He's boisterous, where my mother is reserved."

"You're an only child, aren't you?"

For hundreds of years, the CORE had placed a ban on having more than one child. Except for the ruling class. As a result, most of the influential CORE families had as many children as possible to secure their future bloodlines.

A red hue climbed her throat, eyes darting around to see if anyone was listening. "My father believes rules should apply to everyone."

"Sounds like a revolutionary."

"Hardly," she replied, gaze snapping to his, and there was a note of unease in her tone. "An accusation like that could have him arrested for questioning."

He lifted his hands in mock surrender. "I don't make a habit of reporting people to CORE officials."

Her shoulders slumped. "No. Of course not." She rested her chin on her knees, fingers fiddling with her bonds.

The urge to remove them overwhelmed him, but they'd be a permanent fixture for a long time to come.

She reached for the grass in front of her and pulled, tearing out some blades. "What's the significance of your tattoo?"

The question startled him, but he answered. "It's a family design. My father had his whole back covered in the same pattern, my mother, her wrists."

"Why do some of you get tattoos on your faces?" She mangled the grass between her fingers.

"It's a declaration."

She lifted her head, eyes round. "Of what?"

"To denounce CORE authority. The warrior would rather die than be captured. Once inked, the tattoo is impossible to remove, something about the process." He paused, thinking of the damage to his own ink. "Unless you remove the skin entirely."

Her eyes shuttered, and she returned to pulling grass. He added, "Warriors often get them if a loved one dies in battle. Or often, the warrior gets a prominent tattoo because they weren't born Tellusian and it's their way of declaring they would never go back to the CORE."

There was something about her movements, a jerkiness, which moved him to ask, "Why did you ask that question?"

She didn't answer but let the torn bits of green fall to the ground through her fingers.

"Nia?"

Her head snapped up, eyes narrowing. "You weren't the first Tellusian to take me hostage."

His entire body went rigid. "Tell me."

Keeping his gaze, she propped her hands on knees and rested her chin on the backs of her fingers. "My first post was on a medical aid vessel, the *Diligence*. We were positioned near Jupiter during the alignment. A Guardian was heavily damaged, and we were close enough to help without waiting for medical transports. We docked with it." She closed her eyes. "It was a trap. A Destroyer came out of high speed, attacked, then boarded. They were raiding for medical officers." Her eyes popped open. "You could have been on board that ship."

He shook his head. "I had no part in the raids during the alignment."

"How come?"

He hesitated, not sure how much he should say about their politics. But who would she tell? "At the time, the council was split. There were those who wanted to take advantage of Jupiter's orbit, claim all its colonies, and those who wanted to remain true to the treaties of the time. I belonged to the latter."

"And now? Is there still a split?"

Again, he hesitated. "Right now, there is full agreement among the members." But that wasn't the full truth. He knew of those who would change their stance if certain people had their way, like Admiral Ricker. "Continue with your story," he encouraged.

She settled her chin on her hands again. "I was young and stupid. I should have evacuated with the rest of my bay, but I tried to save the life of my patient. The main power was out, the equipment dead. If I had stopped my compressions, he would have died."

"You were brave. Doing your duty."

She shook her head. "Doing my duty killed my CO and a colleague." A haunted expression passed over her features. "I was the last to leave. I heard them coming, the gunfire and the screams. A warrior found me after I hid. He had a bird tattoo on his face." She touched her eyebrow. "Here." Her fingers trailed down the side of her cheek and jaw. "A hawk frozen in the act of eating his eyeball. He held a knife to my throat and tried to take me. Defenders stopped him. Killed him and saved my life. When you did the same thing—" She stopped speaking, her words choked.

Pain sliced through his chest, chased by the need to track down the man who'd done that to her. There couldn't be that many warriors with hawks on their faces. But his volatile reaction made no sense since he'd done the same thing.

"I would change it if I could."

Her body stilled. She lifted her head, her brow wrinkled. "What do you mean?"

He rushed ahead with the confession he hadn't known he needed to voice. "I should have left you." Silence rang between them, their gazes locked.

Even as he said the words, he wasn't sure he would have been able to leave her if given a second chance.

"Why didn't you?" she whispered.

Excuses froze on his lips. When he'd first taken her hostage, he'd planned on leaving her as soon as she'd served her purpose. His shift in thinking hadn't occurred until the first explosion ripped through *Elara Five*. It had been a subtle change in his plans, one he didn't acknowledge until she'd screamed at him to let her go on the Raven—a demand he found impossible to obey.

Nia swallowed, shaking her head. "If you hadn't taken me, I probably would have died. Or someone else would have taken me, and I would have ended up here anyway."

Both scenarios made his insides clench with pain. Both were unacceptable.

They stared at each other for a long while, searching for answers neither of them could provide.

Then, Nia closed her eyes and flopped onto her back, arms spread wide. Mace remained where he was, watching her, wondering what had happened between them. Would she hate him more because of his confession?

He didn't understand why he cared.

A communique beeped on his vambrace, a personal request from Cache to meet in her quarters. He tensed. It had been a long time since she'd communicated with him in other than a professional capacity, as she would with any of her commanders. With all the side glances she'd been sending him over the past ten days, he knew it wouldn't be about anything good.

His fingers skimmed over the controls of his vambrace, acknowledging the request and calling Elec to him. He couldn't leave

Nia on her own when she'd already gained the attention of the enforcers on duty.

Mace spent the next few minutes staring at his ward. She kept her eyes closed, her expression content as she upturned her face to the artificial light like someone starved for vitamin D. He should tell her he was leaving, but she looked too peaceful to disturb.

When Elec arrived, Mace stood and gave him a nod. And with one last glance at his ward, he left.

Chapter Twenty

Two warriors, Cache's personal guards, flanked the door to her quarters. Mace touched his vambrace, signaling he'd arrived, and her door slid open a second later. He stepped into her personal domain.

The front room of her vast quarters was all business. A circular holotable occupied the center portion, terminals and monitors lining the bulkheads of the oblong space. Cache stared out oval portholes, hands clasped behind her back.

The door slid shut behind him. "You wanted to see me, sir," he said when she still hadn't turned around to acknowledge his presence.

"Yes." Her voice was quiet, so unlike her. He walked around the holotable to stand beside her and stare at the too-familiar view of the minefield.

Cache turned slightly, tipping her head at him, meeting his eyes with her hard emerald ones. "I think we have a problem."

He cocked his eyebrow at her. She returned her gaze to the view, stars twinkling beyond the mines.

"It started with an error in judgment," she began. "My error. I own it. I placed a new team in a dangerous position. That last mission..." She hesitated a moment, then met his eyes again. "It changed you, didn't it?"

Had it? A near-death experience wasn't new. He straightened his shoulders. "I don't think so, sir."

She squared off with him, the tail of black hair flicking over her shoulder. "For fuck's sake, Mace, drop the 'sir.' We're having a conversation here."

"Are we?"

She clenched her fists. If she needed to hit him to get rid of her anger, he'd allow it—not because she was his commanding officer, or even because she was Cache, a friend since they were tyros.

He'd take the hit because he deserved it for everything he'd done to Nia.

She stepped forward, almost toe-to-toe with him. "You took a blasted captive," she said between clenched teeth.

"Yes."

"You attacked a fellow officer with no desire to take his post."

"Did that too," he admitted, and he would do it again. He felt like he hadn't fucked up Foley enough, really.

She stepped back, shaking her head. "You know procedures."

"Then charge me."

She let out a long breath. "Fuck, you piss me off."

"I know."

When he saw the glint in her eye, he realized he'd gone too far. He waited for her next jab, wondering if it would be verbal or physical.

"Taking a captive, shoving them with others of their kind, and reaping the benefits is one thing, but using the old laws to imprison her in your quarters?"

Ah. So that was where all of this was coming from. He thought she would have found out before now from all the whispers.

"What the hell is going on, Mace?" she asked, the volume in her tone rising. "Why would you do that?"

He couldn't tell her the truth. Cache hated the CORE too much, especially the ruling class. She might not ransom Nia if he pleaded with her, but he couldn't take that chance.

He remained silent.

"Is it sexual frustration?" Cache continued, her green eyes flashing. "There's no way you've fucked her already with all this tension and anger in you. I know you too well."

He clenched his jaw so hard that it ached.

But she kept going. "Do you need me to bury the processing interview reports to make her complaints disappear?"

His nerves went numb, and he shook his head in disbelief at what was coming out of her mouth.

"Hell, you only need to crook your finger and half this station would come running. And if it's come to that, you know my door's been open since we were teens."

"Fuck, Cache."

"Is it anger at me?" she asked like she wasn't even listening to his responses. "Your mission was too risky. I admit it and take the blame for those deaths, but stars above, I need the old Mace back."

Nostrils flaring, she turned away and crossed her arms over her chest to stare at the mines. "If you can invoke the old laws, so can I," she said, voice as quiet as it had been when he'd arrived.

His whole body went rigid. "Cache, if you're suggesting—"

"I can and I will. If it threatens the operation of this station, I will remove the problem."

He felt as if his entire body were submerged in sub-zero water. When he'd returned to *Orion*, he'd invoked the Take and Keep law, and his bribe to the processor was supposed to bury Nia's genetic connections. But the same law meant his commanding officer could do the same.

Unless he wanted to battle Cache to the death, she could take what he'd kept.

The need to go to his ward at this exact moment overwhelmed him. He would stand in front of her and kill all those who would try to take her. Including Cache.

"Don't—" His hand drifted to the weapon at his thigh, his mind racing with scenarios. She wore only her gun. He'd be able to take her out, then the two guards, and had enough support on the station to take her command—it was the only way to make it work.

What the hell am I thinking? Challenging Cache? Killing her? Taking over *Orion?* Those were the last things he wanted to do. He removed his hand from his weapon.

Cache spun toward him, whole body vibrating with pent-up energy, eyes flashing in the low light. "Mace, whatever your issues, get your head on straight." She took a step closer. "Whatever it takes. Or I'll be forced to."

She wouldn't do that to him. They'd known each other too long.

"And if I hear about another unprovoked attack on a fellow commander, I'll personally see you in the brig for a year with no chance of probation."

He stayed still, waiting for the next threat, wondering how far she'd really go.

Cache stood taller, turned to the mines and said, "Dismissed."

Mace stared at her profile, wanting to say something clever, but words failed him. Her threat hung between them, but he had to believe she wouldn't go through with it, wouldn't force *his* hand.

All he needed to do was get his head straight.

"Yes, sir." He turned on his heel and left without a backward glance.

I would change it if I could.

Mace's words kept looping in Nia's head as she lay there, soaking up the rays giving the trees their nutrients. Those words revealed regret—an emotion she hadn't thought Tellusians capable of until she came here.

CORE and Tellusians weren't as different as she'd thought. There were differences, cultural ones, but since working in family medicine, she knew Tellusians loved their children as much as CORE parents did, and people wanted to be happy, no matter where they were from.

If only they could live in peace without a war between them.

A shadow fell across her, blocking the warming light. Her eyes popped open. She expected to see Mace, but Elec stood there.

She jolted upright. "What happened?" Her gaze darted to the tree where Mace had been sitting, then around the surrounding area. He was gone. She hadn't heard him move.

Elec shook his head. "The commander told me to make sure you ate something."

An exasperated breath left her. Why was Mace so obsessed with her nutrition? She checked the time on her bonds and straightened when she realized it had been hours since she'd eaten rations in his quarters. Her stomach growled.

"Yeah, okay," she said aloud, climbing to her feet. There'd been food vendors in the main area, some with items she'd never seen before.

The atrium common area remained crowded. Nia stayed as far away from the weapons vendor as possible. Skimming her eyes over the people spread throughout the area, she couldn't see the enforcer who'd watched her earlier. When she looked over her shoulder, Elec remained meters away.

She wasn't sure how to feel about both Mace and him giving her the illusion of space, a false sense of freedom, whether it was thoughtful or insulting.

Following delicious aromas, she headed for the bulk of food vendors and stopped at one roasting skewers of unknown protein.

She tilted her head. Like most CORE citizens, she'd been raised vegetarian. It looked like real meat, but it couldn't be. Where would they keep livestock? It had to be synthetic.

An older man stood behind the counter, his white hair matching the white stripes on his shirt. He asked her a question in Tellusian.

She stared at him for a long minute, decided his face was kind, and held up one finger, pointing at the first row. The skewers smelled way too good not to try. She presented her wrist for the cred exchange. His eyes crinkling, he took her money and passed her a stick of meat.

Nia eyed the skewer. When the man gestured for her to eat, she took a bite.

Her eyeballs pricked with tears. *Too spicy.* But the man watched her with an expectant expression on his face.

"So good," she said with what she hoped was a convincing smile. "Thank you."

From his furrowed brow, she knew she'd failed. She took another bite. "Mmmm." With one last attempt at a smile, Nia headed away from the vendor to circle the perimeter of the common area.

Skewer empty and taste buds burning, she threw the stick into the public reclamation unit on the bulkhead and noticed a narrow corridor she'd missed earlier. It was almost hidden, like the arboretum's entrance. Would she discover something just as wonderful? But no one went inside, skirting the area on purpose. Her curiosity grew.

Moving closer, a foul scent wafted toward her... flesh and rot... it should have repelled her like any normal person, but it pulled her forward. Why would it come through a doorway similar to the arboretum?

The corridor darkened, winding in on itself, then opened into a room almost as vast as the arboretum—some sort of public theater. But it wasn't the raised seating or the blue banners on the bulkheads that drew her eyes. No, it was three decomposing bodies hanging by their wrists on the raised dais. But for their general shapes and some exposed bones, they were unrecognizable as humans.

A large black bird flapped its wings as it pecked away at one of their faces. The meal she'd eaten climbed her throat. None of their eyeballs remained.

Crumpled clothing lay at their feet, dark blue and brown: Tellusian uniforms.

Scalding bile burned her mouth. Without her wanting it to, her brain filled in the information. These people had been stripped, publicly tortured, and killed. Tears burned her eyes.

Every vile story she'd ever heard about Tellusians came back to her. The pictures that the CORE liked to post on the media reels of recovered prisoners. Everything the Mullers had said had happened to them. The body counts. The savagery. The barbarism.

It was all true.

Why had she pushed these facts from her head these past few days?

A hand landed on her shoulder, and she spun around with a scream.

But it was Elec. "You shouldn't be here."

"Who?" It was the only word she could squeeze from her tight throat.

His eyes skimmed to the hanging bodies, then returned to her. "They were traitors, tried and convicted. Commodore Cache likes to leave them up for a while as a warning." He stepped between her and the sight. "The commander wouldn't want you here."

When she didn't move, he turned her with a gentle hand on her shoulder and nudged her the way she'd come. The world around her blurred, unseen, as she placed one foot in front of the other. She wasn't aware of where she was going, only that she'd stepped onto a lift and it hummed around her.

Her brain burned with the image of those bodies. She'd never forget it, her mind continually putting herself in their position. *Traitors.* It looked like their skin had been peeled off.

She didn't know how she'd arrived at Mace's quarters, but there she stood, alone, her hand clutched around the locket at her sternum. She wore a tracker, signaling to any CORE ship on the right frequency that passed close enough.

If Tellusians could do that to their own... what would happen to her if they found out?

Maybe she'd been wrong about some things, like the sex slaves and working captives to the bone, but she hadn't been wrong about others. Tellusians were a merciless race. All they knew was violence.

Mace won't hurt you.

The voice inside her head might be correct, but the memory of those tortured victims buried it deep, making it barely loud enough to hear.

Her bonds beeped, signaling the end of her day off. She covered the light with her hand.

Regardless of what she thought, what she *felt*, she needed to get free of this place.

No matter what it takes.

Chapter Twenty-One

N ia stared at the overhead beams, tapping her fingers to count the seconds. If she closed her eyes, then she saw the shriveled flesh, the empty eye sockets, of the three dead Tellusians hanging on the bulkhead.

Tap. Tap. Tap. She focused on her fingers.

All other attempts at distraction had failed. She'd tried to read in *Orion's* Law Library to learn about the old laws but hadn't been successful. The legal jargon, the "refer to subsection 612," the mind-numbing dryness of the text made it impossible to learn anything.

She'd turned to the History Library instead. That only lasted a handful of minutes before the Tellusian interpretation of events became muddled with the CORE facts she'd learned in school. She couldn't separate the truth from the fiction.

The only thing she could concentrate on was an accounting of the origin of Tellusians. They took their name from Tellus, the Roman goddess of the Earth, and their affinity toward blue came from water and Earth's oceans.

The discord between their peoples began when most of the system's people still lived on Earth. But the planet was dying and couldn't sustain their numbers. Two factions developed. One set of people wanted to move into space to allow Earth to heal; the other, Tellusians, wanted to remain, to give up all technology and industry and return to a hunter-gatherer society.

Having more power and influence, the CORE won the decades-long conflict, forcing everyone to evacuate except for pockets of conservationists. And they herded Tellusians to the outskirts of the system, who claimed Saturn and beyond as their own, and didn't believe the battle for their home planet was over.

Frustrated, she'd given up reading to stare at the overhead beams.

Tap, tap, t—

Abruptly, the lights went out, submerging the room in pitch darkness. Nia lurched upright to sit, seeing nothing in front of her but inky black. A moment later, the lights brightened to quarter luminosity. The doors to Mace's quarters slid open.

Nia pressed a hand to her chest. No one entered, but the doors remained ajar. She stood and glanced at her wrists. Her heart thudded hard. The light was off. No cred exchange or time of day. Nothing. *No security features.*

Nia crept toward the exit, then stuck her head out. Every door along the corridor was open, people coming out with frowns on their faces. A woman had a baby wrapped in a gray blanket on her shoulder and bounced the bundle to an inaudible rhythm.

"If I stop moving, she wakes up," the woman said when she caught Nia staring.

Nia ducked back inside, out of sight.

A low-pitched tone permeated the air. "Attention. We are experiencing isolated power failures. Please remain in your quarters or duty stations. Thank you."

Nia stared at her deactivated bonds. Had someone come for her? She pulled one bond downward, over the hump of her thumb joint. But no matter how hard she yanked, it wouldn't come off.

She quit when her skin reddened from the strain, her bones aching. Tugging her sleeves until they covered her bonds, she stuck a toe over the threshold. Nothing happened. No shock, no pain.

She stepped fully into the corridor, tensing every muscle. Still nothing. Head bent, she strode toward the lift, gaze averted from catching anyone's eye.

Two teenagers stood in front of it, trying to access the inert control panel.

"It's totally dead. Can't jack it," said the one.

"Then let's take the emerg hatch," the other replied. "I don't want to be stuck down here."

Keeping a few steps behind, Nia matched their pace. Ahead, a group gathered around an access hatch. Nia stopped behind the boys, hands behind her back, and tried to act natural.

"You going up or what?" one teenager asked the man at the front of the group.

"As soon as whoever's coming down gets out of the way," he replied, then cleared his throat as a bulky form exited the hatch. "Oh, sorry Commander. Didn't mean any disrespect."

Nia took a step away from the hatch, heart slamming in her ears, stomach dropping into the deck. There was nowhere to hide.

"None taken," Mace replied as he straightened. He focused on her, and his whole body went rigid, expression shuttering.

Every part of Nia tingled in warning.

Mace took one step to her side. "Turn around. Start walking. Don't stop until you're back in my quarters."

Nia couldn't move—even with the heavy threat sinking every word into her gut.

"Now," he added between clenched teeth. He didn't touch her, but the force of the one word made her jump in a half-circle and scurry toward his quarters, the sound of his boot steps following close behind.

"Commander," said the woman holding the baby. "Can you tell us what's going on?"

"Some glitch in the power grid," he replied as Nia stepped over the threshold to his quarters. "It should be fixed shortly."

She spun around, fists clenched, ready to be reprimanded. Mace reached above the door, pumping the manual release until it sealed them inside the dimly lit room.

Nia stayed still, waiting, her breaths shallow.

His posture hadn't relaxed. He paced in front of her like he was trapped. "Do you know what would have happened if a processor or enforcer had found you wandering the corridors unescorted?"

She didn't move but kept tracking his movements back and forth.

"The rights you've earned so far would've been taken away." He ran a jerky hand through his hair. "You'd probably end up in the common holding with all the other captives, and I wouldn't be able to protect you. You might be fine, sure, but then again, you might not."

He dropped his hand and kept pacing. Heat crept up her throat. Her senses prickled at seeing him like this.

He stopped abruptly and turned to her, making her head jerk.

"If you had been in the corridor when the power returned, you would've received a painful shock. Or worse yet, if you'd made it to—oh, I don't know, let's say the docking bay—your bonds would've killed you."

Her stomach dropped. Of course she should have considered that possibility. He'd basically told her so in the med bay. But after today, after what she'd seen in the theater, she needed to get off this station.

The lights returned to full power, and Nia gasped at Mace's expression. Haggard. Tortured.

"What the hell am I doing?" He ran a hand over his face. "Elec told me…" He shook his head and walked away to brace his palms against the bulkhead, head bent.

Heart pounding, Nia stayed where she was, hands by her sides. The lights on her bonds were back on. She swallowed.

When he straightened and turned around, his face had become an impassive mask.

Nia fisted her hands. "Let me go home."

He closed his eyes briefly. "It's impossible."

She shook her head, not believing it. There had to be a way.

Then he met her gaze straight on, his jaw locked. "Unless you want to experience something similar to those traitors, Euphenia Jannex."

All the blood left her head. It was the first time she'd heard her full name since leaving the CORE. Bright light flared in her eyes, her skull becoming weightless. Before she realized what was happening, Mace was there, strong arms around her waist as he stopped her from hitting the deck.

She blinked the fog from her eyes. They sat on the bed, his arms cradling her. Every part of her felt secure. But she knew it was a lie.

"You're safe."

She shook her head at his words.

"I will not allow that to happen to you," he asserted.

"I just want to go home." The raw words exploded from her mouth, painful.

He cupped her jaw in his hand. "I know."

"I *need* to go home." She stared into his icy blue eyes, willing him to free her.

His thumb brushed her cheek.

Tingles spread across her skin. His thumb moved again, creating another wave of sensation that tumbled down her spine. His eyes darkened. She couldn't look away. She wanted to drown in their depths and never resurface.

She gripped the collar of his uniform and yanked him forward. His lips smashed into hers, inelegant, brutal. Heat flared in the pit of her stomach. Shivers exploded across her skin. Every one of her frustrated emotions flooded into the kiss. She trembled, and it had nothing to do with fear.

With a groan, he gathered her closer, his arms tight around her ribs. The shift of their bodies pressed her breasts flush against his chest. Her nipples puckered under the thin material of her top and bra. His mouth took ownership of hers, his tongue stroking inside until she couldn't breathe from the flood of sensation. His masculine scent filled her head, minty and warm. The taste of him stoked a primal part of her she didn't know existed.

She wanted to get closer, *needed* it. Her fingers pulled at the material of his uniform, trying to rip the cloth from his body.

He tore his lips from hers, groaning. She gasped for oxygen. His icy eyes bored into hers. Their chests rose and fell in tandem. The moment hung in time, suspended, until Mace pressed his forehead against hers, hands on either side of her throat.

"What are you doing to me?" he whispered. Their noses touched, breath mingling.

Then he turned his face to the side. In one movement, he scooped her up, set her on the bed, and strode to the door. It closed behind him with a soft whoosh.

She shivered from the absence of his warmth. His abandonment sliced through her stomach like one of those daggers she'd seen today. Conflicting and traitorous thoughts tumbled through her head one after another.

She wanted him to come back.

She wanted to finish what they had started.

Arms wrapped around herself, a sob clogged her throat—one she was determined not to release.

Mace strode from his quarters, his hand scrubbing his face. The way Nia had looked—lips puffy, eyes glistening, her whole body trembling. He couldn't get her out of his head. If he hadn't left right then, he would have had her naked and been inside her within the next few minutes.

The thought did nothing to extinguish the way she made him burn. Her jasmine scent hovered around him in a cloud. He rubbed his lips, remembering how she tasted.

Fucking hell. He needed a cold steam. When he entered an empty corridor, he stopped and stared at the bulkhead.

He wanted to let her go, he really did. Taking her had been a mistake, *a weakness*. He should have left her to die. His chest tightened at his thought. *No.* He couldn't have. Not when those russet eyes had already seared his soul, when her heart beat under his arm, *alive* and full of fight. Not when thinking of her dead along with the rest of *Elara Five* had turned into an unacceptable scenario in those first few minutes.

His mind ran through strategies where he could take her back to CORE space and let her go. But even if she arrived at a CORE-controlled ship or station unharmed, he knew what would happen. She could never return to her old life. They would monitor, restrict, and control her. The CORE never trusted those who returned to the fold and treated them like criminals instead.

The safest place for her to be was in his quarters.

The most dangerous place for her was in his quarters.

He would not turn into something to fear like his ancestors before him. He wouldn't touch her again. Because if he did, if she made those encouraging sounds in the back of her throat that set him on fire...

Fucking hell. He hit the bulkhead with his fist. The resounding crunch filled the quiet.

Chapter Twenty-Two

After the kiss with Mace, Nia rarely saw him. He'd quit escorting her to and from family medicine, instead giving the job to Elec. At least she wasn't required to be bound in the corridors anymore.

Even though she rarely saw him, she couldn't stop thinking about what had happened. When they kissed, she was lost, drowning in sensation. She hadn't cared where she was, who he was, what he'd done... she'd wanted to lose herself completely and forget everything else.

The desire hadn't really left her.

She still wanted him.

And hated herself for it.

The days blurred together one after the other. She might have been surrounded by people in the med bay, but she had never felt so alone. She felt like she lived in a delicate glass ball, and the orb lay in the palm of Mace's hand—he could crush it, and her, at any moment.

By the time she'd earned another day off, she felt like she was going mad.

"It's six hours, same as before," Elec said to her as she stepped off the lift on the ground level of the atrium.

Nodding, she walked parallel to the vendors' shops, skirting all the activity at its center. She only wanted to spend time in the arboretum and didn't check if Elec followed. Her pace slowed when she reached an empty clearing enclosed with sycamores, different from the spot where she'd spent her day off the first time. Her emotions had been too confusing over the past week for her to want to see the tree where Mace had sat and remember the things he'd shared about himself.

With an exhausted exhale, she flopped onto her back on the grass, spread her arms wide, and breathed her tension away. The moist air cleansed her, a healing balm. Some of the larger mines were visible through the bands of lights crossing the dome above. Birds tweeted around her. The stream babbled on her left. She could hear others roaming the space, voices speaking to one another. A laugh barked from a distance away.

She didn't care if she spent all six of her hours in this exact position. Even if she'd been lonely, this type of alone was different. The rustling leaves soothed her. She could almost believe she was on *Jupiter* One, where she was raised.

"Can I join you?"

Nia lifted her head at the feminine voice. Dee stood nearby, her black hair piled on top of her head, and her cream and black dress a swirling mass of pattern clinging to every curve.

"Depends if this is an accidental meeting or if someone sent you," Nia said with her eyes narrowed.

A smile flashed across Dee's face, outlined eyes crinkling. "You're a smart one." Without waiting for an invitation, the other woman sat beside her.

Nia let her head fall back on the grass. "And you didn't answer my question."

"It wasn't really a question, though, was it?"

Opening one eye, Nia turned her head to stare at the woman who had her face upturned to absorb the light's rays from far above.

"Are you here to spy on me?"

Dee's eyebrows lifted. "Spy? No. But someone might have thought you could use some company."

Nia's gaze swung to Elec where he stood on the other side of the clearing, trying and failing to blend in amongst the tree trunks.

Dee snorted. "It definitely wasn't him."

Shaking her head, Nia resumed her previous position. She didn't care if Mace was worried about her. He didn't have a right to be after abandoning her for the past week. "I don't need a pity visit."

"I'm not here out of pity. Just concern."

"Nothing to be concerned about," Nia retorted, her words clipped.

"All right." Dee shifted her position, her clothing rustling in the quiet. "Consider me unconcerned."

Nia didn't need to open her eyes again to know Dee had laid beside her. With an irritated huff of breath, she tried to ignore the woman and reclaim her earlier calm.

Irritation made it difficult, and she opened her eyes to glare above. One yellow leaf descended toward her, slowly flitting this way and that, until it landed on her stomach. Leaning on her elbow, Nia grabbed the stem and twirled it between her fingers.

"Where do your dead go?" The image of those three tortured people rekindled in her mind.

"What?" Dee jolted up, her bangs flopping forward over her outlined eyes.

Nia stared at the leaf, pressing her finger to the pointiest tip. "On my station, everything is connected, and when someone dies, they go to reclamation to become part of the bio-matter on the station."

"Oh." Dee laid down again, brushing her bangs out of her face. "That's how it works here too. Nothing wasted."

"Nothing wasted," Nia repeated, a mantra of the CORE too, everything used again and again. The reclamation chutes were only the beginning of the process.

Had those bodies in the theater been reclaimed yet? Were they being fed into this eco-system as nutrients for the plants in the arboretum? Or were they still hanging there, only bones now, as a message from the Commodore?

If I die here, I'll become a sycamore. But if they found the tracker in her locket, they would make sure to torture her first.

Mace won't allow it.

How could she be so sure? He hadn't condemned the torture and death of those three individuals. And he might say he wanted only to protect her, but he didn't know about the tracker.

Sitting up fully, Nia stared in the general direction of Elec's half-concealed spot and asked, "How long have you known him?"

"I only met Elec last week."

Nia turned her head, giving the other woman an unimpressed stare. Dee only smiled, then sat up too. "I've known Mace for over a decade. My husband was on his team when we married." Her voice was heavy with grief when she added, "Lowe died right before our son was born." A sad smile quivered on her lips.

"I'm sorry," Nia said. "I shouldn't have asked."

"It's okay." Dee bumped Nia's shoulder lightly with her own. "It was a long time ago, and I always knew it could happen. Came with being the wife of a warrior."

Of course Nia knew Tellusian warriors died all the time. So did CORE defenders. She saw it on the newsreels constantly, treated the wounded who survived long enough to make it to *Elara Five*. CORE ships were destroyed. So were Tellusian ones.

This war between their peoples was millennia in the making. And what point did it serve?

What would happen to me if Mace died?

The question made her stomach twist in painful knots. It should have been out of worry that the truth of her lineage would be used against her if he wasn't standing in the way, but she felt sick at the thought of Mace dying—no matter how many times she'd had homicidal thoughts since he'd abducting her.

When Dee spoke again, her tone changed to a pained sort of wistfulness. "Mace was the one who told me Lowe had died in battle."

Nia turned her head. Flat on the ground, Dee had an arm thrown over her forehead, her eyes closed. "I was eight months pregnant. If I'd had a gun right then, I would've shot Mace, and he probably wouldn't have stopped me. Blamed himself for Lowe's death. Probably still does. They were like brothers."

Nia's hands clenched into the grass near her hips.

A rough chuckle escaped Dee before she turned her head to meet Nia's eyes. "Mace was the one in the delivery room with me. He was scared out of his wits, but he stayed in there for me, for Lowe. He helped establish my shop, everything. I'm not sure where we would have ended up if it weren't for him."

Nia's throat constricted, trying to picture Mace in the delivery room. He would have been there to support both friends, Dee and the man he'd called brother. There would have been grief too, a child born fatherless.

The stories on both sides of this war rang with the same sadness.

"So, yeah. If Mace asks me for a favor, I'm going to do it." She turned her head to face the overhead once more, then rubbed the tattoo on the back of her hand absently. "Many of us owe him our lives."

Nia rolled to her feet, unable to listen to more of Mace's attributes. She was already messed up in the head about him, and didn't need someone else adding to it. Without looking behind her, she headed for the atrium's common area, grateful when Dee didn't follow.

Grey had stopped making jokes about him being on edge days ago. Mace understood why. It wasn't funny anymore.

Usually, he had unending patience with the tyros, but now every little fuck up enraged him.

Each night, he slept in the barracks because he couldn't think around Nia. Hell, even when he wasn't around her, he couldn't seem to think. It was becoming impossible to remember when his duty shifts in the command center started.

He knew he was a mess but couldn't seem to fix it. No amount of training, or fights, or how much he bruised and bloodied his knuckles could get his head on straight. He knew it, everyone around him knew it, and they treated him like a plasma grenade about to go off.

It was Nia's day off today, and ten times he'd stopped himself from seeking her out. He mustn't. Because then he'd do something stupid like kiss her again. If that happened, he knew he wouldn't be able to stop.

His only consolation was sending Dee in his stead. At least she wouldn't be alone. Elec gave him regular updates, told him about her deteriorating mood, but Mace knew if he interfered, it would make things worse.

He ran a hand over his face, but it did nothing to clear the haze from his brain. "Freya," he barked. "Don't turn your back on your opponent."

The girl's cheeks reddened, and the reaction made him think of Nia. Stars above, he couldn't get her out of his thoughts. *Fuck.*

Just when he was going to shout at Freya again, the lights in the arena changed and flashed, an alarm blaring. Another proximity alert. Mace whipped his gaze to Grey across from him.

"Battle stations!" Mace yelled as he and Grey ran toward the exit at the same time.

Yellow lights pulsed through the corridor. With Grey at his side, they jogged to the nearest lift, and Mace hit the control panel. He tapped on his vambrace, ordering Elec to make sure Nia got to his quarters safely.

As soon as they stepped into the command center, the proximity alarm stopped. They strode to the holotable, where Cache stood with Sheefra and Gallagher.

"Commodore?" he asked, gesturing to the holo feed with his chin.

"Two shuttles in the field," she said, her attention on the images. "They've broken off and are heading out of the mines."

Mace frowned. Shuttles this far out, even long-range ones, were extremely unusual. "Let me see the replay, sir."

Cache's eyes narrowed, but she complied, retrieving the images of the shuttles weaving through the mines on the outer edge of the field.

Mace's instincts kicked in. "Those aren't shuttles."

Her fingers tightened on the edge of the table while Grey leaned in for a closer look.

"Look at the way they're moving," Mace continued. "Shuttles don't maneuver like that. Those are fighters. Condors would be my best guess, using faceted shielding to disguise their signatures like us." He met Grey's brown eyes, then Cache's green ones. "They're here for us."

A glint of worry passed over her features before her expression hardened. "No. I'll not allow it. They're shuttles."

"Cache. No. First, the Guardian, then the power outage, now this. We need to prepare for the worst. We need to prep *Orion* for flight."

Grey crossed his arms, seemingly undecided on the subject.

Her gaze flickered. "I don't think I'm the one unable to think straight."

There was a warning in her words, and her threat to take Nia away hung between them.

"Cache," he gritted between clenched teeth.

She spun on her heel and walked away.

"Dammit Cache!" He hit the holotable with his fist, but she didn't react and kept walking.

The commanders on the other side of the table gave him a range of expressions, from confused to worried. Mace ran a hand over his face.

"You okay?" Grey asked, concern etched on his brow.

"Yeah. Great. Fantastic," Mace replied, trying to get a grip on his emotions.

Why did it feel like everything was spinning out of control? First, he couldn't concentrate on anything but the woman in his quarters. Now, Cache ignored a blatant threat. Nothing in his life made sense anymore.

Two urges warred within him—the one to make sure Nia wasn't freaking out right now, and the other to stop Cache from following through on her threats.

"I need to finish our training session," he muttered, because both choices would be the biggest mistakes of his life.

But it didn't stop the relief he felt when he read Elec's communique confirming that Nia was safely ensconced in his quarters.

Chapter Twenty-Three

With each passing day, Nia's spirit shriveled more inside of her. The reality of her situation pounded into her brain with every breath she took. The tracker in the locket wasn't working. Maybe because it was a dud to begin with, or she was too far away, or the shielding on this station was too sophisticated.

She wasn't going to be rescued.

When she finally accepted the truth, a numbness settled over her body she couldn't shake. The urge to reach for a suppressant disappeared because she no longer experienced high emotions. She understood she could make a life for herself here, make friends, a career, but she couldn't force herself to crave it, to look forward to something. She just wanted to go home.

The only emotion to sometimes surface through the fog was a seething sort of resentment when she thought of Mace.

He'd abandoned her.

Of course, she wasn't really ever on her own except in his quarters, but she'd never felt hollower. She completed her shifts in the med bay robotically. She never spoke to Elec as he walked her to and from the bay and stopped wondering if he hated babysitting her—stopped wondering because she *knew* he hated it. Who wouldn't?

Another day off, and she found herself on the second level of the atrium, leaning against the railing with Elec a short distance away. She stared at the slowly shifting groups of people below on the main deck but had no urge to join the mass.

She didn't know how long she stood there, lost in her numbness, when a voice rang out behind her.

"I can't take it anymore."

Nia straightened away from the railing and turned to find Dee with her hands on her hips and a frown furrowing her brow. Her yellow and orange dress was extremely short in the front and incredibly long in the back, the whole thing only supported by one strap over her left shoulder. The fashion bruised Nia's sensibilities in every way, but she couldn't find it in her to dislike it.

After staring at each other for a long minute, Nia returned her focus to the crowd below.

Dee moved closer, joining her at the railing. "Look, I know you hate me—"

"I don't hate anyone." She didn't have the energy to hate anymore.

"And I've been trying to give you space," Dee went on as if she hadn't spoken, "But I can't stand by and watch you wither away."

Why not? She didn't voice the question. Didn't care enough to do so.

"Has anyone suggested speaking to the captive psychologist?"

I don't need a psychologist, I need to go home. And she didn't trust anyone here enough to spill her guts to them. "Did Mace ask you to come?" At least it would mean he thought of her once in a while, though she didn't know how he couldn't when she'd taken over his quarters. *Where did he sleep?*

There were indicators he visited while she was on her shifts: a different towel in the bathroom, things being moved around in the refrigeration unit, but she hadn't seen him in at least two weeks. Maybe longer? She wasn't even sure how much time had passed since she'd arrived on *Orion*.

"No. He didn't ask me to come." She leaned an elbow on the railing. "I keep seeing you around, moping, on your days off, and I needed to do something before all the plants in the arboretum shriveled away by association."

"I don't mope," she denied in a flat voice, even though she knew it was the truth.

"If it's any consolation, Mace seems to mope about as much as you."

It should have elicited some reaction from her, but it didn't. *Maybe I should go back to his quarters and nap.* The loathsome nature of the thought made it through her brain fog. She wouldn't willfully confine herself.

"And if I didn't know any better," Dee went on, "I would have thought you two were going through a breakup or something similar."

Her current mood wasn't because of a "breakup," whether or not they'd kissed, but Nia saw no point in voicing the opinion. Her brain was too sluggish to argue.

"But I do know better. It's completely ridiculous, right?"

"Right," she agreed, wanting Dee to stop talking and go away. Out of principle, she would stay here for her full six hours, people-watching, then return to his quarters.

"Anyway," Dee said after exhaling a frustrated breath. "I'm stealing you away from your pity party for the day."

Nia didn't even have the energy to protest the way Dee grabbed her arm and pulled her along. But alarm swept through her numbness when Dee pulled her on the lift—without Elec. "Where are you taking me?"

"Somewhere new. You can't see the rest of the station, so I'm going to show you neat stuff in this quad."

The lift descended at a clipped pace, then the door opened into a plain corridor devoid of people. Nia's nervousness grew. Hand still holding her arm, Dee took her through a narrow corridor. It widened into a space vaster than the arboretum. Nia's disinterest shed from her body like a uniform worn too long. When Dee dropped her arm, she kept walking forward until she gripped the railing tightly.

A helix of rotating metal filled her vision, a pinkish-white energy twisting around it—a power source, but she'd never seen an engine core like it. Looking upward, the reactor chamber seemed to go on forever; looking down, it was the same. She'd known the station was massive. This only confirmed it.

She leaned forward to see better, and Dee settled a hand on her arm. "Watch yourself. There's no coming back from a fall like that."

Truth. Nia couldn't see the bottom from here.

"Is this the only one?" Nia had tried to access a schematic of *Orion* on Mace's terminal but had been unsuccessful because of her limited clearance.

"No. There are four of them, one for each section of the station."

"What are they doing?" Nia asked, pointing to the four people in brown. One was hanging off the edge, inside the cylinder of the construction, making her stomach lurch.

Dee followed where she pointed. "Maintenance."

Another team of four worked farther down. She'd seen similar groupings when she'd wandered on her days off, always four or more together.

"What about radiation?"

"I've been told it's only an issue in the lower decks, where people don't go." Dee shrugged.

Movement behind them made Nia turn. It was Elec, and a look of utter relief crossed his face when he saw them. He braced a hand against the bulkhead and inhaled a deep breath. "Don't do that to me again."

Frowning, Nia turned away. Dee wore the same look of confusion, then she shrugged and rolled her eyes. The comical expression made Nia snort. She focused on the helix in front of her.

The engine core hummed and spun, a strange thing to infuse her with new life, but now she'd emerged from her haze, returning to it didn't hold any appeal.

It became a routine. On Nia's days off, Dee would find her and show her something new. Slowly, ever so slowly, Nia felt the fog around her body lift. A couple of weeks later, she realized Elec wouldn't tail her as long as she was with Dee. A tentative friendship bloomed between them.

And in those quiet moments when she and Dee would lie on the grass in the arboretum or stare at the crowd in the atrium, Nia would ask questions—the things the terminal in Mace's quarters wouldn't reveal to her.

It was one of those times, where they leaned over the railing of the red bridge in the arboretum to see who could spot the most fish, when Nia asked, "What can you tell me about the old laws?"

Dee straightened, her light pink sheath dress catching the light from above. "Oh." Nia stood tall as well, meeting her eyes. "Well, let's see. Where to begin." She stared at the stream, outlined eyes narrowed in thought. "Before modern law, most everything was based on instinct and aggression."

"How long ago are we talking about?"

Dee tipped her head to the side. "Two hundred years? More? But they didn't abolish the old laws completely. They can be invoked in extreme circumstances, like during wartime and such. One I know about is the Mutiny Law. If a warrior feels their commanding officer is unfit for duty, and they have most of the crew behind them, they can take leadership by killing the current CO." Then she shrugged like it was no big deal.

There were laws in CORE society to gain the same results, and no one got killed. "What about captives? This Take and Keep law the processor told me about?"

Dee's brow puckered. "Well, that one's a bit trickier. It had a couple of different meanings. Any weapons, raw materials, or valuables seized in a raid were kept by the warrior who took them. Modern law shares all of this, pooling it into the resources for the entire colony. Makes more sense, really."

Nia's hands tightened on the railing. "And what of captives?"

"Well, even back then, it wasn't like a warrior would keep ten captives in his quarters. There was still the common holding and labor distribution."

"So why would a warrior keep a captive in his quarters, then?"

A rosy hue splashed Dee's cheeks. "Um, I'm not sure I should get into this."

"Spit it out." Nia refused to be brushed aside.

Dee grimaced, closing her eyes. "A warrior would keep a captive when there was a low or unbalanced population count so he could procreate." Dee said it all in a rush, keeping her eyes closed the entire time.

Nia couldn't speak for a minute. "This was okay with everyone?" Her question came out as a squeak. That had to be where all the sex slave stories she'd learned about came from—truth to the rumors, but from a long time ago.

"I know you're thinking really badly of us right now," Dee said, meeting Nia's eyes. "But seriously, no one has done this in centuries. I mean, it's barbaric. We're not like that anymore."

"So all this time I've been in Mace's quarters, people thought—"

"No, I wouldn't think that. I mean, it's Mace we're talking about. Yeah, it's a bit shocking because he's so against people farming."

The way she said it made Nia zero in on her again. "What aren't you telling me? There's something else, isn't there?"

Dee caught her lower lip between her teeth. "Um, I'm not sure how it applies now, I haven't studied any laws of late, but in the old laws, if a warrior kept a captive, it sort of meant—it *did* mean, I should say—they were legally bound together."

Nia blinked. "Legally bound."

"Yeah. You know—"

"Married?" The word came out in a shriek.

"Um, yeah, back then it did. I'm not really sure how it works these days." Dee's cheeks blazed pink.

Nia pressed her fingers to the bridge of her nose. "I'm not married."

"Right. Definitely not married. I totally agree with you." Dee emphasized her statement with a nod. "Wait. Were you married before you came here? Had someone special?"

Nia shook her head. "No. Too busy to concentrate on that."

Her mind went to Calvin, the last person she'd dated. It was strange, but she hadn't thought of him in days, weeks even. Her old, CORE life seemed so far away. But now that she was so removed from it, she thought of their interactions and shuddered. How had she stayed with him for so long? Why had she accepted it, taking enhancers to make it more bearable? The whole concept seemed absurd.

Nia rubbed her forehead, a headache pulsing in her frontal bone. "I'm not married," she said again. She couldn't get married without knowing it, right?

It was completely ridiculous, and she needed to know the truth. "Where would he be right now?"

"Who?"

"Mace," she said between gritted teeth.

"Oh. Ah." Dee swallowed, turning to get a good look at Nia. The pink hue of her cheeks disappeared as the color drained from her face. "Either training or the command center, I would guess. The command center is off-limits to civilians, so we can't—"

"Then we'll check this training place first."

When Dee didn't move, Nia gestured with her hands. "Now."

Chapter Twenty-Four

T he grappling session had turned brutal.

It was supposed to be a demonstration, but with all of Mace's pent-up frustration, it turned into something else. Keeping his gaze locked on Grey, he wiped the corner of his mouth with the back of his hand, and it came away smeared with blood. Mace's torn uniform hung from his shoulders, and he removed it entirely, throwing it to the side.

His friend had finally lost his patience with him, and the look in Grey's eyes promised a beating of a lifetime. Mace wholly embraced it. He needed it. Maybe it would finally clear the fog hovering in his brain for the past few weeks. But he also wouldn't take it lying down.

Cracking his bruised knuckles, then his neck, he squared off with Grey, fully aware of the tyros cloaked in tense silence, surrounding them in a loose ring. Blood trickled from near Grey's eye and the corner of his mouth.

Equally matched, they circled each other, searching for an opening. In their emotional states, if one of them made a move, they'd better make sure they had an advantage.

When his movements aligned him with a clear view of the entrance, he froze. Nia gripped the railing at the top of the landing, staring at them. His eyes drank her in. Curly hair framed her face in wild disarray. She wore one of the outfit styles she seemed to prefer, beige leggings and a long sweater dress in burgundy. Dee stood at her side.

Mace saw the flash of movement a second too late. Grey slammed into him with the force of a Destroyer at maximum speed. They tumbled to the mat, and Mace's instincts kicked in, not allowing Grey to get the upper hand. But the damage was already done, and within moments, Grey had Mace pinned in an unbreakable hold.

"Yield," Mace said, slapping the mat with his free hand.

Releasing him, Grey rolled onto his feet and extended a hand. The look in his friend's eyes said it all: distractions would get him killed. Ironic, since it was something Mace spouted to the tyros almost every day.

Mace took the offered hand and jumped to his feet, wiping a frustrated hand over his face. He had no excuse.

"I hope you all learned something there," Grey said to the spectators, but Mace had already returned his attention to the women near the door.

It had been too long since he'd seen Nia. He'd stayed away to protect her. She was too appealing, too enticing... and she shouldn't be. Not to him. No matter what the old laws said, he had no right.

That didn't stop the contentment pumping through him at seeing her with his eyes. Of course he knew she was fine, Elec sent him updates all the time, but his chest settled at the sight of her.

When he strode toward her, she flew down the stairs—like she couldn't contain her excitement at seeing him. His heart leaped in his chest. But as he neared, he noticed her flushed face, clenched jaw, and fisted hands. His steps faltered.

Her shout echoed loudly across the space. "Are we married?" She stopped in front of him, her chest heaving and chin raised.

All movement, all sound, abruptly halted around them. Mace felt every eye in the matted arena.

His gaze shot to Dee trailing behind her, whose eyes were widened with unease and apology. Whatever conversation she and Nia had, the damage was done.

Stepping forward to block the tyros' inquisitive stares, he took Nia's elbow in his hand. "Let's go somewhere—"

She yanked her arm out of his grasp, eyes flashing. "I will *not* be misdirected, or handled, or managed, or whatever else you think you will do here. *Answer me.*"

Her body vibrated, feet firmly planted, and fists pointed at the ground. Short of throwing her over his shoulder, he doubted he could make her move without answering her question.

Keeping her gaze, he said in an even voice, "Technically speaking, we are legally bound."

A primal sound erupted from her throat. She threw herself toward him, arms outstretched, like she intended to strangle him. He moved quickly, redirecting her aim using her momentum, and clasping both her wrists in his hand. They'd rotated until he held her back to his front and faced a room full of wide-eyed tyros, his arm banded around her ribs. Grey stood to the side with a dubious expression, his head tilted.

Nia's chest heaved in front of him. With another cry of outrage, she tried to break free, but he held fast, waiting for her rage to burn out. When she kept struggling, he realized it would not happen anytime soon. Her passion felt Tellusian and ignited his own.

"Let me go, you waste-humping bastard," Nia gritted between clenched teeth, then threw her weight like she wanted to headbutt him. All she hit was his sternum.

Without thinking too long about it, he adjusted his hold, and tossed her over his shoulder, his arm trapping her thighs so she wouldn't kick him in the face—an identical position to the one he'd forced her in the day he'd taken her. His chest tightened painfully.

"Hope you all noted how to subdue an unarmed civilian," he shouted to the tyros as he headed for the exit. "As you were." Dee's jaw dropped as he passed her by.

He bounded the steps two at a time. Nia spat obscenities. She wouldn't stop struggling and dug her fingernails into the skin of his back so deep, he had no choice but to touch his vambrace and bind her hands.

An outraged shriek surged from her chest. While she flailed against him, he ignored the astonished stares of the warriors he passed in the corridor leading to the exit. She didn't let up, even when they stepped out into the atrium.

"Put me down!"

He headed to the nearest lift. "Not likely when you'll attack again." The door opened, and he stepped inside, careful not to bang her head on the door frame. The trip to his quarters felt long with her writhing and screaming at him the entire time.

He didn't set her on her feet until the door to his quarters closed behind them. Face red, she backed up two steps and glared at him.

"I hate you."

"I know, *izar.*" He touched the control on his vambrace to separate her wrists.

Her body seemed to deflate, her shoulders caving in. "How could you do this to me? How could you *marry* me without my consent?"

"It was the best way to protect you."

"Protect me? *Protect me?*" Her breaths left her in quick gasps. "You were the one who brought me here. I was *protected* on *Elara Five.*"

"Not nearly well enough."

A frustrated groan left her lips, her arms flying up in exasperation as she spun around to stare at the bulkhead.

He took a step back and turned to press the control to open the door. Now that she seemed calmer, he could return to training.

"No," she said, her voice forceful.

"No, what?" He glanced over his shoulder to find her glaring at him, fire flickering in her eyes.

"I won't allow you to do this to me again."

He faced her fully. "Do what?"

"I won't allow you to foist your responsibility onto others. You can't take me from my home, say you're going to protect me, then ignore me for weeks at a time!" By the time she finished, she was shouting again.

Disbelief shuddered through him. "You don't want me to ignore you?"

Her expression changed, as though she hadn't realized what she'd said, then she fisted her hands. "No. I don't want you to ignore me."

He stepped fully into the room, and the door closed behind him. "Then what do you want?"

Her breathing turned ragged, fingers flexing at her sides. She looked around his quarters, eyes almost wild, then they settled on him.

He took a step closer. "What do you need, Nia?" If it was in his power to provide it, he would. He wanted her to find some sort of peace on *Orion*.

She placed a hand flat against her stomach and shook her head. "I don't know." Then her fingers curled into a fist and lifted her chin. "How do I end this marriage thing?"

Even though it wasn't an unreasonable request, his heart squeezed so tight it hurt to speak. "I revoke the old laws and place you in common holding."

She tensed, a stillness hovering around her body. He closed the last two steps between them and cupped her cheek in his hand. "I'll see it done."

If this was what she needed to feel safe here, he'd do it. He would need to remain diligent that no harm befell her in common holding, and would pay off whoever he needed to.

Her russet eyes searched his face. No denial left her lips, and he understood then that it was the right thing to do. He should have done it sooner.

With the weight of that truth settling inside him, he nodded once and took a step back.

She stopped him by covering her hand with his own. Tingles spread down his arm at the touch. The memory of the kiss they'd shared resurfaced, how she'd pulled him with non-CORE-like passion.

Her eyes flared like she was remembering too, then her other hand rose and pressed against his bare chest. Prickles pulsed through his skin. He inhaled a sharp breath when her fingernails curled into his skin.

He grasped her elbow with his free hand. "What do you need, Nia?" he whispered, his throat too tight to speak properly.

The hand on his chest moved, inching its way upward to leave a scorched path in its wake. Her fingers wrapped around his nape, then traveled further until they delved into his hair. Russet eyes darkened; her lips parted. Her gaze flicked to his mouth, then returned to his eyes.

"You," she said, and pulled his face to hers.

Nia didn't know what she was doing.

Earlier, she'd been so furious, so full of rage at being married without her consent, she'd attacked him in front of everyone, screaming like she'd gone completely mad. And now it felt like all those emotions had been funneled into a state of desire so potent she had no way to fight it.

His lips crashed against hers, brutal and exactly what she needed. She didn't want gentle. Anger directed at herself coursed through her veins. She shouldn't have wanted this but couldn't fight it. She blamed it on being separated from CORE society for so long, for all the mood modifiers she used to pump into herself being out of her system. Her emotions dictated her actions, just like every other Tellusian.

But no excuse could justify the way she felt when Mace claimed ownership of the kiss, like a man starved, and she the only ration in sight. His tongue swept in, hungry, and ate her up.

Fire crept through her body, all-consuming. Her tongue reciprocated the exploration with an urgency she didn't know she possessed. Heat settled between her thighs.

He pulled her against his body with enough force that her lungs emptied with an *oomph*. She grabbed his shoulders and hung on tight. Mace's hands traveled her spine to her bottom, pressing her against him. She plunged her other hand into his hair, and her legs found their way around his hips. He growled encouragement, fingers curling into her buttocks.

His grip tightened almost painfully as he pushed her against the table. *More of that.* She needed the sting to take away the guilt.

But it was like he'd heard her say the opposite, and his touch and kiss gentled. She couldn't deal with tenderness. Not now. She bit his bottom lip. Hard.

He gasped and tore his mouth away. A dangerous glint entered his eyes, and she shivered, then dove back in, hands roaming over his shoulders, biceps, then up again. He lifted her onto the table. His nostrils flared as he leaned closer, inhaling the scent of her throat. Her breath caught in her chest, tingles spreading low in her body.

"*Izar*," he whispered against her skin, "you have taken over my mind, body, and soul, and I cannot escape."

A wave of heat washed over her to pool in the center of her body. His frantic hands lifted her shirt, caressed her breasts through the thin material of her bra. She arched her spine, gasping. The throbbing heat in her center turned into a stab of pain.

He bit her nipple through the fabric, and she cried out. Nia held onto his hair. Her legs spread wide at the press of his knee. He kissed her abdomen downward until he breathed hot air on her swollen clit through her leggings. She almost orgasmed right then, a low moan rolling through her body.

"Mace, please." She wanted him to satisfy the burning need inside her.

With his face pressed between her thighs, he stiffened.

Distress cut through the haze of her passion.

No. Whatever internal battle he fought, she wouldn't allow him to leave her like this. Her fingernails dug into his shoulders.

"This isn't what you want," he said as he leaned over her, hands braced on either side of hips, his expression haggard.

Desperation made her voice sharp. "Of course it's what I want. Stars above, Mace, if you can't tell when a woman is in acute need, I'll give you some blasted lessons, but don't you dare stop."

He shook his head. Her nails scraped his skin as he pushed away from the table, leaving her cold.

"Mace." His name came out ragged as she watched him leave.

A new fury swept through her. She wouldn't allow him to run away this time.

Chapter Twenty-Five

Striding toward the lift, Mace held onto his sanity by a thread. His heart raced with the realization of what he'd almost done, his body throbbing with unfulfilled desire.

He turned at her shout of anger. A petite ball of fury launched herself at him, legs wrapping around his waist and fingers digging into his hair. He hugged her to him, reveling in the feel of her supple body against his. Her soft and hot center settled over his painful erection.

"You're not," she said, kissing him savagely, "leaving me," her mouth slammed into his again, "like this."

His fingers dug into her muscles beneath the thin material of her clothing, the heat in his body flaring. He returned to his quarters, the door sliding closed behind them. When he broke the kiss, she yanked his head back down.

"You hate me," he groaned, pushing her against the bulkhead.

"You asked me what I needed," she moaned, but not denying it. Her teeth scraped his jaw. "Give me what I need." She ground her pelvis against his.

He couldn't think with her center thrusting against him, all reason snatched away with her touches. He needed to consume her as she consumed him.

He took her lips with his, his hands roving all over her body like he'd always wanted to. Each of her gasps stoked the fire inside him. He skimmed his hands against her flesh beneath her shirt, her skin soft, addictive. Beneath the material of her bra, her breasts fit perfectly in his hands. He squeezed and stroked, needing to get closer.

She reached between them, skimmed her hand into the front of his pants, inside his underwear, and firmly gripped his cock.

All the restraint he thought he'd attained these past few weeks crumbled to dust.

His mind blanked, with only one thought remaining. He needed to be inside her.

Using his thigh between hers, he braced her against the bulkhead and ripped her leggings down the middle. She gasped, but her lips recaptured his in the next instant, encouraging. His hand cupped her pussy, and she pushed against him in invitation.

Two fingers sank inside her. *So wet.* Her walls clenched around him, greedy, and she moaned, the sound vibrating like an electric shock through his body. She squirmed and bucked as he thrust his fingers in and out, her mouth traveling wherever she could reach. Her hands squeezed his rock-hard cock, almost painful in its strength.

He loved it and pumped his hips into her hand.

"I need more." She panted against his neck, fingers tightening around him in pulses.

Her other hand gripped his scalp, frenzied. Shivers cascaded down his spine. Adjusting his angle, he sank another finger inside her.

"Yes," she moaned, then shook her head. "No." She squeezed his cock again. "I need *this*. Deep. Hard. I need you." She freed him fully from his pants.

Frantic, he slid her underwear to the side and entered her in one swift thrust. *Tight. Hot. Sweet.* The world darkened around him. She was perfection clenching around him. He couldn't hold still and fucked into her over and over again.

Her legs hugged him to her. Her shouts and moans of ecstasy bounced off the bulkheads. Wild, frantic fingernails gouged the skin of his chest, arms, and neck.

His pleasure built, tightening his balls, about to explode out of him. He reached between them, found her clit slick and swollen, and stroked with his middle finger.

The sounds coming out of her mouth turned feral. He recaptured her lips, his tongue sweeping inside to taste every inch of her. His finger stroked around her, circling. The tension between them grew, stretching tight, climbing to a breaking point.

With a scream of pleasure, she convulsed around him, pushing him over the edge. An explosion of light blazed behind his eyes. His body shuddered, spilling inside her. Every part of her squeezed him tight.

He collapsed forward, her slight body pressed between him and the bulkhead. His legs felt like liquid, his head floating and empty of thought. Breaths expelled through his lips in ragged gasps, mixing with hers.

Still inside her tight, hot sheath, he braced his elbows against the bulkhead. Russet eyes stared at him, dazed, a high flush riding her cheeks. Mussed curls spiraled everywhere. Her fingernails dug into his biceps to keep balance. He didn't want to move; no place in this universe had felt more like home.

The staggering thought shattered his peace. What had he done?

He'd stayed away from her so this wouldn't happen. He'd failed. Self-loathing thrummed through him at his weakness. Settling his hands on her hips to keep her steady, he pulled out.

Nia exhaled a stunned breath with parted lips. She seemed frozen in shock.

Breathing through his nose, he pressed his forehead against hers and closed his eyes. His skin stung where she'd scratched him. The scent of their intercourse filled his head, making it almost impossible to think.

"This can't happen again."

An oppressive silence followed his statement. Someone coughed in the corridor. Nia stiffened in his arms. The fingers on his biceps tightened, then she pushed him away with a half-shout.

He tucked himself into his pants. Her shredded leggings lay on the deck. Her top covered her to mid-thigh.

"You bastard," she whispered, and his stomach sank.

He deserved whatever she was about to scream at him.

She clenched her hands like she were readying to punch him. "You're going to fucking abandon me again, aren't you?"

The truth in her words froze him. Every time their passions exploded between them, he left. He'd told himself it was to protect her, because she was the one in the vulnerable position, but what if it had had the opposite effect? What if by leaving, he'd only hurt her?

Conflicting emotions tumbled through him, freezing him to the spot as he watched her hands clench and release beside her, like a ticking bomb counting the seconds to detonation.

Then don't abandon her.

He stepped toward her. She stiffened, her fingers becoming still, eyes narrowing.

He extended his hand. "Come," he said softly.

Indecision furrowed her brow, but she placed her fingers in his. Gently, he tugged her toward the washroom. The door slid open, but instead of going inside, he turned her to face him. She kept his gaze as he took the hem of her top in his hands and pulled it over her head. Next, he undid her beige bra and slid it off her arms, then slipped her matching underwear down her legs, until the only thing she wore was her locket and bonds.

Fully naked, she was stunning, but it wasn't what this was about—no matter how much his cock stirred at the sight of all her bare flesh.

He tugged her through the washroom and into the steam shower. It was only built for one, and he stayed in the doorway as he turned it on. The high-pressure air and moisture rushed through the space, encircling them both.

Mace kept her in there until her hair was fully damp, then turned off the pressure. He reached for the nearest soap, realized it was the one he used, but squirted the foam into his palm anyway. The entire time, she kept her eyes on him, watching like she wasn't completely sure what was happening.

He didn't understand what the hell he was doing either.

Starting with her shoulders, he slid the foamy soap across her skin. Down her silky arms, across the natural swell of her belly, between her satiny legs—he tried to keep it professional, but when she panted softly, all he wanted to do was take her again.

Standing, he tried to ignore the glazed look of passion in her eyes as he finished with her hair, then pressed the control to start the rinse. Within ten seconds, he became as soaked as she.

He shut off the steam and stepped out of the stall, grabbing the biggest towel from the wall compartment. With quick movements, he rubbed the residual moisture off her body, then dried his chest. Wherever his hands traveled, her eyes followed. He tried to squeeze as much moisture out of her hair as he could, then wrapped the damp towel around her body, tucking it securely beneath her armpits.

Taking her hand, he walked backward, tugging her out of the washroom. As soon as she was free of its confines, he swept her into his arms. She let out a gasp.

Before she could protest, he settled her on his lap on the bed—and held her.

His pants were damp. Her hair dripped onto him. His body still sang with the scratches she'd given him. But for a few quiet minutes, they sat together. Her body relaxed, sinking into his. With that relaxation came awareness.

The towel had ridden up until it barely covered anything below her navel. The skin of her shoulders was incredibly soft beneath his fingers. He'd seen her naked and wanted to explore more. They'd had a quick fuck, and now he wanted a slow one.

And if he stayed any longer, he wouldn't be able to stop himself.

It pained him to say his next words. "I'll do as you wish." His throat was so tight it hurt to speak. He didn't want to let her go and pressed his lips to her temple. "I'll sever the legal bond and take you to common holding after your shift tomorrow. You will be free of me."

Nia stiffened in his arms.

Over the past few minutes, she'd existed in a state of dazed contentment, her body warm, her mind calm.

Now Mace's words brutally yanked her from that headspace. She scrambled off his lap with the towel clutched tight to her body. Tenderness throbbed between her legs as a reminder of what they'd done. Every breath she took into her lungs was a struggle. He remained seated, hands braced beside his thighs. She stared at him, lips parted, and couldn't for the life of her explain the panic taking hold of heart.

He was doing what she wanted. They wouldn't be married any longer. Why did his words feel like a betrayal?

The urge to scream made her clench her jaw. "I need to get dressed," she said between gritted teeth.

Mace stared at her for the longest time, then stood. When he walked by her, he paused, and she tensed. She thought he was going to touch her again, but he kept walking. The door to his quarters whooshed open, then closed.

Tears pricked her eyes. Nia blinked them away, determined not to lose her shit after everything. He'd given her what she wanted—a quick fuck and a promise to rescind their marriage. *I will not cry over this.*

Straightening her spine, she dropped the towel and strode to the compartment under the bed where she kept her clothes. As she put on a similar outfit to what she had on, but this one black and green, Mace's scent wafted over her. She was covered in it.

Nia pressed a hand to her stomach and closed her eyes. The buzz of her orgasm was long gone, but what an orgasm it had been. Never in her life had she experienced sex like that. Even with enhancers, she'd never come close to a state of euphoria with any of her former partners. Wild and frantic, she'd wanted a release and had received more than she'd bargained for.

Her bonds beeped, making her glance at them. An hour remained of her day off, then she would be trapped in here once more, the scent of what they'd done lingering everywhere.

Mace already stole her sanity. She wouldn't allow him to thieve her time.

No one waited in the corridor to escort her. Ever since Dee had taken to hanging out with her on her days off, Elec had made himself scarce. Would someone materialize when she arrived at the atrium?

She stepped onto the lift and stared at the control panel, unsure of where she should go to find some sort of peace. The door closed, but the lift remained stationary without her input.

She didn't want to be babysat. She didn't want to face Dee after what had happened. She didn't want to be questioned. But she also didn't want to stay in Mace's quarters.

She remained frozen in indecision for so long that the lift moved on its own. It ascended, then sped across a section of the station before descending once more. She had no idea where she would end up when the door opened. Four brown-clad maintenance workers stared at her. She stepped off to let them on, and surprise flickered through her when she recognized the location. This was where Dee had shown her the engine core on one of her other days off.

Nia strode forward. When the corridor opened into the vast space, she was once again struck by the incomprehensible size of *Orion*. To think there were four powering this station. The resources needed to construct it staggered her. It would have taken decades to build. It rivaled terrestrial stations when she'd been educated to believe Tellusians lived like savages on their Destroyers.

They were a brutal race, but they also created wonders.

She braced her elbows on the railing and looked over the edge, then startled back when a maintenance worker hung only a couple of meters away accessing a panel. She peeked over again. He glared up at her.

"Sorry," she mumbled, strolling further along. When she looked over the edge again, he was gone.

Exhaling a slow breath, she braced her elbows on the railing and watched the helix-like structure twist in on itself. She closed her eyes and listened. A pulse. *Orion's* life force. Even as it soothed, her mind churned with what had happened between her and Mace. Stars above, what she wouldn't give for a suppressant right now.

"What are you doing here on your own?"

She straightened at the voice, every limb tensing. Nia turned around to find a man wearing a warrior's uniform. A gun was strapped to each of his thighs, and knives littered his belt. It took her a second, but she recognized him because of his long nose and the way one section of hair swooped over his forehead. He was the one who'd visited family medicine for the self-inflicted cut on his hand.

His eyes swirled with malice and something else. Unease skittered through her. Swallowing, she stepped away from the railing.

Chapter Twenty-Six

Nia scanned the empty space around them, her stomach plummeting into her toes. There wasn't anyone else around.

His eyes hardened. "Answer me."

"It's my day off," she said, hating her unsettled tone.

He stepped toward her. "But why are you *here* on your own?"

She shook her head, not having a good answer. "I wanted to be alone." She'd seen other captives with bonds like hers in common areas. Since Elec had stopped guarding her on her days off, no one told her she couldn't be by herself.

"You're very much alone, aren't you?"

Apprehension shivered down her spine at his tone. His eyes scanned their surroundings, and when they landed on her again, he flashed her a smile that didn't reach his eyes.

She took another step away from the railing, and he countered with a step toward her. Nia froze in place.

"I never properly introduced myself before," he said, his sharp gaze making her heart beat with anxiety. "I'm Commander Foley, head of security, and I take my job very seriously." His fingers twitched where they hovered near his gun.

Head of security? He was in charge of all the enforcers? Nia felt the blood drain from her face. Her heart beat erratically against her ribs. This man exuded lethal grace, and every instinct inside her screamed for her to run.

"And you're like any CORE person I've ever met. You think you're important, don't you?"

Did he know who she was? Was that what he meant? More panic infused her limbs.

When he stepped toward the railing, no longer blocking her exit, the tension in her body eased. But it only increased again when he circled around her. The opening to the corridor was in sight, but he was close enough to grab her if she made a break for it.

Nia swallowed around the growing dryness in her throat. "It's a beautiful station," she said, her voice cracking.

"It is, isn't it?"

He stopped in front of her and glanced at her wrists. She followed his gaze, and a sharp breath escaped her. The light on the side was flickering instead of being a solid blue.

"It's interference from the engine core," he said, and her eyes snapped to his. "Gives a bit of privacy, doesn't it?" His lips quirked. "Sometimes captives come here to commit suicide, and all that's left of them is charred bonds at the bottom of the chute."

"How do you know it's suicide?"

He grinned fully then. "Some think it would be better if you disappeared."

Her insides turned to liquid. When she stepped to the side to move around him, he blocked her path. Clenching her jaw, she fisted her hands and prepared to defend herself.

Mace knew the tyros stared at him from the corner of their eyes. He knew Grey's held questions. But he ignored all of it in favor of pretending he hadn't carried his ward out of here kicking and screaming an hour ago, then returned with his pants soaking wet and scratches all over his body. He'd put on a new uniform as quickly as possible.

The messed-up thing was that what they all thought had happened, *had* happened. Only no one knew she'd practically ordered him to fuck her.

If he declared to everyone around that she'd asked for it, how would that sound?

The old laws were so twisted. Despite the speculation shot his way, no one would do a blasted thing for her. The only people who would listen to complaints were the processors, and Mace could pay them to look the other way.

Nia was right to condescend.

He wiped a hand over his face and glanced at his vambrace for the tenth time since returning. Her tracker showed movement as she headed away from his quarters. Some of the tension in his body relaxed. If she were on the move, then she was doing okay. She wouldn't mope alone for the rest of her time off.

Though Dee had been clear a couple of weeks ago not to call it moping.

As Mace watched the tyros grapple in pairs, using the new skills they'd learned, Grey stopped beside him with his arms crossed and sent him a look.

"What?" Mace spat, knowing whatever his friend wanted to say, it wouldn't be good.

"I'm thinking you're not setting a good example for the youngsters." His eyes lingered on the exposed scratches on Mace's throat.

"For fuck's sake, Grey, I didn't hurt her."

His friend raised an eyebrow, expression skeptical.

"You can ask her yourself," Mace went on. "I'm sure she'd love that. You can find her in—" He stopped speaking when he glanced at his vambrace again.

The connection to her bonds had been severed. He didn't have a location tag.

Panic made him run towards the stairs. He touched his vambrace to send Dee a communique and slid the comm device from his vambrace to his ear. He took the steps three at a time and was almost to the exit when she responded.

"What do you mean, 'Where is Nia?' You were the one who carried her away kicking and screaming."

His trepidation grew as he stepped out onto the fifth level of the atrium. "I left her in my quarters. She's not there anymore, and her tag stopped working. I was hoping you were with her."

"No. I'm in my shop." There was a rustling of movement before she asked, "What did you do to her?"

Over the railing, he scanned below, hoping to spot her. "I didn't—" He stopped speaking because his protest would have been a lie. He'd fucked her and left her alone.

He ran a shaky hand over his face. "Where would she go?"

"I don't know. We've been to tons of places."

"Tell me them all." Why would her bonds stop sending him a signal?

"The arboretum, the museum, the aquarium, Tchocho's Place for drinks a couple of times. She really loves the arboretum, though." He moved toward the lift, intent on checking the arboretum first, when she added, "I took her to the engine core once, then we went—"

"That's it." There would be enough interference from the energy output to mess with her signal. He slapped the lift's control panel. "Thanks, Dee."

"I'll help you look."

"No, I've got it." He didn't want her to feel like they were teaming up against her.

The lift descended, too slowly for his taste, and opened at the central deck of the engine core.

The hum of the engine core pulsed toward him, almost like a living thing. He sometimes thought of it that way, the heart of *Orion*. Or four hearts, each section independently powered by its own core. *Orion* wouldn't exist without them, only a hunk of metal floating in space. The engine cores gave it life.

Mace strode through the corridor, his unease at being separated from Nia's tracker increasing with each step. The overhead disappeared as he stepped into the reactor chamber. He quickly scanned the deck, but it was deserted. His eyes moved upward, and his heart seized. She stood too close to the railing, and she wasn't alone. Foley stood in front of her, head bent as if he were telling her secrets.

Heart threatening to burst out of his chest, he raced back the way he'd come, found the service ladder, and climbed it as fast as he could. The thin metal bars bit into his palms. His boots slapped against the deck as he jogged the narrow corridor, and it once again opened into the voluminous space of the reactor chamber. When he stepped into Nia's line of sight, he didn't imagine the relief in her eyes.

"Foley." The word came out in a harsh bark, and the other commander tensed and straightened. The bastard had his hand on her shoulder, thumb pressing into the delicate center of her throat.

Mace's vision blurred. His hand went to his gun on his thigh, but Foley let go of her, and she skirted him to rush toward Mace.

"Are you okay?" he asked when she stood in front of him.

She gave him a quick nod, but her face remained wan. He brushed his hand against her shoulder, attempting to erase Foley's touch. A small, pink oval stood out against Nia's pale skin where he'd pressed her throat. Fury raced through Mace.

Tucking Nia behind him, he stared at Foley, who leaned against the railing overlooking the engine core shaft like he hadn't a care in the world.

"What are you doing here?" Mace asked, calculating all the ways he could kill the bastard right now.

Foley smirked. "Shouldn't you ask your ward that question? Unlike her, I have reason to be here." He smiled, and it wasn't nice. "I was making sure she wasn't contemplating suicide. She seemed distraught. What *is* happening behind closed doors, Commander? I've received some reports about screaming from your section of the quad."

Mace wouldn't take the bait or the deflection, not when Nia tightly gripped the hem of his shirt. Was it to hold him close, or because she didn't want him to beat the shit out of his colleague?

Foley pushed away from the railing and sauntered past them. "Take care of your ward, Commander. Wouldn't want anything to happen to her." He left the reactor chamber whistling.

The need to go after him and beat him into a pulp almost overwhelmed every other thought.

"What did he say to you?" Mace asked her when Foley's whistling had faded.

Eyes aimed at his chest, she shook her head. "Not a lot. Tried to scare me or something." She lifted her eyes to meet his. "I think he might know my identity."

Impossible. If Foley knew, Nia would already be in the brig because he'd want a cut of her ransom. But realizing she'd caught his personal notice... Mace ran a hand over his face. Could he even send her to common holding now? If he'd been worried about her safety before, now he was doubly so.

"Come," he said, hand skimming her spine to rest on the small of her back.

She stepped closer until her shoulder pressed against his ribs. His chest squeezed at the accepting action.

Gently, he guided her to the corridor leading to the lift. She kept quiet during the ride to his quarters, but her body stayed close to his.

He shouldn't have left her earlier. He should have let her dress in private, then returned to make sure she was okay.

He kept making mistakes when it came to her.

The door to his quarters slid shut behind them, enclosing them in silence.

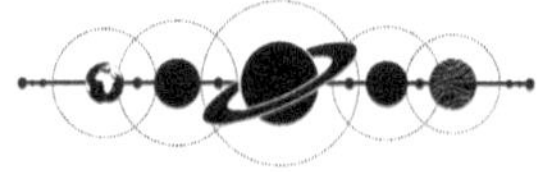

Nia lifted her eyes to look at Mace. She hadn't felt warm since the other commander had found her in the engine core, Mace's body heat the only thing keeping the cold at bay. She stepped closer and grabbed his forearm, fearing he would once again leave her.

The movement snapped him out of whatever thought had frozen him. He closed the small gap between them, swooped her into his arms, and carried her to the bed. They settled together, front to front, her head tucked under his chin on his shoulder, his arms tight around her.

The position loosened something inside her, and an exhale shuddered through her body.

"I'm sorry, Nia." His fingers brushed gently where Foley had gripped her throat. It hadn't been hard, but effective. With a bit more pressure, he could have done severe damage to her larynx.

She swallowed, lifting her gaze to Mace's from the cocoon of his arms. His icy blue eyes brushed over every feature of her face, searching. She wasn't sure what the apology was for, their bout of sex against the bulkhead? The underlying threat coating the other commander's words? Or taking her from her home? His gaze seemed to hold all of that.

And if someone had told her before coming here that a warrior could apologize, she would have laughed for an hour.

But sincerity lived in his expression, making her chest squeeze and her throat tighten. She was tired of battling her feelings for Mace, tired of feeling guilty for every morsel of peace she found here.

With a small nod, she accepted his apology.

His expression relaxed, and he pulled her closer. She couldn't stop herself from snuggling deeper, reveling in how his body surrounded hers so completely.

"I don't think I should go to common holding," she whispered against his chest. Then, because it wasn't the complete truth, added, "I don't want to go."

His arms tightened around her, then relaxed. "All right."

Her bonds beeped, and she glanced downward. Her day off was over.

Chapter Twenty-Seven

The soft beep of his vambrace woke him. It took Mace a second to realize where he was, why contentment enveloped him, warm. Why tranquility felt like a protective shield.

He'd been sleeping in the barracks so long, his own bed felt unfamiliar.

Nia's cheek rested against the curve of his shoulder, her lips against his chest. Her fingers curled into the fabric of his uniform at his sternum, preventing his escape, and her knees were wedged between his thighs.

Stars above, he never wanted to move. It felt too right, too perfect.

He'd tried to stay away from her. All it did was cause problems. He'd always listened to his instincts before this, and they'd never led him astray. He should have listened when it came to Nia too.

They screamed at him to keep her as close as possible.

His vambrace beeped again, and he shifted his body enough to see the panel. Incoming communiques, morning announcements, the automatic reminder his tyros started training in a few minutes—it all marked the beginning of the day, one he'd rather ignore if it meant he could keep holding Nia.

But his not returning to work after leaving without an explanation would only create more problems, giving Cache more reasons to follow through on her threats. If adhering to their regular schedule kept Nia safer, then that's what he needed to do.

"Nia?" He lifted his hand to run his knuckles along her cheek. Her eyes remained closed, her lips parted.

Sleep made her appear younger than her years. The guilt, the thought he should have left her behind, tried to reemerge, but he pushed it away. Regret had no place between them anymore.

He cupped her cheek, then pressed his lips to her forehead. "Nia."

"Mmmm?" she murmured, snuggling deeper into the fluffy bedding.

The action made his chest feel like it wanted to explode. She trusted him.

He ran his hand along her arm to her fingers and took them in his own. "It's time to get up, Nia."

Her eyes popped open, body stiffening. For a split second, he thought she would push him away and scramble to her feet, but she relaxed into his embrace.

A small smile curved her lips. "Morning."

"Morning." He tucked a curl behind her ear. "I need to get to work soon."

She furrowed her brow. "What were you doing when I found you yesterday? Dee called it training."

"That's what I do. I train tyros to become warriors."

Her eyes widened. "Mace," she said, her tone stern. "How old were they?"

He thought about it for a moment. "That group ranged from about twelve to fifteen."

She lurched upright, her breaths shortening. "The stuff the CORE says about child soldiers is true?"

He placed a comforting hand on the back of her neck. "They'll train for years and won't be sent into battle until their age of majority."

"Please don't tell me the age of majority here is sixteen."

"Nineteen."

Tension eased from her spine. "It's still so young."

"And the same age as CORE soldiers."

She shook her head even though she must have known he was right, then scrubbed her hands over her face. "Ugh! I hate this. I hate it all. I hate the death, and the torture, and the violence." Her breath left her with a whoosh.

Mace ran his hand over her spine. "If I could change reality for you, *izar*, I would."

A strained chuckle left her lips, then she looked at him over her shoulder. Her eyes were sad, but there was something else there too. "That's probably the nicest thing anyone has ever said to me." She pushed herself to stand, and his hand dropped away.

"You should receive more compliments."

"Oh, I've received compliments," she said as she headed toward the washroom. "But no one's offered to alter the solar system for me before." The door closed behind her.

Mace remained where he was, listening to her move around inside the washroom. She might have thought his words insincere, but they were true. If he had the power to change this war between their people, he'd do it for her.

Brushing the thought aside, he stood and went to the refrigeration unit for rations. He thought about pulling something for Nia as well, then decided to let her choose her own. She'd never shown favoritism toward her morning meal, picking something different every time he'd shared it with her.

She emerged from the washroom a few minutes later, face pink like she'd scrubbed it clean, then scurried to the kitchen. Grabbing some rations out of the unit, she came to sit across from him.

They ate in silence. It wasn't awkward like it had been before, but companionable. Nia's eyes kept darting to him, then away, the small smile she'd given him earlier returning.

He felt his own lips curl.

The door to his quarters beeped, signaling someone on the other side. While Nia took their ration containers to reclamation, he strode over and touched the control panel.

Elec stood on the other side and straightened to his full height when he saw him.

"Oh, Commander. I didn't realize you'd be here." The younger warrior's gaze skimmed to where Nia moved behind him, then resettled on Mace—then the scratches at his throat. His eyes bulged.

Mace pressed his lips together. He really needed to get his hands on a regenerator to heal those marks. Just the visible ones, though. He liked the rest.

Nia's hand slid into his, and his whole body twitched before he returned the squeeze of her fingers. Elec tracked the action, his head tilting to the side.

Mace didn't look at Nia when he said, "Meet us at family medicine."

Elec jumped to attention. "Understood." Then he made a quick and unnecessary salute. "Sir." Shaking his head, he hurried away.

They followed, but Mace kept their pace slow so they'd ride the next lift. All the way to the medical bay, Nia kept her hand in his. He remembered how she hadn't wanted to be touched when she'd arrived, even through clothing.

In front of the med bay doors, he turned to her and settled his hands on her shoulders. "I'll pick you up at the end of your shift."

Her gaze met his. "You don't have to if you're busy."

"I want to."

The corner of her mouth quirked. "I'd like that," she said, the color rising in her cheeks.

He couldn't resist. Mace pulled her close and brushed his lips across her temple, not caring who in the corridor saw them. When her hands grasped his forearms, fingernails biting through the material of his uniform, the urge to really kiss her made him grip her shoulders tighter.

Instead, he stepped away, touched the control for the door, and ushered her in. A line of people waited at the side of the room, every med bed with someone on it. Nia glanced at him one last time, her small smile returning, before the door slid shut between them.

After a beat, Mace continued on to training, his chest feeling lighter than it had in weeks, years even.

The tyros were already warming up when he arrived at the matted arena, one group running laps, the other doing a range of stretching.

"Switch!" he yelled, though he didn't know how long they'd been in their set. From the grumbling, it probably hadn't been long.

"You're in a good mood," Grey commented, coming to stand beside him.

Crossing his arms over his chest, Mace side-eyed him. How could Grey tell? He'd only been there a couple of minutes.

His friend shrugged. "You've been doing an hour or two in one of the rooms before lessons, but today you've only just arrived. Switch!" he shouted.

Instead of addressing Grey's observation, Mace shot him an "I don't care about your opinion" glance and joined the tyros running the outer edge of the mats. He pushed on some speed, taunting them to keep pace. They didn't disappoint.

The day progressed as any other. Warmup changed to sparring. Grey and he took turns with smaller groups, improving their skills.

It was the first time Mace had felt engaged in a lesson in weeks.

The tyros broke into pairs to grapple. Grey and he circled around the mat, giving pointers. Mace opened his mouth to praise Shand when the deck beneath his feet rumbled.

All the tyros halted to look around. Instinctively, Mace braced his legs apart. Another explosion shuddered closer, the boom loud enough to hurt his ears. Tyros tumbled to the ground, losing their balance. Heart beating fast, he met Grey's wide eyes. This wasn't some sort of malfunction.

Mace glanced at his vambrace. "Fuck." Information streamed from the command center, Cache calling warriors to arms.

A third explosion rocked the station. The bulkheads groaned under the strain, then the lights dimmed to quarter luminosity.

Battle-readiness raced through him. "Everyone to the weapons lockers!" Mace yelled over the next explosion. "Tyros, you're with me."

He had to get to Nia. Her tracker light remained in the med bay, connected to *Orion's* systems. He sent a message to Elec, telling him to protect her at all costs.

Warriors and tyros scurried, grabbing weapons, armor, and forming teams. Mace checked the charge of his weapon and added a second thigh holster to his arsenal, along with a pulse rifle strapped to his back.

The explosions stopped, an eerie silence remaining in the aftermath. Mace received one last communique from the command center: Four engine cores blown. CORE contact confirmed. Weapons and shields down. Enemy forces boarding. Station-wide evacuation order—

The feed cut off.

Fuck.

Spiro and Betel met them in the main corridor. The tyros held weapons they hadn't been cleared to use yet, their eyes betraying their excitement and fear. Mace glanced at the youngest in the group. Freya stared back at him, a glint of determination in her eyes.

He'd told Nia he wouldn't put a child in battle, and he hadn't. The CORE had done it for him.

He broke the tyros into four groups, led by Grey, Spiro, Betel, and himself, then addressed his students. "We are your unit leaders. Follow orders. We'll take any civilians we find along the way. Under no circumstances do you play the hero. Your main objective is to get off this station alive and meet at the rendezvous point. Understood?"

"Yes, sir," they said in unison.

With a nod to his three friends, he pressed his back to the bulkhead next to the door. Another warrior was at the ready with a smoke grenade if they needed it. Mace opened the door. All was silent in the corridor. He poked his head out. Nothing.

He and two warriors fanned out on the fifth level of the atrium, scanning above the barrels of their weapons, searching for the enemy. Besides a few Tellusians scrambling to get to their evacuation ships, there were no defenders.

"Clear," Mace said, and the groups of tyros and warriors entered the corridor.

They couldn't take the lifts, not with their numbers, and not during an attack with low power. Warriors secured ropes to the railings within seconds, throwing them over.

Mace glanced at his vambrace, watching for any unknown life signs as the first of the tyros and warriors climbed over the railing to rappel. Nia's light moved toward the evacuation bay.

The last of the tyros rappelled over the edge. He and Grey followed. Wind whistled lightly as they flew down the rope. Mace's feet hit the deck, his gun up in the next second as he scanned the area for threats. He jogged over to the tyros in defensive positions at the edge of the deserted main-level vendors.

Mace signaled the group to move out, but Grey stopped abruptly, turning. Mace felt it too: a heartbeat of absolute quiet.

Enemy fire burst through the atrium.

Chapter Twenty-Eight

As soon as Nia had arrived in family medicine, she didn't have a minute to herself. It had been the same at all her former posts. One day would be quiet, the next non-stop. Unfortunately, Kessy had the day off, making the day even more challenging when dealing with Faas and Mayra's enduring antagonism.

On the positive side, the bustle didn't allow her even a second to examine how her relationship with Mace had changed over the past day—and what that would mean for the future.

Because she really couldn't deal with that right now.

Frowning, she ran a scanner over her patient, a baby with a fever, one more time. Such a wee thing. Nothing conclusive emerged on the screen, frustrating her. Give her a broken bone or a lacerated appendage any day. Maladies like these, especially in one so small, were always a guessing game.

"Where are you hurting?" she murmured to herself, then looked at the mother. "Maybe it's a growth thing?" The woman didn't look happy with the vague explanation. "I'll lower her fever, then maybe it's best to keep her here for observation." It was the only thing she could think of.

This was why they shouldn't have placed her in family medicine. It annoyed her to no end that she would have to ask Faas or Mayra for their opinion.

Turning, she sought to make eye contact with one of them when the deck rumbled beneath her feet. She tensed, hands tight on the scanner.

Another rumble, and a collective gasp echoed through the med bay. Nia's eyes flew to Elec, whose focus was on his vambrace. Then his other hand reached for the weapon at his thigh.

Boom. The blast rocked everyone to the side. Shouts of alarm collided against the bulkheads; supplies cascaded off the shelves onto the deck. Her infant patient cried. The mother curved over her baby in a protective cocoon. Children whimpered in fear. Her heart racing, Nia tightened her hands on the med bed, trying to keep her balance.

Another blast roared through the space. Nia pitched to the side, hit her elbow on the med bed, and fell to the deck. People screamed. Above the ringing in her ears, the metal around them groaned with strain.

The lights went out, and the emergency lights turned on, dim and red. Using the med bed for support, she staggered to her feet.

"Everyone to their evacuation zones and get off the station," Elec shouted to the people in the bay. "Hurry!" he added when everyone seemed frozen. "CORE are boarding."

Cries of fear and dismay echoed as everyone hurried to the exit. One more explosion rumbled farther away, then the station stilled.

Nia's heart pounded hard in her head as she clenched the edge of the med bed. The CORE was here. She grabbed her locket and squeezed it tightly. They'd finally come.

But instead of the thought elating her, dread swirled in her chest, and her head felt disconnected from her shoulders.

Elec gripped her elbow. "We need to go."

"Where's Mace?"

"We'll meet him at the evacuation bay."

She nodded, her stomach roiling with fear. Elec cleared her bonds to leave, and they entered the corridor. The dim, flashing lights made it hard to see. Shouts resounded further along, people giving orders, others panicking. Elec hurried her forward, her elbow in one hand and weapon in the other.

"We can't take the lifts," he said, gesturing to where others entered an emergency hatch. "We'll need to climb up to deck forty-two."

They waited at the back of the line, and she recognized some patients from the med bay climbing inside the hatch ahead of them. *Evacuation zones. They'll get off safely.* She swallowed against the dryness in her mouth, her heart feeling like it was trying to escape through her throat.

It took forever before it was their turn.

"In you go," Elec said as he helped her inside the emergency shaft, where she stepped onto a ledge and grabbed hold of a ladder rung. Her stomach leaped into her throat. The space below her plummeted unendingly, similar to the engine core. She looked up and could see the outline of the people climbing above her in a tube about the same size as the lift. A baby cried, the sound bouncing within the bulkheads.

Elec followed close behind when a shout down the corridor made him turn. Laser fire erupted, blinding against the dark of the shaft.

"Climb, climb, climb!" Elec shouted before he shut the door behind her, sealing her inside and him out.

Heart galloping, palms sweaty, Nia tried to climb as fast as she could. The thick hatch muffled the weapons fire. Sounds of distress echoed from above as people climbed faster.

Elec... he didn't enter the shaft behind her.

A sob clogged her throat as she continued to climb. The shaft's bulkheads felt like they closed in on her. The echoing movements, the rustle of clothing, disoriented her senses the higher she went. When she passed another access hatch, she saw which deck she was on: nineteen.

A whimper escaped her. Her hands were already sore from the thin metal bar, but she didn't stop, moving as fast as the man above her—which felt about as fast as a hundred-year-old shuttle only using half a thruster. The hatch below could open at any moment, exposing them to the defenders who'd attacked Elec.

Her pace faltered. Should she go back down? Defenders were supposed to be on her side. *What is my side?*

She kept climbing, desperation clogging her throat. Was Elec alive?

An ear-splitting sound, weapons fire, ripped through the shaft from above. Screams of terror echoed, then thumping noises, bodies hitting bodies. Someone was shooting at them from a hatch above. The man above rammed into her, an unavoidable force in the small space.

Nia screamed, losing her grip. She fell, the narrow rungs of the ladder scraping against her body, until her elbow caught against one of them, nearly ripping her arm off.

Bodies pushed past her as they fell, and she had no way to determine if they were dead or alive. She pressed herself against the bulkhead, trying to make herself as small as possible, squeezing behind the ladder, her shoes slipping then holding. They kept falling and falling, ramming against her body, scraping. The weapons fire continued on, a never-ending barrage assaulting her eyes and ears as she held on as tightly as she could. Her forearm burned with sharp pain.

The laser fire stopped. The screaming stopped. The only thing Nia could hear was her heavy breaths. She held perfectly still, afraid to move, terrified that if she did, the shooting would start again. Shouts from a long distance above made her flinch. Hot tears coated her cheeks.

Time passed slowly as she waited for silence. When it descended, its oppressive weight constricted her throat. Had no one else survived? She closed her eyes and thought of those who'd been ahead of her in the line. Bile rose, the taste coating the inside of her mouth. She could hear nothing from below, no groans or gasps that someone was injured and needed treatment. Her eyes tracked downward, but there was no movement, just the unending shaft disappearing into the black. *No one to help.*

Swallowing against the acidic taste that grew in her mouth, she searched the bulkhead in the dim light and realized she'd stopped between two decks. It took an excruciating long time to get her limbs to co-operate, to release the rungs enough to rotate to the front of the ladder.

Her arm throbbed painfully. Her body shook as she moved as quietly as possible. With her damp hands and trembling legs, each rung she grabbed took her whole concentration. One wrong move, and she'd plummet like the others.

Listening for anyone else, Nia climbed a rung at a time until another hatch appeared. She wouldn't ascend farther—not if it meant being shot. Stepping onto the ledge, she pressed her hands against the metal, uncertain how to open the hatch. For a panicked moment, she thought she was trapped, then saw the handle at the bottom.

Careful not to slip and fall, she braced her body against the bulkhead and gripped the handle. Her damp palms slipped on the smooth surface. Gritting her teeth, she wiped them on her leggings, grabbed with both hands, and pulled.

A hiss of air escaped the seal, then the shaft turned into a wind tunnel as the corridor's fresh air battled with the stagnant stuff in the shaft. Nia froze. Had that been too loud? Was anyone on the other side of the hatch? When she heard nothing, she pushed the door open.

The corridor's deck glared red under the emergency lights. Nia stepped one foot out, waiting for something to tell her if it was safe or not. When only silence remained, she climbed out the rest of the way. Heart in her throat, she leaned against the bulkhead, willing the strength back into her legs.

This corridor looked exactly like the one Mace's quarters were on, except the numbers on the doors began with CUL24.

Where was Mace? *Is he even alive?* What about Dee or Kessy?

Her chest tightened painfully, bile rising in her throat once more. She stared at the shaft she'd exited and gripped her locket. Defenders had fired down indiscriminately...they were supposed to *defend*. It was in their name. None of those people had been armed, some children, *babies*, and the defenders hadn't cared.

Her vision blurred. She'd done this. She'd killed all of them as assuredly as if she'd pulled the trigger herself. Her chest felt like it was shrinking. She couldn't breathe.

Her liquid legs collapsed beneath her, the bulkhead her only support as she sank to the deck. Darkness seeped into the edges of her vision. The baby's cries echoed in her head, paired with the thumping of the bodies as they fell. Her body shook.

Footsteps stomped along the next corridor. Nia froze in place, unable to move. They kept getting closer, the heaviness of their steps matching how hard her heart pounded. She gasped as two defenders rounded the corner, then scrambled to her feet. Their helmets were opaque, their white and silver uniforms splattered with blood, and their weapons aimed straight at her.

Nia lifted her hands in surrender, exposing her bonds.

"She's CORE," said the one, his voice generic through his helmet's interface.

"You heard our orders," the other one replied, his head tilted over the sight of the weapon. "Leave no survivors."

A shout of pure terror burst from her throat. Nia spun and ran, hugging the side of the bulkhead so the open hatch door would block her. This wasn't a rescue mission. It was a siege. Her feet stumbled beneath her, and she braced for the pain of death.

The shots never came. She kept running.

Two more defenders turned the corner in front of her. Nia screamed, skidding, falling on her bottom at their feet. They aimed their weapons above her and fired.

Another weapon blasted from behind her, connecting with their personal shielding, making it ripple in stress. But it was the sudden appearance of a knife, plunged to the hilt, that captured her gaze. The blade was wedged in the space between the helmet and uniform of the defender on the right. She blinked, and a matching wound appeared on the other defender.

They both fell to the deck.

It felt like her body had turned to iron. She couldn't move, breaths bursting past her lips at a ragged tempo.

A scuffing noise behind her broke through her daze. She turned her head.

Mace strode toward her. One side of his face was splattered with blood, and his blue uniform was covered in weapons and body armor. The first two defenders she encountered lay dead behind him.

She gasped a breath, relief blending with her fear and panic. He passed her by, knelt beside the dead defenders, and pulled the knives from their bodies before wiping the blades on their uniforms. Red smeared against silver.

He tucked the two knives away into his belt with a *snick*, then stood and extended his hand.

Chapter Twenty-Nine

Mace shook, his eyes roving over Nia. He noted a laser burn on her arm, but otherwise she seemed unscathed. He strove to get his emotions under control.

She slumped on the deck where she'd fallen, her face pale with shock, eyes glazed, and stared at his hand like she didn't know what to do with it. Her gaze slid to the dead defenders behind him.

"Nia." He kept his voice gentle, but her body jerked anyway, eyes widening as if seeing him for the first time. "We've got to go." And they had to hurry. Any living Tellusians were leaving the station in the last of the evacuation transports right this minute.

It was tempting to stay and fight, to regain control instead of evacuating. Even with their communications impeded, he knew Cache would have thought the same thing. For her to order a full evacuation meant the battle was lost before it had begun. The CORE had timed it so that there were no Destroyers nearby. There was at least one traitor on *Orion* who'd facilitated it all.

"Nia." This time his voice held more force, and she reached out. Mace pulled her trembling body against him for a quick squeeze. Taking her hand, he retraced his steps past the two defenders whose throats he'd slit. Nia inhaled sharply. Their helmets had disengaged, the man and woman staring unseeingly at the overhead with their blood puddling on the deck.

So he'd cut a little deeper than necessary. They'd sealed their fates when they'd aimed their weapons at Nia. She'd almost died.

Mace gripped her hand tightly as they hurried down the corridor, Mace focusing on the dangers ahead, but aware of the woman beside him.

When the defenders had swarmed the atrium, he and the tyros almost hadn't made it out of there. Both tyros and warriors had been injured, but they had lost no one in their escape. It wasn't until they'd gotten to the evacuation zone that Mace had a moment to contact Elec again.

And he hadn't received a response.

Terror clenching his chest, he'd followed Nia's tag to deck twenty-four. When he'd seen those defenders aiming at her... he must have aged a decade.

"What happened to Elec?" he asked quietly, tugging her along, but keeping his senses open. When Nia didn't answer, he cast her a quick glance. She shook her head, all color leached from her face.

Fuck. He didn't have time to grieve for the young warrior, because a flash on his vambrace indicated movement ahead. The place was crawling with defenders. He pressed his back against the bulkhead, Nia doing the same beside him. They waited. He couldn't take on a large group of defenders and keep her safe at the same time.

He looked down at her bent head. She gripped his hand tightly, knuckles white. When the corridor cleared, he pulled her along, then stopped again at the next one over. There were at least two defenders blocking their way, protecting a key junction. Mace ushered Nia to the side, thinking.

Shit. He was going to have to leave her alone for a minute, or else they were fucked.

He bent to her level. "Stay here," he said, then because he couldn't resist, he pressed his lips to hers. Life returned to her eyes when he pulled away, a flush gathering in her cheeks. Mace nodded. *Better.*

He didn't bother with his gun. He hadn't been able to crack the autonomous shielding frequency of the defenders' uniforms yet. A quick peek revealed their attention was in the other direction. His jamming signal was still working.

He darted out. The one turned, saw him coming, and aimed. Mace threw his knife, the blade sinking into the sweet spot at his throat, between his helmet and the top of his uniform. The other defender got a shot off, grazing his shoulder, but Mace kept running. He barreled into the woman and sliced her throat on the way down.

Mace stood and caught his breath. A strangled sound came from Nia at the end of the corridor. He didn't have time to do this gently, to shield her from battle. As a surgeon, she would have seen thousands of wounds, but that didn't mean she had much experience on the front lines, seeing war in real time. He turned to calm her, then froze.

A defender had her in front of him, a knife to her throat. It had already pricked her skin, a drop of blood running down her neck.

"Is this yours?" the defender asked, his helmet disguising his face and voice. *Coward.*

"Drop your weapons," the defender ordered, keeping Nia in front of him.

Mace nearly laughed out loud. It would take ten minutes to remove them all.

"Drop the knife!" the defender shouted.

Mace didn't have an opening. He spread his arms wide, the bloody knife on the tips of fingers about to fall. The defender stepped from behind Nia to aim, and Mace shifted, flicking the knife into his palm, turning and throwing it as the heat of the laser singed the hair by his ear. His knife landed true between two ribs.

Mace ran toward Nia. Her body shook as the dying defender squirmed and tried to grab hold of her ankle. Her blank eyes stared straight ahead.

On one knee, Mace slit the defender's throat to finish him, glad the man had been in pain at least those short seconds before death. The bastard made Nia bleed.

Mace stood and took a quick look at her wound. Superficial. He grabbed her hand.

"You've been shot." Nia's voice sounded hollow.

Mace glanced at his shoulder. A gouge only, in almost the exact place she had hers. The laser burn stopped most of the blood loss.

"No time." Those shots would bring more defenders. "We've got to go."

Nia's icy hand felt small in Mace's much warmer one. She drew strength from him and let it ease the tremors in her body.

They passed the bodies of the two defenders, and Nia averted her gaze. It wasn't their deaths making her reel. It was her lack of emotion at having witnessed them. She felt nothing. No guilt or disgust. Not even remorse for lacking the emotions. She couldn't allow herself to feel, or she'd lose the little calm she'd regained with Mace's presence.

She followed behind him, focusing on his back and the way he silently moved ahead of her. They passed more bodies, both Tellusian and CORE, all with fatal wounds and vacant stares, their blood pooling on the deck.

Nia swallowed. *People are dead because of me.* If she allowed the truth to settle into her soul, she knew she would start screaming and never stop.

She forced herself to focus on staying alive. Her fingers squeezed Mace's. He gave her a quick glance and returned the gesture. It was enough to settle her stomach.

Quiet filled the corridors, and Nia kept looking behind them, expecting more defenders. When Mace stopped, she almost barreled into his back. He pressed his hand against the control panel next to a wide door, and it slid open.

They were in a bay filled with empty landing pads, only a handful of ships remaining in the otherwise deserted space. Mace led her to a ship similar in size to a Raven. It sat angled on a platform, and Mace pushed her up the ramp to help her in.

Nia used the railing for leverage until she'd reached the cockpit, sliding into the co-pilot's seat. The scent of newly washed metal composite filled her head. Every surface gleamed. Mace sat beside her and touched the controls. The ramp whined closed, and the vessel's engines hummed. Mace buckled himself in, and Nia followed suit.

Shields rippled around them. Mace gripped the controls. The ship lurched forward, and Nia's head snapped back. They shot out into space.

Right toward two Guardians.

Stomach plummeting into her toes, she gripped the arms of her seat until it felt like her fingernails would break off. Weapons fire streaked red and orange against the black of space as fighters and other combat vessels flew in some type of preordained chaos. A huge portion of the mines was missing where they'd been thick on her arrival, the two Guardians occupying the resulting space.

Laser fire came right toward them, and she flinched at each shot, the shields rippling from the contact. Mace veered out of the path of a Condor at the last second. "Fuck," he muttered under his breath.

The panel flashed a warning in front of him, but Mace kept heading toward the Guardians.

"What are you doing?" Nia asked. The warships grew in size as they neared. They should be trying to get away, not heading to their deaths.

"It's the only way out. We don't control the mines anymore."

Nia tried to swallow around the dryness in her mouth. They were so close to the one Guardian that she could see the individual windows on the port side. "But what about the—" A loud *thunk* cut her off. "—grappling hooks?" she finished. The magnetic grappling hook punched through their shielding.

"A little too close." He had the nerve to sound unconcerned.

Their trajectory abruptly changed, throwing Nia's nauseated stomach into her throat. Bile coated her tongue.

When they were captured, Mace would be executed as a Tellusian terrorist. *No.* She couldn't accept it. There had to be a way out.

Mace unbuckled his restraints first, then hers. He stood, tugging Nia to her feet. The cabin darkened as they were pulled into the mouth of the hangar. He took his gun out of its holster, changed the settings, and pressed her clammy hands on the stock. He forced her to aim the weapon at his stomach.

"Shoot me," he demanded.

Nia dropped the gun. "What?"

Two more low *thunks* echoed through the ship as stabilizer cables connected with the outer hull.

He snatched the gun, shoving it at her again. "Shoot me. It's the only way we can play this. Like you're trying to escape."

Nia backed away, refusing to grab hold. The cabin brightened as they entered the hangar. "I can't shoot you." More bile rose in her throat.

Defenders hurried around the ship as they were taken further and further into the Guardian's belly.

"Shoot me, goddamn it!" he yelled, forcing her finger on the trigger.

"No," she whispered a second before the ship jolted and hit the deck. Nia fumbled, the gun pressed between them. A shot went off, and he crumpled.

What had she done? Nia couldn't move as someone from the outside forcibly lowered the shuttle's ramp. Her gaze remained fixed on Mace's inert body. So lifeless.

Lights flashed in her face from the defenders' weapons as they swarmed the ramp. They screamed at her, but her head was in a fog, and she didn't understand the words.

"Drop your weapon!" One voice broke through her haze.

She jerked, not realizing she still held the thing, and let go of it like it were an infectious disease. She placed her hands on her head.

Her eyes shifted to Mace. Was he okay? He was so still.

Through the yelling, she heard a voice demanding she identify herself. That she could do.

"Surgeon Lieutenant Colonel, Euphenia Jannex, *Elara Five*, ID number 435801."

She squinted against the lights in her face, heart pounding. Mace's weapon had been set to stun, right? He wouldn't have made her really shoot him, would he? She couldn't see any blood, but he lay face down and could be hiding a true wound.

A defender stepped forward, blocking her view of everything except the width of his chest in his silver uniform. She looked up. Her blood-splattered face reflected off the defender's visor. He grabbed her wrist.

Unadulterated panic bubbled in her chest. She rolled her eyes back into her head, imitating the loss of consciousness as best she could. *Fewer questions to answer.*

Nia fell, not expecting the defender to let go. When she bashed her head against the side bench of the ship, stars exploding behind her eyelids, she hoped to hell the performance had been worth it.

Chapter Thirty

The familiar beeps and clicks of medical tools should have comforted Nia, but they didn't. She'd been feigning unconsciousness for a while. How long could she continue the façade?

Once she'd been deposited on a hover bed in the hangar, they'd secured her with metal restraints, making her heart race with panic. She hadn't dared open her eyes to see what was happening to Mace, but heard the slurs against him, the dull thuds making her think they kicked him while unconscious. It took everything in her to remain limp and lifeless when all she wanted to do was scream and attack.

The hover bed wound through corridors, onto a lift, then back out until she arrived at what sounded like a medical bay or lab. A scanner hummed over her head and torso, all the way to her feet. Someone loosened her Tellusian bonds, the organic metal parting from her skin. Nia resisted the urge to rotate her wrists.

The bed's restraints remained. A regenerator buzzed, healing the cut on her throat, then the laser burn on her arm. She thought there was more than one person in the room, but no one spoke.

A few minutes later, a door whooshed open and closed. A masculine voice barked, "You two out. You stay." Feet shuffled, and the door opened and closed again.

"Report," the same voice demanded.

"The usual, sir," a feminine voice from beside Nia answered. "Tracker has been removed, ocular implant deactivated. There was a cut to her throat and a laser burn on her arm, which I've healed. Preliminary scans showed evidence of recent sexual assault, confirmed by untreated scratches on other parts of her body."

"Revive her."

"She's already awake, sir."

Nia's eyes flew open. Two men stood on one side of her. The sandy-haired one with shrewd brown eyes had four emblems on the shoulder of his silver uniform, indicating a high rank in the military. The man beside him wore the black of a medical officer, his features bland and cold.

She swallowed, her eyes going to the woman on the other side of the hover bed also wearing black. The doctor wouldn't meet her gaze.

From her position, Nia couldn't see much of the room, but it looked like a lab. The smooth, white architecture of the place made a block of ice settle in her stomach instead of being comforting.

"Euphenia Jannex," the first man said, grabbing her attention. "You were declared missing and presumed dead forty-five days ago along with a third of *Elara Five's* medical personnel."

Her eyes blurred. A third of her colleagues? Almost a thousand people would have died or been taken. Had Ezra made it?

"I'm Major General Forna," he continued, "also the administrator of this vessel."

Swallowing the tears choking her, Nia gave him a nod of respect, acknowledging his position. She recognized the last name. The Forna family were benefactors of the Lunar Medical Academy.

He glanced at his PALM, and Nia blinked. A strange disconnect filled her at seeing one.

"I'm here with Slattery," he said, tilting his head to the side. "He's a specialist. Do you know what that is?"

Nia's heart raced, her mouth going dry as she stared at the other man. She'd never met a specialist but had heard whispers of them when stationed on a medical aid vessel years ago—those who specialized in interrogation.

"I haven't done anything wrong," she said, her voice croaky. The skin of her wrists burned as she pulled against the restraints.

"Of course not, no," Forna said, his voice an affectation of sympathy. It exacerbated her panic. "We're here to ask you a few questions." He gave her a thin smile, and Nia stilled her movements.

"Please contact my family."

His eyes crinkled in a semblance of a smile. "Perhaps if you do well with these questions. Until then, I'll only need your cooperation, and this will be all over." The fake smile dissolved. "I've been in contact with *Elara Five*." Her heart tripped over itself. "And know Calvin Autry well. He'd like you returned to him, but understands procedures, of course."

What the hell was he talking about? She yanked at her wrists. "Tell my father I'm alive." That was the only procedure he needed to follow.

"In due time." Forna glanced at his PALM again, eyes narrowing on her. "Do you know the name of the Tell you arrived with?"

Her heart skipped a beat. What were they doing to Mace? She shook her head.

"I don't believe you," he said in a flat voice.

Nia licked her dry lips. "They only called him Commander or Sir," she croaked, her throat aching with the need to scream. "I never knew his name."

Forna's face hardened, and Nia glanced at the specialist. He hadn't moved, his gaze frozen on her like some sort of disturbing, lifelike statue.

"I don't think you understand the gravity of your situation," Forna said, reclaiming her attention. "You're presumed dead. I could throw you out an airlock, and no one would know the difference. What is the name of the man who held you hostage?"

Nia clenched her jaw and closed her eyes. "I don't know."

There was silence around her for a moment, making her heart beat faster. Something touched her forehead, and her eyes flew open. The specialist stood on the other side of her, securing a device to her temple with a *click*.

She gasped. When he leaned to do the same to the other side, she saw what he held—an odd-shaped cortical node. Nia shrank back, trying to get away, but Forna wrapped a hand around her throat and pressed her against the table. The second one clicked into place with a pinch. Warmth spread through her forehead and face, then settled into the space where her spine met her brain.

"There." Forna said the word like a weight had been lifted from his shoulders. He let go of her throat to sit on a stool. "These nano nodes are the specialist's pride and joy. They've been programmed with one purpose, to infiltrate the brain and impede a person's ability to lie. As long as the nodes are attached, the nanos can do their work. Mind moles, we like to call them."

"That's illegal," Nia gritted out. The other doctor stood behind him, looking as if she wanted to run away.

One corner of his mouth quirking, Forna nodded at the specialist.

For a second, Nia felt weightless, like she floated in a regeneration bath. Pain didn't exist, and stress didn't have a definition. She sighed, happy to relax. Her mind drifted to a safe place in her brain, when her parents were still together, laughing as each held a hand and swung her between them. Nia smiled.

"How do you feel?" someone asked, and her eyes snapped open to find Forna leaning over her. She couldn't remember why she'd felt threatened by him.

"Perfect," she murmured, wanting to sleep the day away on this beautiful cloud. Then she screamed when the sensation was ripped away from her. She plunged into a vat of ice water, every part of her prickling with pain. Nia gasped for breath.

"He can add pain to the process or take it away," she heard someone say from a great distance. The sensation of needles in her skin turned into knives stabbing her everywhere, not a piece of her body untouched. The blades turned molten hot, ripping her apart with every jab.

A lifetime passed before the stabbing stopped. The bulkheads of the lab echoed with residual screams. Sweat beaded on her skin, her clothing sticking tight to her body. Rawness coated her throat as if someone had taken a laser scalpel to it. She searched for an escape.

Then it struck her that no time had passed at all. She felt ancient, like years of her life had been sucked from her limbs. Her lungs wouldn't work, wouldn't take a proper breath. But the pain had stopped, and she would do almost anything for it never to happen again.

"What's your name?" Forna asked, his gaze focused on his PALM.

"Euphenia Jannex," she said, her throat raw from screaming. "People close to me call me Nia. You can call me your living nightmare as soon as I get off this bed. I'm going to take that laser scalpel over there and stab you in the head."

"The Tells have made you violent," he murmured, but didn't seem concerned by her threat. "What is the name of the terrorist we found on the ship with you?"

"Mace. He's a big, scary commander, and he's so good at hurting people, he trains others how to do it." She hated the words coming out of her mouth, but couldn't stop them. Another rush of relaxation from the nanos had her not hating herself so much.

"What else can you tell me?"

"You should get your receding hairline fixed. There's been so many advancements in follicle technology. Maybe there's a correlation between hair loss and the small penises of cowardly men. Someone should do a study—"

She gasped, another wave of pain halting her opinions.

"Let's get focused again," Forna said after the wave subsided. "Tell me about your captivity. Don't spare me any details. Let's begin with what this Mace," he practically spat the name, "did to you."

"He took me from my home and kept me."

Forna raised an eyebrow. "What else did he do to you?"

"He ignored me."

"He ignored you?"

Nia nodded. He'd ignored her for weeks. *Bastard.*

Forna's eyelid twitched. "He didn't touch you?"

"He did touch me." Forna leaned forward, eyebrows raised as he waited for her to continue. "I liked it and wanted more."

"Level two," Forna gritted between his teeth.

The specialist pulled her muscles out of her body through her pores. She screamed so hard that her voice disappeared. Her brain disconnected from her spine. She must have blacked out, because the next thing she heard was the hum of a regenerator near her throat.

Her body throbbed, but the pain in her throat receded. *How long have I been here?* It must have been a hundred years since she'd lived with Tellusians. Sweat trickled in the crease of her neck and into her hair.

A frantic beeping cut through the haze of pain. The regenerator stopped. When she opened her eyes, the room blurred around her.

"Secure the door." Forna's voice came out harsh, laced with alarm.

"It's Mace, isn't it?" Nia whispered, her brain still wrapped in fog. "He's going to kill you. I'm not sorry."

There was a gasp, then a scream cut short. Nia turned her head toward the door. Mace filled the entrance, his face a mask of rage. Forna stood beside the bed, but something was wrong with him. Nia realized the hilt of a knife protruded from his eye, his left hand shaking. The specialist was already on the deck, dead.

The doctor had stopped a meter from the door, shaking, Mace's weapon pointed at her. "To the bed," he ordered. "Release her."

The woman scurried, tears on her cheeks, and undid the restraints with trembling hands. As soon as Nia was free, she rolled off the bed—and almost collapsed when her feet hit the deck.

Mace was there in the next instant, his arms wrapping around her body to hold her upright. He cupped her face with his free hand, still aiming his gun at the doctor with the other.

"Did she hurt you?" he asked in a quiet voice.

The doctor whimpered, crouching behind the table.

Nia shook her head. "No." Her voice came out scratchy. "She watched and did nothing."

Mace made a sound low in his throat, then lifted his hand to her brow. "What are these?"

"Mind moles." Her hands still shaking from the torture, Nia touched them, trying to find the release, but they wouldn't budge. "They make me tell the truth." His eyebrows arched, and she nodded. "It's a lot of verbal garbage, really. Whatever pops into my head, I say it aloud and—"

He covered her mouth with his hand. "I'm getting off this ship. If you stay, you're free, but—" He looked around the medical lab. "You'd need to get to your family as soon as possible, off this ship, and I wouldn't be able to help you with—"

Nia removed his hand, halting his words. Her chest had gone tight at the concern etched on his face. He didn't want to leave her here, but he'd do it if he must.

"I want to go with you," she said simply.

His face relaxed, and he nodded. Noise outside the corridor had him tensing once more. "They're here." He pressed her against the bulkhead, out of sight from the corridor, then grabbed a device out of his pant leg. A round orb, similar to the one he'd used on *Elara Five,* sat in his hand.

When he threw it out into the corridor, it didn't make smoke. Repetitive weapon fire filled the air. Then silence.

"Let's go."

Holding her hand, he poked out his head. After two heartbeats, he pulled her after him into the corridor.

They stepped over bodies.

"I really wish you wouldn't kill all these people," Nia said, unable to stop the words from leaving her mouth.

He gave her hand a squeeze. "It's what I do, Nia."

"I know, but I don't like it. They have lives and families, and you killed them all. They aren't mindless clones or drones. Or at least they used to be before you killed them, and that makes me feel awful. But then again, some of them could be horrible like Major General Forna. And the Slattery guy. I'm not sad *they're* dead, deranged assholes—"

Nia stopped her words at Mace's incredulous look over his shoulder. She slapped her free hand over her mouth. He turned around, and they continued. He fired down the next corridor, making their way around more bodies.

Nia tried to focus on Mace's broad back, but her eyes drifted lower. She dropped her hand from her mouth.

"You have a nice ass."

"Thanks." A tinge of disbelieving laughter laced his tone.

"I noticed in the beginning. When you kidnapped me and threw me over your shoulder. There has to be something wrong with me for noticing, right? I mean, you shouldn't be admiring your kidnapper's bum, should you? I should probably be psycho-analyzed or something—"

When he cast another look in her direction, she clapped her hand over her mouth again. Amused or not, she had to remember they were in a dire situation and she needed to be quiet. *Yes. Very quiet.*

Chapter Thirty-One

Ever since Mace had heard her scream in agony when he'd arrived on this deck, he'd been shaking. The need to kill every last person on this ship dictated his every action.

He pulled Nia to the side at a junction. One more corridor to go, but it was blocked by defenders.

Out of the corner of his eye, he watched Nia pull at the nodes on her head with one hand, her mouth covered with the other. Her eyes held a shimmer, like she'd drunk too much alcohol.

"You aren't going to start spurting blood out of your head when you yank those off, are you?" he asked, frowning at her.

Her hand dropped, eyes widening comically. "God, I hope not. I should have asked how to get them off. They're not like the cortical nodes I've used before. I wouldn't want the nanos to take permanent residence in my brain. How would I ever keep my secrets, then? That would be horrible. And I see the way you're looking at me right now. I'm supposed to be quiet. Okay, how's this? My voice is really quiet right now. Pretty good, right?" She finished on a whisper.

Shaking his head, he returned his attention to the corridor. His stomach fell. He was going to have to leave her again. A firefight would bring more defenders, and right now they had the advantage of his jammer. He took his secondary weapon from his left thigh and handed it to her.

"Take this and shoot anyone who comes from that direction." He jerked his chin the way they'd come.

Her hand dropped from her mouth. "Mace, I can't. I'm a doctor, not a warrior."

He touched the panel on the side. "It's set to stun."

"Okay. I can do that." She held the weapon aloft, face flushing.

Mace returned his attention to the threat ahead. The first corridor was clear. He sprinted, then stopped at the junction. He waited. Footsteps. *Just about there.* Mace lunged, incapacitating the first with a slice to his femoral artery before turning to the second. The third farther along only startled him slightly. He slit the second's throat and threw the blood-coated knife at the third, hitting the sweet spot.

The first wasn't dead and was making too much noise. Mace took a knife out of his boot and slit his throat. All without getting a shot off.

And they'd changed to teams of three. *Good to know.*

He hurried to retrieve Nia. Once he turned the corner, he pushed the barrel of the gun out of his face.

"You keep that, but don't shoot me."

"Okay."

He grabbed her hand, and they jogged down the corridor. She tsked when they stepped over the dead.

"I really wish you wouldn't kill all these people."

He shot her a look, hoping to keep her quiet. She frowned at him and said, "Why don't you stun them all?"

Fed up, he grabbed her by the shoulders and met her at eye level. "Because if I let them live, they'll be the ones to kill me in battle tomorrow. Understand?" He used the same firm teaching voice he used with his tyros.

When she shook her head, he knew he had failed. He sighed. "Just keep quiet."

She nodded.

They kept going, her hand in his until they reached the launch bay. Mace set Nia with her back against the bulkhead near the door.

"Watch in both directions. Shoot anyone you see. We have no friends here."

He didn't wait for her response but sprinted inside. The internal security of a Guardian was laughable. They were arrogant and assumed no one could breach their warship. No security protocols on the doors except for a PALM swipe, and he'd confiscated one off the first defender he'd killed in the brig.

The launch bay contained one security detail and a handful of maintenance workers. Mace made quick work of the defenders and incapacitated the rest. No need to keep quiet now. They were almost out.

Once he was sure the bay was clear of threats, he jogged to retrieve Nia. She stood staring down the corridor, her face beyond pale.

"I shot a doctor," she said, her words faint.

A crumpled mass of black lay slumped at the end of the corridor. He took the gun from her. "And they'll be fine when they wake. Let's go."

"Where are we?" she asked as they hurried toward a Condor.

"This is where they launch their fighters."

"Truly? I should probably learn more about ships. Until I met you, I never thought my education was deficient. I had no idea there were—"

She stopped talking when he shot her another look. They stopped at the bottom of the Condor, its ladder already extended.

"Up you go." He ripped the stolen PALM off his hand and dropped it on the deck. He had no use for it now.

Nia climbed ahead of him, then paused at the top. "It's a one-seater. We're going to have to find another one." She almost sat on his face in her haste.

"They're all one-seaters. Get in," he said, giving her bottom a push.

She yelped, then climbed over the edge, bracing her feet against the edges of the seat.

"Stay like that until I can slide in with you." Mace climbed over the edge, stowing his guns behind the seat. He pressed his body against hers, his arm across her middle. They slid into the seat together, her floral scent wrapping around him. He almost groaned aloud.

Ignoring his body's response to her proximity, he read the control panel over her head and powered up the fighter. The canopy closed above them, and he initiated the shielding and viewer.

"This isn't going to work," Nia said quietly, resting her hands on the tops of his thighs.

"Why?" Mace asked, distracted as he berated himself for not grabbing helmet clips from one of the dead to interface with Condor's systems.

"I'm getting turned on sitting like this," she replied in a matter-of-fact tone.

His arms gave her an involuntary squeeze. Another body part of his body sprang to attention at her words. "One thing at a time," he said, voice hoarse.

The entrance to the bay overflowed with defenders, their weapons fire bouncing off the Condor's shielding. Mace put them in a hover, setting it in line with one of the launch tubes. The shots from the defenders rocked the ship.

"Hold on."

Nia's fingernails bit into his thighs, doing nothing to ease the hard-on she'd created with her confession. He initiated maximum thrust, the tube increasing their acceleration. As they were about to breach the tube, he dropped a live missile.

Flames followed them out, licking upward around them until they shot into space, the vacuum extinguishing the explosion.

"What was that?" she asked, turning to see through the canopy's viewer.

"A gift."

She sagged against him. He was momentarily surprised she didn't give him hell for killing more people.

He banked, and *Orion* came into view. The sight of his childhood home made him swallow. He didn't know if there was anyone left on the station to fight, but the battle in the minefield was lost. A Guardian sat docked on the outside of the station, its lighter coloring contrasting with the black that comprised *Orion's* design. Nothing had ever looked so wrong.

In front of him, Nia's shoulders shuddered, but he didn't have any time to console her. Marauders were on their tail. Mace headed into the densest part of the minefield on the other side of *Orion*. Without control of the mines, it was absolute insanity to escape in this direction, but they had no other option.

Nia's fingernails dug in deeper as he wove them in and out of the mines, trying to outmaneuver the fighters behind them. He banked close to a huge mine. Her scream pierced his eardrums. The Marauder didn't recover fast enough, exploding behind them.

Two more to go.

He checked the rear feed, then reversed propulsion. The two ships shot ahead of them. He fired, accelerating at the same time. The one on the left exploded. They flew through the debris field a second later. Nia yelped as their shields sizzled, gripping his thighs tighter. He fired and nicked the second fighter on its wing. *Good enough.*

Mace weaved out of danger, toward the corridor they'd created in the mines, leaving the damaged Marauder to its fate bouncing around a minefield. As soon as they were clear, he engaged maximum thrust, aiming out of the sector.

Nia didn't relax in front of him, and the farther they flew from *Orion*, the more her breaths shortened, until she was almost hyperventilating. His arms tightened around her.

"What's wrong?" he asked, even though it was a stupid question. So much had gone wrong.

"I need to destroy this necklace. It's a tracker, Mace. *Orion* was attacked because of me. I killed all those people." Her last words left her in a ragged sob, her body shuddering in front of him.

Her confession brought a rush of cold over his skin. A tracker? How had it passed the scans? The proximity alerts, the power outage. All had happened after Nia had arrived. Had she somehow caused it?

If her tracker started it all, then *he* was the one responsible for losing *Orion*. If he hadn't taken her from *Elara Five*, then none of this would have happened.

Logic intervened. A tracker of that size wouldn't have broken through *Orion's* shields.

But his brain kept itching with possibilities, and made him ask, "Why were you in the engine core yesterday?"

She sniffed. "What?"

"Why did Foley find you in the engine core? Why did you choose to go there?"

She turned slightly. "After we fucked—" He twitched at the way she said it with her accent. "I didn't know what to do with myself. I stepped on a lift and didn't tell it where to go. It moved on its own and took me there. Then I watched it because it's beautiful."

The tension in his chest eased at her admission. She hadn't been there for sabotage.

"It was more than fucking," he murmured against her hair.

After a moment, she nodded. "Yeah." Then her hands flew to her neck. "Take it." She struggled with the clasp. "Destroy it."

Putting the ship on autopilot, he brushed her hair away from her nape and took the clasp in hand. With a flick of his thumb, he opened it. "The reclamation unit is on your right."

She took it and shoved it inside the small compartment like it were diseased. Her nape still exposed, he couldn't stop himself from leaning forward and pressing his lips against the warmth of her skin. Her scent filled his head.

She stiffened, then relaxed against him.

"Let's get these nodes off you too," he murmured against her skin.

Turning a bit, she met his gaze, her eyes still shiny with tears. "There should be a recall button somewhere."

He took her chin in his fingers, tilting her head. He found the small switch near the top and pressed it.

She gasped.

"Are you okay?"

She cleared her throat. "Yes. It tingled." She turned the other way so he could see her left side, and he did the same with the other. She gasped again.

"Get rid of these too, in case there's a tag on them."

With shaky hands, she shoved them into the reclamation chamber with the necklace, then hit the "deactivate and disassemble" button. A hum, then silence.

She sniffed again. "I feel like shit," she murmured, swaying in front of him. "Those things drained everything out of me." She sniffed again. The next one turned into a sob.

Realizing she was about to lose it completely, Mace adjusted their trajectory and wrapped both arms around her. His body armor got in the way. While he unclipped the sections and fumbled them over his head, her crying intensified. Shoving the weight of the pieces behind the chair, he pulled her close.

She resisted a moment, then turned her face into him, cheek pressed against his chest. Her whole body melted as the next sob escaped her lips.

Fingers clenched into his uniform. Her curls tickled his chin, giving him a dose of her sweet scent.

Tears dripped onto his chest.

"You weren't responsible for *Orion*," Mace murmured against her hair. "It was an inside job, four engine cores blown at the same time." But she kept crying. He held her tighter.

The whole time on *Orion*, she'd had a tracker blaring her position, and she hadn't said a thing. Of course, she hadn't. She was CORE. At every turn she'd told him she wanted to go home. She'd never hidden that.

His chest cracked at the thought of letting her go.

But when they arrived at their next location, there might be the opportunity to give her what she wanted, get her home in the safest way possible—as a civilian, and smuggle her to family who would have the power and influence to protect her. Hopefully Lexi could help.

Would he be strong enough to go through with it?

Did he have a choice?

This thing between them... he couldn't think straight when he was around her, made problematic choices. But the bigger question of trust pressed down on him. Would she have told him about the tracker if those nodes hadn't been attached to her head?

Because if she hadn't, with the place they were going next, he didn't know if he would have been able to forgive her if she'd brought the CORE to them.

CHAPTER THIRTY-TWO

Nia tried to stretch, stiffness cramping her muscles. Her elbow hit something hard, making her eyes fly open.

The canopy's viewer showed the never-ending view of stars dotting the black of space. A masculine and minty scent enveloped her. Shifting her weight, she turned. Pain shot through her nape and spine from being so scrunched. Mace's biceps flexed beneath her cheek.

Her parched and swollen throat screamed when she tried to swallow.

"Here," Mace murmured, the timbre of his voice rumbling through her body. He passed her a thin ration tube.

Twisting off the cap, she sucked back the gooey mass. It moistened her tongue and throat while settling the growling in her stomach. She shoved the leftover packaging into the reclamation compartment.

Mace wouldn't allow her to hold her body away from his and pulled her flush against his chest. Resting her head on his shoulder, she relaxed. A flutter erupted in her stomach when his lips brushed her ear.

"How long was I asleep?" she asked, her voice heavy with fatigue.

He touched the front panel, and it beeped. "Sixteen hours."

A long time. Maybe it had something to do with the mind moles. *Or the guilt.*

The arms around her middle and the lips against her head couldn't erase what had happened, how she might have had a hand in it despite Mace's assurances.

"What did they do to you?" he asked quietly against her ear.

She shook her head, not wanting to talk about it, but when his arm squeezed gently, she knew she had to give him something. "It hurt, but it was all mental. All in my head."

His body shifted beneath hers, like he would demand more, when she saw the melted patch of uniform on his arm.

"You're injured." She sat up straight, bumping his chin.

"It's just a graze."

"Is there a med kit in here?"

"Probably behind the seat. It's not worth fussing over."

"Are you trying to win the martyr-of-the-year award?"

A breath puffed against her forehead. "All right." He jostled her forward, reaching, then pulled a med kit from behind him.

She didn't waste any time peeling his uniform away from the injury and regenerating the damaged tissue. After she finished, she gave him the kit and snuggled into his chest.

"Where are we headed?" she asked after a while.

"Somewhere safe to lie low for a while."

She frowned at his vague answer. Leaning forward, she read the nav display. Unease skittered through her. "Are we flying through CORE space?"

"Yeah." His arm flexed around her.

Nia's heart beat uncomfortably in her chest. CORE space. A month ago, she would have been elated. Since yesterday, she didn't want to have anything to do with the CORE.

And they might be in a CORE fighter right now, but the protection of its camouflage would only last for so long.

Trying to shed the apprehension creeping through her body, she leaned into Mace's chest. Her heart throbbed painfully at what had happened, what she'd done. The CORE had control of *Orion,* and she didn't see how that would change anytime soon. Two Guardians protected it, with probably more to come. Thinking of defenders and administrators swarming all over *Orion* unfettered made her skin crawl.

Instead of allowing those imaginings to take over her brain, she turned slightly to study Mace.

Stubble across his jaw gave him a scruffy appearance. His hair was mussed, and on *Orion* she'd seen him run his hands through it. Concentration pinched his features as he monitored the ship's systems. Nia barely resisted the urge to smooth his brow.

His piercing blue eyes flicked to hers and softened.

"Are we still married?" she blurted.

His eyebrows jumped. "Technically..." She narrowed her eyes when his voice trailed off. "Yes. Our situation stands. You'd own everything of mine if I died."

The words so casually spoken made her stomach drop. "Don't say that."

"You always deserve the truth, *izar.*" He tucked a curl behind her ear.

"What does that word mean?"

"*Izar?*"

She nodded.

"Light. My light." He pressed his lips against her hair.

A sigh escaped her unbidden, and Nia closed her eyes.

After a while, he said, "You're not my captive, Nia. Not anymore."

Relief tangled with dread in her chest. She should have been happy to hear those words, but they created more questions than answers.

She couldn't trust anyone—except maybe the man holding her.

"Why do you go by Nia?"

A half-laugh puffed between her lips. "Wouldn't you if your name were Euphenia?"

"My full name is Macedenia, and I don't go by Nia."

Shocked, she spun around as much as she could. "Really? That's your full name?"

Humor crinkled his eyes. "No. Not really."

With a disgusted exhale, she turned around again. "Not funny."

"I thought it was a little funny."

She shook her head, then turned her head to meet his eyes again. "Why do I only hear one name for Tellusians? Never a last name?"

"Tellusians only use one name. Long ago, it was to have a bit of anonymity from the authorities. We've stuck with it all this time."

She faced forward again. It was strange to keep the tradition when genetic testing could identify anyone.

After a while, Mace cleared his throat. "When I first learned of your lineage, I did some research."

Tension climbed through her body. "What did you find?"

"Your father is Bret Jannex from *Jupiter One*. He's fifth in line for the Chancellorship, which makes you nineteenth."

Pressure continued to build in her chest. "You know more than I do. I've never kept track."

"And it was hard to find images of you," he continued. "You don't go to any of the events the rest of the ruling class seem to favor."

She didn't have an answer because it was true. She'd never enjoyed the opulence most ruling-class children took advantage of on a regular basis.

"It got me wondering why a ruling-class socialite served on a medical station during high conflict." He kept his tone mild. "I would have thought you'd be gearing up for an administrator position in the Lunar colonies."

Nia choked out a laugh. "You sound like my mother." Then she shook her head. "I wouldn't call myself a socialite. Politics isn't my thing. I became a doctor to help people, not to sit in a cushy chair behind a desk. That's what my mother wanted, not me."

His arms gave her a gentle squeeze, and she sank into his chest. When he didn't continue with his questions, she closed her eyes. Despite her sixteen-hour sleep, her mind needed to shut off. She dozed in and out of consciousness, between bad memories and fear for the future.

The front panel buzzed. Nia straightened to read the nav display. "That's a CORE outpost."

"I know the person in charge," Mace said against her temple. "And I'm hoping they'll be able to help. I need to send you home, Nia."

Her stomach dropped. The words should have comforted her. Thoughts of home were the only things that kept her sane these past weeks... the only thing she'd wanted.

But after what had happened on the Guardian, she didn't feel like the CORE was the safety net it once was. Those two men had *tortured* her when she'd already been forced to speak the truth.

Her tension didn't ease as they neared the distinctive design of a deep space outpost, its conical shape bulging in the middle. Mace didn't signal the station but flew underneath beside a docked shuttle. The outpost was too small for a shuttle bay but had docking clamps. The clamps grabbed on with a *thud*, and a moment later, a docking tube descended to the canopy, the stars disappearing from sight.

The tube sealed, and as soon as the fighter showed a stable connection, Mace retracted the canopy. A ladder descended.

Mace lifted her by her hips. "Climb on up."

As soon as she entered the narrow construct of the tube, Mace elevated her so her foot could catch on the lowest rung. The memory of what had happened in the emergency shaft on *Orion* swept through her. Panic squeezed her chest. She heard the screams again, the thumping of bodies hitting one another as they fell. She couldn't move. Her breath wedged in her throat.

Then Mace was there, his arm wrapping around her hips, face pressed into her lower back. "I've got you." His body heat settled her. "One foot in front of the other."

Swallowing around the asteroid in her throat, she did as he said, concentrating on the next rung, pushing the screams out of her head.

It seemed a long time before she emerged through the docking hatch and caught sight of two pairs of standard-issue CORE boots.

"I'm right behind you," Mace encouraged from below.

Nia pressed her elbows on the deck. Strong hands grabbed her upper arms, lifting her and settling her on her feet.

A man and a woman regarded her with puzzled expressions, each wearing the beige and white of CORE science officers. Both tall and lean, the man sported a goatee, while the woman's straight black hair brushed her shoulders. Intelligence sparkled in her angular eyes, mixing with her confusion.

When Mace's head became visible out of the docking tube, the woman let out a whoop, her face exploding into a dazzling smile. As soon as he got to his feet, she threw her arms around him in an enormous hug.

"I can't believe you're here." Her Common accent hailed from the Lunar colonies, unlike Nia's Jovian one. The woman stepped back, holding Mace at arm's length, a frown puckering her brow. "Why are you here? You wouldn't be in a Condor unless something bad happened."

"They've taken *Orion*," Mace said, voice hard.

The woman gasped and paled. The man beside her stepped close to place a hand on her shoulder, but his eyes were on Nia.

"How?" the woman whispered, hand covering her mouth, and Nia realized they both wore PALMs. It seemed so strange to see them now. So unnecessary.

Mace shook his head. "We'll get into that later. First." He took Nia's hand and pulled her closer. "I want you to meet Nia. Nia, this is my sister, Lexi."

His sister. Once he said it, Nia could see the similarities in their features and coloring. "I'm pleased to meet you," she said, giving her a nod and slight bow of greeting as anyone CORE would.

The pair in front of them froze. "You're CORE," Lexi murmured, then returned her gaze to her brother. "Why? What's she doing here? What's going on?" A Tellusian accent started to emerge in her words.

Reflexively, Nia touched her wrists where her bonds used to be, instinctively trying to hide them from sight before she remembered they had been removed. Both scientists in front of her tracked the action.

Lexi's expression turned horrified. "No. Mace. Say you didn't."

Mace stepped close behind Nia, his hand on the small of her back. "I won't get into it right now."

His sister's mouth opened and closed like she couldn't get words out, then she closed her eyes briefly before turning to the man beside her. "This is Justice, my colleague."

Justice nodded to both of them, holding himself respectfully, but Nia became aware of how he stared at her, his piercing eyes making her uncomfortable.

"When's your next scheduled maintenance?" Mace asked.

"Two days," Justice answered, his tone hinting at anger. "And I don't think I need to tell you what would happen if you're found here."

"It's terrible timing," Lexi said, taking a step closer to Justice. "The worst, really."

"Because of what you're working on?" Mace asked.

She gave him a nod. "We'll discuss more. You two look tired." She jerked her head to the right. "This way. I'll show you some quarters."

They followed her up the ramp, over the top of a green space that contrasted with the beige and black glossy surfaces of the outpost's construction. The lack of gray metal composite was startling, unnatural. They stepped into a circular lab, and Nia examined the assorted equipment, wondering what they were doing out this far.

Lexi kept walking, navigating the circumference of the outpost, until they reached the habitat level. "There's only one extra room," she said, stopping at the third door.

She gave Mace another hug, but the frown never left her face. "It is good to see you, even under the circumstances." She pulled away. "We'll talk when you're ready. But don't take too long."

Mace nodded. "I owe you one."

"I know." A small smile played on her lips, then her eyes flicked to Nia, and it disappeared.

Nia's stomach churned. *I'm not welcome here.* Whatever safe haven Mace thought they would find, he was wrong. Her presence put both scientists on edge so much that she wanted to leave.

Chapter Thirty-Three

Their temporary quarters were designed the same as those Nia had on *Elara Five*. A surreal sensation wrapped around her as she stopped in the middle of the room. She placed a hand against her stomach to ground herself. Built only for one, it had a narrow bed, a washroom with a steam shower, a table built into the bulkhead, and a handful of wall compartments stacked on top of each other.

She jumped when Mace's hands settled on her shoulders. A gentle tug, and the small of her back pressed against his abdomen. She relaxed into the hold.

"How are you doing?" he asked, voice rumbling through her body, hands skimming her arms to take hold of her elbows.

She leaned her head against him and closed her eyes, reveling in the tingles running through her scalp at his touch. So much had happened since she'd woken this morning in his arms. Her brain couldn't process it all.

"Nia?"

"I need a steam." It was one thing she could focus on. After spending hours in a fighter, she could smell herself without lifting her arms. But she didn't move, didn't want to separate from him. Mace was the only solid thing in her life right now, and she clung to the sensation. Her sanity depended on it.

"I could use one too," he agreed. His hands skimmed to her shoulders and cupped the sides of her throat.

Shivers spread through her body, settling into the base of her spine and bottom. She closed her eyes, remembering how it had felt to have him wash her after they'd had sex the first time, how no one had ever taken care of her like that before. She hadn't been able to move, or react, or speak, just drowned herself in the experience.

Maybe she should return the favor. He'd saved her from Forna and Slattery when he could have left her there to save himself.

He could have left her on *Orion* to die, but he cared enough to find her.

Turning in his arms, she placed her hands flat against his chest. "Let's go then." With a shift of her body, she got him moving backward to the washroom. It was smaller than his on *Orion,* no way for both of them to fit.

Not allowing her plans to be thwarted, she began to undress him outside the doors.

"Nia?" he asked when she slid the zipper of his uniform down his ribs.

"Yes?" She slid her hands beneath the material and slipped it from his shoulders.

"What are you doing?" His top puddled around his feet with a light *thwap.* Despite having asked the question, he didn't move.

"Undressing you." She moved her fingers to the zipper at the front of his pants.

"Lexi told us not to take too long."

"Okay." Since their first encounter might have been the fastest fuck she'd ever had, she didn't think they'd have a problem with speed. It had also been the most mind-blowing fuck she'd ever had, quick or not.

It was more than fucking. That's what he'd said on the way here. She agreed with him but couldn't say *why* it was more.

Guiding his pants lower, she licked her lips when his cock bobbed in front of her face, hard and ready. She looked up at him from her stooped position. Heat flooded her abdomen at his expression, his eyes hooded. She broke eye contact only long enough to undo the fastenings of his boots.

He stepped out of his boots and pants, and her fingers twitched to grab him. Instead, she settled her hands on his hips and pushed him the rest of the way into the shower.

"Max pressure. Medium temp," she said, when she realized there were no controls on the bulkhead.

Steam rushed in around them. She took a moment to undress. Mace kept his eyes on her, and she couldn't look away as the steam billowed, the scent of soap swirling out the open door.

He was beautiful. He was dangerous. He threatened. He protected. What had once scared her drew her near.

Naked now, she stepped inside. His black hair, heavy from the moisture, hung in strands around his face. Slinking close, but not touching him, she pressed her hand to the dispensary, and CORE-issue soap foamed in her hand. She kept his gaze as she started with his shoulders, then chest, feeling each muscle, making sure he was thoroughly coated.

His eyes darkened the more she touched him. Her hands traveled lower, breaths leaving her lips in quick bursts. Everywhere she caressed, satiny skin covered muscles as hard as steel. Her fingers trailed through every dip and valley, loving the way he twitched beneath her touch.

She stepped closer still, her breasts brushing his abdominals as she stroked his back, then over his buttocks, which clenched beneath her fingers, to the crack of his ass.

"Nia," he said, his tone full of warning.

She liked the sound and smiled. Her fingers returned to his front, and she succumbed to the need to grab him.

A breath hissed from his lips. Then he groaned when she squeezed and stroked. The sounds he made fueled the fire burning between her legs, spreading heat across her skin.

He moved, and she thought he was going to touch her, but he braced his hands on either side of her head.

She dropped low and took him in her mouth. A string of curses left his lips as she sucked and played, squeezing his balls with her free hand, and reveling in the way his body shook. Steam swelled. The grooves in the tile pressed into her knees. The swirling blue ink of his tattoo mesmerized as the muscles of his abdomen shifted and jerked. She took him to the back of her throat again and again.

Velvet and steel filled her mouth, but the sounds of his pleasure filled her heart. After everything, she wanted him to feel good, to explode with pleasure. She wanted to push him to the brink and beyond.

His breath became erratic, his movements unsteady. Tension climbed through his body, and she squeezed his sack. The roar that followed reverberated through her body. He unloaded in her mouth, and she drank every last salty bit of him. His continuing gasps echoed off the bulkheads until he grabbed her shoulders and hauled her roughly to her feet, wrapping his arms around her.

"I'm starving for you," he growled in her ear.

Then she was moving, her feet lifting off the deck as he took her into the main space.

"End!" she shouted at the bathroom so they wouldn't waste the outpost's resources. Her damp curls stuck to her cheeks.

Each of his hands gripping her thighs, he spread her wide as he tumbled her onto the bed, then buried his face between her legs. Lapping, licking, he left no place untouched by the scorching heat of his tongue. All thought left her head. His tongue circled her clit, driving her higher. He ate at her like he hadn't had a meal in years.

Hands keeping her legs locked in place, he thrust his tongue inside her. A moan ripped past her lips as she tilted her hips back and forth, banging her shoulders against the smooth bulkhead.

A long lick from taint to cleft, then he focused all his attention on her clit, giving light licks one on top of another. She grabbed his hair with both hands, holding him in place, making sure he wouldn't stop. The heat inside her built. A flush swept through her body. Her orgasm trundled toward her.

Fingernails digging into his scalp, she held on for dear life. Until the dam broke, and she couldn't think anymore.

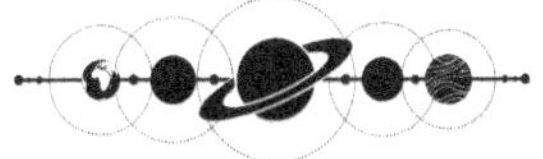

Every touch made his heart crack more. This could be their last time together. He would send her home. Lexi would help. Nia would be safe with her family.

The thoughts kept looping in his head, making every second precious.

With her hands biting into his hair, Nia's body quivered with her orgasm. He brushed his nose into the curls crowning her pussy and inhaled. *Fucking amazing.* He would never get enough of her taste and would never have the chance to try.

His heart twisting, he lifted his head and absorbed her satisfied expression. Spread wide for him, glistening—he didn't think his cock could get harder. He ran his hands over her stomach, arms, breasts, her soft skin tickling his palms.

Scooping her up, he sat on the edge of the bed and settled her over him with her legs straddling his hips. She draped over him, limbs loose and pliable. He cradled her face in his hands. She met his gaze, eyes glazed in pleasure, and her lips parted. With a groan, he took her mouth with his own, swept his tongue inside. Sharing her scent was a new level of erotic.

Her tongue stoked his, becoming more insistent, demanding. She bit his lower lip, and he moaned. The blazing heat of her pussy hovered over his hardening erection. He adjusted his position, his cock kissing her entrance, then trailed his hands downward until they kneaded her ass.

His lips keeping hers captive, he lowered her onto him. They groaned together. She clenched her walls and rolled her pelvis, taking him deeper. Breaking their kiss with a moan, he leaned forward and pressed his face into her neck, inhaling her fragrance.

They settled together, not moving, experiencing each other in a way they hadn't the first time. He lifted his head to see her face. Russet eyes shone at him, full of wonder and passion.

She rotated her hips, hands stroking his shoulders, and a spear of pleasure shot through the chest. She chose the pace. He met her soft movements with ones equally gentle.

His lips brushed across brow, traversing her cheek to nip at her ear. Leaning forward, he licked her collarbone, his tongue leaving a moist trail. Lower he laved, until she leaned back and he could take her perfect nipple in his mouth. He swirled the hardened nub, loving the catch of her breaths. He took a biting nibble. Her moan made him thrust harder. Then he tongued lower, scraping his teeth along the underside of her breast.

He paid equal attention to her other breast, and her movements became frantic. Taking hold of her hips, he increased their pace. Her face flushed, and her lips parted as he plunged into her again and again. Tilting her head back, she closed her eyes.

So beautiful. "I want to watch you when you come, *izar*. I want to see your eyes."

Her eyelids flickered, and she met his gaze. Licking her lips, she trailed her fingers over his chest, toying with his nipples, lightly grazing the skin of his abdomen. Nia squeezed her knees against his hips, pushing, demanding he go deeper.

Every time he plunged inside her, the pleasure escalated. Mace watched the blossoming flush of her cheeks and throat as he continued to pump his cock. She held his face in her hands and kissed him, her tongue rubbing his in and out, mimicking the movement of his cock inside her.

Her breathing shortened as she pulled away. He watched her climax build, his balls tightening. She grabbed his shoulders and arched her back. A primal groan wrenched from her chest. Her eyes keeping his, she clenched around him. Her body jerked forward, fingernails digging in as her whole body convulsed.

Mace couldn't hold back. His orgasm rose from the base of his spine and exploded into his brain. One more deep thrust and his cock emptied inside her, her tight walls wringing every shiver out of him.

She collapsed forward, arms wrapping around his head, face buried in his throat. He leaned against the bulkhead, taking her with him. Their rapid exhales mingled.

Mace squeezed her to him, inhaling the sweet and salty fragrance of her skin, then brushed her curls away from her face to kiss her. Her mouth opened, her tongue stroking his, her thighs clenching his hips. She pulled away, fingers on his cheeks, and gave his bottom lip one last nip.

His chest squeezed so tight that it hurt. Everything about her was perfect.

How was he supposed to let her go?

Chapter Thirty-Four

The door to their temporary quarters shut, blocking Mace's view of Nia sleeping on the narrow bed, naked except for the thin, CORE-issue blanket covering her body.

He stood there a moment, staring at the blank beige of the door, his body tense and his mind racing. There was a large part of him that wanted to say *fuck you* to the universe, to steal Nia away from both the CORE and Tellusians, to screw responsibility. For it just to be the two of them, together, where politics and lineage didn't matter.

But common sense intruded. Where would they go? They were still too far away from anything Tellusian to use the Condor for the journey. The outpost's shuttle would have even less range. There was no place in CORE territory that would be safe for him, and no place in Tellusian territory that would be safe for her after what she'd confessed. And traveling to Calypson territory... they might as well commit suicide if that were their only option.

With the weight of everything pressing down on him like a thousand asteroids, he'd held Nia for as long as he could, for as long as he thought he could get away with, before his sister would pound on their door demanding answers.

Swallowing, he turned away and started down the ramp. On the lab level, Lexi stood at a terminal, one arm braced above her head, her black hair swooped over her shoulder. She lifted her head when he neared. Eyes narrowing, she straightened, then strode to meet him at the bottom of the ramp.

He spoke before she could. "I need to get Nia to a safe CORE location as quickly as possible."

Lexi released a laugh tinged with hysteria. "Are you out of your ever-loving mind? We don't have the time or resources to coordinate a soft re-entry for her, not with the maintenance crew arriving in thirty hours."

Panic squeezed his chest. He needed to get Nia to safety. With her possible participation in *Orion's* seizure, unintentional or not, she wouldn't be safe in the Tellusian fleet.

He settled his hands on her shoulders. "It needs to be done."

"That may be so, but not from here." She shrugged off his hands and took a step back. "You've got to know it's a mistake to let her go. She's seen this place, met us, she'll sell us all out."

"She won't."

"She might not want to, but they'll get her to talk whether she loves you or not."

His chest squeezed tight, and he swallowed. "That's why I need her to get to her family first."

Lexi shook her head. "I can't believe you put us in this situation." She didn't raise her voice, but it sounded like she wanted to.

"I didn't have a choice."

"Explain," she demanded, crossing her arms over her chest.

Mace paced in front of her. "We didn't make the first rendezvous to receive the coordinates for the second. The Condor we stole wasn't fully charged. If I hadn't come here, then we'd be adrift right now, at the mercy of anyone who came upon us."

Her expression softened, arms dropping to her sides. "Why didn't you make the rendezvous?" She jerked her head toward the sitting area next to the lab.

They walked side by side. "We were picked up by a Guardian."

Her head whipped to him on a sharp inhale, the color leached from her face. "A Guardian? How did you escape?"

They settled opposite each other on a U-shaped sofa. "I overpowered the four guards they sent with me to the brig. They'd thought I'd been stunned. Then I found Nia in a lab." He shook his head, a hard lump growing in his throat. "I heard her screams across the whole deck. They'd been torturing her mentally." He hung his head. "She won't talk about it."

Lexi's hand covered his. "I'm sorry she went through that, but it doesn't change the fact that having you here, especially her, is extremely dangerous."

He couldn't deny it, but if there'd been an alternative, he would have taken it. "I need to make contact with the fleet as soon as possible and couldn't do it from a Condor."

But Lexi was already shaking her head. "It's too risky. I wasn't going to deliver my latest report until we took leave in two weeks' time. Anything sent from here can be retraced. I can't jeopardize our position like that. Not now."

Her gaze moved over his shoulder, and Mace turned to see Justice walking toward them. Something about the man put him on edge—and it wasn't because it was clear he and Lexi had some sort of relationship.

"How was *Orion* taken?" Lexi asked, recalling his attention when Justice sat beside her.

"It was an inside job," Mace said after a moment. "Well-planned, with multiple people working together, or they would never have been able to pull it off." Nia's confession came back to him, and he wondered again if she'd played an unintentional role. "All four engine cores were blown, power diverted, shields disabled—" He shook his head in disbelief. Saying it aloud highlighted how enormous the undertaking was. How many traitors would it have taken to co-ordinate? *Too many.* "And two Guardians waiting to swoop in. They detonated a massive portion of the minefield to get through. We'll have no foothold in the sector from now on."

The nauseated expressions on the pair's faces matched the feeling inside Mace's stomach. He and Lexi had been born and raised on *Orion*—and now their home was in the hands of the CORE.

Mace cleared his throat. "What would you have sent in the next data stream?"

The question snapped Lexi from wherever her mind had gone, and she cast a quick glance at Justice. "They have us working on something huge. Big enough they're being cautious, not allowing us to see the complete picture. I was going to send you our new research and experiments. Maybe your experts could piece it together with other data you've attained."

"Is it bio-weapon related?"

Lexi perked up. "How did you know?"

"Because of what we recently found on a smuggler's ship." He described the weapon Cache had shown her commanders.

Brow furrowing, Lexi turned to Justice. "It could be connected."

Justice rubbed his goatee, leaning back in his chair. "Possibly. I'd always thought we were working on something larger than a hand-held gun, a weapon built for a ship's systems, but anything is possible when we've been kept in the dark about so much of this project."

"What more can you tell me about it?" Mace asked.

"It's genetic-based," Lexi explained. "We're isolating markers that differentiate between races."

A cold sensation washed over him. "The payload would be able to tell the difference between a CORE soldier and a Tellusian warrior? Kill one and not the other?"

Lexi scowled. "In short, yes. But there are more similarities between us than the CORE would want us to believe. It could also focus on the differences between someone CORE and someone Calypson. That's why I was going to send the information sooner than our usual check-in date."

"I can take it with me and save you the trouble."

She let out a short laugh, but she wasn't smiling. "Don't think this absolves you of your transgressions."

"What transgressions?" The question was reflexive, defiant in the face of his older sister's censure.

Lexi's eyes darkened to the point where if she'd been holding a gun, Mace was sure she would've shot him. "What transgressions?" she repeated through clenched jaws. "Mace. What the hell is wrong with you? If Mom were alive, she'd put a knife to your throat herself. You took a captive. You fucked a captive. You brought your captive *here* and fucked her again, when you know you shouldn't even trust her. Please tell me what part of that *isn't* a problem!"

Mace clenched his teeth, battling the discomfort her words created. He didn't ask how she'd known he and Nia had been intimate before arriving here. His sister knew him too well.

On a slow exhale, Lexi's eyes flicked to the level above, her expression shuttering.

Unease swirling in his chest, Mace turned to find Nia there, her hands gripping the railing so tightly her knuckles were white, and realized Lexi had shouted everything in Common.

Nia's heart beat a wounded rhythm in her chest, her cheeks burning like lava. She knew she wasn't welcome here, but to hear those things shouted about her made her wish the deck would swallow her whole. Her fingers ached where she clutched the railing.

Mace stood, and still Nia couldn't move. Behind him, Lexi glared at her brother with her arms crossed over her chest.

Straightening her spine, Nia pushed away from the railing. She wouldn't hide. She wouldn't cower. If it had been up to her, she would have remained on *Elara Five*, the station unharmed from Tellusian attack, and she would have known none of this life.

The thought panged something strange in her chest. If she'd remained on *Elara Five*, she would be doing the same thing each day, every day. *Wake up. Work. Stimulants. Superficial relationships. Sleeping aids. Repeat.*

Even though she'd seen and experienced horrific things over the past month, she'd never felt so alive.

Her eyes followed Mace as he walked up the ramp to her. He was the one who breathed the most life into her. Whether she wanted to attack him or devour him, he was the one person who set flame to the buried spark in her chest.

Stopping in front of her, he took her hand. "She's angry with me, not you."

Nia shook her head. Her feelings weren't important, and Lexi was right. No one here should trust her. Look at what she had spilled as soon as those nanos had taken residence.

He tugged on her fingers. "Let's get you something to eat."

When her stomach answered with a growl, his eyes crinkled into a smile. He led her down the ramp, past where Justice and Lexi sat, to the dispensary beyond.

"Veggie pasta number three isn't bad," Lexi said over her shoulder, words clipped.

Nia cast her a glance, and the other woman's glare softened into a resigned expression.

Mace ordered two servings and took them to the nearby table. While they ate, Nia couldn't help but overhear the conversation between the other couple.

"We can hide them until the maintenance crew leaves," Justice said, his tone rational.

"You know it won't work. The crew always scans. They would be found within ten minutes. And how would we hide the fighter?"

"The Condor won't make it to Saturn or another Tellusian settlement on one charge," Justice countered.

There was a beat of silence, then Lexi asked, "What do you suggest?"

"We can send Mace's message through the new encryption program. I know we haven't tested it yet," Justice added quickly, "but we don't have a lot of other options. This way, at least they'll have a heading."

Nia flicked her gaze to Mace, who was listening as intently as she was. Swallowing his mouthful of food, he turned to meet his sister's eyes.

Lexi squinted at him. "You can make your long-distance communication. We have an encryption we'll bounce through about fifty hubs before it reaches your destination, hopefully keeping us in the clear."

"That sounds like it'll take time."

"It's a downside, but safer." Slapping her thighs, she stood. "Which means we should do it now, or you won't receive a response before we need to throw you out." With her lips pressed together, she led the way to a terminal on the far side of the lab, Mace following.

Nia watched for a moment, then focused on the man still sitting on the couch. Justice stared at her... strangely, his face expressionless, but his eyes full of calculation. A shiver of apprehension raced down her spine.

"It sounds like you've had quite a journey," he said after a time.

She cleared her throat. "You could say that." Not wanting to talk more, she stared at her meal and tried to finish.

But after the Tellusian food she'd eaten, it tasted like bio-matter in her mouth.

Chapter Thirty-Five

L exi grumbled the whole time they used the long-distant lascom to send Mace's message. He kept the communique short, using encoded information to verify his identity and guarantee the message wasn't being sent under coercion—a precaution both Grey and Cache would expect. Mace counted on at least one of them receiving it. His chest pinched. If neither of them had survived the siege, he didn't know what he would do.

When the message was finally sent, he took hold of Lexi's elbow and turned her toward him. "I wouldn't have come here if I'd had alternatives."

"I know." She exhaled a long breath. "I *do* understand that. And I wouldn't want the pair of you drifting and running out of air. But with everything..." Her voice trailed off, a grimace marring her features.

"It's the bio-weapon stuff, isn't it? It's got you on edge."

She threw her hands in the air. "How can it not? I wake up in cold sweats, wondering what the hell we're doing out here, if there's even a purpose to it all anymore. I think, 'What if we destroy it all?'" A mirthless laugh shuddered through her. "But there's no point. The information won't be lost. They'll have backups. And we're replaceable. Another CORE outpost would be built. Another batch of CORE scientists would take our place. And if we're not here, then Tellusians become uninformed. I know we save lives." Fingers twisted together, she hung her head. "But I've been here so long, I sometimes forget I'm Tellusian."

"Ah, Lex." Mace wrapped his arm around her neck and pulled her close, his cheek pressed to her hair. Against her ear, he spoke his next words in Tellusian. "Your courage inspires the stars."

A small sob left her, then she straightened quickly, shrugging off his arm. "You're so sentimental." Turning to the terminal, she tapped on the glossy surface.

He grinned at the deflection, then became serious. "It's time for you to come home."

Her fingers slowed.

"You've done your duty," he continued. "Don't let Cache or anyone else convince you differently. You finish the time you've promised here, and that's it. You're done."

Mace thought she would refuse and insist she was handling it, but she surprised him when she swallowed and agreed with a nod.

Tension eased from his spine. His big sister would come home. Even if *Orion* was lost, she'd return to Tellusian territory, to safety. She'd endangered herself for far too long, neglecting her own happiness. He couldn't begrudge her whatever contentment she'd found with her colleague.

Lexi cleared her throat and refocused on the terminal. "I'm going to download everything from our last months here for Cache. The Condor should be able to hold a file that size."

Leaning a hip against the terminal, Mace watched her work. After a while, Nia joined him, and he pulled her into his embrace. His sister shot her a glance, but otherwise didn't stoop to her earlier hostility.

It took three hours, but they received a response, Grey's ID embedded in the code. Relief that his friend had made it to the rendezvous lightened more of the load on his shoulders. But what of Cache? The message was a set of coordinates, but it would have been foolish to expect anything else. It gave them a target.

Then there was nothing left to do except say goodbye.

Standing in the docking hatch, Lexi embraced him, wrapping her arms tightly. "You be careful." She pulled back and stared at Nia for a beat before hugging her too. "You take care of each other."

Over Lexi's shoulder, Nia's eyes widened in surprise. Lexi's temper ran hot, but forgiveness always followed. Amusement flickered through him when she patted Lexi's shoulder awkwardly before his sister released her. Cheeks pink, Nia stepped away and tucked a stray curl behind her ear.

Justice moved into his line of sight, extending a hand. Mace grasped his forearm in the Tellusian way.

"Your engine coil is fully charged," Justice said. "Be well."

"Thank you." Mace nodded. "Same to you."

After a self-conscious wave, Nia climbed down the docking tube ahead of him. With one last nod to both scientists, Mace followed. He slid in behind Nia, and she shifted forward to accommodate his size.

"Stay safe, brother," Lexi murmured above them, the sound echoing before she locked the docking hatch.

Powering the Condor's engines, a sense of unease grew inside him, along with the need to tell his sister to come with them, to fly the shuttle to the fleet and leave this place for good right now instead of waiting. He had nothing to substantiate the feeling, but it buzzed beneath his skin all the same.

They separated from the outpost with *clink clank* and accelerated away. The farther they flew, the more Mace's stomach churned. He couldn't put his finger on why he was so on edge.

They traveled a long while in silence, Nia shifting and turning, trying to get comfortable in front of him.

When he settled a hand on her hip to keep her still, she huffed out a breath. "How long will it take to get to the rendezvous?"

He touched the panel. "About eight hours."

Another heavy breath left her as she settled more fully against him, leaning her head onto his shoulder. With nothing to break the monotony of space flight, he thought she dozed off, but she asked, "Can you teach me to fly?"

He tilted his head, and his cock twitched. "Is that a euphemism?" Though it would be virtually impossible to have sex in such a small space.

Slowly, she turned until she met his gaze, her eyebrow raised, lips pursed. "Not a euphemism. I want you to teach me how to pilot this thing."

"Now?"

"Do you have somewhere else you need to be?"

His lips twitched. "No, I guess not."

"Well, then." She gestured to the controls.

Affection lightening his heart, and since he couldn't think of a good excuse not to, he began to teach her the basics. He started with pre-flight checks and how to initiate the engines. Then how to see if there was a full charge and how to engage the shields. Nia caught on quickly, and before he knew it, he let her take the controls.

She put them in a spin.

"Wow, that was harder than I thought," she said with a hand to her stomach once he'd righted their position. "You make it look so easy."

"I was ten when I took the controls of my first ship. I've had a bit more experience than you." He kissed her neck.

She tilted her head to give him better access. "How many different ships can you fly?" His lips tasted the skin of her throat. "I mean, I've seen you in what, three so far? Or are they all similar?"

"No." He pulled away slightly. "They're all different, especially between the CORE and Tellusian ones. But I haven't been in a ship I couldn't fly, even if I've never seen it before." He shrugged.

She captured his gaze over her shoulder. "So you could fly a Guardian? Or a Destroyer?" she asked, tone disgruntled.

He smiled, kissing the side of her brow, smoothing its lines. "If I had to, but there has to be more than one person on the bridge. They have many systems working in tandem."

She turned back to face the front. "My stomach feels better now. I'd like to try again."

"Keep your eye on your thrust balance. If one is firing hotter than any other, we'll spin again."

"Got it."

He gave her the controls. This time she kept them steady. After a few minutes, she developed a feel for the craft and had them banking in turns. *Quick study.* It sometimes took tyros weeks to achieve the same success.

"The tricky bit is navigation," he said, lifting her hair for another kiss and inhaling deep.

"Is this how you teach all your students?" He heard the smile in her voice. "With reward kisses?"

"Yep."

She shook her head. "Why is navigation tricky? Don't you use the nav system?"

"Yes, but you can't take it for granted. If it fails for any reason and you're out too far, far enough the sun looks like another star, and you can't chart on your own, you're fucked. You could fly out of the system instead of where you want to go."

"I've never considered that. Guess I'll be studying my orbital parameters."

Mace displayed their current position on the viewer and waited, letting her read the information on her own.

She stiffened. "Doesn't that mean we're in Calypson territory right now?" she asked, voice tight.

"Yes, but only on the edge. They won't bother us."

She looked out the viewer, like she could see the Calypson nebula so far away with her own eyes. "How can you be so sure?"

"Experience."

The first time he'd cut through their territory as a kid to avoid a CORE patrol was a day he'd never forget. He was so sure they'd follow him and suck his brains out—or whatever they did to change people—he didn't go home for an extra two days. But they hadn't pursued him then or any time after when he needed to shoot across their territory in extreme circumstances.

The front panel blinked. Dread filled him, and he took the controls from Nia.

"What's that?" she asked.

"A communique from my sister's outpost."

If she was breaking comm silence, it meant something bad had happened.

Mace touched the controls, and his sister's image filled the screen. An angry red mark colored her cheek, the imprint of fingers visible. Her eyes were puffy from crying.

"Justice!" he roared. He was going to cut the man's balls off and feed them to him. Then beat the shit out of him until he was nothing but a puddle of blood.

"He's gone," Lexi said with a sob.

"What happened?" Nia's softly spoken question broke through the haze of Mace's rage, making him focus.

"I overheard his communique with the CORE. He's an agent, Mace. All this time, and I had no idea. I'm a blasted idiot. He played me from the start." Her learned CORE accent disappeared in her upset. "He thought he knocked me out, but I was able to tag the shuttle. Sending you the marker now."

This was his fault. He'd done this. Their arrival had spurred whatever Justice had planned, whatever his reason for being at the outpost.

Mace adjusted the controls. "We're coming back for you."

"Don't!" Lexi almost stood when she said it, then sat in her chair. "A Guardian is almost here. He must have signaled it as soon as you arrived. You'll be captured too if you return. I wouldn't fit in the fighter, anyway." Her voice broke.

"I'm not leaving you to the mercy of those people," he said between his teeth, his clenched jaw throbbing.

"You're going to have to, little brother. Your mission ahead is bigger than me. You free *Orion*." She ran a shaky hand over the mark on her face. "Everything you sent and received from Grey will be compromised. I'm sending you and him alternative rendezvous coordinates now."

"Lex," he whispered, impotent with the need to help her. The coordinates came through, and he changed trajectory.

She jumped, then looked behind her. "They're here. Take care of yourself, Mace. I love you. Don't come after me."

The feed went black.

"No!" he yelled, the sound ripped from the deepest part of him. Fingers digging into the sides of his seat, he tried to tear it apart with his bare hands.

Nia turned her body until her face rested against his chest, fingers clutching his shirt.

He took gasping breaths. If he thought about what would happen to Lexi, he would implode.

"I think I'm going to be sick." Nia clutched his shirt tighter. "I'm so sorry."

His big sister.

Mace couldn't stop his silent tears.

Chapter Thirty-Six

With the Tellusian fleet in sight, Nia's heart pumped an anxious rhythm in her chest. The sight of two Destroyers, their armaments glinting in the light cast by the other smaller ships around them, made her stomach clench in a tight knot, adding to her nausea.

Lexi. Oh no, Lexi.

She couldn't get the sight of Lexi's bruised face out of her head. Her stomach threatened to empty itself. Would Lexi be suffering like she had with those mind moles? Would her throat be raw with screams? Could something worse be happening to her?

Nia couldn't stop the morbid cycle of her thoughts.

She and Mace hadn't spoken as they'd traveled to the new coordinates Lexi had sent. Those were some of the longest hours of her life.

Panic had clawed at her as they'd waited for some sort of communique. Thoughts of all the ways they would suffer if stranded in deep space bombarded her. Running out of food, air, freezing to death—it became a never-ending loop of doom.

When Grey finally got in touch, she'd never been more relieved.

With the Tellusian fleet in sight, each of the smaller ships became more distinct as they neared.

"That's a CORE freighter," she murmured, leaning forward. "How would you get one of those?"

"We have our ways," Mace said, voice flat and his body rigid. His hands moved over the controls, then his vambrace.

Every part of her ached for him. Her battle-ready warrior could do nothing for his sister, and he'd only had time to think about it on their journey here.

"This is what's going to happen," said Mace as he drew nearer to the one Destroyer, his arms tight against her shoulders and his voice soft in her ear. "I'm not bringing you aboard officially. We'll get you emancipated, then you'll stay out of sight until I can get you on a transport. Understand?"

She nodded, her throat too tight to speak. After all her insisting she wanted to go home, his words stabbed her heart.

Mace circled around one Destroyer and flew the Condor into the starboard aft hangar, passing through its shielding with a sizzle. Shuttles, fighters, and smaller transports lined the deck and inner bulkheads. Once between two shuttles at the rear of the hangar, Mace lowered their ship.

Two warriors stood by, both looking about as deadly as anyone could in a casual way. The fighter's hum disappeared to nothing as Mace powered down, then the canopy opened. Besides a few maintenance workers, the hangar was quiet.

Hands on her hips, Mace lifted her over the edge. Glad to get out of the cramped fighter, Nia climbed out and descended the retracting ladder.

Her feet hit the deck with a satisfying *thud*. She turned, eyeing the two warriors.

The one on the left, tall and lanky, wore dark glasses that concealed his eyes. Tattoos wrapped around his neck. The other warrior was shorter and stocky. A wicked scar sliced downward into his eye socket.

How could he have survived such a wound?

The one with the glasses raised his eyebrows at her frown, and the other stared at her with an assessing gaze. Once Mace joined her on the deck, they stepped forward to embrace his forearm in turn.

Mace spoke in Tellusian, his eyes sliding to her before he stepped closer and ran a hand down her spine. She leaned into him.

"Everything is arranged," Mace said to her in Common. "We need to take you to processing."

Her heart leaped at the word. He must have seen the trepidation on her face, because he added, "It's where we need to go to emancipate you officially. I want there to be no question you are free if someone were to happen upon you before you get on a transport."

She nodded even though her stomach clenched and churned at the thought of leaving.

Mace tipped his head to the two men in front of them. "This is Spiro," he said, indicating the one with the dark glasses, who gave her a nod. "And Betel." The other man only grunted. "You can trust them." He turned to his friends. "Did Cache survive? Did she pick up the shuttle my sister tagged?"

"Cache is still kicking," Spiro said. "We know nothing about a shuttle."

"Who's planning the offensive?" Mace asked.

"Admiral Krispin," Betel answered, his voice coming out like a scratchy bark.

"Good. There isn't another I'd trust more with my life. What about the tyros? How are they doing?"

"Recovering," Spiro answered, his mouth grim. "They weren't ready for battle."

"No," Mace agreed.

Nia swallowed, remembering the young ages of Mace's trainees.

"What of Lexi?" Spiro asked.

Tension snapped through his body. "A Guardian picked her up."

Betel growled at the same time as Spiro cursed in Tellusian, making her jump. Mace gave her a reassuring squeeze on her shoulder.

"We won't rest until we get her back," Mace said, his voice harder than she'd ever heard it.

The other two nodded their agreement.

"Let's go," he said to Nia, sliding his hand to her hip. She tucked herself into his side and headed out of the hangar.

Everything was quiet as they stepped into the corridor, the lighting dimmer for nighttime hours. They traveled in a strange formation, Mace at her side with Spiro in the front and Betel at the rear—like all three of them expected trouble on their own ship.

They didn't encounter any as they took a lift downward. With Mace at her back and the other two in front, the lift felt incredibly small.

Processing had the same feel as it did on *Orion*, sterile and impersonal, a medicinal scent hovering over everything. A shiver of apprehension tickled her spine when the processor, a woman with long brown hair, took them into one of the small rooms. Nia sat on one side of the table, the processor on the other. The three warriors behind her formed a formidable wall, and the processor kept glancing at them as she went through the emancipation procedure.

Every so often, like when the processor asked her about her missing bonds, Mace would bark a response in Tellusian back at her. The tension in the room kept escalating, the processor's expression more shuttered. Long minutes later, Nia was given a palette, a clean uniform marking her as a civilian, and an ID number attached to her one name.

It was over. She was free, a Tellusian citizen.

The processor scurried from the room as if it held a plague.

Standing, Nia turned and regarded the three warriors.

These were her people now. *Until I reach home.*

Swallowing the panicked feelings bubbling in her throat, Nia took Mace's hand when he offered it and followed the other two out. They traveled to another deck, then the pair who'd met them at the hangar gave Mace a nod before leaving them in front of a door.

"These are my assigned quarters," Mace said as he scanned his hand. "You'll be safe here until your transport."

The quarters were small, about the same size as the ones she'd had on *Elara Five*. There was one narrow bed, a refrigeration unit, and a desk-type table and chair affixed to the bulkhead on the other side.

Tugging on her fingers, Mace sat on the bed and pulled her between his legs. His hands stroked her arms when he spoke.

"Your transport leaves at oh-nine-hundred. Don't leave this room until then. Go straight to the hangar, board using your new ID. Keep your palette close. You'll need it to make your connections. Don't talk to anyone. They'll know your CORE right off from your accent, and they'll expect bonds, or for you to speak Tellusian. They'll test you if they're suspicious. And if you're put through the system again, the way I've gone about things to keep you safe, I don't think they'd bother to contact me. Don't get caught."

She licked her dry lips. "What do you mean? What things?"

"When you first arrived on *Orion*, your DNA was flagged as ruling class, and I had to pay to bury it." A haunted expression crossed his face. "I'm not proud of how my people treat captives, but I can't change it. Not overnight. You don't deserve any of this."

He pressed his face into her stomach, holding her close. "I couldn't have released you before, not safely. But if you keep your head down, this will work." He tipped his head to meet her eyes. "Betel contacted assets for your journey. Everything is set up on our end until you reach a hub closer to Jupiter. From there, you need to get to your family. No military. No administrators. Do you understand?"

She nodded, her throat so tight she couldn't even ask questions.

"I would send a warrior detail with you, but it would draw more attention. You need to do this as quietly as possible." His fingers squeezed her hips. "And when I leave here tonight, I won't be returning. We're going to take back *Orion*. This is our goodbye, Nia."

Fear for him, of his upcoming mission, assailed her. He'd disregarded his people's laws to see her free. She lifted her hands from his shoulders and sank them into his hair. Closing his eyes, he groaned and pulled her to him, his cheek against her sternum.

Tears pricked her eyes. This was it. Her last few hours with him. Then she'd never see him again.

How had her perspective changed so much in such a short time? How was the thought of leaving this man wounding her like no other pain in her life? How was the idea of returning home filling her with more apprehension than remaining with the people who were supposed to be her enemies?

Releasing a slow breath, she leaned away enough to take the hem of her shirt and pull it over her head. She cupped his face in her hands, the short growth of his facial hair tickling her palms.

"I need you," she whispered, throat tight, then kissed him with all the desperation climbing through her chest.

He moaned against her lips, tongue sweeping inside. She yanked at his uniform, fumbling with the zipper, relieved when he took over to reveal his gorgeous chest and arms. Wherever she touched, she tried to memorize every detail, to imprint the essence of him on her mind.

Frantic, they tore at each other's clothes until naked. They tumbled sideways onto the narrow bed, a tangle of limbs. Every place their skin made contact induced gasps, shivers pebbling her skin.

His touch never demanded, only coaxed and guided. These hands she'd seen kill handled her as if she were breakable. Every tender stroke made her heart ache.

Their lips drank from each other, the edge of desperation never diminishing. It only increased, but in a reverent way.

She would have almost rather this had been as wild as their first time—to ease the anguish overtaking her chest.

When he finally entered her, thick but gentle, tears leaked from her eyes.

He shifted their positions, rolling, until she was on top. Trying to make it last as long as possible, she rocked against him with subtle movements. She should run away from this man and every lethal part of him, but she couldn't. She loved him. With how everything started between them, it made little sense, but it was the truth.

The realization did nothing to ease her anguish. With a ragged moan, she rocked faster. Her fingernails bit into the skin of his chest. His hips met hers, but never pushed them over the edge of frantic.

Keeping their eyes locked, he cupped her breast, his fingertips toying with her nipples in light squeezes. Pleasure swirled through her, taking over her mind. She could only feel and stare, his icy eyes full of emotion, mesmerizing.

Her breaths became staccato, heat crawling up her spine. Pressure built inside her chest and stomach. He reached between them, thumbing her clit, and she came with a cry of surrender. Pleasure rushed through her, hot and tingly, then she collapsed forward, burying her face into his neck.

Fingers dug into her hips as he thrust, more aggressively now. His groan turned into a shout, body shaking, as he came inside her. She kept rocking against him, taking each one of his tremors, then bit his jugular gently.

With or without enhancers, she'd never experienced intimacy like this before, and doubted she would again. Forevermore, this man had changed her.

Their breathing leveled. Pulling out, he rolled, taking her with him until they cuddled front to front, her legs tucked between his. She lifted her chin to meet his gaze, and more tears pricked her eyes.

The way he looked at her... her throat constricted.

He kissed her forehead, her cheeks, then settled on her lips with the gentlest pressure before pulling away again. "For as long as I live," he whispered, his voice ragged, "I will never love another as I love you."

Her chest squeezed so tight she thought her heart shattered.

Chapter Thirty-Seven

Hand on Nia's jaw, he studied her sleeping features, memorizing them. How was he supposed to let her go?

But he had to. For both their sakes. She wasn't safe here.

Brushing his knuckles against her cheek, his hand moved lower, stroking her arms, then hip and spine, engraving her curves into his mind. She sighed, snuggling closer. His heart had never felt so full, or so broken at the same time.

When his vambrace beeped with a summons from Admiral Krispin, he knew their time had come to an end.

He couldn't move for the longest time, but knew if he didn't, he never would. The inner voice screaming for him to hold tight was the same one that had shouted for him to take her on *Elara Five*.

Gently, he disentangled their limbs, careful not to wake her. It would only make it harder. He'd said everything he could with his mouth and body over the past few hours, taking her twice more.

He tucked the blanket around her and kept his gaze averted as he dressed. If he didn't, he was liable to slide in next to her and make love to her one last time. His vambrace beeped again, spurring his movements.

It wasn't until he stood by the door that he took another moment to stare at her. Tucked securely in his bed, she looked like she belonged there. If only he could return after retaking *Orion* and find her in this exact same spot.

Throat tight, he touched the control to the door and stepped outside. It slid shut, blocking his view. Clenching his jaw, he swallowed all the emotions wanting to erupt from his chest and headed toward the bridge of the *Phalanx*.

The door to the lift opened on deck one. The expansive bridge covered two decks, with three holotables at its center. People moved in all directions. Terminals lined the outer bulkheads, systems monitored by men and women wearing techie uniforms. Repetitive beeping sounds of system checks intermixed with voices.

Images floated above the holotables, including one of *Orion,* as Mace headed to the briefing room on the port side: the war room. On the edge of one holotable lay the bio-weapon Cache had found on the smuggler. A team of techies examined it.

Scanning his hand, the door to the briefing room slid open, and he stepped into a long space filled with warriors. A bank of portholes lined the hull on one side, a gray bulkhead on the other. Through the thick, oblong glass, smaller ships moved between the larger vessels of the fleet, stars glinting behind them.

Cache stood at one end of the holotable, Grey beside her. Her head jerked when she saw him, eyes narrowing but shadowed in relief.

Mace strode toward them. Commanders and sub-commanders from *Orion* and others from the *Rebel* and *Phalanx* conversed, the room buzzing. Mace nodded to those who acknowledged him, a few he hadn't seen in years. Foley was there, standing beside Poole, and when their eyes met, momentary alarm swept through Mace.

If there was one person Nia needed to stay clear of, it was Foley. The urge to go over there, shoot Foley in the head to take care of the problem, made his steps falter. *Not the time.* They needed every person they had, even the homicidal ones, for the upcoming offensive.

Foley grinned at him, but calculation filled his eyes.

"I didn't realize you'd returned," Cache said with a frown when he stopped beside her. She narrowed her eyes at her vambrace.

"Or you would have already issued a formal reprimand?"

"Yes." She tapped her vambrace, and his beeped in response.

He could take it as her being petty, but knew he deserved it. Instead of evacuating with Grey and the tyros, he'd gone after Nia. From a professional standpoint, he should regret the decision, but he didn't. If he hadn't gone after her, she'd be dead. His chest squeezed.

Cache crossed her arms, and Mace knew she had the urge to yell at him, could feel the rage pulsing from her.

"What happened to Lexi?" Grey asked, and Mace knew he would have had questions as soon as he'd received the message directly from her.

"A Guardian took her into custody." His tight throat made the words hoarse.

Cache's eyes softened for the briefest of moments. "We'll find her."

Mace gave her one nod. He would stop at nothing to see his sister safe, even if he had to take on a whole Guardian by himself. But they had to find out where they held her first.

Cache's formidable expression returned. "Was she able to send the information about her work?"

"Yes. Everything is in the Condor's database I arrived in."

"I'll get a team on it."

"Did you pick up that shuttle she tagged?"

When Cache nodded, his heart raced. The need for blood consumed him.

"He's in the brig." She put a hand on his arm when he made to leave right then. "It needs to wait until after the briefing."

He knew she was right, but the urge to take every bit of his rage out on the coward overwhelmed him. Mace clenched his fists, pressing them against the edge of the table to ground himself. Justice wasn't going anywhere.

The briefing room door slid open, and Admiral Krispin entered. All the warriors straightened their postures. Conversations halted mid-sentence as he strode to the other end of the holotable. The admiral's eyes surveyed everyone as they gathered on both sides.

His eyes settled on Mace for a second before he passed his hand over the surface of the table. Images of *Orion* and the sectors surrounding it materialized in the middle of the holotable.

Krispin spoke, voice hard. "We have only one chance to reclaim *Orion* and we need to move quickly. Our attack includes Captain Litka of the *Rebel*," he nodded to the woman on his right, "and Captain Ionadi of the *Mercenary* who will join us in two hours."

Good. Ionadi was a hell of a captain. Mace wouldn't want to be on the receiving end of her weapons.

Krispin touched the holotable, and an image of *Orion* rose at its center. The same two Guardians Mace had seen during their escape flanked the station. The CORE had cleared a larger path in the minefield, a corridor wide enough for warships to move easily. Two more Guardians protected the edge.

"These are the last updated positions we have of CORE forces defending *Orion*—or *Obsidian Station*, as they have renamed it. Two more Guardians, the *Alliance* and the *Prestige*, will be here in thirty hours."

A rumble went through the group. Three Destroyers against four Guardians was doable. But six?

"Our siege will begin in twelve hours. Commodore Cache will be coordinating the infiltration team. Commodore…"

"Thank you, Admiral." Cache touched the table's surface, and the minefield and the Guardians protecting it disappeared while *Orion* enlarged, showing the inner workings of the station. "I'll be leading a covert team of eight to infiltrate *Orion* to regain control of her command center and fly her out of the system. We have apprehended a CORE freighter stocked with Marauders. We'll use the freighter to bypass their security and gain access to the station." She highlighted the docking bay in Section A. "The infiltration team, led by Commander Mace, will cut a short path to the command center."

Mace raised an eyebrow, which she ignored. He would never shirk a mission given to him, but it would have been nice to get a heads up.

Cache continued, "I'll also have a technical team with me. We'll gain access to the main terminal and use the emergency systems to vent the atmosphere, clearing most of the station's defenders in one maneuver."

Mace frowned. It was an extremely risky operation with a lot of holes.

"What about the survivors on the station, sir?" One of the sub-commanders asked this at the far end of the table.

Admiral Krispin answered. "From what we understand from multiple sources, when they took the station, they used extreme prejudice. We're expecting no survivors." Hisses and growls rumbled through the group. "Which brings us to our frontal assault. I'll be coordinating with Captain Litka and Captain Ionadi to destroy the Guardians protecting the corridor." He touched the panel and *Orion* shrank, replaced by the image of the two Guardians, the mines columned on either side. "We will begin the attack once the freighter has landed. The frontal assault will serve as a distraction and aid the infiltration unit."

"What of the two Guardians docked to the station?" Commander Sheefra asked. Beside her, Foley stood with his arms crossed over his chest. His hard eyes assessed as he stared at the images of the Guardians.

The admiral enlarged the image of *Orion* once again. "From our intel, we know most their crews were deployed to the station, leaving skeleton crews aboard the docked ships. It's unlikely the Guardians would undock and join the fight in the corridor in the timeframe we're implementing."

"However, they each have a full detail of Marauders at their disposal. That's where our third prong comes in. Commanders Sheefra and Foley will launch Strix and lure their fighters into the minefield. Once Commodore Cache has control of the station's systems, the technical team will use the mines against the Marauders as well as the Guardians."

"How do we know they don't have control of the mines already, sir?" Foley asked.

The admiral looked to Cache.

"We were able to lock key systems before evacuating," she responded. "One of those was the remote mines. We don't believe they circumvented the override because they used a controlled detonation to create the corridor." She paused a moment to enlarge *Orion's* command center. "Once in control of the station, my team will unlock those same systems and use them against the four CORE Guardians."

Foley was still frowning. "And how do we know they won't use the station's weapons against us, sir?"

"The weapons were disabled by the virus implanted by the same traitors who blew the engine cores. Even then, as a precaution, we locked out the CORE's ability to access the weapons." Cache cocked her hip to the side. "Unfortunately, we were rushed, and once we regain control, it will take some time to get *Orion's* defenses up and running."

"Some time, sir?" Foley asked with eyebrows raised.

Cache didn't respond.

"Sir, what of the Marauders on the freighter? Can we use those?" Commander Sheefra asked.

"Unfortunately, no," Cache answered. "We need the entire quantity, so scans of the freighter won't betray us. As well, we can't exceed their crew complement, eight in total. I have three on my technical support team. Commander Mace will have three others on the infiltration team."

Krispin checked his vambrace. "The freighter will disembark in five hours and ten minutes. Be prepared to reclaim *Orion*. Dismissed."

The group scattered, their voices punctuated with restless adrenaline. Admiral Krispin indicated he wanted to speak with both Mace and Cache. They walked through the departing warriors to the end of the table.

"Sir," Mace said once he stopped in front of him.

"It's good to see you, Commander, even under the circumstances." He extended his arm, and they clutched each other at the elbow briefly.

"You too, sir." A close friend of his father's and nearing his nineties, Krispin was war-weary. Mace knew he would much rather be with his wife, kids, and grandchildren than coordinating a high-risk offensive.

Krispin frowned at Cache. "There seem to be a few details left out of your plan. Are you prepared?"

"We will be by the time we depart, sir," she assured him.

The admiral narrowed his eyes at Mace, then looked to Cache. "Do not make this a suicide mission. I would be extremely irate if it turned into one."

"Yes, sir," they said in unison and turned to leave.

The admiral's voice stopped him as they made their way to the door. "Commander Mace, one more thing." Cache paused mid-step, then continued out while Mace stood before the admiral.

Chapter Thirty-Eight

Once alone, Krispin gave him a hard stare, then took Mace by the shoulders and into a fierce bear hug, slapping him on the back.

"It is good to see you, son."

Mace returned the gesture, throat tight. After everything that had happened, the truly affectionate embrace almost did him in.

One more slap on the back and Krispin pulled away, scowling at Mace from arm's length. "Now, tell me the truth of it. How long have you known you were leading this offensive?" Krispin let his arms drop.

There was no reason to lie. "When Cache announced it at the table, sir."

The admiral's eyebrows rose. "Cutting it close, aren't we?"

"I wasn't able to make the rendezvous."

Something in his tone tipped off the admiral. "What's happened?"

He cleared his throat. "Lexi's been taken into CORE custody."

Krispin swore, hitting the holotable with his fist. The image of *Orion* disappeared. "How long?"

"Since yesterday." He clenched his fists, his thoughts turning to Justice in the brig. Mace owed him a slow, agonizing death. The man's screams would fuel him throughout his upcoming mission.

"There's still time then," Krispin said. "I'll contact my people and see where she's being held." The admiral's eyes bored into his. "We'll get her back."

"I know." Thoughts of what could happen in the meantime were what tortured him.

With a nod, Krispin turned to go, but Mace stopped him by saying, "Sir?"

His superior turned around with his eyebrows raised.

Mace ran a hand through his hair, positive he shouldn't even be asking this question. "Is there a way to protect a captive if they were from the ruling class?"

Tipping his head to the side, Krispin narrowed his eyes. "Context?"

Mace let out a frustrated breath. The more he talked about Nia's circumstances, the more danger she would be in. But he trusted Krispin with his life. More than that, he trusted him with the lives of the people he cared about.

"Does a ruling class captive always have to get sent back to the CORE in pieces?" Saying it aloud made his stomach churn with acid.

Krispin crossed his arms over his chest. "I'd heard you'd taken a captive and didn't believe it, told the person they were a dirty fucking liar, actually. Are you telling me she's part of the ruling class?"

Mace clenched his fists. "She's no longer with us, sir."

"Ah," he said, like it explained everything when it really didn't. "This is a theoretical question, then?"

"Yes."

"Theoretically, yes." Those two words lightened the oppressive load on Mace's shoulders. Krispin went on. "Violence against the ruling class is a more recent development, relatively speaking. It wasn't until Chancellor Feering's rule, when he started making public executions, that we wanted to return the favor. But I remember a time when CORE citizens could ask for amnesty, choosing to join Tellusians in our fight to regain the resources taken from us. I believe the law can still be invoked, even for the ruling class, especially if someone influential were to sponsor the individual."

Mace's mind raced. He could have given Nia the choice to stay. He almost wanted to return to her right now and tell her. But since the beginning, she'd said she wanted to go home. He couldn't take that away from her, no matter his feelings.

"Thank you, sir. I appreciate the information."

"If you study the old laws, it should be there." Krispin straightened. "It's too bad your ward is no longer with us. I would've liked to meet the woman you couldn't leave behind." With another nod, he left.

Mace stared at the closed door for a good long while, thinking. Would it have been possible to protect her properly from the start? The processor should have told him. They were the ones most well-versed in the old laws—but of course he hadn't. He'd wanted the creds Mace could give him instead.

With a sound of disgust, Mace strode toward the door. He had someone to visit in the brig.

Grey was waiting for him. They fell into step as Mace headed toward the lift. "You don't need to hold my hand," he said as he slapped the control panel.

"Cache ordered me to make sure you didn't kill him."

"A direct order?" The lift door slid open, and they both stepped inside. He touched the control for the brig.

"Yeah," Grey said, facing the door. "Apparently, someone from the top is taking an interest. Not Krispin, though."

His instincts tingled. Who would care if Justice lived? Grey's eyebrow arched like he wondered the same thing.

The need to kill Justice for what he'd done to Lexi burned through him like a supernova. But there was also Grey to think about. A direct order meant there would be repercussions for him as well.

As much as it pained him to say, Mace gritted, "I'll just talk to him." But there was only one thing he needed to "talk" about—he needed the name of the ship or station where they took Lexi.

"Of course," Grey replied, his voice mild. "I wouldn't have thought otherwise."

The lift door opened onto a dimly lit corridor smelling of death. It wasn't the same scent as in a med bay, but one laced with desperation and fear.

They stopped at the take-in desk manned by one enforcer. "Which cell for the newly apprehended CORE agent?"

"Interrogation room six," she said. "But Commander Foley's already in with him, sir."

Mace clenched his fists. "Under whose orders?"

"His own, sir."

Passing her, he strode down the corridor. Mace didn't bother with the observation room, but scanned his hand and opened the main door.

Shirtless and bloody, Justice sat with his wrists bound to the table in front of him, his feet secured to the deck. Foley leaned over him, a hooked instrument pressed next to Justice's eye.

Blood coated the tools on the cart beside the table. Cut lines covered Justice's chest and arms, oozing crimson. He had two black eyes. Red-tinged saliva ran from his mouth and through his goatee before dropping onto the table.

"Foley," Mace growled. "Out."

Foley hesitated before straightening. Shrugging, he tossed the instrument onto the metal tray next to the interrogation table. The surgical tools clattered.

They both stepped into the corridor, the door closing to block Mace's view of Justice.

"I thought you would have an interest in this one," Foley said, his knowing tone grating against Mace's nerves.

"I'm taking over." Not wanting to hear Foley speak again, Mace scanned his hand and re-entered the cell, knowing Grey would wait on the other side of the window.

Justice lifted his head, saw him, and spat a gob of blood to the side. "You've come to relieve that coward? Piece of Tell shit hits like he's flirting." Another gob of blood flew onto the deck.

Even with Justice's damaged state, Mace only had to envision Lexi's face to want to do worse to him. And he should have realized the moment he stepped foot on Lexi's outpost that Justice was an agent. It was his eyes. Too steady, too trained, they took in everything without trying to. And right now, Justice's eyes urged him to kill him and get it over with.

Mace paced in front of the table. He would return him to Foley's tender care before allowing Justice the easy way out.

"Where are they taking Lexi?" If he had a starting point, it would make it so much easier to track her. They must be taking her to a prison station, but there were so many, and they stripped people of their names upon arrival, giving them only a number.

"You're not very good at this shit, are you?" Justice said, his voice too calm. "You've told me what you want in the first five seconds. Now I won't give it to you until I get what I want. The other guy might be a pussy, but you're an amateur." His Lunar accent was probably real too, unlike Lexi's learned one.

Mace didn't care about his mind games, only wanted some clue as to Lexi's position. "Where are they taking her?" he gritted between his teeth.

"I've been wondering," Justice said in a lazy tone, one at odds with the blood streaking from his body. "Do you know who your girlfriend is, and you're protecting her? Or are you as stupid as you look?"

Mace stiffened, his heart rate kicking inside his chest. As an agent, Justice would be required to know everything related to CORE politics.

He would have recognized Nia. But had the fucker told Foley about her ruling-class heritage before Mace arrived?

And Mace had brought her here, where she could be harmed, and left her on her own.

Justice's bruised lips broke into a wide smile. "You Tells are so easy to read, so emotional. You've been protecting her, and now you're wondering if I told the other guy." He turned his head to the observation window. "Maybe he's out there listening right now."

No one knew Nia was here. She was safe. And Mace wouldn't allow him to lead this conversation. "Where are they taking Lexi?"

"What would he do to your girlfriend? I know you Tells like to flaunt your savage reputation as much as possible, scare the masses with your might and all that. What would he do before sending her home broken? Beat her? Mindfuck her until she doesn't remember her own name? String her to a bulkhead and remove her skin a centimeter at a time?"

Rage threatened to consume him at the suggestions, but Mace couldn't allow the agent to fuck with him. Nia was safe. She was going home on a transport today, in under an hour. Betel's contacts were solid. He would *not* lose focus to this man's head games. "Where are they taking Lexi?" he repeated.

"Lexi who? I don't know a Lexi," Justice said in a lifeless, computerized voice. Then his smile flashed again, his eyes glancing at the tray of tools next to him. "You Tells aren't nearly as creative as CORE specialists. During training, they practice on us agents. It's a great time, I can assure you."

Pressure squeezed Mace's chest. A fanatical light entered the agent's eyes. Justice wouldn't break. Mace had seen the expression too many times. There wasn't enough fear there to work with. Justice knew he wasn't getting free and truly wanted to die right here and now.

He wouldn't confess Lexi's location no matter how much Mace asked, and no matter how many cuts Foley gave him.

Desperation made him brace his hands against the table, lean forward, and say, "If you have even an ounce of affection for my sister, you'll tell me where they're taking her."

Justice grinned and leaned forward. "Affection? Yeah, she was a good fuck."

Jaw clenching, hands fisting, Mace closed his eyes and tried to tamp his anger. But all he saw was Lexi's bruised face behind his eyelids.

"Do you know how often she begged me to put my dick in her?"

He could not appeal to Justice's humane side because he didn't have one.

"Tell slut couldn't keep her legs together for anything. Rank whore."

Mace pushed away from the table in an effort not to take one of those tools and stab him through the ear canal.

But Justice wouldn't shut up. "She would always scream, 'Harder! Harder!'"

Mace closed his eyes. He knew the man was manipulating him but couldn't stop the rage. The door opened, and his eyes popped open to find Grey standing there, his expression full of warning. It barely made an impression.

He needed to leave. Grey could finish. He'd handle it properly.

Then Justice's next words made him stop cold.

"The arresting general assured me that every defender on board his Guardian would make it as *hard* as possible."

With a roar, Mace vaulted over the table, took the agent's head in his hands, and twisted. The pop and crack ricocheted off the bulkheads. In the resulting silence, Mace's ragged breathing echoed off the bulkheads.

He let go, and the body slumped forward, leaving a trail of blood down his arm. Chest heaving, hands clenched by his sides, he stared unseeingly at the bulkhead. Visions of Lexi, of the horrors Justice had painted with words, flashed in his brain. He couldn't stop it.

"We've been summoned," Grey said from behind him, cutting the quiet. "Walk it off. I'll take care of this and make the necessary reports."

Mace spun away from the body. This would be another mark against him, but he couldn't conjure the proper remorse. He lifted his eyes and saw only understanding in Grey's gaze.

A communique from Cache waited to be acknowledged on his vambrace. He'd been so involved with Justice, he hadn't heard it.

Straightening his uniform, he stepped into the corridor, then tensed.

Foley stood against the bulkhead, arms crossed, and a disgusted expression on his face. "You've got to be the shittiest enforcer in the sector."

For once, Mace was glad of the insult. It meant he wasn't a vindictive sociopath like Foley. And it also meant Foley hadn't gone off to find Nia. Whether or not Justice told Foley about Nia's lineage, the only people who knew she was on board were Spiro and Betel, and they'd stab themselves before betraying him. As long as Mace didn't contact her, then she'd stay safe.

With an irreverent salute, Mace turned on his heel and strode toward the lift.

Nia would be gone from the ship soon, Foley none the wiser.

Chapter Thirty-Nine

She was returning home. The truth should have been exhilarating, but the sick feeling in Nia's stomach hadn't dissipated since she'd woken.

Mace's quarters were empty. He'd left without saying goodbye. Her heart cracked and wouldn't stop throbbing in pain. He'd told her everything he needed to say last night. He'd said he loved her.

When a sob passed her lips, she pressed them tightly together. *I will not cry.*

She'd already dressed in the generic civilian uniform she'd received from the processor. An alien sensation infused her as she stared at her reflection in the digital mirror she'd found in one of the wall compartments. The garment was mostly gray but had blue trim, the same blue worn by warriors and technical personnel.

Sighing wearily, she took the palette she'd been given and sat on the bed, her spine pressed against the bulkhead with her knees bent. Ship updates scrolled across the top, but none told her where Mace was or what he was doing.

Tellusian newsreels scrolled at the bottom of the screen. Most were about what happened on *Orion*, the death toll, the missing persons, and whether there was hope of the station being returned to Tellusian control. It all made her heart beat an uncomfortable rhythm in her chest.

A while later, a message appeared on the screen: *Your registered transport leaves in thirty minutes. Confirm your seat.*

Below the "confirm" icon was a "delay ticket" option. Below the delay icon was a list of four other transports. Nia's fingers hovered over the screen. Mace had told her to get on the first transport. But the next one wasn't much of a wait, only thirty minutes.

The thought of leaving now, of stepping onto a transport and never seeing Mace again... she swallowed against the lump in her throat. Maybe he would come back here one more time.

She pressed the "delay" icon, chose the next transport, and hadn't moved from her spot when its reminder appeared on her screen thirty minutes later.

She pressed the delay icon again.

It wasn't until there was only one transport remaining that she finally left Mace's quarters.

Throughout the entire planning session, Mace felt Cache's knife-like gaze cut through him. The schematic of *Orion* lay between them, but the distance might as well have been a crater. Every movement of hers was tense with restraint, and she probably would have struck out if they'd been alone—because she'd have to answer for Justice's death as much as him.

Six other infiltration team members surrounded the briefing room holotable. Grey, Betel, and Spiro stood to his left, with the three techies on his right. Taking non-warriors on this mission tripled the chance of failure, but he understood they needed them if they were to unlock *Orion's* systems. He didn't have to like it.

Mouse had been on an op before, but the other two were green. Mouse had earned his name because of his enormous eyes. They almost gave him the look of someone of lower intelligence. Until you had a conversation with the guy—his brain operated at a level not attained by the average population.

Newton specialized in hardware. Mace had never worked with him before but knew him from the bridge. He had short, curly black hair, and his Adam's apple bobbed every other minute when he swallowed.

Callista was the last of the tech team, a software genius new to *Orion*. He'd heard her name a few times since she'd arrived, all compliments. She kept her head bent, her honey-brown hair tied at the base of her neck.

When Cache's gaze flicked to him, her eyes narrowed. He met her stare straight on, unapologetic. Anything else would show weakness, and he couldn't afford that right now.

Because Nia was never far from his thoughts. *She should already be gone.* His stomach clenched, and he resisted the urge to make sure she'd taken her transport. He didn't want to leave a trail to her now that she was safe. With Foley's resources, Mace had even more reason to keep his distance—no matter how much it pained him to do so.

Cache broke his gaze, leaning forward to brace her hands on the surface of the holotable. He focused on what the techie, Callista, was saying. This wasn't the time for him and Cache to be unaligned. The only thing he should be focused on right now was liberating *Orion* from the CORE.

They solidified the plan, then went over it again. They changed the plan, then scrapped the plan and started over.

"Commander." Cache's biting voice made him lift his head. She'd obviously asked him something, and his mind had drifted.

The mission. He had to concentrate on the mission. If he let anything else distract him, they'd all get killed.

Heart aching with each step, Nia followed the map of the *Phalanx* on her palette to the transport hangar. The farther she traveled through the corridor, the more people she encountered.

She kept telling herself she wasn't safe here to make her feet move.

Following the crowd, she stepped into the hangar. Tension crept from her shoulders to her ears. People filled the place from bulkhead to bulkhead.

Maybe it hadn't been such a great idea to wait for the last transport. It wasn't possible to take a step and not bump into someone. Nia hugged her palette to her chest, trying to stay out of the way as she searched for the correct ship. The mass of bodies moved at a crawl's pace.

"What's the hold-up?" A voice asked from behind her, speaking Common. She turned slightly to see a portly man wearing a dark green suit, his pale skin reddening with agitation.

"There are medical crews readying to go to *Orion*," said a woman wearing a feathered yellow hat, the matching striped dress hard to look at for too long. "I think it's just a matter of waiting for them to be organized, then the line will move again."

Nia continued on, reading the hull numbers on the ships, searching for hers, then paused when a group of doctors clad in their white jackets walked toward her. She scanned their faces, wondering if she knew any from the time she'd spent on *Orion*. When her eyes rested on someone familiar, her heart leaped. But confusion quickly set in.

How did she know that man? He wasn't from her med bay, but she definitely recognized him from somewhere. The group passed by, and his gaze landed on her, eyes widening almost imperceptibly in recognition before his placid expression returned.

Nia stopped, her heart beginning to race with perplexing dread. How did she know him? He'd recognized her too, but acted like he hadn't. Her mind ran through every medical officer she'd met but drew a blank. She didn't know him from her life before, did she? From *Elara Five* or the *Diligence*? Or even Medical Academy?

Then, it clicked. The day in the engine core, when Commander Foley had threatened her. She'd seen a man doing maintenance in the engine core when she'd looked over the side. *That* man. In the wake of the events, she hadn't thought of him again.

But he'd been wearing a maintenance uniform. And he'd been alone.

Mace had told it was an inside job, that they'd blown the engine cores at the same time. When those mind moles were inside her head, he'd asked her why Foley had found her there that day.

Swallowing, Nia turned, looking over her shoulder at the group of doctors. The man had stopped too, the rest of the medical crew continuing past him. He stared at her with a cold, detached expression on his face. It reminded her of the way Justice had stared at her.

Her heart pounded a warning in her head, drowning out all the other noise in the hangar. When he took a step in her direction, Nia spun around, her breath catching in her throat.

He was a traitor. *An agent.* She'd been the only one to see him in the engine core. Her feet moved quickly, weaving in and out of the people as fast as possible. He'd kill to keep her information quiet. She could scream, shout for help, but Mace's warnings hung heavy in her mind.

Nia darted to the side, through a line waiting for a transport. People grumbled as she pushed her way through, trying to flee from the man who'd been responsible for the deaths of so many.

And he's returning to Orion *as a medical officer.*

She needed to tell Mace. He was the only one who would know what she was talking about, the only safe person on this ship. Was he still on board?

Her palette tight in her fingers, she lifted it to contact him, but stepped the wrong way. A woman moving her arm smacked it out of her hand. Nia's chest seized as it flew into the air.

The woman said something in Tellusian, her tone apologetic. Waving her comment aside, Nia turned, searching for where it had fallen. Her eyes landed on the man pursuing her. He was way too close, only a few meters away. Her palette lay at his feet. He bent to snatch it, his eyes never leaving her.

Spinning around, Nia left all pretense of being polite behind and charged through the crowd, her only intent to get away from this man who looked like he could hurt her without feeling an ounce of remorse. Bodies jostled; people unknowingly stepped in her way. She squeezed between them, bumping and pushing. Someone shouted something behind her, but she didn't stop, didn't turn around, her momentum focused on escape.

Her heart pounded as she neared the exit. The crowd thinned, and her stomach churned. It wouldn't be a good idea to leave the safety of numbers, but she couldn't stop now. Her feet wouldn't let her. The door slid open as she neared, and she stumbled into a deserted corridor.

With no clue where it led, she took off at a run, the gray bulkheads whizzing by her. Nausea rising, she chanced a glance over her shoulder when she neared a corner. The man paused outside the door to the hangar, hands empty of her palette. Nia tripped, then righted herself, turning to sprint.

Why was there no one around? This was a Destroyer, shouldn't it be full of people? Maybe it was because all the civilians had left already, taking earlier transports like rational people, while she and the rest of the last-minute idiots scrambled.

There had to be another way to contact Mace. If nothing else, she'd return to his quarters and wait for him—as long as she could lose the man following her.

Not looking behind her, she turned another corner, then another, becoming more disoriented.

When a stitch stabbed her side, she stopped and bent over, gasping for breath. Had she lost him? The corridor behind her was empty, with a lift nearby. If she went to another deck, it would be harder to follow. Hopefully, she could find other people. Someone might tell her how to get in touch with Mace without her palette.

The hair on her neck stood on end. Nia straightened. The man stepped into sight ahead of her at the other end of the corridor. Panic squeezed her throat. She stumbled and turned to run, passing the lift and trying to retrace her random route. Could she find her way back to the hangar and onto her transport? Maybe find her palette wherever he left it? Getting off this ship seemed the best way to escape the traitor following her, but she needed her palette to make her connections.

She'd taken two turns by the time she realized she'd gone a different route and was thoroughly lost. A narrow corridor caught her eye.

With one last glance over her shoulder, she escaped through it, the metal corner scraping her arm as she made the quick turn. A hum pulled her forward. She tripped into a vast space. A more compact version of *Orion's* energy core towered in front of her, the helix narrower, the rotation faster.

Scrambling, Nia followed the railing around, looking for a place to hide. She needed the man to stop pursuing her, then she could find her way back to the hangar and her palette.

The agent stepped in front of her. Nia screamed, stumbling back. Spinning around, she searched frantically for the nearest escape, a corridor like the one she'd come through. A hand gripped her nape with such strength, her body jerked in the opposite direction. She reached, trying to break free, but his fingers dug into the sides of her throat so tightly it felt like he seared holes into her skin. Her limbs thrashed as he shook her, brain rattling in her head. She couldn't breathe. The railing of the engine core slammed into her stomach. Stars dotted her vision.

She might have heard someone shout from far away, but she wasn't sure. Weightlessness consumed her as her body went over the railing. Then she was falling, falling, falling... *Thwack*. Her side hit something hard, her breath leaving her body. Her hand reached out, trying to stop her descent. *Thwack*. She hit something else, a flash of light blinding her. Another solid object slammed into her ribs.

Splash. Everything stopped.

Chapter Forty

The cockpit of the CORE freighter gleamed black and beige. Mace strode to the pilot's seat, Grey beside him. Nervousness exuded from the techies as they took their places on the narrow bench at the back. A bulky beast, the freighter was made for transporting cargo, not passenger comfort.

Cache's eyes assessed her techies as she sat in one of the two crew seats on the side, Spiro taking the other. That left Betel to slide between Newton and Callista.

Mace touched the control for the comm, keeping it audio only. "We're ready to depart, Admiral."

It took only a moment for Krispin to respond. "Safe journey. Out."

Grey monitored the ship's systems while Mace engaged the engines. Once fully powered, Mace flew them away from the fleet, trying to keep his focus. They hit maximum speed, and an alert stillness settled over the eight of them.

The resulting silence made Mace's mind wander. Ever since he'd realized Nia's transport had departed, his chest ached. If it hadn't been for this mission and his fear for his sister, he would have been a useless mess—whether it acknowledged a weakness or not.

The urge to find Nia wherever she landed and ask her to return consumed most of his thoughts. If she would even consider the possibility, she could come back on her own terms, ask for amnesty and receive sponsorship from Admiral Krispin. Then Mace could ask her to marry him properly.

His body stilled. *Shit.* He hadn't divorced her during the emancipation process. Why hadn't the processor said anything? He wiped a hand over his face. It probably had to do with the threats he'd given her if she spoke of Nia's emancipation to anyone.

Obtaining a proper divorce was as good a reason as any to go after his wife. A small grin stole across his face.

Cache spoke over his shoulder, jerking him from his thoughts. "Radio silence in five people."

Mace nodded, then cut the feeds. Time to focus on the mission.

Over an hour later, the *Mercenary* dropped out of maximum speed behind them. Its first shot hit them dead-on, the sound cracking through the cockpit. The freighter shuddered. The Destroyer fired again, a terminal popping with sparks beside Mace.

"Shit." Grey tapped at the controls. "I know you told Ionadi to make it look good, but come on." They all rocked with another hit.

Mace tried to keep the ship steady and on course, but the navigation systems were out of whack.

"There's something off in the engine room," Grey said. "Not getting clear readings."

"Betel, Grey, go check it out," Cache ordered. She took Grey's spot when they'd left. "Environmental is on the fritz." Her fingers ran over the terminal.

Five minutes later, Grey signaled the cockpit. "It's not good. We've got a leak in the engine casing, and we're venting atmosphere."

"Can you fix it?" Cache asked.

"Betel's using sealant right now. It'll slow the air loss, not halt it altogether. The only way to fix this behemoth is at a space dock."

"Do what you can, then return. We need to close all the hatches to save air." Cache leaned back. "At least she stopped firing."

The *Mercenary* hit them again, everyone bucking forward.

Mace raised an eyebrow at her. "You spoke too soon."

She smiled, her green eyes ablaze, then laughed outright. "I probably should have let Ionadi win at poker last night. She's always been a sore loser."

Grey strode through the hatch, and Cache rose. She didn't return to her seat but remained standing between theirs. Once all eight members of the crew were accounted for, Mace sealed the door and rerouted all the oxygen to the cockpit.

"How much atmosphere do we have left?" Callista asked from the bench, her voice wavering slightly.

Mace checked the environmental panel. "Enough to get us there, but just barely. No deep breaths, people." He accelerated away from the *Mercenary*, and the warship followed.

He kept his hands on the controls, hoping the *Mercenary* wouldn't take another shot. From the warnings flashing along the panel, he didn't know if the freighter could take it.

Their aggressive escort kept pace until the two Guardians in front of the minefield came into visual range. The *Mercenary* immediately broke off its pursuit. One Guardian pursued it. The other aimed its weapons at the freighter.

"Callista, you're on," Cache said in a murmur. The young techie's fingers were already flying across her palette.

Changing course, Mace headed directly toward the remaining Guardian. The panel beeped, wanting a security code. He turned to Callista.

"Um. Just a sec."

Cache whipped around to her. "We don't have 'a sec'."

Callista swallowed. "Try six, six, seven, two, B, P, H, one, nine, Q."

Grey punched it in. Everyone waited, silent, as Mace flew alongside the colossal ship.

The comm crackled. "Gamma Niner Charlie Foxtrot, we do not have you on any work orders. Please re-confirm your code."

"Callista." Cache's tone was a low warning.

"It *should* work. Try it again."

Grey sent it again. Everyone held their breath.

In the rear viewer, the second Guardian returned to its position in the mine corridor, having broken off its pursuit of the *Mercenary*.

The comm channel returned to life. "Please proceed to docking bay B3. Land and await inspection. Out."

Mace severed the comm connection.

"Good work," Cache said to Callista. "But fuck, we wanted Section A."

"Be glad they're letting us land." Mace said as he flew them through the mine corridor and straight to *Orion*.

They all stared silently at the two Guardians flanking the oblong station.

"That's just wrong," Grey spoke, his tone drenched in disgust.

Cache leaned forward, her face between theirs. "There's so much more wrong with this situation than Guardians docked with *Orion*."

They passed through *Orion's* outer shielding and under one of its docking arms. Another shield, and they entered the bay, the deck thick with defenders.

Cache dug her fingernails into the headrests of Mace and Grey's seats. "Anytime, Krispin. Anytime," she muttered.

The freighter settled onto the deck with a *thud*.

The world shuddered around her. Nia tried to move, but her body ached like she had gone through reclamation. A moan echoed around her before she realized it was her own voice. *Where the hell am I?* Her head pounded. Her back throbbed. She coughed, moist air choking her.

A bulkhead curved in front of her, shiny. Uncomfortably warm metal pressed against her body. Caustic steam swirled around her, making her eyes water and her throat close.

A hum reverberated around her, a familiar noise she couldn't place. On the heels of the confusion came bone-deep dread. Her body stiffened. *The agent.*

She lifted her head, and heat speared through her leg like she'd broken something. Pushing the pain aside, she twisted as best she could, searching for where she'd landed. She was in some sort of cylindrical shaft, a meter wide, with water sloshing beneath her through a metal grate. Her clothes and hair were soaked, and moisture dripped down the bulkheads. Looking up, she peered at the opening of the shaft meters away. The glow of the engine core shone brightly.

Stars above. She was in a section of reactor containment. The water may have broken her fall, saved her life, but it couldn't be good for her to be down here. She would need to be treated for radiation.

Her first urge was to scream, to call for someone to get her out. But what about the agent? She didn't know how far she'd fallen. Maybe he thought she'd died. It wasn't much of a stretch. If she'd seen someone thrown over the railing, she would have thought them dead too. This tube was probably full of water when she'd landed—a fluke she hadn't drowned.

Using the bulkhead as support, Nia rolled to her knees, every joint groaning in protest. When she tried to put weight on her foot, she gasped, pain making tears prick her eyeballs.

Bracing her spine against the bulkhead, she rolled up her soggy pant leg and found her skin turning purple around her ankle. A sprain or a break? Either way, it would be impossible to climb out of this tube. If she didn't want to die here, she'd need to call for help, whether or not the agent was near.

"Hey!" she shouted, her throat dry, making her wonder how long she'd been out. "Is someone there?" Her voice ricocheted inside the cylinder, then echoed back to her.

A *ker-klunk* answered, the noise so loud her eardrums ached. The sound of rushing liquid followed. The cylinder began to fill with scalding water. It rose over her feet. Panic squeezed her chest so tight she could only take gasping breaths of chemical-filled air.

Tipping her face upwards, she shouted, "Help!" The water was already up to her thighs. She couldn't swim well, having had only a couple of lessons at a lunar resort when she was a child.

With the water at her shoulders, she frantically splashed, trying to stay above the rising tide. Her feet lifted off the metal grating, and she kicked, her injured ankle spiking in pain. She sank below the waterline and got a mouthful of the foul liquid. It dripped down her face as she surfaced again. Her eyes burned. The opening of the cylinder rushed toward her. The water pushed her up and out, but it didn't stop rising.

Now she was in a bigger vat of liquid. Eddies pulled at her, trying to drag her lower. She kept kicking, her ankle sore and tired. The engine core loomed above.

Then, like someone had turned off a tap, the water started to drain. Nia thrashed, her heart beating as if she'd taken too many stimulants. She wouldn't allow herself to get stuck in one of those cylinders again. Her feet hit something solid. Her fingers connected with metal. She gripped it tightly. The water kept draining, gurgling, then quieted until the only sound was the hum of the engine core above her.

Caught on the metal between two of the cylindrical drains, Nia rolled and exhaled a relieved breath. She had to move, couldn't stay here, but exhaustion kept her in place. Water dripped from her body, tinkling as it hit metal. Steam rose around her.

The thought of the water rising again made her scramble to her knees. Her ankle screamed when she stood, and she almost fell inside the tube.

Carefully, she shuffled between the cylinders to the edge of the chamber. Her heart sank. How was she supposed to get out of here? The bulkhead was solid, smooth metal, with the first railing a dozen meters above her.

Before she had time to think of other options, another *ker-klunk* echoed. Water sloshed below, and in no time at all, it rose to her ankles. Swallowing her panic, Nia stayed close to the bulkhead. There had to be a way out of this thing.

Far above her head, grooves were etched into the metal, then above that, the first railing. When the water reached her shoulders, she kicked, keeping close to the bulkhead and her eyes on the indentations. She floated upward, but not far enough before the water receded.

Terrified she'd be stuck forever, she pushed against the bulkhead with her good foot. Her fingers caught on the edge of the groove. She held on tight, but as the water lowered, her body became heavy. If she fell, she'd probably break her neck.

By the time the water had receded past her body, her fingers ached with the effort to remain where she was. One slip and she'd fall. When the gurgling stopped, she knew the water had finished draining.

The worst idea I've ever had. She wouldn't be able to stay here long.

Then, weightlessness overtook her body. For a second, she thought it was because she'd slipped. But in the next moment, she lifted as though a gentle hand carried her upward. The droplets around her rose in bubbles.

They suspended artificial gravity. Was the *Phalanx* traveling at maximum speed? If it was, she didn't know how much time she'd have before gravity would return to non-essential areas.

Using the grooves in the bulkhead, she pulled herself upward as fast as possible. With the first railing within reach, she pushed herself over, then used the overhead to guide herself to the nearest corridor. Righting herself, she tried to remain close to the deck.

When gravity returned, it felt like she'd gained a thousand kilograms. The deck rushed to meet her good foot, and she tumbled the rest of the way, landing on her knees, then hands. Behind her, the water returned to its cylinders with a thundering *splash*.

Wincing, Nia stumbled to her feet and limped her way to the closest lift, tension in her spine at the thought of the agent resurfacing. Her shoes squished and sloshed with each jerky step. She needed a med kit to heal her ankle.

The lift door opened. *Find Mace.* But he wouldn't be on this ship anymore. He'd said they were taking back *Orion*. She had to find someone in command to tell them about the agent.

She pressed the control for deck one. A message appeared on the screen: Access Denied. Snarling, she tried deck two, but the same thing happened. It didn't allow her to go anywhere above deck five.

"This is why Tellusians need voice-activated systems!" she screamed at the overhead.

She would have been able to tell the computer it was an emergency and to contact the necessary personnel.

Fine. She pressed the control for deck six, and the lift finally moved. When it stopped, the door slid open. Someone wearing blue ran past the lift as if the ship were on fire. Nia stepped onto the deck.

Boom. The sound was so loud it felt like it came from inside her head. Yellow emergency lights pulsed along the corridor. There weren't many people on this deck, but the ones she could see were rushing here and there.

The ship rocked with another blast, and Nia braced her hand on the bulkhead. What was happening outside?

"Excuse me," she said to a passing technical officer, but the woman ignored her to continue on her way.

"Can you—?" Nia stopped speaking when the next person did the same thing.

Frustration choked her. She couldn't go above this deck on her own, and everyone was too busy to help.

Nia hobbled along until the door on her right opened. For the first time since she'd lost her palette, she recognized where she was. It was the hangar where she and Mace had arrived. And there sat the Condor they'd flown in.

Wet and shivering, Nia limped her way toward it, not seeing any other options for how to get off this ship.

Chapter Forty-One

The infiltration team gathered at the freighter's hatch. Each of the techies stared at Mace with wide eyes, their hands either clamped around their satchels or palettes. The tapping of Callista's fingers was the only sound until Grey lifted a pulse cannon to his shoulder and Spiro snorted.

Grey shrugged. "Never leave home without it."

"Autonomous shielding?" Cache asked Callista.

The techie swallowed, her face pale. "Sending you the frequencies now."

Cache nodded to him, and Mace took point. Their vambraces beeped as one. The warriors adjusted the settings on their weapons to the frequency of the defenders' personal shielding.

"All right, people." Cache stared at each of them. "Let's get this done."

Weapons aloft, Mace opened the hatch. As they'd hoped, the *Phalanx's* frontal assault had distracted the defenders. All CORE personnel in the bay ran to battle stations, no one paying attention to the freighter.

They'd gotten halfway to the exit when they were noticed. In rapid succession, Mace took out the three defenders closest to them. Laser fire erupted behind him, but he trusted Spiro, Betel, and Cache to take care of it while he cleared the path ahead. Beside him, Grey used the pulse cannon, wiping out five defenders with one blast.

As the last of the weapons fire behind him died down, a shadowy silence followed them out the bay and into the corridor. A pair of defenders cornered ahead, and Mace fired two shots, taking them out. Each corridor they cleared brought them closer to the command center.

Their luck ran out in the Section B atrium, the area laid out almost identically to the one in Section C.

Backs pressed against the bulkhead, Mace stared at each of his team members, mind racing. He should have expected it. They were trapped. Defenders guarded every angle of the atrium, and they'd taken defensive positions behind them as well. Those pairs of defenders, easily neutralized, had only been decoys.

Right now, they had no place to go. If Mace stuck his head out, his brains would be splattered against the bulkhead.

"Any suggestions?" Cache asked beside him. The techs on her other side vibrated with fear.

It was such a blasted mistake to bring them. He glanced at Grey, who shook his head. Betel and Spiro didn't share any ideas either. Mace settled his eyes on Cache. "I have one, but you're not going to like it."

"Try me," she said, her tone edged.

"Blow a hole in the lift and rappel twenty decks."

Cache's eyebrows arched with understanding. "I actually do like it. Subtle."

He cocked his head to the techs.

"They'll be fine," she said in answer to his silent question. "They're tougher than they look."

Mace shook his head. If they were any less tough, they would be a puddle of piss. "Grey, open up the lift on my mark. Cache, get the techs secured with bungees." He looked at Spiro and Betel. "What are you two hoarding?"

"A little of this. A little of that," Spiro said, pulling out a smoke grenade from the vest he wore.

Betel grunted and took a flash bomb out of his pants pocket.

Raising his eyebrows in appreciation, Mace waited for Cache to secure the last techie, then nodded to Grey. His friend aimed at the main lift and fired. A deafening blast echoed a second later, shattering the lift's walls.

"Eyes," Mace said in a low voice.

Everyone looked away as Betel and Spiro threw their toys. An earsplitting *boom* accompanied a blinding flash. Smoke billowed everywhere.

Cache ran the techies through the chaos, adding her cover fire. Their bungees stretched tight as they fell through the chasm Grey had created. Mace heard one of them scream the entire way, thought maybe it was Newton. The five warriors used ropes to follow a second later, landing on a heap of rubble covered in dust.

"Seal that," Mace ordered Grey, motioning for the techies to get as far away as possible.

"Fire in the hole." Grey tossed a grenade upward, then ran for cover as Mace ducked around the corner with the others.

The explosion rocked through them, raining more debris until the shaft was totally unusable.

"That was fun," Spiro said, stepping away from the bulkhead.

"You're all insane," Callista murmured. She sat against the bulkhead like her legs had given out, her breathing labored, head bent between her knees.

Spiro shrugged. "Probably."

"Shouldn't we have gone in the other direction?" Newton asked, his voice sounding raw as he pointed to the overhead. "Like upward."

"Come with me," Cache said and led the team under a low corridor—even the shaky-legged Callista—ducking under a low beam.

The engine core pulsed its hum nearby. In its outer cylinder, they wouldn't see it in the next part of their journey.

"We're in the scrubbers," Callista breathed, wiping the soot from her cheeks.

The small robotic creatures collected condensation, clicking against the metal framework, and were oblivious to the station's change in command.

"And sixty decks above is the command center," Mace said, coming to stand beside her.

"Sixty?" Newton asked, voice weak.

Mace pointed to the ladder disappearing into the dark space. "Let's get climbing."

Panic clawed at Nia's throat. The *Phalanx* rocked again as she gripped the ladder on the side of the Condor. Every second step upward was pure agony as knives stabbed her ankle. No one stopped her, everyone too busy with the battle happening outside. When she got to the top, she pushed herself over the edge with her good foot but landed on her bad with a hiss of pain.

The inside of the Condor was so much bigger without Mace behind her. Too big. She could barely reach the controls if she sat in the seat properly. Mace hadn't told her how to adjust the seat, but she searched.

Something clacked behind her as the seat moved forward. She took a quick look and saw a med kit. A whoop of joy left her lips. She could fix her messed-up ankle. Her movements jerky, she grabbed it.

Propping her foot against the control panel, she used the scanner and regenerator to heal her ankle. It only took a few minutes, and the swelling disappeared, the pain easing. But during that time, the *Phalanx* rocked around her in a continuous rhythm, like it was being bombarded nonstop. It didn't bode well for her getting off the ship.

Nia tried to calm her jumpy heart as she went through all the pre-flight checks she could remember. The canopy closed with a whine. Once closed, her view of the bay blocked by the inactive viewer, she stared at the control panel in alarm.

How was she supposed to get clearance to leave without being shot down?

This is a stupid idea. She should have tried to head for the bridge. The ship rocked again. Maybe there wasn't a bridge left to go to.

She touched the viewer control. Her eyes blinked at all the information streaming in front of her, disoriented. In the bottom corner of the feed, an image of the *Phalanx's* exterior made her gasp. Guardians fired continuously, like they were trying to punch a hole through the shields, and the *Phalanx* wasn't moving out of the way. *Orion* beckoned in the distance. She was so close!

Her heart in her throat, Nia touched the comm. "Um, hello? I need clearance to leave the *Phalanx*. Can someone help me?"

The comm crackled, then a masculine voice echoed over the line. "Identify yourself. Why are you using the emergency bridge channel?"

"The bridge! That's what I needed. I'm Nia in the CORE Condor, shit, I don't remember what the call numbers are, um, requesting to depart from the starboard aft hangar. I'm Commander Mace's former captive. Oh, blast. I wasn't supposed to say that. Okay. Here's the truth. I saw a traitor. One who was in the engine core the day the CORE attacked. He's headed to *Orion*. I need to identify and stop him. And I know Admiral Krispin is in charge of this vessel, and Mace said he didn't trust another man more with his life... and so I'm trusting him with my life. Stars above, this sounds so stupid. Mace said he was going to *Orion*. The traitor was going to *Orion*. So I need to get to *Orion*, okay?"

Silence echoed on the other end of the comm, and Nia banged her forehead against the control panel. She'd never sounded less intelligent. What the hell was she doing?

When she lifted her head, two Tellusian warriors were making their way toward the Condor. *Oh, shit.* This was it. She was going to be arrested and put in bonds.

But they stopped a few meters away.

The voice on the comm made her jump. "Condor Echo Two Six Two, you are cleared for departure. Safe journey. Out."

Nia let out a breath. How had that even worked? Fingers shaking with adrenaline, she engaged the thrusters and hovered above the deck. The ship hummed and groaned. Why hadn't it made those sounds when Mace flew it? And she wasn't pointed in the right direction. Monitoring her thrusters, she turned the ship between the two shuttles. She'd almost accomplished the task without incident when the tip of the fighter's wing grazed the one shuttle. She over-corrected and banged into the other one. The sound reverberated through her skull and made her fingers tingle on the controls.

Finally, she pointed in the right direction, and with a deep, fortifying breath, she punched the accelerator. Her head slammed into the seat as she jerked forward, through the shields and out of the hangar.

Laser fire erupted in front of her. Marauders, Strix, and mines careened everywhere. Nia screamed, banking one way, then another. A Guardian drifted at an odd angle, incapacitated. Escape pods shot out from its sides.

A mine headed right toward her. She over-corrected, and the Condor spun, making her stomach leap into her throat. It took her too long to get it oriented.

"Thrust balance. Thrust balance," she repeated to herself.

Her comm crackled, then a feminine voice said, "Echo Two Six Two. Stay on this trajectory. We are here to escort you."

Two Strix flanked the Condor, and Nia's shoulders relaxed a fraction. Out of nowhere, orange bursts came at her, bouncing off the shields, then the Strix's on the right. She accelerated, trying to get away. The Strix burst apart, debris raining toward her. Nia had no time to mourn the death because the orange fire hit her shields over and over again. A Marauder headed straight for her. The repetitive screeching beep of a weapons lock echoed within the fighter. Her control panel displayed shield strength at eighty-five percent.

The Marauder blew apart, chunks of metal composite sizzling against Nia's shields. She banked to get away, almost hit the other Tellusian escort, and righted the ship as another Strix took the place of the destroyed one.

Orion drew closer and closer. Her stomach no longer lived in her body.

Another worry toppled all the others. *I don't know where to land.*

Thank the stars Grey had brought the pulse cannon. Defenders guarded the command center three deep. Mace and the rest of the team stayed out of sight near the disabled security checkpoint. They'd already thinned out the enemy ranks but needed one last push. A stunning blast from Betel's grenade, followed by Grey's second last shot from the cannon, and they broke through the line protecting the entrance.

As soon as he stepped into the command center, a shot narrowly missed Mace's head. He dove for cover behind the secondary terminals, Spiro beside him. Using hand signals, he communicated with Grey across the space behind another bank of terminals. Cache remained in the corridor, protecting her tech team.

Four defenders remained in defensible positions near the main holotable, their CORE techies huddled along the far bulkhead whimpering. Mace's hand tightened on his gun.

Laser fire shot overhead, sparks cascading. As soon as the volley ended, Mace signaled Grey. He and Spiro broke around the terminal in opposite directions. Weapons fire blazed toward them. Spiro hissed. Mace dropped low, aimed, and shot a CORE general right between the eyes, leaving a wide hole through his forehead. Another brief burst of fire followed, then silence.

"Grey, report," he barked, fearing for a moment one of his friends was hurt or worse.

"Clear."

Grey came into view, and Mace stood to appraise the situation.

"Spiro, clear the rest of the area. Make sure there are no surprises. Grey, make sure the CORE techies stay put. Take their PALMs." Mace jerked his head to the half-dozen men and women trembling in the corner before he walked back to the corridor and gestured to Cache. "The command center is yours, Commodore. Welcome home."

A satisfied gleam entered her eyes before she herded the tech team in, all business. "Mouse, start unlocking key systems. We need weapons and navigation. Callista, check if they've hidden any survivors."

Mace joined her and the techies at the holotable.

"There are Tellusians in the brigs." Callista lifted her head to meet Cache's eyes. "They're not doing well."

"As soon as it's safe, we'll send for the medical teams," Cache said with a nod.

"Can we see the outside feeds?" Mace asked the techies.

"Give me a second," Mouse responded.

The viewer flickered, went off, then every screen flashed with images of the outside battle. Mace focused on the *Phalanx*. Surrounded by six Guardians, they fired nonstop at the Tellusian Destroyer. It looked to be adrift.

"They're dead in the water," Cache said, almost in a whisper. "We need to help them." She turned to the techies. "We need those mines online now."

"Working on it," said Callista and Mouse at the same time. Newton hadn't resurfaced since going under the table.

"Oh, hell," Callista breathed, her eyes panicked. A countdown started on the main viewer: Self-Destruct 29:59

29:58

29:57

29:56

Chapter Forty-Two

"I did not order the self-destruct!" Cache shouted, her hand slapping the table.

"It started on its own!" Callista shouted back. "I hit some sort of tripwire beneath the systems."

"Can confirm," Mouse interjected quickly, like he wanted to stop murder—which was possible. "It's part of the virus they've planted and wasn't deliberate."

Cache pointed at Mouse, her features hard. "You. Return to unlocking those systems." She pointed at Callista. "You. Fix what you did and turn the fucking thing off. If we all die, it'll go on your report."

Callista jerked, her brow furrowed in her confusion. "But won't I be dead along with—?"

"Get to work!" Cache shouted.

Mace strode over to where Grey monitored the CORE techies. Hands on their heads, the scent of their fear and desperation wafted toward him.

He pushed away his pity, and thoughts of Nia, of what she would want him to do in this situation, to ask, "Which one of you can turn off the self-destruct? Lie to me and die. Work with us, and we will treat you with respect."

Grey's eyebrows lifted. Okay, so it sounded less threatening than the situation warranted, but it seemed to have the desired effect. While most of them continued to shake and blubber, one woman held up a tentative hand.

He stepped toward her. "You can turn it off?"

She shook her head frantically. "I heard General Duval say that if the self-destruct was tripped, it would be unstoppable." Her voice shook as she spoke, her Common accent different from Nia's. She ended on a sob, her eyes sliding to where they'd stacked their dead commanding officers.

"No one here designed it?" Grey asked.

She shook her head again. "We're all bridge crew from the *Triomphe* and arrived this morning."

"*Tais-toi*," the man beside her spat.

She turned to him, her face twisted in anger, and said in French, "We're either going to die or become sex slaves, Reggie! I'd rather cooperate if it means some respect!"

A couple of the others nodded, two looked close to fainting, and one at the side reached for her left hand, her missing PALM, like he'd seen Nia do a hundred times. The center of his chest stung.

He would not get any more help here and returned to the holotable just as Newton poked his head out.

"They've done a lot of shit to this thing," he said, running a hand over his face. "It's going to take about a dozen teams a few days to fix everything. They weren't intending to fly *Orion* out of here."

"Are *we* going to fly?" Cache asked, hands braced against the holotable.

"I think so?"

"That was a question?"

"Yes?"

Cache glared at him as he disappeared under the holotable, then met Mace's eyes. He knew what she was thinking.

If they couldn't get the station out of the sector, they were dead. More CORE would keep coming.

"Mouse?" she asked the techie near him.

"I've accessed most of the main systems," Mouse replied, "but the same virus is slowing us down. I have re-established communications."

"Can we contact the *Phalanx*?"

"Their comm is down."

"Weapons?"

"Still working on it. I'm almost ready to clear the station. A couple more minutes."

They stared at the viewer. The *Phalanx* could use their help right now. Transports left the hangars. They were evacuating. The *Mercenary*, *Rebel*, and Tellusian fighters were offering as much cover fire as they could to the survivors.

"Callista?" Cache asked.

No reply, and when they looked at her, Mace noted the sweat beading on her brow.

The clock continued.

22:34

22:33

22:32

Mouse perked up, a smile on his face. "I have control over the mines."

Finally. Mace moved to tactical control on the left while letting out a measured breath.

"Aim at those Guardians," Cache ordered.

The panel lit up beneath his fingers. Using targeting control, he activated the mines' propulsion systems and sent a cluster of them toward the Guardian attacking the *Phalanx*.

They hit all at once, making its shields ripple. Something vented into space.

"Don't stop," Cache said, her voice hard. "The *Phalanx* is dying out there."

"Sir!" Mouse shouted. "There's a communication coming from a Condor. It has a Tellusian escort."

"Let's hear it."

Mouse put the audio over the comm. When a hesitant voice echoed in the command center, Mace's fingers stilled over the controls, his stomach plunging.

"*Orion*. Mace. Commodore. Whoever! This is Nia in Condor Echo Two Six Two."

He met Cache's wide eyes. All the blood drained from his body at the sound of Nia's voice.

"I can identify a traitor trying to gain access to *Orion*," she went on, her voice edged in panic. "Please advise me where to land. Please. I'm really bad at this flying thing. Shit. Mace, why didn't you show me how to use the weapons?" She finished in a near shout, then paused. "Did I already say please? Forget that part and tell me where to land."

"Cache," he whispered, praying his commanding officer and friend would know how to stop Nia from killing herself.

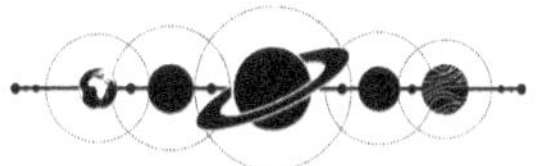

Focus. Focus.

Nia gripped the controls so hard her fingers ached. One of *Orion's* arms cast a shadow across the canopy.

A silence followed her frantic declaration. Did her message even get through? She swallowed to combat the nausea climbing in her throat.

The comm crackled and a male voice said, "Condor Echo Two Six Two, land in docking bay A1. Be advised we still have hostiles in that part of the station. Out."

"Awesome." All the moisture left her mouth. "I was looking forward to some hostiles. Where the hell is docking bay A1?" Her nausea increased while she tapped at the screen in front of her, trying to find some control where it would say "schematics" or something.

"Okay," she said when nothing obvious appeared. She had no more time to look since the station towered ahead of her. "A1 has to be near the top. Section C was at the bottom." She aimed the fighter toward the apex of the station, hoping her guess was right.

Heart pounding, she circled the station twice before noticing an open bay door. "Here goes nothing," she muttered, then lined up as best she could.

A guidance system materialized on her screen, directing her with an option for an "automated landing." She pressed the icon, and the program took over.

A long breath left her, and she sat back a bit. "They're just going to need to manage if this isn't A1."

She passed through *Orion's* shielding and entered the wide bay. Her heart leaped into her throat. It was filled with defenders. She ducked out of sight. So far, they seemed to think she was a friendly because she was in a Condor. But rising panic made her breath short. The fighter kept descending. They'd find out she wasn't a fellow soldier soon enough. If she landed, and the automated system dropped shields and opened the canopy, then she was dead.

Nia pressed the icon to turn off the automated landing, and the Condor nearly crashed. Sheer luck kept her in the air. But the defenders moved frantically to surround her and fired.

Stomach rolling, she watched her shields ripple, holding at eighty-one percent. She could take a lot from the defenders' weapons, but the shield strength wouldn't last forever.

The pressure in the bay changed so abruptly Nia almost let go of the controls. The defenders were firing at her one second, then flying out the bay's doors the next, along with anything that wasn't secured. *Whap, whap, whap.* Bodies hit the sides of the fighter. Nia winced, her shoulders up to her ears.

When the bay's shielding returned, the Condor dropped. She yanked on the controls. *Thwack.* The landing gear slammed into the deck, the sound echoing inside her head.

Nia sat staring at nothing, her heart rate slowly lowering. Blinking twice, she forced herself to let go of the controls one finger at a time, then shook out her arms.

Peeking through the viewer, she affirmed she was the only one left in the bay. She pressed the control for the canopy to retract. It whined, the vastness of the bay greedily sucking the sound away. When the strength returned to her arms, she pressed the control for the ladder, pushed herself over the edge of the fighter, and clumsily half-slid, half-slipped down the rungs.

Her feet hit the deck, and she fell to her knees. Gasping for breath, she dry-heaved. Twice. How had she survived her flight? She had no clue. Some celestial being must be watching out for her.

Silence pulsed, disturbing in such a large space. Legs shaking, she stood and searched for an exit near the rear of the bay. Several lined the bulkhead along with lifts. Which one led to Mace?

She headed to the closest one, then stopped when the swishing sound of a door opening hushed farther along. Turning toward it, her heart jumped into her throat when Mace stepped through, his uniform splattered in blood, a gun in his hand, and Betel right behind him.

With a shout, she ran and launched herself at him. Her body slammed into his, and it felt like coming home. Disregarding everything else, she wrapped her arms and legs around him and heard his weapon thump to the ground a second before his arms encircled her. She buried her face in his throat and squeezed him tight, inhaling his minty scent entwined with the acrid smell of weapons discharge.

"Ah, Nia," he said, hugging her close. "*Izar*." His lips skimmed her ear. "I don't think I can let you go again."

Her heart squeezed at his words, and she held him tighter. "I don't think I want to be let go."

A tortured sound emerged from his chest as he returned her embrace and pressed his cheek to hers. She closed her eyes and let the moment wash over her. The disquiet she'd been feeling since their separation disappeared. She was safe and protected, and had never felt more whole.

All too soon, Mace set her on her feet and held her at arm's length with his hands on her shoulders, his expression severe and eyes haunted. "What the hell did you do? You were supposed to be far from here."

She covered his hands with her own. "There was a man." Beneath hers, Mace's fingers flexed. "He stopped me from getting on my transport, almost killed me because I saw him in the engine core the day Commander Foley threatened me. He was doing something inside the chamber."

Throughout her explanation, Mace's expression became more murderous.

"He was alone?" Betel asked from beside her, his voice gravelly.

She nodded, meeting his eyes.

"There aren't supposed to be solo maintenance crews," Mace said, the planes of his face hard. "Tell me more."

She told him everything about what had happened on the *Phalanx*. "I think—" Nia finished, swallowing against the dryness in her throat. "I think he's a CORE agent."

Mace pulled her close and turned to Betel. "Do you know the status of those medical crews?"

"Still on standby as far as I know."

Mace bent and grasped his weapon. "Come," he said, his hand skimming her spine. "We need to get to the command center."

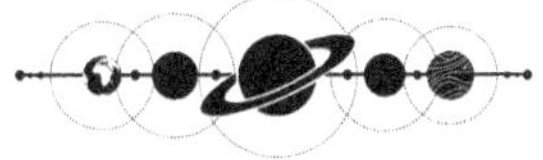

Mace didn't think his heart rate would ever return to normal. When he'd heard her voice over the comm, his heart had stopped dead. Thinking about her flying across a battlefield with nothing more than an hour of the most basic instruction...

He couldn't stop touching her as they made their way out of the docking bay, needing affirmation that she was safe—that she'd returned to him.

His hand on her spine, he focused ahead. Mouse may have been able to clear most of the station of defenders using the emergency environmental systems, but it didn't mean he'd gotten everyone. There could be pockets where defenders survived.

With Betel taking point, they headed the way they'd come. Mace kept his senses alert. He wouldn't be able to breathe easily until they'd returned to their defensible position. The empty corridors echoed with their footsteps.

A few of the lifts were working, courtesy of Mouse, and they returned to the one they'd taken to the docking bay. As Betel reached for the control panel, Mace's instincts hummed, hair pricking on his nape, and he turned.

Laser fire erupted in his peripheral vision. In the next instant, he twisted, shielding Nia with his body and returning fire.

Blistering heat scalded his back. A shout erupted from his throat. He tried to protect Nia, cover her, as the haze of pain overtook his vision.

Chapter Forty-Three

Circumstances changed so fast, she wasn't sure what happened. One moment she'd been tucked securely against Mace. In the next instant, weapons fire exploded around them.

They crashed to the deck, Mace's arms around her ribs. Her breath left her in one big whoosh, her head smacking the hard surface. Stars danced in her eyes. Mace flattened her, a solid, motionless mass.

"Mace?" she croaked, turning as much as she could to see his face. His eyes were closed, and sweat beaded his brow. Her stomach twisted with nausea.

"Move!" Betel shouted from nearby. Amidst more weapons fire, the acrid scent overwhelming, she tried to follow the order, to squirm out of Mace's grip, but his body pressed her against the deck. A panicked sob escaped her lips.

His body jerked forward, rolling, but his eyes didn't open. Then his arms fell away enough to allow her to wiggle free.

She lifted her head. Betel dragged Mace by his collar, one centimeter at a time, toward the lift. His weapon fired nonstop in the direction they'd come.

The next round of bursts made her flinch, and she ducked instead of getting to her feet.

"Take his gun!"

She turned and saw the two defenders using the bulkheads as cover, firing blindly toward them. Mace's gun lay near his feet. She dove for it, pressing the trigger as soon as it settled into her hands. Her body jerked with the force of the recoil.

The laser blasts gouged holes in the bulkheads, sparks flying. But her chaotic aim had the desired effect of making the defenders retreat. She spun, scrambling after Mace as Betel pulled him fully onto the lift. The door closed behind her. Betel slapped his hand against the control panel, and the lift ascended.

It was the first time she got a look at Mace's injury, and a shout broke from her lips. She clambered closer. A laser burn cut across Mace's spine, melting his uniform to his body. The wound was too deep, too wide. He was losing too much blood. He needed immediate stasis and surgery.

Nausea swirled in her stomach. "I need a med kit!" she shouted, swallowing against the bile rising in her throat. She pressed her fingers to Mace's neck, felt a weak pulse, and exhaled a quick, relieved breath.

"There'll be one in the command center," came Betel's rough reply.

The lift door slid open to reveal a wide corridor equipped with a biometric tunnel.

Betel dragged Mace out by the collar. "I need some help here," he shouted to the right.

Spiro came running from an arched doorway. Nia moved out of the way, and Spiro took his feet.

Her heart aching, she followed them the way Spiro had come. The doorway opened into a space mimicking the atrium in shape and layout, with a holotable at its center. Viewers ran along the circumference, ones full of images of the battle outside, violent with laser blasts, mines exploding, a debris field scattered everywhere. Nia's breath caught. She'd flown through that.

"What happened?" asked a woman with black hair swept into a tail at the top of her head, her expression hard. *Must be the commodore.*

"Stray defenders," was all Betel answered as he and Spiro carried Mace to the side.

"Keep him face down," Nia ordered, following, her heart beating a rapid rhythm in her chest.

Her gaze skimmed over the rest of the people in the command center. Six dead defenders were piled in one corner, two of them with high-ranking uniforms. A small group of bound CORE technical officers huddled near them. She recognized the Tellusian warrior, Mace's friend from the training center, standing near the CORE officers, his concerned gaze aimed in her direction.

Standing across from the commodore, three Tellusian techs stood shoulder to shoulder, their fingers frantically skimming the surface of the holotable, their faces pinched with worry. That's when Nia noticed a countdown hovering above its surface:

16:39

16:38

16:37

A self-destruct? The acid churning in Nia's stomach climbed her throat. She swallowed and returned her focus to Mace. He was the one who needed her help most right now—whether or not they were all about to explode.

She collapsed to her knees beside him and widened the melted and charred material of his uniform to get a better look at the injury. Her hands shook. Nerve damage. He might not walk again.

"All three of you, get the damn thing turned off, and get it turned off now," the commodore's voice cut through the tension. "Or we'll die before we get a chance to see if this beast will even move."

Betel shoved a med kit at Nia, and she opened it, letting out a slow breath to calm herself. Thank the stars it was fully stocked. She grabbed two cardiovascular nodes, a laser scalpel, the transfusers, and a regenerator.

"Will Mace live?" The commodore's voice cut right to Nia.

She swallowed and met the commodore's gaze. "He needs stasis."

"Do your best. We can't move anyone right now." She broke Nia's gaze and focused on her technical officers.

"It's the virus, sir," the one woman said, voice shaking. "It has nothing to do with which systems we've unlocked."

"Then figure out a way to remove it," Cache said, her words clipped.

Nia looked up at Spiro, who remained close by. "I need him on his side for a moment."

The warrior crouched and helped her roll him. With quick movements, she cut away his top with a laser scalpel and attached the cardiovascular nodes to his chest. They laid him flat once more, then she inserted the blood and fluid transfuser portals into his arm. Each hummed as they worked.

She took a length of regeneration gauze and wadded it to stop the bleeding where the laser weapon had failed to cauterize. Her gaze flicked upward.

15:01

14:59

14:58

Spinal damage. Nia took out the fine detail regenerator, willing her hands to steady. Her hands hovered over the worst of the damage near the base of his neck. *Focus!*

She turned on the fine detail regenerator. It buzzed as she addressed the most sensitive area of the injury. She stopped listening to the voice in her head that told her if she'd seen this injury on *Elara Five*, she would have sent him straight to palliative.

Minutes counted down. An oppressive silence hung over everyone in the command center, with only the small noises from her machine and the beeping of the techs working to cut through the tension. While she worked, she tried not to look at the numbers counting down above the table. Her gaze flicked upward anyway.

8:23

8:22

8:21

Her stomach clenching, she kept healing Mace. If they exploded, at least they would explode together.

"I think I've found a backdoor," one tech said, voice soft. "Give me a couple of minutes."

"We don't have a couple of minutes," the commodore responded over top of her, her tone incredulous.

Nia healed the spinal cord and the tissue around it, trying not to think of what would happen if she did it wrong or rushed the process. Seconds ticked by, seconds she knew they didn't have.

"Got it!" the same tech shouted.

Nia flicked her eyes to the holotable. The numbers above continued to decrease.

5:37

5:36

5:35

She refocused on Mace's injury but couldn't help looking at the countdown every other minute.

"Callista..." The commodore said, the one word a warning.

A collective breath swelled around them.

Nia paused in her task and grabbed Mace's hand.

1:26

1:25

0:00

Simultaneous exhales filled the stifling silence. The three technical officers stepped away from the table, visibly shaken. The commodore braced her hands on the holotable and hung her head like she needed a minute.

Nia lowered her shoulders from where they'd lifted around her ears.

"No time for breaks," the commodore said not a minute later. "Return to what you were supposed to be doing."

There was still an air of urgency swirling in the command center, but the sick sensation of impending doom had faded. Adrenaline easing from her body, Nia focused on healing Mace's muscles a strand at a time. By the time she was done, his back would be more synthetic than not.

"Sir!" shouted a technical officer at the holotable. "I've got *Orion's* weapons online."

"Fire at those Guardians," Cache ordered.

An overwhelming hum filled the command center, followed by an internal groan and a hollow *clank*, as though a giant flicked its fingers against the outside of *Orion*. Nia lifted her head to look at the viewer. A spear of red shot from the station and connected with the closest Guardian. She gasped.

The weapon cut the ship in two like a knife through flesh.

"Target another Guardian," Cache ordered without missing a beat.

The station hummed again, and the beam of light cleaved another ship.

All those lives. Nia blinked the moisture from her eyes as she refocused on Mace's wound. This was what the war had brought them to: two peoples who'd destroy each other with the flick of a switch. Her throat tightened painfully.

"Betel," the commodore ordered. "Destroy all the Marauders about to make suicide runs."

"I've got navigation," said one tech over top of Betel's, "Yes, sir."

"Get us the hell out of here."

A moment later, *Orion* shuddered, and Nia pulled her tools away from Mace's wound to brace herself against the deck. She stared at the information scrolling across the holotable's surface. The ship she'd been on, the *Phalanx*, imploded on the way by, scuttled.

Orion lurched around them, moving forward with a groaning jerk, then accelerated to high speed, absolutely still. The amount of power needed to move a station this size boggled Nia's mind. The reason for the four massive engine cores was suddenly quite clear.

"You three," the commodore's voice rang out as she addressed her warriors. "Clear the rest of this station a deck at a time until reinforcements can be brought over. Grey, take these CORE techies to the brig until they can be processed."

Three "Yes, sirs," echoed as Nia continued to heal Mace's wound. Now that they were safe, the noise of the command center faded into the background as she concentrated.

Nia was finishing with one side of his back when she realized the commodore drew near. She lifted her head when the imposing woman squatted beside her.

"How's he doing?" the commodore asked.

Hands bloody, Nia pushed the hair away from her face with her forearm. "Better. I need to take him to a sickbay. He needs more fluids and blood. He also needs a large bulk of tissue synthesized, but I've healed the worst of it."

The commodore nodded, but worry lingered in her eyes. "You said something about a traitor."

Nia nodded, then focused on Mace's wound. What she was about to say... it would sentence the man to a horrific death and go against everything she'd believed in.

But when she thought about what he'd done to her... all those deaths he'd caused on *Orion*...

She swallowed and kept her gaze on the blood on her hands while she moved the regenerator over Mace's spine. "There was a man on the

Phalanx, one who I thought was an agent. I saw him alone in the engine core the day before the attack, and from the way he was trying to kill me, I'm pretty sure he was the one responsible for *Orion's* breach in security."

"You can identify him?"

"Yes, and he wore a doctor's uniform, was supposed to be heading here to provide medical aid. At least that's what I heard someone say in the hangar."

"Mouse!" The commodore's shout made Nia jump.

"Yes, sir?" the tech with huge eyes came closer.

"Have all medical personnel heading here detained for questioning. Don't let anyone leave for any reason. Keep them in B2 for now."

"Yes, sir."

Cache said nothing for the longest time, just stared—long enough for Nia to ask, "What?" belligerently without looking up from her task.

"Since when have you known how to fly a Condor?"

"Mace taught me yesterday."

Cache expelled a bark of laughter. "I can see why he kept you."

Nia's hand pulled back. She shook her head, then resumed her task. "I need to focus here."

"Yeah," Cache agreed, then asked, "Are you sure he's going to be okay?"

"He'll live," Nia said with a small smile, the truth making her heart light. "He'll live."

Chapter Forty-Four

Fire enveloped his back unlike anything Mace had ever experienced. An agonized bellow worked its way through his lungs and lodged in his throat. Broken images filled his brain: the infiltration team, Nia arriving in a Condor, the attack from defenders. *Fuck.*

Must be dying. He'd come to the end of his run. It had been a good run, full of family, love, and successes, but he regretted not being able to share more of his life with Nia. If only he could see her face one last time...

Breathing through the pain, inhaling a medicinal scent, he opened his eyes. The room around him blurred. An outline of a med bed sharpened, gray bulkheads beyond. He tried to move, but only lifted his head, then gasped when new agony shot through his spine.

Hurried footsteps neared. Legs came into focus with small feet in flat black shoes. He knew those feet. Nia's wan face came into view as she crouched in front of him, her eyes shiny with tears.

It's true. I'm dying. She wouldn't look so anguished otherwise.

He lifted his hand, tried to touch her face, pull on a curl, but all he got was another stab down his spine.

"Lie still," she said, pressing a cool hand to his cheek. "The less you move, the better."

He tried to say her name, but a rasped sound escaped his lips instead.

"This will help." She twisted off the top of a ration tube and held it to his mouth. Relief filled the insides of his cheeks, and he swallowed. Soothing goo slid down his throat. Mace closed his eyes, then opened them again to make sure she hadn't left.

If he was dying, if his remaining time was counted in minutes, then he needed to say a few things. "Nia," he whispered, the word shaky.

"Shhhh." She touched her finger to his lips, then pressed a dermal syringe into his neck.

Mace blinked. She'd shushed him? The thought melted away, the pain in his back receded, and his eyelids drooped. "Dona wanna sleep cuz imma dying."

"You're not dying." The words preceded the hiss of another dermal syringe in his neck. "You might have, but I saved you." The room brightened, then she added, "But you saved me first, so I guess we're even." A tinge of humor laced her words.

The bulkheads of the medical bay came into sharp focus. "What did you give me?"

"A stimulant. It will give you a few minutes of lucidity before the painkillers kick in again."

When she was about to move away, his hand snaked out to grab her wrist. She gasped. He pulled her close. "Why does it feel like my back has been ripped off?"

"Because it was." She brushed her knuckles along his cheek. "You've got a sizable amount of new tissue growing right now, and you're covered in regeneration gauze. You need to stay still," she asserted. "Doctor's orders."

Mace took a deep breath, his spine protesting the expansion of his lungs. "You returned."

His words brought her to eye level. She rested her chin against the med bed in front of him. "I had to. There was an agent after me. I couldn't get to my transport, and—"

"And you'll go as soon as you have the chance? You'll use Betel's contacts to return to your family?"

She huffed a breath and shook her head. "No, I'm not going to do that."

His fingers clenched around hers. "Why not?"

Her throat bobbed in a swallow. "Because... I'm not going anywhere." Her hand cupped his jaw, and shivers spread through his skin. "I love you, and I don't want to leave. You scare me, and aggravate me, but when I'm with you I've never felt more alive."

He closed his eyes, his body slumping against the med bed. She wasn't going anywhere. When he opened his eyes, a smile quirked her lips.

"Does that sound about right?"

Mace nodded. "We're still married."

"What?" She stood, pink highlighting her cheeks.

He turned his head to keep her gaze. "I didn't divorce you during the emancipation process. I forgot. Or maybe I didn't want to. I don't know." Each word came out like a flood. "But I want to marry you again. Properly. I want to make you mine the traditional way."

Her expression softened. "That sounds about right." Leaning forward, she brushed his lips with hers.

Electricity shot through his body. When she straightened, her gaze darted over him, cheeks darkening with color.

He tugged her closer with his hand. "There's someone else in the room, isn't there?"

"It's Betel." She cupped his cheek. "He's been watching over you."

Betel grunted.

Mace was glad it was someone he trusted because of what he wanted to say next. "Admiral Krispin said there's a way to protect you even with your lineage. I know he'd help as a sponsor, or whatever we need."

A frown puckered her brow. "Someone said the admiral was hurt and is in surgery."

His stomach dropped, and he realized his eyelids were drooping again. He squeezed her fingers tighter, not wanting her to leave him, even for a minute.

"Where are we?" Mace didn't recognize this sickbay.

"*Orion*. Section A. We're headed to Saturn with the *Mercenary* and *Rebel*."

So they'd gotten the thing moving. If anyone could have done it, it was Cache. She was too fucking stubborn to fail at anything.

"How long have I been out?"

She glanced at the control panel at the head of the med bed. "A little over an hour."

"What about the traitor you saw?"

Her brow furrowed, a tinge of fear entering her eyes. "He wasn't on board any of the medical vessels. He might have changed his plans after he saw me. Or maybe he wasn't heading here at all. I don't know. But he's not on board. Cache made me look at all the personnel files of those who've returned."

Mace's chest seized at the thought of having the man go free, someone who'd tried to kill Nia and almost succeeded. He deserved to die just for touching her. A long, agonizing death.

The door opened behind him where he couldn't see, and Nia jumped, letting go of his hand to raise hers surrender-style.

What the fuck? He tried to lift his head to see what was going on, but the drugs she'd given him were taking effect.

"Euphenia Jannex, you're under arrest for treason. Hands on your head."

The male voice wasn't familiar. Mace struggled to sit up, to protect her, but his brain was too foggy. Whatever she'd shot into his neck made his limbs weak, refusing to cooperate. "Betel," he mumbled, knowing his friend would understand.

Hands on her head, Nia's eyes flicked to his, and Mace saw the fear there. His anger mounted.

Then Betel was beside her, partially shielding her body.

"Stand aside, Lieutenant," the same voice said. "If you interfere, we're going to have to take you down."

Betel's hand hovered over his weapon.

"It's okay," Nia said, expression tight but resigned. "I don't want anyone to get hurt. I'll go with them."

"No." The word was wrenched from Mace.

Thankfully, Betel didn't listen to her. "She's not going anywhere," he said, his gravelly voice cutting through the sickbay.

"Stand down, Lieutenant. This isn't any concern of yours. The charges have been formalized. She will stand trial."

"Like hell." Mace tried to push himself up again, moving his arms under his body.

"Mace, stay still." Nia stepped toward him but stopped when the sound of a weapon charging echoed in the sickbay. "You're going to rip your back open." She replaced her hands on her head.

Steps moved toward her, and Betel pulled his weapon.

Nia shouted, "No!" at the same time Mace did. Shots echoed. Betel crumpled. Two warriors came into view, one grabbing her upper arm, the other holding bonds.

"Don't touch her," Mace shouted, pushing against the table.

"Sorry, Commander. We have our orders."

"I rescind your orders."

"You'll have to go through proper channels, sir. We're taking her."

They pulled Nia to her feet, and she met his eyes with a wobbly expression before they took her out of sight.

His heart ripped from his chest. "Let her go!" He tried to scream the words, but they came out wrong. His back speared with pain as he raised himself.

The door slid shut with a whoosh.

"No!"

Mace struggled, ignoring the burning sensation through his spine, the tearing of newly formed flesh. He shifted his weight, bringing his legs to the side. Excruciating tingles shot through every part of his body. He had to get to Nia. He had to stop them. Nothing else mattered.

His feet swung over the edge. The sensation of his back ripping in two felled him. His legs gave out on a groan. He fell on top of Betel, his head hitting the deck with a *thunk*. Pinprick stars dotted his vision, then blackness.

Mace tried to stay conscious, didn't know how long he lay on his lifeless friend when the door opened again, feet hurrying toward him. "Nia?" he asked, voice hoarse.

Cache came into view. "You're bleeding all over the place," she said as she squatted beside him.

"Cache. What did you do?"

Her hands stilled in the air as they reached for him. "Fuck. You think I had something to do with this? I came here as soon as I heard, thought I could put a stop to it." She rolled him into a seated position, pain lancing through his shoulders where she touched him. "Shit. Seriously, stop bleeding. That's an order."

With a groan and a hiss, she hoisted him up, her shoulder under his, staggering under his weight even though she was as tall as him. Cache leaned him against the med bed. Once he nodded that he could stand on his own, she bent to check Betel's pulse.

"Stunned."

"If you didn't issue the warrant, who did?" Mace wanted blood so badly he could taste it. For the charges to be formalized already, they would have had to have been in the works since before the *Orion* op.

Cache's face paled. "I thought you knew."

Not much could faze Cache, and the look she was giving him solidified the dread resting in his stomach. "Knew what?"

"The warrant came through Admiral Ricker. Foley's behind it. He took her off station."

Mace roared, blood rushing to his head. He pushed away from the bed.

"You can't even walk, fuck, slow down."

"Nia. I've got to get to Nia." His heart hammered in his chest like it never had before, threatening to break free.

"We'll get her, but you need to be able to walk first."

Shaky but standing, he pushed away from the bed. He needed to get to Nia. "Krispin can pardon her. He has the power. The old laws will protect her." Getting anyone else would take too long. As soon as Foley had Nia alone, he'd—

"Krispin's in surgery. Has been for a while."

The way she said it made it sound as though she didn't think Krispin would come out of surgery either.

No! No! No! He had to get to Nia. He had to stop Foley, the sick fuck. "Then pump me full of something. We're in a sickbay. They've got every kind of drug here. Adrenaline-synth will work."

"If I pump you full of something, you'll probably die."

Mace grabbed her by the shoulders. "You do this for me, Cache. You get me there. I will not lose her. Not like this."

He stared into Cache's eyes—green eyes he'd known for close to three decades—and willed her to understand. If Nia got hurt, if Foley touched her, he wouldn't be able to go on.

Cache gave him one nod. "You won't lose her."

Chapter Forty-Five

Nia tried to calm the racing of her heart. Her hands were bound in thick metal, much different from her old bonds, and secured to the table in front of her by a short chain. She tested its strength again, pulling. No give, not even a little. Palms clammy, she rolled her fingers into fists.

The two warriors who'd come for her had shoved her onto a prison transport, taken her to another ship, and stuck her in this cold cell. No one had stopped them. Leaving *Orion*, leaving Mace... her panic hadn't subsided.

She kept her gaze away from the metal cart of crude surgical instruments beside the table. She'd tried to kick it over, but her legs wouldn't reach, even when she'd pulled so hard the bonds cut into her wrists. A bulkhead of opaque glass stretched in front of her.

She closed her eyes. The look on Mace's face as they led her away would forever be burned into her memory. She'd never seen him look so frightened. Not during any of the dangerous situations they'd been through together. His fear escalated her own. The memory of those bodies in *Orion's* theater made her swallow against her dry throat. They'd been labeled traitors too.

Would Commodore Cache order her tortured in front of a crowd? From how Nia had saved Mace's life and her cooperation in trying to track down the agent, she hadn't thought Mace's commanding officer hated her.

But if Cache wanted to publicly torture her, why hadn't she kept her on *Orion*?

Nia pulled on the bonds again when the door opened. She straightened. Commander Foley entered, his hair swooped over his forehead, his eyes alight with something that made her heart skip a beat.

Not him. Her stomach squeezing tight, she held his gaze and lifted her chin. She wasn't a coward.

"Euphenia Jannex." He almost sang her name. "You've found yourself in a predicament."

He gripped a fist-sized container in his hand. She snapped her gaze back to his face, not really wanting to know what it held—not when she could see the cart of tools out of the corner of her eye.

"I'm not sure if you know what kind of trouble you're in, but I'll enlighten you. As your arresting officer, it's my duty to inform you of the charges, the evidence, and the repercussions if you're found guilty."

"But I'm innocent until proved guilty, right?"

He smiled a lazy smile. "Not exactly. The law doesn't work here the same as it does in the CORE."

"May I receive counsel? Would someone assign me an advocate?"

"Not with the charge of treason."

How was that fair? She sensed he enjoyed her discomfort and tried her best to keep her face blank.

Setting the container on the edge of the table, Foley pulled out the chair opposite her, the legs scraping against the deck in a grating pitch. Her shoulders hunched, trying to deflect the sound.

He spun the chair around and sat with his legs spread and arms folded over the back. "Let's start with the penalty. If you're convicted of treason, you'll be publicly tortured for days and eventually sent out an airlock if you don't die from your wounds."

Stomach twisting, she pulled on the bonds, the metal cutting into her wrists.

"Now that you understand the consequences of your actions, let's move on to the proof."

She froze as he reached for the container, opened it, and dumped the contents onto the table. Metal pieces tinkled, bouncing, before settling on the surface. They glinted gold at her, one shard large enough to see the etched vine design of her old locket.

Her breath caught in her throat. How had he gotten it?

"We've retraced this item's power signature all over *Orion*."

Swallowing, Nia stared at the pieces, her mind scrambling.

"I can see your confusion, so let me explain." He set the empty box on the corner of the table and closed the lid with a *snick*. "When a maintenance crew flushed the system of the Condor you arrived in, they found these." He gestured to the table. "Even though you'd sent it through reclamation, part of the device still emitted a signature. A marvellous piece of tech, really. It had gotten through initial scans when arriving on *Orion*, and didn't even die properly when reclaimed. Sometimes CORE tech impresses me."

He grinned, and her heart beat faster. Her mother always liked quality.

"I'd already been looking for the device that had pinged against our security hubs and had the signature flagged. Lucky the maintenance crew did their due diligence and contacted me."

He stood and pressed his hands flat on the table. "The movements of the tracker also coincided with the movements of Commander Mace."

The remaining moisture in her mouth evaporated. Foley leaned closer, hands straddling the gold bits and pieces. She resisted the urge to move away.

"I'm of the belief that you were the one with the device, but if I'm mistaken and it was Commander Mace, I'll lay the charges against him instead."

No! Nia stared at the disassembled locket, her eyesight fogging around the edges. Mace would take the blame for her without flinching. To know he would be publicly tortured and executed—her exhales left her in panicked bursts.

"Do you remember a man named Justice?" Her head snapped up, and Foley sent her his unfeeling smile. "Lovely fellow. He recognized you. Said you were ruling class. But that couldn't be. If you were ruling class, you would have been flagged for ransom the second you stepped foot on this station."

Foley pushed away from the table to walk toward the torture tools. "Justice is dead, by the way. Mace brutally murdered him while he was bound. Broke his neck." Her head snapped to him, and he tipped his head at her. "I also had a lovely chat with the man who processed you on your arrival."

Lovely chat? Nia swallowed around the rock in her throat. What had Foley done to the man who'd processed her? Was he in a room like this? Beside a cart full of surgical tools?

"Tell me Mace knew." He stroked the handle of a blade. "Tell me he's been protecting you."

She shook her head, all the warmth leaving her body. Chills raced over her skin.

One side of Foley's mouth quirked upward. "It seems Commander Mace broke a lot of rules to keep your identity secret. Should we add the tracker to the list of charges?"

"It's mine," she croaked, her throat feeling as if she'd swallowed the pieces of her locket. "If I'm ruling class, you can ransom me. You don't need to execute anyone."

"But you're not ruling class anymore." He picked a blade from the tray. The hook at the end glinted in the overhead light. She couldn't look away. "Your ID shows a different lineage entirely, a stolen one." He stepped closer. "You want to know the funny thing? I couldn't take proper legal action against you until you were secretly emancipated."

Nia's lips parted.

He smiled, his teeth flashing in the light. "As a civilian, you can be charged with crimes. As a captive, you only lose rights, especially when the commander invoked the old laws. You were protected then. As a civilian, you are subject to all the rules and regulations the rest of us are."

There wasn't anything funny about it at all.

"So." He leaned a hip against the table and twirled the blade in his hand. "As your arresting officer, I have two choices. I could go through the motions. Take you in front of a jury—and trust me on this one, they'll convict you. Or," he stood, "I could reveal your true identity and petition the council that you're better off as a bargaining chip. We could free Tellusian POWs in trade. I have a couple of friends who haven't been shot out of a CORE airlock yet." He shrugged, tossing the blade into the air and catching the handle in his palm. "What do you think I should do?"

"I think you should put that down." The force of her own words surprised Nia.

He circled behind her. She turned her head slightly, not wanting to lose sight of him. Abruptly, he dug his fingers into her hair and jerked her head back. Nia cried out. The cool metal of the blade pricked against her throat.

Above her, Foley's face filled her vision. He blocked the lights above, his narrow nose cutting his face in half.

"I'll tell you a secret," he said, bits of spittle landing on her face. She tried to shrink away, but he held on too tightly. "Usually, I get the information I want out of prisoners within the first ten minutes. Just like this. I don't need any more from you. The rest of the time, I play." The metal stroked her skin.

Nia refused to cry or beg. "Mace is going to kill you for touching me."

He tightened his grip on her hair. "He could have as your warder under the old laws, but not when you're a free civilian."

He brought the hook to her face. The cold of the metal pressed against the white of her eye.

"He's my husband," Nia choked out, hoping it protected her even as a civilian.

His knuckles relaxed against her cheek. Foley backed off, separating the tool from her eye. "You're lying."

She latched onto his doubt. "I was emancipated, but he didn't divorce me. It's the old laws. He's still my husband."

When he stepped back, his hold on her hair lessened. The relief swelling through her body made her bold. "You should have done your research, asshole."

He jerked her head, and she cried out. It felt like he'd ripped out a chunk of her hair.

The door slid open, and Mace tumbled in with Cache and Grey. A flurry of movement between the three of them, and a knife shot past Nia's head. With a *thud* and a scream from behind her, the hold on her hair released.

Mace stumbled toward her, his eyes wild, and collapsed with his arms around her waist, face buried between her breasts. With her hands bound to the table, Nia could only close her eyes and lean into him, rubbing her cheek across his silky black hair.

Grey circled behind her, and Nia turned her head. The knife was lodged through Foley's eye, the man dead and slumped against the bulkhead.

"Quite a throw," Grey said. He yanked the knife out. Nia winced at the squelching sound.

"I was aiming for his hand," Mace muttered, the words muffled against her chest.

Cache released Nia's bonds. With her hands freed, Nia buried her face in Mace's throat and wrapped her arms around his shoulders. Her fingers came away bloody.

"What the hell are you doing?" she yelled, pulling away. His glazed eyes filled with confusion. He shouldn't have been able to walk on his own. "You've wrecked all the work on your back. You've lost too much blood already. What did you give him?" She turned accusing eyes on Cache. "How is he standing?"

The commodore lifted her hands in surrender. "Nothing. I was going to, but I didn't want to kill him. He's been pushing himself like this to get here." Cache stared at Foley, a disgusted expression twisting her face, and shook her head.

Nia caught Mace's face between her hands and said, "Mace?"

His glazed eyes partly focused on her. Her breath caught in her throat at the raw emotion swimming there. He kissed her cheeks one at a time, cradling her face.

"I thought I'd lost you." His hands shook.

Nia pressed her forehead to his. "I'm here, *izar*. I'm here."

His embrace wrapped her so tightly she couldn't draw a proper breath. She let him crush her, melting into his chest. Breathing wasn't so important right now, not when his strength surrounded her.

His grip lessened, and Nia pulled away to look into his icy blue eyes. "Now, get your gorgeous butt to a med bay so I can fix your back."

Chapter Forty-Six

S omeone must be playing a joke on her.

Nia stared at Dee, the most obvious culprit. But she and Kessy were both adamant this was how Tellusians got married in the "traditional way."

All three of them stood in Dee's shop. Her friend had closed it for the day so they could prepare. Nia understood their cultures were different. But this...

With her hair piled in loops on top of her head, she wore only the smallest of underwear—she would have had more coverage holding a palette in front of her—as Dee and Kessy *painted* her. Blue swirls covered her body from the tips of her toes to her ears and spiraled everywhere in between. Her arms, legs, stomach, and breasts were all decorated in the pattern of Mace's family.

"If you think I'm going out there in only blue paint, you're—"

"No, no," Dee insisted. "There's the traditional gown too."

Some of her tension eased, but she resentfully stared at the blue dresses the other two wore. While Nia stood practically naked, Dee and Kessy were swathed from throat to wrist to ankle entirely in blue. The material hugged all their curves, leaving nothing to the imagination, but at least it covered their skin. Their hair was also piled on top of their heads in large curls.

Her friends' gazes focused, they continued to paint. The process was taking forever, and Nia fidgeted, though tried not to for fear of smudging the paint before it dried. All she could do was stand there and think. And worry. And fret.

It had been a month since *Orion* had begun orbiting Saturn. During that time, Nia accepted that this was her new home. The urge to return to the CORE, to *Elara Five*, had dissolved into nothing. She missed her parents and being able to communicate with them whenever she wanted, but consciously allowing her old life to slip from her fingers had been... liberating.

Her new life wasn't without obstacles. With Commander Foley's death, Mace became the head of security for *Orion*. He also refused to give up teaching the tyros. Each day was a struggle for him to find balance. From what Nia had seen of his interactions with Cache, his CO was about ready to intervene. But that worry was for another day.

For the time being, Nia had decided to remain in family medicine, taking full shifts instead of abbreviated "captive" ones. She couldn't say why she'd kept her original post. Since being emancipated, she could apply for other positions. Perhaps it was just stubbornness, since Mayra and Faas kept trying to make her life difficult, and she refused to let them drive her away.

Because both she and Mace were so busy, some days they only saw each other in bed. There wasn't a night that went by that they didn't take advantage of being together, of showing how much they loved one another. With what had happened with Foley, and Mace's injury, both of them almost touching tragedy, they didn't want to take a second of their time together for granted.

Tragedy... the most painful part of their lives was that Lexi was still missing.

They couldn't find Mace's sister—not even word of her execution. Mace had used all of his contacts and assets, everyone close to him doing the same, including Admiral Krispin, who'd made a full recovery, but no one could find out what had happened to her. She vanished from the system, like she'd been launched in an escape pod, never to be seen or heard from again. Nia's stomach churned at the thought.

That didn't mean they'd given up. *Far from it.* Nia swallowed the new batch of nerves bubbling up her throat. Tomorrow would begin a completely new adventure.

Dee and Kessy stepped back, admiring their handiwork. From their expressions, they seemed pleased, but Nia looked down and all she saw were her nipples covered in blue.

"I can *not* go out like this." She loved Mace with her whole being, but this was asking too much.

"Oh!" Dee hopped up and scurried to the rear of her shop. "I'll grab the dress," she said over her shoulder. "Newly fabricated this morning."

Kessy's mischievous smile should have warned her. When Dee returned with the garment, Nia's jaw dropped.

"You've got to be kidding me."

It wasn't a dress; it was a blue mesh bag.

Dee frowned. "What's wrong with it?"

"It's entirely see-through! Everyone can see *everything!*"

Her friend's frown morphed into a grin. "That's the point." She stopped in front of Nia and motioned for her to lower her head. The light material fell onto her shoulders, cascading down her body.

Surprisingly, Nia did feel more covered than she would have thought. Everything was still visible, but it felt like she'd donned shielding.

"Mace is going to lose his shit when he sees you," Dee murmured.

If it were only him, Nia wouldn't hesitate walking through the door and heading straight to the arboretum where he waited. But knowing other guests waited with him made her bare feet stick to the deck.

Thankfully, she'd been told the ceremony would be small. She hoped "small" meant the same thing here as it did for the CORE.

"Ready?" Kessy asked from beside her.

Was she ready to marry Mace?

Technically, they were still married, but Mace kept saying he wanted to "do it right" then would quickly add, "but only if you want to."

There wasn't anything she wanted more.

"I'm ready."

With her friends on either side of her, they left Dee's shop. The bracing temperature of the deck against her bare feet made her move fast. A few people walked the level, going about their day, but when they saw Nia, they stopped and stepped to the side to wait.

Tension climbed Nia's spine.

"Don't worry," Kessy whispered beside her. "That's normal. It's out of respect for the bride."

Even if everyone only stopped out of respect, it didn't erase the embarrassing reality that they could see her nipples—whether or not they were covered in blue paint. Swallowing her nerves, she followed the two women who led the way around the atrium to the third-level access of the arboretum.

Tiny butterflies danced in her stomach as they walked through the narrow corridor and onto a catwalk that ran the circumference of the arboretum. Moist air wafted around them, saturated with the scent of the trees and earth. It was quiet up here, the dust and rocks of Saturn's rings reflecting through the crisscrossed lights above. Birds chirped and cawed, the noise of the atrium floating away behind them.

Nia followed Dee along the catwalk, then down a metal staircase, with Kessy right behind her. When she stepped onto the composite path that would lead them to her marriage ceremony, the dancing butterflies tried to escape through her throat.

Their clothes rustled as they walked. Nerves crept through her body, unstoppable, but her feet kept moving. She pressed a hand to her stomach and took a deep breath. Each of her heartbeats was as loud as a weapon's blast in her head.

Then, through the trees, she heard voices and saw patches of blue. Dee met her gaze over her shoulder and smiled. They turned the last corner. Up an incline and in a circle of sycamores stood Mace.

Everything else melted away.

He wore the same sort of mesh garment as she, naked beneath except for a small strip of underwear. His skin was painted too, the lines melding with the tattoo that covered his abdomen, becoming one unending swirl. Her lips quirked when she realized his nipples were blue. His hair was slicked back from his face. It made Nia want to go over there and muss it.

Taking a deep breath, she walked toward him, keeping her gait even instead of running over there and throwing herself at him.

A hush settled on those present as she neared. The grass tickled the soles of her feet. Cache stood at the top of the incline wearing a formal uniform of dark blue lined with white, a short cape falling from her shoulders. Her black hair was styled in loops on top of her head. Despite the dress uniform, the commodore looked softer than Nia had ever seen her.

On Mace's left stood Grey, Betel, Spiro, and a handful of warriors who she didn't know well yet.

Dee and Kessy joined the group on the other side of the clearing. Sorley and Kilian were there. Next to them stood Lokin, Dee's son, who was almost the same age as Kilian. All of them were smiling.

But it was Mace's smile she needed to see. His eyes crinkled, the icy blue warming as his gaze swept her from top to bottom. She lived for his smiles now, to see his joy. It filled her like nothing in her life ever had before.

All the tension in her body disappeared. She was making the right choice.

Lifting her chin, she strode forward until she stood in front of him.

"You look amazing," he said, hands on her shoulders as he pressed his lips to her temple. When he pulled back, his eyes held so much heat, she knew he wanted to carry her off and have his way with her.

She swallowed as an answering warmth settled low in her stomach.

Mace took her hand, and they turned to face Cache. Everyone else formed a circle around them.

"Welcome," Cache began. Then she spoke on the themes of water, life, and connection, first in Tellusian, then translating in Common. The words flowed around them, lyrical and poignant. Nia looked at Mace out of the corner of her eye and found him staring at her, eyes full of emotion.

After that, she couldn't look away.

When Cache completed the officiant's portion, Nia and Mace faced each other. They stood palm to palm, breath to breath.

Mace spoke first. "Nia. You are my strength. I am nothing without you. I will spend the rest of my life protecting you and would die in your stead."

She'd been told they would exchange a vow, had memorized the one she'd made by heart. But after hearing Mace's declaration, all thoughts left her head. She could only stare at him.

"I don't want you dying in my stead!" she blurted.

An awkward chuckle rippled around them, and Nia's cheeks burned. She'd basically refuted his vow. *I make a horrible Tellusian.*

Amusement crinkled Mace's eyes, and he gave her fingers a squeeze.

Shaking her head at herself, Nia took a deep breath, trying to remember the vow she'd been practicing all week. Staring into Mace's eyes, seeing the love there, it all came back to her.

"Mace. I came to you empty, and you filled me with life. You have given me hope for a different future. I vow to walk alongside you, to hold your hand, to live up to your strength, and to face all obstacles together. Always."

His lips parted, and she swallowed at the intensity in his eyes, as if he wanted to devour her. Right now, that seemed like a pretty good idea.

Cache cleared her throat, forcing their eyes on her, and said, "Tellus guide us now and through the veil."

Then Mace swept Nia into his arms and kissed her like his life depended on it. Everyone in the circle hollered their approval, clapping.

When they broke apart, Mace pressed his forehead against hers. "I love you so much, Nia."

She squeezed him tightly. "I love you more than I can say." Burying her face in his neck, she hugged him as hard as she could. They had tonight—their last night of safety and calm.

Because tomorrow... After two weeks of planning, *tomorrow* they would head into CORE space to find Lexi. If they couldn't find her from Tellusian territory, then they would need to work from the inside.

And there was only one CORE official Nia trusted enough to help them: her father.

Thank you for reading!

If you liked STAR-CROSSED CAPTIVE, I would absolutely love it if you would leave a review at your favorite retailer.

Not ready for this story to end?
Join my reader community for your exclusive FREE copy of STAR-CURSED ODYSSEY, the story behind what really happened to the *Calypso* all those years ago.

GET IT HERE
https://bookhip.com/VZTJHTD

All of J.E.'s books can be found at:
https://books2read.com/jemcdonald

Glossary

administrator – This is a member of the ruling class who works under the Chancellor and has control over a smaller territory—usually a station or ship. Administrators can also be in the CORE military but it's not a pre-requisite.

agent – An operative of the CORE military, they work alone, often used for assassinations.

AL-22 – The standard weapon of a CORE defender.

anti-grav lift – A one-person machine that floats to reach high objects.

autonomous shielding – Shielding that protects a person from laser fire. Does not protect against slower moving objects like blades. Standard in a defender's uniform but can also be a portable clip (often used by agents and enforcers).

battle-suit – What defenders wear when engaging the enemy. It is entirely enclosed so if they were shot out into space, they would survive.

biodome – An area of a ship dedicated to growing plants. Its circular construction is made of transparent aluminum.

biomatter – Any matter/waste that comes from a living thing.

bio-suit – A suit used to walk on a planet of moon with an atmosphere that is hostile to humans, or can be used in labs while conducting unsafe experiments.

blast doors – The physical doors that protect docking bays, hangars, and viewers beyond the shielding.

bulkhead – The walls of a ship or station.

Calypson – The *Calypso* was the first inter-stellar vessel to carry humans to another solar system: Epsilon Eridani. Its intended mission was to research the first planet of the system and begin the terraforming process on its moon. The crew is presumed lost in space until they return over a hundred years later...

cardiovascular node – Same thing as the cortical node but used in the area of the heart.

cargo ship – A vessel used to haul cargo.

Chancellor – The most powerful person in the solar system. He/She has veto power over everything. Think of the Chancellor as the Prime Minister of the solar system.

comm(s) – Communications, communique. This is how people communicate with each other audibly. Sometimes there is a visual aspect.

Common – The language universally spoken by all people no matter their origin.

composite – A man-made material like metal created to withstand the pressure of space.

CORE – Collective Organization of the Regulated Establishment. A civilized government body which has control over the terrestrial planets and Jupiter and all resources therein (Sectors One to Three). This government took control of the population through evacuating Earth and making the population dependent for its survival thousands of years ago, and was born from four major corporations known as the Corps before the evacuation. The only people who live on Earth now are conservationists trying to heal it.

CORE Military – The military force which, for the most part, protects CORE citizens from Tellusian raids. Ranks follow the current day American army but other terms are listed below.

cortical node – A device (the size of the tip of your thumb) placed on the head which can analyze brain activity, and send electrical impulses or nanos through the brain.

cred(s) – A monetary unit. Tellusians and CORE have separate identifiers for their currency but they both call them creds.

deck – The floor of a ship or station.

defender – Any rank of soldier in the CORE military. Their uniforms are white and silver and have autonomous shielding. This shielding works against laser fire but not blades, which is why Tellusian Warriors like knives so much.

dermal syringe – A futuristic version of a needle/syringe. It's placed against the skin to transfer narcotics or nanos into a person's system.

Deimos – One of Mars' moons. It's a large rock.

dispensary – The automated machine behind the walls of a ship or station that makes either food or drugs.

enforcer – A Tellusian warrior who works security, uses brute force a lot, not afraid to kill.

fighter – A small armed vessel used for precision fighting and attacks.

flight-suit – A space-worthy suit used to do outside maintenance on a ship and has autonomous propulsion.

freighter – A large vessel used to transport large things such as a new batch of Marauders.

Gibbous – A phase of the moon, but in this case either the name of a space station or a mild curse word.

grav bar – The future version of a barbell used in weight training.

grid – The future equivalent of the Internet but it connects all things, encompasses the whole of CORE space by a network of relays, satellites etc.

hovercart – A surface vehicle. Made for two people with a back bed for gear, doesn't have a roof, so if on Earth, the persons would need to use UV suits to drive it.

investigator – Works under the Chancellor. They investigate anything from mundane crimes of station life to larger problems, but leave all the heavy lifting to the military.

jack – To override controls to gain access to a room, compartment, or airlock.

lascom – Long-distance communication utilizing laser technology relays.

laser scalpel – A laser that is used for cutting. Quite small.

laser weapon/gun – A generic term for the weapons used by defenders and warriors. There are many types of laser weapons.

lifeline – A tracker which a person would purchase with their own money. Used especially by the ruling class.

lift – A multidirectional elevator used in ships and stations.

long-range shuttle – A small utilitarian vessel which can go longer distances on a single charge.

marker/markings – The documentation to declare ownership of a ship.

med bed or hover bed – A bed that can read a patient's stats and where a lot of the medical "action" takes place. Information is displayed on a control panel at the head or side of the bed, depending on the design. A hover bed is movable, a med bed is stationary.

med kit –A portable kit used to hold medical tools.

medic – Someone with the basic understanding of first aid.

medical aid vessel – A vessel with the sole purpose of saving lives. Often wounded would be transported to a medical station for specialized care.

medical assistant – Someone who is trained in medicine to aid doctors, a nurse.

nanos – Nanobot technology. They can be programmed to do a multitude of different tasks within the body.

ocular implant – This is a device implanted into the eye of CORE citizens at a very young age. It connects to the PALM and shows information in front of the right eye. It can be turned off but most CORE citizens are so used to it, that it stays on indefinitely.

overhead – The ceiling of a ship or station.

palette – This is a hand-held computer similar to our tablets but it's much more advanced. The Tellusian version of a PALM.

PALM – Personal Automated Link to Media. This is an extremely thin, transparent film and a collection of sensors which is worn over the palm of the hand and links the person to media, and any other information that is vital to their lives on the "grid." Information is displayed both in two and three dimensional form and is also connected remotely to an ocular implant. CORE citizens only use this, not Tellusians or Calypsons.

processing – this is the term used for when a CORE citizen is taken in a raid and then given rights as a captive. Their biometric information is recorded, they're given identifying bonds on each wrist before being placed in either a work pool for manual labor or a post specific to their occupation with the CORE.

pulse cannon – Similar to a rocket launcher but it delivers pulses of energy as its payload. Held over the shoulder and has limited charge, five shots max.

pulse rifle – Slender gun good for long-range situations.

reclaimer – The compartment in the wall/bulkhead/ship where the item is received into the reclamation system.

reclamation – The recycling process of all ships and stations. Materials are disassembled in their base parts to be reused in different ways. Used for both inorganic and organic matter.

regeneration bath – A rejuvenating bath of thick medical fluid that repairs skin and is otherwise quite enjoyable when a person is immersed in it for ten minutes or more.

regeneration gauze – A fabric-like substance that helps skin heal and reduce scar tissue. Sort of like a super-advanced band-aid. (Some scars are not repairable. It depends on the extent of the damage.)

regeneration tool or regenerator – A tool which sterilizes, stimulates, and repairs damaged tissue. A **fine detail regenerator** would be used for small things like veins while a **broad spectrum regenerator** would be used for large areas like skin.

robocleaner – A robotic device used to clean up solids and liquids. An advanced vacuum that works by itself.

ruling class – This group of people stems from the original Corps and is responsible for all law-making and non-military control over the population. They have control in the military as well. Birth lines dictate who the next Chancellor will be.

scanner – A handheld device which scans a patient's vital statistics.

scribe – A recording device usually found on the overhead.

Sector Ten – Consisting of a man-made nebula, it is the area which is occupied by the Calypsons and avoided by everyone else.

sectors/hemispheres – The solar system is divided into sectors and hemispheres (based off of the Sun and Earth's positions) for navigation purposes. The CORE has complete power over sectors one through three.

shuttle – A small utilitarian vessel used for short distances: ship to ship, station to ship.

sluice – A laundry chute which cleans and folds laundry within minutes.

SNAP shielding – The automated shielding system that initiates when there is a loss of pressure/atmosphere on a ship or station. Very important for the CORE when Tellusians make forced airlock entries.

specialist – An operative of the CORE military who specializes in interrogation techniques and torture.

steam shower – Also referred to as a steam. An attempt to save water, steam and pressure clean the body with a burst of air to dry the body afterward.

sterilization – The process of sterilizing a surgeon's hands before surgery, inserted into a rectangular shaped device usually located on the end of a med bed.

sterilization film – A thin transparent film used in transporting sensitive medical equipment like prosthetics.

suspension chamber – A patient with severe injuries needing extensive surgery would be placed in this cylindrical pod so their condition doesn't worsen.

synthesizer – A tissue cloner (not a musical instrument). Where there is a void of tissue, a synthesizer can "replicate" new tissue to fill the void. There needs to be sufficient existing tissue for the bonding process.

tag – A digital marker Tellusians use to track enemy ships.

tech – This has two meanings, one is just a short form of the word technology. The other is the short word for technician. So either a person or a thing can be referred to as (a) tech.

techie – This is a slightly derogatory term usually used by warriors/defenders to someone with a technical mind.

Tell – This is a term used by the CORE toward Tellusians. Tellusians find it offensive.

Tellusian – The Tellusians resisted the evacuation of Earth arguing if the human population got rid of technology and advancement, Earth would not need to be evacuated and therefore would be able to sustain life. They were deemed terrorists and eventually run to the edges of the solar system. They developed into a fierce Warrior race. The have control of Saturn (their biggest asset), Uranus, and Neptune and mine each for their resources. They also steal what they can from the CORE, including people.

tracker – A chip used by the CORE to trace its officers, usually implanted in the flesh of the shoulder blade.

transfuser – A portable device with a store a fluids/blood product for emergency situations. Has a finite amount of material and can run out quickly.

transparent aluminum – It looks like glass but it's as strong as metal. (Yes, I stole this from Star Trek. Sue me.)

transport – A large passenger vessel used for long distances. Would need creds to secure passage.

tyro – A novice training to be Tellusian warrior. A student.

vambrace – Technology made of metal composite worn around the forearm of a Tellusian warrior. Used as a communication device, can detect life signs, and has a multitude of tactical uses but is not a weapon.

viewer – The monitor at the front of a ship that allows sight beyond the ship. Can either be a window or a screen depending on how it's used.

ward/warder – The relationship between the captive and the warrior who takes them.

warrior – A Tellusian soldier. They begin training very young and there is stiff competition to become one. Anyone who wants to be a Warrior goes through intensive training and "games." They have to be the best of the best. They have a penchant for knives.

CORE Ships:

Cruiser – A luxury shuttle which the wealthy and ruling class use as pleasure vehicles, a "space yacht."

Condor – A single-person long-range CORE fighter.

Guardian – A CORE warship. The biggest, most heavily armed of the bunch. Used to fight Tellusians.

Marauder – A single-person short-range CORE fighter.

Raven – A multi-person CORE scout-vessel. Has weapons and is used mostly for reconnaissance.

Tellusian Ships:

Destroyer – a Tellusian warship, similar in size to a Guardian, but with more exterior/visible armaments. Made of black composite metal so it blends in with space.

Cetan – A Tellusian stealth scout vessel. It's designed to house a Griffin that can separate and then work independently of each other.

Griffin – A one-person long-range Tellusian fighter.

Strix – A one-person short-range Tellusian fighter.

Tellusian Pod – These come from a Destroyer during raids to attach and force an airlock to ships and stations so Tellusians can people farm. They're round in shape and several captives can be taken and then stored in one until they are delivered to the Destroyer and processed as captives.

Star-Crossed Captive Playlist

These were the songs I listened to while writing this book:

1. Anvil by Lorn (Vessel)

2. Roll by ZABO (Roll)

3. Beat and the Pulse by Austra (Feel it Break)

4. Breathe by ZABO (Breathe)

5. Slow Match by Moderat, Paul St.Hilaire (Moderat)

6. Renaissance by Ujo (One More Day – EP)

7. Innerbloom by RÜFÜS DU SOL (Bloom)

8. Run For Your Life by Big Grams (Big Grams)

9. Les Grandes Marches by Moderat (Moderat)

10. With You (Are these feelings even real) by Aloboi (With You, Are these feelings even real)

11. Codex by Radiohead (The King of Limbs)

12. Sleep Awake by Mother Mother (O My Heart)

13. On My Knees by RÜFÜS DU SOL (On My Knees)

14. i like the devil by Purity Ring (Womb)

15. Undertow by Warpaint (The Fool)

16. we were never young by Raised By Swans (no ghostless place)

17. Another Life by Jadu Heart (Another Life)

18. Emptiness by One True God, Ronlit (Emptiness)

19. Water Plant by aYia (aYia)

20. Between Two Points by The Glitch Mob, Swan (Drink The Sea)

21. So Far Away by Faunts (Feel.Love.Thinking.Of.)

22. Fairy Tale by Ekali, Elohim (A World Away)

23. Violence – REZZ Remix by Grimes, i_o, Rexx (Miss Antropocene)

24. So & So by HANA (So & So)

25. Do Not Break by Ellen Allien, Apparat (Orchestra of Bubbles)

26. Arcadia by Apparat (Walls)

27. Water – Farves Remix by Trey Mirror, Henry Green, Farves (Water – Farves Remix)

28. Untitled #6 – Jacobs Studio Sessions by Sigur Ros (2022 Remaster)

29. MORE LOVE by Moderat (MORE LOVE)

30. begin again by Purity Ring (another eternity)

31. Trampoline – Jauz Remix by SHAED, Jauz (Trampoline – Jauz Remix)

Acknowledgements

It seems a million years ago that I started writing a book I called Blueshift, though I guess it's closer to fourteen years. It was the first BIG IDEA I had for a novel. In that moment, I was well and truly bitten by the writing bug, and the itch hasn't gone away since. It also seems a very long time ago that I asked SO MANY people for help with it over the course of 3ish years, only for the manuscript to be trunked out of sight as I worked on other things. (I'd been told by agents there wasn't a market for it, and I wasn't ready to self-publish at that time.)

So my first big thank you is to the YONDER team. Without you approaching my publisher, I might never have dusted this baby off and revamped it in the short space of two months.

There were a lot of people who read that first, second, third, forth, fifth (you get the picture) drafts in those early days. Every bit of feedback helped me grow as a writer. Paula Jane, you brought me down to reality in your gentle way. (Things I needed to hear!) Coline, you've always been my number one cheerleader, love ya. Melodie, it was you who challenged me to do NaNoWriMo in the first place, and you've been an amazing beta reader ever since. And thank you to Amanda B, Dave O, and Pearl K. Your insights helped me bring this book to the next level, even years after the fact. (I'm sorry if I missed anyone. It's been a while!)

A huge thank you to Darcy M. You allowed me to barrage you with medical questions, and my favorite bit of feedback you gave is still, "If this guy lost this much blood, he'd be dead." (Cue the invention of the transfuser!)

Thank you to my group of amazing author friends who have been an inspiration as they embark on their own self-publishing journeys. You Owls are truly amazing!

And to my local TBA Writers' Group. Your loyalty and advice keep me fortified no matter what the obstacle.

As always, thank you very much to my whole family, immediate and extended, who continue to be such an enthusiastic support system. Love you all.

And why did I name this book (and now subsequently the series) Blueshift? Metaphor, baby! Nia's mindset shifted toward Tellusians the more immersed she became in their culture—the good and the bad.

Lastly, I wanted to address my dedication. The seed for this book came to life while watching a television program. I wanted the doctor and the warrior to get together, but alas, the TV writers chose to put the doctor and the scientist together. (Good on the scientist, he deserved some happiness too, but it wasn't how I wanted the romantic arc to go!) Though this book can't be considered fan fic because I never based these characters off of those two or set it in that existing world, it never would have happened if I hadn't had that burning urge to rewrite the story. (I mean, it was Jason Mamoa. *Come on.*) The fic writers get it! Thank you for being awesome.

More Works by J.E. McDonald

https://books2read.com/jemcdonald

WICKWOOD CHRONICLES

Ghost of a Gamble
Ghost of an Enchantment
Ghost of a Summoning
Edge of a Shadow, Part One
Edge of a Shadow, Part Two
Ghost of a Beginning (Prequel)

GOLDENLACH RIDGE SHIFTERS

Captive Wilderness
Caged Fury
Conquered Betrayal

BLUESHIFT

Star-Crossed Captive
Star-Born Anomaly
Star-Cursed Odyssey (Prequel)

About The Author

J.E. McDonald was born and raised in Saskatchewan, Canada, The Land of the Living Skies. As a child, she was either searching the clouds for identifiable shapes, or star-gazing way past her bedtime. She's an anti-morning person who wakes up at 5am to write. Needless to say, coffee is a morning requirement. She cut her teeth watching Star Trek, James Bond movies, and reading the Harlequin novels her mother left in the bathroom—which resulted in an extremely skewed sense of sex education by age eleven. All of these factors contribute to her love of writing paranormal romance with humor, mystery, and lots of spice. J.E. resides in Saskatchewan with her husband and three daughters.

www.jemcdonald.net
Facebook: /JEMcDonaldAuthor
Instagram: /jemcdonaldsk
TikTok: @jemcdonaldsk
Threads: @jemcdonaldsk